WATCHERS
OF
TIME

ALSO BY CHARLES TODD

A Test of Wills
Wings of Fire
Search the Dark
Legacy of the Dead

WATCHERS OF TIME

An Inspector Ian Rutledge Mystery

CHARLES TODD

BANTAM BOOKS

WATCHERS OF TIME

A Bantam Book / November 2001

BOOK DESIGN BY GLEN M. EDELSTEIN

Library of Congress Cataloging-in-Publication Data
Todd, Charles.
Watchers of time : an Inspector Ian Rutledge mystery / Charles Todd.
p. cm.
ISBN 0-553-80179-1 (alk. paper)
1. Rutledge, Ian (Fictitious character)—Fiction. 2. Police—England—
Fiction. I. Title.

PS3570.O37 W38 2001
813'.54—dc21   2001035272

Published simultaneously in the United States and Canada

Bantam Books are published by Bantam Books, a division of Random
House, Inc. Its trademark, consisting of the words "Bantam Books" and the
portrayal of a rooster, is Registered in U.S. Patent and Trademark Office
and in other countries. Marca Registrada. Bantam Books, 1540 Broadway,
New York, New York 10036.

PRINTED IN THE UNITED STATES OF AMERICA

BVG   10 9 8 7 6 5 4 3 2 1

For Elayne K. McCullough—

For whom traveling the world was a joyous adventure
And whose friendship was a treasured gift.

And for Bill and her family, who brought her so much
happiness.

Bon voyage . . .

WATCHERS
OF
TIME

CHAPTER ONE

SEPTEMBER 1919
Osterley

DR. STEPHENSON TURNED AWAY FROM THE bed where the dying man lay breathing so lightly the blanket over his thin chest barely stirred. His bony, restless fingers plucking at the edge of the wool were the only signs of life and awareness. Twice the young woman sitting on the bed beside him had tried to still them, covering them with her own, but her father's hand picked up the silent tattoo again, like a drummer remembering his place, as soon as she released it. He had already frayed an inch of the binding. She gave up and sat back, sighing.

His face was grooved by illness, and a stubble of beard emphasized the lines, like a rough landscape of suffering below the sun-weathered skin of forehead and nose. Shaggy gray eyebrows hung heavily over the sunken lids. Age weighed him down, but there was a certain strength there as well, as if life had made him fight for all he had, and he had not forgotten the battles.

Catching the eyes of the man's sons, who were standing on the far side of the bed, faces in shadows cast by the scarf draped over the lamp's shade, the doctor nodded toward the window across the room, out of earshot of the patient. The young woman looked up as they moved away, but stayed where she was. She didn't want to hear what was being whispered.

Another gust of wind swept the front of the house, and rain was driven heavily against the panes, rattling them. The storm had stalled, as they sometimes did here along the coast, reluctant to move inland and lose itself in the hilly terrain there. For three hours or more it had hovered over the village, flailing everyone and everything out in the open.

The older of the two brothers bent his head to catch the words as Stephenson said softly, "He's moving comfortably and peacefully toward the end. There's nothing more I can do. But he might wish to have Mr. Sims here? And I should think your sister would be comforted as well."

Mr. Sims was the Vicar.

The younger brother answered, "Yes. I'll go for him, then." He went quietly across the room to the door. The scarf that shaded the lamp by the bed riffled as he passed, and the light flashed once across his face. There were wet trails of tears on his cheeks.

His sister reached out and briefly took his rough hand.

The other brother sighed. "He's had a long life, Pa has. But not that long. Sixty-four. We'd thought he'd be with us another five, ten years. His own father lived to just past eighty. And Uncle Tad's young for seventy-six." He shook his head.

"Your uncle Thadeus has the constitution of an ox," Stephenson agreed. "He may well outlive your grandfather's years. But your father's heart has given out, and his body must follow." He studied the grieving man's face, noting the deep lines of worry and sleeplessness. Hetty Baldwin, his housekeeper's daughter, was getting a good man in Martin Baker, the doctor told himself. Much like Herbert in character— God-fearing, with strong ties to his family and a fierce sense of duty. It was a sound match. "Everything happens in God's own time, you know. Even this. And it's a kindness that he won't linger." He spoke the words as comfort, then nodded toward the bed. "See if you can persuade Elly to rest a little. She's hardly stirred from his side since yesterday morning. We'll call her if there's any—urgency. She will only wear herself into collapse, driving herself like this."

"I've tried, to no avail." Martin turned toward the window, lifting the curtain and pulling aside the shade a little to look out. Rain ran down the glass in rivulets, pushed against the house by the wind. A filthy night, he thought. A fitting night for death to come. . . . He dropped the shade back in place and said to Dr. Stephenson, "There's naught to be done to make it easier on her?"

"I'll leave something. A sleeping draught. Give it to Elly in a glass of water, when your father is gone. And, Martin—see that Dick doesn't insist on being one of the pallbearers. That shoulder of his is not fully healed, and the socket will never be as strong as it was. He's not out of the woods yet. He could still lose the arm if he's not careful. The army surgeons can't work miracles without a little help!"

"I'll remember."

"Good man!" A clap on Martin's shoulder for comfort, and then Stephenson walked back to the bed. He reached down and touched Elly's hands, folded tightly in her lap. They were cold, shaking. "Your father is comfortable. He would want you to be the same. Let Martin fetch you a shawl, at least."

She nodded, unable to reply. The gray head on the pillow moved, first to the right, then toward the left. Herbert Baker's eyes opened, and focused on his daughter's face. He said in a gravelly voice, "I want a priest."

The doctor leaned down and replied reassuringly, "Yes, Dick has just gone to fetch Mr. Sims."

"I want a priest!" the old man repeated querulously.

"He's coming, Papa!" Elly said, fighting her tears. "Can you hear me? He'll be here quite soon—"

"Priest," her father demanded. "*Not* Vicar."

"Herbert," the doctor said soothingly, "let me lift you while Elly gives you a little water—"

The dark, pleading eyes shifted to the doctor's face. "I want a priest," the dying man said very clearly this time, refusing to be distracted.

The bedroom door opened and Dick was ushering in the Vicar. "I met him on his way here," he told them. "Coming to see if we had need of him."

Mr. Sims was taller than Dick, thinner, and not much older. "I've been sitting with Mrs. Quarles, and thought it best to call on you before going home," the Vicar explained. Herbert Baker had taken all day to die. Most of the town knew the end was near, a matter of hours at best. Sims had stopped in twice before.

Sims reached out to touch Elly's arm, saying easily, "Ellen, do you think you could find a cup of tea for us? We could use the warmth on such a wet night."

She flushed shyly. "Tea? Oh—yes. I've just to put the kettle on."

Smoothing the blanket over her father, she got up, leaving the room with reluctance. Sims took the place on the bed that she'd vacated and squarely met the intent eyes of the old man. "You've had a good life, Herbert Baker. You were married to a fine woman—a caring wife and a devoted mother. Both your sons survived the War, and have work. Elly is a lovely girl. God has been kind to you."

"Thank'ee, Vicar, and I'll have you say a prayer for me after the priest goes!"

The Vicar looked up at Martin, then said, "Dr. Stephenson?"

"He's been asking for a priest. Just now, before you came in. I don't know why—"

Dick said, "Father James is the only priest in Osterley. He's a *Catholic*—"

"That's right—he's the one!" Herbert Baker said with more will than strength. Something in the depths of his eyes flared with hope.

Martin said, "If that's what he wants, humor him, then. Dick, go and see if Father James will come here." His brother hesitated, glancing uneasily at the Vicar, as if he'd just been asked to commit heresy. But Mr. Sims nodded encouragement, and Dick went out the door.

Martin said, "You'll stay?" to Sims.

From the bed came the single word "Stay." The lined face was exhausted, as if speaking was a greater effort than he could manage.

Sims replied, "I'll go to the kitchen, then. From the look of her, Ellen is more in need of that tea than I am!" Rising from the bed, he added gently, "I'll be within call, Herbert. Never fear." His smile was reassuring.

Herbert nodded; his eyes closed. The wind had dropped again and on the roof overhead the rain seemed to fall softly now, with a summer patter.

Dr. Stephenson said quietly to Sims, "He's sound enough in his mind. But dying men often have whims like this. Best to humor him!"

"Yes. I knew a wounded man in the War who wanted to be buried with his little dog. Only he didn't have a dog. But when they came to bury him, his arms were folded across his chest as if he'd held one as he died. Strange comfort, but who are we to question?"

The Vicar went out the door, shutting it quietly behind him. There were voices on the stairs. Sims speaking to Ellen. And then they went down again together.

The room was silent. Martin watched his father for a time, and then said anxiously to Stephenson, "It'll be an easy passing?"

"As easy as any. His heart will stop. And his breathing will follow. He will be asleep long before that. I didn't expect him to wake at all. I thought he'd reached the last stage."

Herbert, roused by their voices, said, "Is the priest here, then?"

"Not yet, Papa," Martin answered, lowering himself to sit on the bed. "Dick's gone to fetch him." He gripped his father's hands, unable to say anything, a plain man with few graces. But the warmth of his fingers seemed to give a measure of peace to his dying father. Martin cleared his throat hoarsely, warmed in his turn.

The silence lengthened. After nearly a quarter of an hour, Dick came in, bringing a short and balding man of middle age in his wake. Father James greeted Stephenson with a nod and came to shake Martin's outstretched hand. His fingers were cold from the night air. "I understand your father has been asking for a priest," he said, his face showing only concern.

"I don't know *why*, Father—"

"Nor does it matter. I'll speak to him, then, shall I?" It was a question asked gracefully, setting Martin at his ease. The priest turned quietly to bend over the bed. After a moment he said, "Mr. Baker? Herbert? It's Father James. What can I do to help you?"

Baker opened his eyes, seemed to have difficulty focusing them, then blinked as he looked up at the white clerical collar, clearly visible against the black cloth. "Father James, is it?"

"Yes." As a thin, trembling hand came out from under the blanket, Father James reached for it and the claw seemed to lock onto his.

"Send them away!" Herbert Baker said. "Just you and me."

Father James glanced across at the anxious faces of Baker's two sons and then at Dr. Stephenson. The three men nodded briefly, walked to the door, and went out, their shoes loud on the wide boards of the passage, then moving together down the stairs.

Father James, waiting until they were well out of earshot, looked around to collect some impression of this man lying in the bed waiting for death to come. He knew who the Bakers were, but had seldom exchanged more than a word or two with any of them.

It was a big room set under the eaves, with simple but sturdy furnishings, and a worn carpet on the floor. Someone had painted watercolors of the sea and framed them for hanging. An amateur's hand, the sunrises and ships vigorous, but showing an untrained eye. The family had taken pride in them, to frame them. The single window faced the street, the shade pulled against the night and the curtains drawn across it.

So many houses in the town had this same air of working-class austerity, Father James found himself thinking. Osterley's years of prosperity lay in the past—well before Herbert Baker's time. No one starved, but people here worked hard for their bread.

As the priest turned back to the bed, he saw the woman's photograph on the table beside it. The soft whisper of the rain faded, then revived as a squall, the wind sending a gust of drafts into the house and making the lamp dance to its fitful tune. Baker's wife? She had died before the War, as he recalled, and this must have been taken some ten years before that. The daughter—Ellen?—looked much like her. The same dark hair and sweet face, staring at the camera with trusting and expectant eyes.

He sat down carefully on the bed's edge, where Ellen and the Vicar had sat before him, and said in the voice that was his greatest gift as a priest, deep and steadfast, "I'm here. We are alone in the sight of God. In the name of the Father, the Son, and the Holy Spirit, tell me how I may serve you?"

Nearly half an hour later, Father James walked down the stairs of the Baker house, and found the family, the doctor, and the Vicar waiting for him in the small, very Victorian parlor. Tea had been brought and poured, but the cups were still more than half full, sitting forgotten. Wind rattled the shutters, a theatrical announcement of his appearance, like a drumroll.

Every face had turned toward the priest, all eyes pinning him in the doorway, concern mixed with weariness and not a little curiosity in their expressions. Father James cleared his throat and said into the expectant silence, "Your father is resting quietly now. He has asked me to reassure you that he wishes to be buried in accordance with his own beliefs, with Mr. Sims officiating. I have served him by giving him a little comfort. If he should require me again, you've only to let me know. And now, if you'll forgive me, I must go. It is late—"

He was offered refreshment, he was offered the gratitude of the grieving family. Prevailed upon by Mr. Sims, he sat and drank a cup of lukewarm tea, out of kindness. Dr. Stephenson, watching him, was struck by the tension around his eyes, putting it down to the awkwardness of being in an unfamiliar household among strangers not of his faith. The two of them, doctor and priest, had shared many long watches together over the years, and Stephenson had always found him a strong and dependable ally in the business of offering peace to the dying and solace to the survivors. Even so, the face of death was never commonplace. One learned to accept, that was all.

Father James behaved with sympathetic courtesy toward Herbert Baker's children, that deep voice bringing a measure of comfort to Ellen, as it had to her father. Dick and Martin, both slack-faced with exhaustion, appeared to find a renewal of strength in his assurance that Herbert Baker had made his peace with his God and had not changed his faith. Simple men, they couldn't fathom their father's odd behavior, and were half embarrassed by it. Father James, understanding that, said only, "Your father was not frivolous. At the end, we are all in need of God's grace, like a child before his father. I'm some years older than the Vicar. Perhaps to a man of Herbert Baker's age, it mattered." He smiled across the tea table at Sims.

The Vicar looked up. Tansy, the liver-and-white spaniel sitting by his chair, patiently waited for Sims's fingers to resume scratching behind the curly ears. He said, almost diffidently, "In the War it was the same. They were so young, most of them. But old in experience that I couldn't match. I sent more than a few of them along to the Methodist chaplain, who was closer to their fathers' age than I was. That seemed to be the best thing to do for them." Then he turned the conversation, adding to Father James, "You must be thanking God that this weather held until after your Autumn Fete at St. Anne's. It was a blessing. . . ."

Ellen said, "Martin went with Hetty to the bazaar. He brought me a brush for Tansy, and a new lead." A smile lit her pale face, and then faltered. "Papa was well enough to go last year."

"So he was," the Vicar answered, returning her smile. "He has been a rock of strength each spring at Holy Trinity, too. I always took pleasure in working with him."

As soon as it was decently possible, Father James rose and took his leave. Martin Baker escorted him to the door and thanked him again. The priest stepped out into the night. The rain had dropped off once more, and there was only the wind to keep him company on his long walk home.

Dr. Stephenson, climbing the stairs once more, found that the priest was right: Herbert Baker seemed to be resting quietly, slowly losing his grip on life.

In the small hours of the night, the man died peacefully, his family gathered about him. His daughter, Ellen, sobbed quietly and his two sons watched in anguish as he drew several short, uncertain breaths, then stopped breathing altogether, only a thin sigh passing his lips. The Vicar, by his side, prayed for Herbert Baker's soul as the sigh faded.

The funeral was well attended, and Herbert Baker, coachman by trade, was sent to his eternal rest with the goodwill of a village that had known him to be an honest and plainspoken man with no vices and no outstanding talents, except perhaps for loyalty.

A week after the funeral, Dr. Stephenson returned to his surgery late one afternoon to find Father James just walking out the door.

"Well met!" Stephenson exclaimed, with pleasure. "Come in, let me pour myself a drink, and I shall be at your service. First babies are not to be hurried! This one kept his mother and me awake all of the night and well into the afternoon, and I've missed my breakfast, my lunch, and my usual hours." He led the way back through the doorway, down the passage, and into his private office. The room smelled of wax and disinfectant, a blend that Father James found to be a sneeze-maker. He dragged out his handkerchief, sneezed heartily three times, and grinned crookedly at Stephenson.

"You should hear me when they've waxed the pews and the confessional at St. Anne's! The blessing is, I'm not bothered by incense."

The office was small, painted a pleasing shade of blue, and offered three chairs for visitors as well as the more comfortable old leather one behind the doctor's broad wooden desk. Dr. Stephenson settled into that, and Father James took his accustomed place in the ancient wingback. As Stephenson lifted the bottle of sherry and offered it to him, the priest said, "No, thank you. I've another call to make, and she's temperance-mad. I'll lose my reputation if I reek of good sherry."

Stephenson grinned. "How does she manage communion wine, then?"

"It's consecrated, and the evil of the grape has been taken out."

The doctor chuckled, then poured his own glass. "Yes, well, the mind is a wonderful thing, wonderful."

"It's about the mind I've come," Father James said slowly.

"Oh, yes?" Stephenson sipped his sherry with relish, letting it warm him.

"I'd like to ask you if Herbert Baker was in full control of his faculties when he called me to him on his deathbed."

"Baker? Yes, well, that was an odd business, I daresay. But he was dying of congestive heart failure, and his mind was, as far as I could tell, clear to the end of consciousness. Any reason why you feel it might not have been?" His voice lifted on a query. Stephenson was a man who liked his own life and that of his patients as tidy as possible.

"No," the priest replied. "On the other hand, I'm seldom asked to second-guess Mr. Sims's parishioners. Or he mine, for that matter. It was curious, and I found myself wondering about it afterward. Baker most certainly *appeared* in full control, though understandably weak. Still, you never know."

"Which reminds me," Stephenson said, turning the subject to something on his own mind. "There's one of your flock I do want to talk about. Mrs. Witherspoon. She's been refusing to take her pills again, and I'm—er—hanged if I can understand it."

The priest smiled. "There's a challenge for you. At a guess, I'd say that when she feels a little stronger, she's convinced she doesn't need them. Then she feels unwell again and quickly takes two to make up for it. A good-hearted woman, but not overly blessed with common sense. If I were you, I'd have a talk with her husband. She pays more heed to what he says than to anyone else. The sun shines out of Mr. Witherspoon, in her view."

The ironmonger was the most lugubrious man in Osterley.

Stephenson laughed. "The eye of the beholder. Well, there's a thought. That woman will make herself seriously ill if she doesn't heed someone!" He looked at his wine, golden in the little glass. "I had a patient once who swore that sherry was Spanish sunlight caught in a bottle. Never been to Spain myself; I'm hard-pressed to escape for a few hours in Yarmouth. But there's most certainly medicinal magic in it." He finished the wine, then said, "How are those triplets of yours?"

Father James beamed. The triplets were his younger sister's children and lived some distance away. "Thriving. Sarah is coping, with the help of two nuns I found for her, and every member of the family we can dragoon into service. I've done my own turn walking the floor at night. I expect those boys will be holy terrors by the time they're eight. Their father was something of a devil himself at twelve!"

Stephenson said, "Aren't we all? But responsibility comes soon enough."

The priest's face changed subtly. "It does. I'll be on my way, then. Get some rest, you look as if you could use it!"

Watching him out the door, Stephenson had the curious feeling that Father James should take his own advice.

Nearly two weeks had passed since the funeral. Stephenson, rested and busy, had long since put Herbert Baker out of his mind when he took his wife to visit friends.

It was a dinner party like a dozen others the doctor attended with some enthusiasm whenever he could. There were eight couples, and he'd known all of them for years. Comfortable with each other, sharing a common history, they had found in one another a companionship that had few boundaries. Stephenson could count most of them as his patients, and his wife had sat on committees of one sort or another with every one of the women—church bazaars, flower arrangements, food baskets for the poor, spring fetes, charity cases, visiting the sick, welcoming newcomers to Osterley, and generally forming an ad hoc social group that was as small as it was select.

He couldn't have said afterward how the subject arose. Someone asked a question, another guest expanded on it, and a wife raised a laugh by adding her own views. Stephenson found himself picking up the thread, and the next thing he knew, he was telling the story of a dying patient who had wanted to hedge his bets in the next life by seeing both the Vicar and the priest.

One of the guests leaned forward. "Was that old Baker? My wife remarked to me that she'd seen Father James walking out of Baker's front door one night in a pouring rain, saying good-bye to young Martin on the step. I told her she must have been mistaken—Baker was sexton for seventeen years at Holy Trinity!"

Richard Cullen said, "Had the right idea, though, didn't he? Who was it that said Paris was worth a Mass?"

That dissolved into a debate over whether it was Henri IV and progressed to a recital of the opening lines of "The Vicar of Bray." Herbert Baker had been forgotten once more.

It was late in the evening on the second of October when Father James returned to the Victorian Gothic house that served as St. Anne's rectory. He let himself in through the unlocked kitchen door, grateful for the lamp still burning on the small table by the window, and sniffed appreciatively at the lingering aroma of bacon. He crossed the room to peer into the oven. His dinner was sitting on the rack in a covered dish. Lifting the lid, he saw that the contents were a little dry but certainly still delicious. There were onions as well, and what appeared to be a Scotch egg.

The housekeeper, Mrs. Wainer, had—as always—remembered that the body needed nurturing as well as the soul. He could feel the saliva flow in his mouth. Onions were his greatest love.

Father James set the lid in place and closed the oven door. Tired from a long vigil by a very ill parishioner, he stretched his shoulders as he straightened his back. The chair by the bed had been too low, and his muscles had knotted. But the man had lived, thank God. His family needed him.

He went down the passage that led past the parlor and the small music room that he had converted into a parish office. In the darkness he moved with the ease of long familiarity. As he reached the hall by the front door, he could hear the clock in the parlor cock itself to strike the hour, the *whirr* of the gears a soft sound that stopped him, one hand on the newel post at the foot of the stairs.

The clear golden chimes always reminded him of the house where he had grown up—the clock had come from there—and the laughter of his mother and father, sharing the reading of a book as the children sprawled at their feet. It had been a nightly ritual just before bedtime, and it was something he himself, celibate and alone, missed. Mark had died in the War, killed on the Somme, and Judith had died of the influenza, taking her unborn child with her. But Sarah had brought her triplets alive into the world, and he looked forward to the day when their rowdy spirits and lively voices would brighten the silence of the old rectory. Sarah had already promised them for a week each year, though they were not yet three months old. He smiled to himself at the thought. Mrs. Wainer, bless her, would probably quit in dismay.

As the chimes echoed into silence, he went on up the stairs to his study on the first floor. The lamp on the desk wasn't lit, but one in his bedroom was burning, a low flame that guided his movements. He went through the bedroom door to put his case and coat away, and then wash his hands before dinner.

Coming back into the dark study, he failed to see the shadow that stood immobile in the deeper shadows beside his private altar. The gold chain on the priest's chest gleamed in the moonlight pouring through the windows. Noticing that the draperies hadn't been drawn, Father James crossed the room to pull them to, reaching high over his head to move the heavy velvet across the wooden rod. The first pair were only half shut when the shadow stepped out directly behind the priest. In the figure's hand was the heavy crucifix that had always stood on the altar between a slender pair of candlesticks. It was lifted high, and the base of the cross brought down with stunning force, straight into the bald head that seemed, in this light, to be tonsured and unnaturally white.

A target that was so clear it seemed to draw a sigh from the priest. He began to crumple, like old clothes falling to the floor. The crucifix was lifted again, the base flashing in the pale light as it descended a second time. As the priest hit the carpet with an ugly *thump,* the bloody scalp was struck a third time.

Then, with efficient grace, the shadow stepped back, dropped the crucifix from a gloved hand, and set about silently, swiftly, wrecking the room.

The police, summoned the next morning by a distraught Mrs. Wainer, took note of the food left untouched in the oven, the black blood pooled beneath the priest's head there by the window, and the state of the room: the paper-strewn floor and the scattered contents of the desk drawers. They examined the tin box that lay upside down and pried open with scissors, emptied of parish funds. And came to the conclusion that Father James, returning home unexpectedly, had been attacked by someone he'd disturbed in the midst of a burglary.

Not a target. A victim.

He'd heard a noise in the house, they concluded, discovered there was an intruder upstairs, and gone to the window intending to see if there was anyone at home next door. The neighbor had three nearly grown sons—it would have taken only a few seconds to unlatch the window and call to them to come and search the house with the priest. The alarmed thief, very likely concealed in the bedroom just behind the study, must have seen Father James at the window and hastily reached for the first weapon that came to hand—the crucifix—striking the priest down from behind to stop him from calling for help. In his terror he'd hit the priest again, and then fled, the money from the box in his pocket. Muddy shoe prints near the lilac bush showed a worn heel, a tear in the sole near the toe. A poor man, then, and desperate.

As luck would have it, the house next door, usually noisy with three generations of family, had stood empty the previous night. Taking even the elderly grandmother with them, they'd traveled to West Sherham to meet the girl one of their sons wished to marry. But the thief couldn't have known that.

If the family *had* been at home, they'd have arrived in force, very likely in time to glimpse the fleeing man. It would have been satisfying to have a description of the killer.

The townspeople of Osterley, whether members of St. Anne's, Holy Trinity, or no church at all, were shocked and horrified. They gathered in little clusters, silent for the most part or carrying on conversations that ended in head shakes and stunned disbelief. A few women wept into their handkerchiefs, red-eyed with grief and misgivings. Children were shushed, told to go to their rooms, questions unanswered. It was a *wicked* thing, to kill a clergyman. No one could recall even having heard of such a crime happening before in Norfolk—certainly not in living memory! Osterley would be the talk of East Anglia. . . .

Mr. Sims, trying to minister to his flock as well as the murdered priest's until the Bishop could send someone else down from Norwich, heard the same litany again and again. "He was such a good, caring man! He'd have helped whoever it was, given them the money, done his best for them—*there was no need to kill him!*"

A growing aura of suspicion spread through the town, as people tried to second-guess the police.

Then it slowly began to occur to inhabitants, one after another, that the killer couldn't be a local man. Not someone they *knew*. It simply wasn't possible.

Still, eyes turned suspiciously, glanced over shoulders, followed this man or that down the street with furtive conjecture—an unease spreading like a silent illness through the town.

Mr. Sims found himself thinking that there *was* a reason for killing Father James, if he'd seen the face of the man invading his home and threatening him with the crucifix from his own altar. Recognition was knowledge—and there were some who might be afraid that even the compassion of a priest had its limits.

Fear was seldom ruled by reason; it reacted to danger first and logic afterward. The first blow must surely have been fear—the succeeding blows could have been fear, or could have been cunning, the need to silence. How was anyone to know, until the priest's killer had been found?

Sims tried not to look into the faces of the people of Osterley and speculate. But he couldn't stop himself from doing it. Human nature was human nature. He was no different from the rest of his neighbors.

The War had taught Sims that frightened men did whatever they had to do to stay alive. And in the trenches, killing had become a natural reaction to peril. He wondered if the priest's attacker was an unemployed former soldier, one so desperate that he'd felt no compunction about taking life.

One man in Osterley came close to meeting those criteria. Sims refused to entertain the likelihood that he would ever kill again.

The Vicar scolded himself for such unchristian speculation. Surely not even a war-hardened veteran would kill a *priest*!

All the same, how far would the few pounds stolen from the rectory go? How long before empty pockets drove the killer—whoever he was—to strike again?

That night—for the first time since he'd come to Osterley nine years before—Mr. Sims locked his doors. The vicarage stood behind a high wall in an expanse of wooded lawn, old trees that had always been his pride and given him a sense of continuity with those who had served Holy Trinity before him. Now the house seemed isolated and secretive, hidden away and intolerably vulnerable.

He told himself it was merely a precaution, to lock his doors.

In bitter fact, he was coming to terms with the unexpected discovery that the Cloth, which had always seemed his armor and his shield, was neither, and that a man of God was no safer than any other householder.

CHAPTER TWO

OCTOBER 1919
London

RUTLEDGE CUT HIMSELF SHAVING AND SWORE.

His sister Frances, sitting in the chintz-covered chair by the window, winced but said nothing. When he did it again, she couldn't stop herself.

"Darling, must you carve up your face on your own? Or could I do it for you? Surely I'm a better butcher than you are?" The words were light, intentionally.

He shook his head. "If I'm to return to work, I must learn to manage." He was on medical leave from the Yard, and it was dragging on, day into endless day, chafing his spirit.

She regarded the heavy bandages that swathed his chest, still binding one arm close to his body. "I'm surprised the Yard will allow you back until that comes off. Surely there are regulations? You can barely button your own shirt, and I've done up your shoes for you all these weeks. A half-dressed policeman is hardly a proper representative of the majesty of the law?"

"Frances. Shut up!"

"Yes, I know, it isn't a pleasant reminder, is it? I'm sorry. But I do think you may be acting prematurely."

He put down his razor, splashed water on his face, and groped for a towel. The razor went sailing across the room. This time he swore silently.

Hamish, reflecting his anger, said, "Aye, it isna' a brave thing you do, merely foolhardy."

Rutledge said, "I am going *mad* cooped up in these rooms." The words served to answer both of them.

Frances said, deliberately misunderstanding him, "Yes, you must be. I did ask you to stay longer at the house. It's still warm enough to sit in the gardens in the afternoon, or walk across the street into the square. You can come back again, if you like." She had brought him there from hospital, and found a nurse to care for him until he could fend for himself, then taken over the chore of getting him dressed and undressed each day while he impatiently healed. Wounded tigers, she had thought more than once, would have been less of a handful.

But in the beginning, when she'd been summoned north, she had been terrified that he'd die before she got there. She'd only just got used to him being home and safe, with War's end. After four bitter years of killing, her brother had come back to her alive and so she had let her guard down at last. Policemen weren't *supposed* to be shot in the line of duty. The shock had left her breathless. Still, she'd done her best not to fuss over him. . . .

Rutledge, who understood the unspoken concern that lay behind his sister's efforts to keep him under her eye, had found it impossible to explain to her that he preferred his own flat, where he could swear at the pain or pace the floor at night or simply sit with his eyes closed until the worst had passed. Instead he'd merely said that he needed to learn to do for himself again.

Now he gingerly stooped and picked up the razor, then turned to grin at her. "Frances, you are the most capable woman I've ever met. When it comes to dealing with a crisis, you have no peer. All the same, it's easier, sometimes, not to have witnesses."

She smiled. "Yes, Father was just the same. I can't remember a time when he was ill that he didn't want to find himself a burrow somewhere and crawl off until he was better. It drove Mama to despair." The smile faded. "But returning to work, Ian—is it wise?"

Rutledge studied her. She knew, a little, what he'd been through in the War. Not all of it. She knew that he had been shell-shocked. But not that he had brought back from the Western Front the living voice of a dead man, Corporal Hamish MacLeod. Nor did she know what it was like to order a man shot, or to send weary and battle-worn men into certain death. To walk on the maggot-ridden bodies of corpses, or watch a friend die hideously, screaming. Nothing deadened such memories. They stayed bottled up. Raw, brutal, barbarous. The stuff of nightmares that the mind scrambles to bury deeper and deeper, just to survive, until there was no way to exorcise the demons that had seized possession of part of him.

There were stories he could tell when friends or colleagues asked "How was it over there?" And these were tailored to each listener. For some, humorous accounts of the incessant rain and sucking mud. The lack of water for bathing. How necessary it was to shave, so that the gas masks fit properly. To others he spoke of acts of bravery he'd witnessed, or the kindness of the nursing sisters. To a few he was comfortable discussing the shared danger that had turned men who had almost nothing else in common into brothers. But seldom the whole truth for anyone, only a small measure of it. It was, he thought, better that way.

"This is no' a wound of war," Hamish reminded him now. "You made yourself a target, on purpose."

Yet in some ways the confinement of this healing had once again left him vulnerable to all the horrors he'd fought these past five months to overcome. Now they were creeping out again in spite of him, reaching out to pull him back into the morass of despair and hopelessness he'd struggled so fiercely to leave behind. In the distraction of work, the subsequent exhaustion that brought him dreamless sleep, the concentration that kept Hamish at bay, he had scraped together a measure of peace.

"Until Scotland." It was a refrain that Hamish had dinned in his head day and night for the past three weeks. *Until Scotland . . .*

Rutledge told his sister lightly, forcing the shadows out of his conscious mind, "There's sanity in work. I've a desk full of papers to get through—hardly a test of endurance. And I *am* on sick leave, not permanent disability. This will heal, in good time." Unlike the spirit . . .

"It's little more than a week early."

Frances was that rare woman who knew when to stop persuading and start encouraging. "All right, then, let's try a compromise. You can manage your own breakfast, and find yourself a midday meal, but come to me for your dinner. At least I can be sure you're eating properly. You don't, you know. You are far too thin, still—"

But it wasn't eating improperly that kept Rutledge thin and drawn. It was so many hauntings . . . Hamish. The War. The impossibility of forgetting, when England was full of wounded men, struggling to go about lives that years in the trenches had altered irretrievably. People looked away from such men now, embarrassed by them, unable to think what to say to them. The War was finished. Over and done with. Except for the crosses in Flanders's Fields. And the living reminders no one quite knew what to do with. He saw himself a dozen times an hour on the streets—among the amputees, the blind, the ugly coughing of the gassed—even though he'd come home from France whole in body. *His* wounds were invisible, yet he shared the misery of such men. Even now he could see clearly the poor devil he'd watched from his window that very morning, clumsily managing his crutches and attempting to steer a reasonably straight course among the passersby. Or the hideously burned face passing under the street lamp three nights ago, long after dark. The man had tried to hide the worst of his scars with a scarf. But with one ear missing, his hat had settled awkwardly . . . A pilot, shot down in flames and unlucky enough to have lived through it.

As he had lived through Scotland . . . somehow.

Hamish said, "Ye ken, I wasna' ready for ye to die!"

To silence his thoughts, Rutledge agreed to dinner with Frances. The prospect of working a full day again *was* daunting; he knew quite well he hadn't regained his full strength. All the same, it would do no harm to try, and possibly offer him some little respite from Hamish's morbid concentration on Scotland.

Rutledge didn't want to think about Scotland.

Scotland had haunted him while he was recovering from surgery. It had filled his drugged dreams. It had brought him upright, drenched with sweat and pain, in the darkest part of the night when defenses were at their lowest ebb. Words, faces, the sound of pipes, that last day of rain when nothing stayed dry . . . It was all there in his mind when he was most vulnerable—on the edges of sleep, waking in the predawn hours—fighting the overwhelming pain for fear the doctor might give him more drugs if anyone guessed how much he suffered.

He'd never wanted to go back to Scotland. Too many Scots had been killed in the trenches—he had given the orders that sent hundreds of them charging into No Man's Land through gunfire that was pitiless, inhuman. He had watched them scream, he had seen them drop, he had stepped in the thick red blood where they had crawled in agony toward

their own lines. He'd heard their last fumbling words as they died. It
was a burden of guilt that still burned like live coals in his conscience.
But the Yard had seen fit to send him north, whether he wanted to go or
not. Barely a month ago, he'd done what he had sworn he would never
do. And he didn't want to think about it now.

There were letters from his godfather, David Trevor, who lived near
Edinburgh, lying in his desk across the room. Unopened. He didn't want
to read them until he was well, until he was back at the Yard and his
mind was filled with other problems. He didn't want to hear how it had
ended. He wished to God night after night that it had never begun—and
knew that he lied even as he said the words. *He had had to stay—*

But Hamish reminded him of those letters day and night, and he'd
ignored the voice until his head ached. When he was *healed,* fully
healed, he'd read them. . . . Not until then. Hamish be damned!

Oh, God. *Scotland be damned—!*

Frances was watching his face, and he dragged his thoughts back to
the present before she could read them.

Much as he disliked admitting it, she was right—one-armed, he was
worse in the kitchen than he was with a razor. And his cooking would
keep her happy, too. Less likely to chide him for looking like a scarecrow.

"Now let's see about that tie. Then I must go, I've a party tonight
and nothing to wear." She smiled as she rose and crossed to the wardrobe. "This one, I think, with the gray suit."

Chief Superintendent Bowles was not happy to see him. But then
Bowles never was pleased to find Inspector Rutledge at his desk. The
Chief Superintendent had hoped Rutledge might die of septicemia.
Foolish of him to get himself shot in the first place! It went to prove that
Rutledge was neither dependable nor competent to deal with police
work. All the same, one could hope that the next time he was fired
upon, the bullet would fly true.

There was already talk in certain quarters about the possibility of a
promotion. Bowles had squelched it, saying, "Too soon, too soon. He's
not been back at the Yard half a year yet. Give the man time to find his
feet!"

Bowles greeted his returning Inspector with what could best be described as subdued enthusiasm, and set him to clearing up files, going
over paperwork for the courts, looking at the disposition of cases.

Wouldn't do to have Rutledge out on the streets, fainting in the midst of an inquiry. He'd told his superiors that as well. Wait until the man's healed! Time enough then for him to take on a new case.

Rutledge, in fact, didn't care. The mind-numbing concentration needed to finish each report or check every document kept Hamish at arm's length and silent. It was respite in the form of inescapable boredom, and he embraced it with prodigious gratitude.

The other urgent requirement was to rebuild his stamina, depleted by enforced idleness. And so he began a regimen of walking each day. To breakfast in a dark-paneled pub, chosen because it lay several streets above Trafalgar Square. To lunch at any one of several pubs on streets that ran toward the Tower, and then an ever larger loop that would bring him back to the Embankment. Frances, under the impression that he was prudently taking the Underground, said nothing about his gray face each evening. But the thought of walking down into the crowded, noisy tunnels turned him cold with nerves. It was too much like being buried alive in the trenches.

The first day, Rutledge arrived back at the Yard shaking from the exertion, and still made himself take the stairs two at a time. Even on the weekend, he refused to stay indoors and rest. By his third day at the office, a Tuesday, he could walk without the black shadows of exhaustion clouding his mind to the point that he was a danger to himself and traffic in the streets. On the afternoon of the fifth, he was able to breathe reasonably well, and stop to look about him. His legs, he thought wryly, belonged to him again. Their tendency to wobble in his weakness had angered him more than the arm strapped to his chest.

There was work being done on a plaster War Memorial in the middle of Whitehall. The construction had snarled traffic for some time, and before returning to the Yard, Rutledge decided to have a look at it. Simplicity had been the goal, but the memorial seemed inadequate, he thought, to hold the memory of so much spilled blood and so many ruined lives. Depressed, he moved on toward St. Margaret's Church, to stand on the corner of Bridge Street for a time, looking up at Big Ben and watching pigeons wheeling against the sky. Reluctant to return to his desk in his stuffy, ill-lit office, he listened to the traffic on the Thames, and considered crossing the busy bridge.

Hamish, relishing the wind from the river and a sudden gust of rain that swept down on them, was lost in his own reflections.

The sound of voices, like small birds twittering in a bush, brought

Rutledge's eyes back to St. Margaret's, and his thoughts back to the present. A group of young women, stylish in black, stood waiting at the door for another, just descending from a motorcar in the street. She waved and hurried toward them, the wind catching the skirts of her coat, as if sweeping her out of his reach.

He recognized her walk before he heard her voice calling to her friends. It was Jean—

She caught up with the others, and laughter surrounded them, her face holding the pale light for an instant before they turned and went inside the church. Her cheeks were flushed with excitement and warmth.

Her wedding was to be held at St. Margaret's in a fortnight's time.

Jason Webley had told him that, coming to visit him in hospital at the end of September and after a time awkwardly turning the subject to the woman Rutledge had once been engaged to marry. "I say, old man, have you heard? Jean's set a date, end of next month." Webley paused, then added, "She asked Elizabeth to be in the wedding party. Elizabeth asked me what her answer ought to be, and I told her I thought you wouldn't mind."

"No." But he had minded. Not because he begrudged Jean her happiness, but because she'd taken away so much of his. He could still remember the day, nearly eight months before, when she'd told him, haltingly, in another hospital ward, that she wished to end their engagement. And he'd seen the fear in her eyes, the dread of being tied to a broken man. . . . He hadn't yet begun to recover, a silent, empty man in the grip of nightmares she couldn't understand, and she'd believed that he never would be more than that. An object of pity for the rest of his life.

Hamish reminded him, "It was a near-run thing!"

It had been. But Rutledge was as unprepared for her desertion as he would have been for a slap in the face. He'd needed comfort, a gentle reminder of that normal life he'd lost somewhere in the trenches. Jean couldn't have chosen a worse time to break her engagement to the man she'd once sworn she loved above all others. A week or two more—a month— Would it have made a difference if she'd offered him the compassion of waiting a little longer? Held him in her arms and told him it didn't matter, she loved him still—even if it was a kind lie?

He would never know. Jean had scuttled out of the hospital room in undisguised relief, grateful that he'd been willing to set her free. By August she had become engaged to a diplomat and was looking forward to a new life in Canada, where the man was taking up his next posting.

Blithe, unshadowed, she had brushed away the war years as if they were a bad dream. Shallow, Frances had called her—a woman who would never have made him happy.

Staring at the church door, Rutledge found himself thinking that he was, after all, a lucky man. He hadn't married Jean in that golden haze of 1914, when war was gloriously linked to romance and adventure, not to suffering. She had tried to persuade him to agree to a hasty wedding then: uniforms, crossed swords, and a hero off to fight the Hun. And he had reminded her that she was far too young and lovely to find herself a widow. . . .

He wondered what kind of life they might have shared these past seven months, after he'd finally been released from the clinic, still a prisoner of his own terrors. And how deeply they would have come to hate each other, finally. Or if she might have found herself wishing that the bullet he'd taken in Scotland in September had put an end to their pretenses.

Hamish said, "She'd ha' been bonny in black."

Certainly she would have carried herself with great courage, impressing all his friends, trailing behind her the whisper of great passion and love lost, where neither had ever existed.

Still, he was swept by a sense of loss as he watched her pass through the door of the church, oblivious. She hadn't felt his eyes or his thoughts. She hadn't sensed his presence and turned to look for him. There was a loneliness in that.

By the end of that week, Rutledge told himself that he'd made rather remarkable strides from the crippled man struggling to shave one-handed while his sister watched. The throbbing in his shoulder and chest muscles had begun to subside into a dull ache that he could put out of his mind. He could do without the sling now for hours at a time, although the arm was still tightly bound.

Another week, he told himself, *and I'll be fit again.*

The dinners with his sister were beginning to wear thin. Much as he loved her, enjoyed the variety of her cooking, and appreciated the fact that she did not fuss, Frances worried about him, and he found it difficult to smile and ignore that. On the other hand, before the War, it had been Rutledge who had worried about her. And he knew too well the signs of unspoken concern. Of skirting around issues that ought not to be discussed—what had happened in Scotland, Jean's approaching wedding, mutual friends who were in worse straits than he was. He had reached the point of wanting to blurt out, if only for the sake of clearing the air between them: "Look—I know David is worried that I haven't written him—I just can't face it yet. Don't ask me why! And as for Jean, I wish her well, I'm not heartbroken. I'm lonely, that's all, but I don't want to meet a dozen of your suitable friends. For God's sake, that's not the answer!"

Hamish reminded him, "Ye're no' fit company for yourself, much less a lassie. Get drunk and get it o'er with!" As advice, it wasn't bad.

But that Friday there were more pressing matters to consider. Chief Superintendent Bowles, after a consultation with the police surgeon, considered his options, then went to see Rutledge.

"It's a matter of setting the Bishop's mind at rest. He's worried about the death of one of his people. Catholic priest, murdered in some backwater of Norfolk called Osterley."

"A priest?" Rutledge repeated, surprised. In the eyes of the law, killing a clergyman was no more heinous a crime than killing a shop girl or a fishmonger. The penalty was the same—hanging by the neck until dead. But in the eyes of society, a man of the Cloth was protected by his calling, set apart. Inviolate.

Hamish reminded him that priests had once been burned at the stake. But that was another day and time. With no bearing on 1919.

Bowles was shaking his head. "We lost our way in the War, you know." It was one of his favorite themes. "No good ever comes of change. Women doing men's work—it isn't natural! The lower classes getting above themselves. I shouldn't wonder if we'll see worse before we're done. Society breaking down, Bolshevism on the loose. Now a priest's dead."

He peered at the sheet of paper in his hand. "Struck down with his own altar crucifix in St. Anne's rectory, to be precise. The local police haven't caught the villain yet. The priest walked in on a thief, apparently. It's probable he could have recognized the man, and was murdered for that reason. The police are looking at that as the primary motive, for now. Still—we may have a madman in our midst, who's to say differently? Little wonder this Bishop wants reassurance that we're doing all we can."

"What was the thief after?" Rutledge interjected. There were more likely choices for breaking and entering than a church office or rectory. A poor box and a priest's pockets were notoriously bare. Madman indeed!

"A paltry sum collected at the church harvest festival, I'm told, which means everyone at the festival, in the village, and in the countryside for miles around knew there must be money in the rectory."

"That broadens the inquiry considerably," Rutledge agreed. "Did the priest have a housekeeper? How did an intruder get past her?"

"She'd already gone home for the day. And the priest himself should have been in the church to hear Confession, but had put up a notice there saying he was away at a deathbed and might not be back in time. Clear sailing, the thief must have thought. But Father James came home and went up to his study, and the intruder panicked. A shame, but there it is. It could happen to any householder."

It could—and often did.

"Word has come down from the Chief Constable in Norfolk that it's politic to send an officer," Bowles said. "You're to show the Yard's concern and have a look at the evidence. Speak with this Bishop or one of his people, assure him that the local police know what they're about, and once he's satisfied that everything possible is being done, come back to London. From what I hear of the local man, Blevins, he's competent and has a good reputation for using his head. Shouldn't take you more than a few days. And October in the Broads is usually fine."

Rutledge remembered that it was often wet, but said nothing.

Hamish said, "It's no' a holiday, mind. Watch your back! You canna' trust the man. He doesna' want you in London."

"It's more likely a diversion," Rutledge answered silently, "to take pressure off Blevins. While everyone is watching me, he'll be free to get the job done."

Hamish grunted, "Have ye forgotten Scotland already?"

Bowles was saying, "Leave now, and you'll be there tonight. Anything I ought to know regarding those, before you go?" He gestured to the files spread across Rutledge's desk. "Parker can deal with them."

"No, I'm finished with this lot. In fact, I was about to hand them over to Sergeant Williams. He'll know which are to be filed and which distributed to the officer in charge of the investigation."

"I'll send Williams up to collect them. There's a train at half past ten, you can make it if you hurry!" Bowles smiled in encouragement. Rutledge was reminded of crocodiles. The same cold yellow eyes.

"Very well." He stood up, took the pages Bowles handed him, tucked them under his good arm, and went to open the door. "I'll report by telephone, shall I?"

"No need. It's a courtesy visit; you won't be getting involved."

The doctor, taking the bandages off Rutledge's chest for the last time, looked at the wound, poked and probed at it—making the patient wince—and then nodded in satisfaction.

"You were damned lucky," Dr. Fleming said, "that no deep infection set in. Still, it won't hurt to have a small plaster over it. A matter of prevention. How do you feel?"

Rutledge, looking down at the raised, raw scar in the matted hair on his chest, replied, "I can breathe without discomfort." He flexed his arm. It felt like a soggy rag. "I doubt I could take on a child of six in a brawl."

Fleming chuckled. "Nor should you. But that arm will be like new, once you begin using it. Never fear! Just don't overdo it for the first few days—don't carry anything heavy or push at anything that doesn't want to budge. Again, a matter of prevention. I have found in twenty years of treating patients that Nature is a good doctor, too, given half a chance. The problem is, we seldom give her credit and therefore come to regret it."

It was, Rutledge knew, one of Fleming's favorite homilies. "I'm off to Norwich. Which shouldn't be strenuous."

"Cheating the ratepayer, are you? I'd take the train if I were you. Less demanding on the chest muscles than driving."

But Rutledge left London in his own motorcar, his claustrophobia still rampant. It was not possible for him to sit in a compartment jammed hip and knee into other travelers. The compulsion to stand and scream for air would be as violent as it was unreasonable.

By the time he reached Norwich, his chest muscles were in open rebellion, Mother Nature urging them on. Hamish, worse than Dr. Fleming at pointing out Rutledge's shortcomings, reminded him that he had made the drive against advice.

As a compromise, Rutledge found a small hotel on the outskirts of town and stayed the night there, not prepared to face the traffic of Norwich at the end of the day.

Hamish, who had alternately raged at him and baited him for miles of the way, was as tired as he was: The familiar voice was silent over dinner.

Rutledge slept hard from fatigue. Hamish never followed him into sleep—the voice in his head lived in the waking mind, a bitter and hourly reminder of the bloody offensive in 1916 on the Somme, where so many men had died not by the hundreds or thousands but by the tens of thousands, their lives thrown away in wave after desperate wave of futile attacks. Where he himself had been buried in mud and saved from suffocation by the body pressing down on him. He'd been told over and over again that Corporal Hamish MacLeod had saved his life. But the blood caked like a second skin all over his face and hands had come from the English firing squad and the coup de grâce Rutledge had had to deliver personally in the instant before a direct hit had blown the salient to bits. Hamish hadn't died from German fire, and Rutledge had been too shaken, too lost in the depths of shell shock to set the record straight: that Corporal MacLeod had been shot for refusing a direct order on the battlefield the night before that final dawn assault.

The tangled skeins of truth and official reports had left Rutledge with silence, with memory, with a waking haunting that had nothing to do with ghosts. Only with the broken mind of a man who had been sent straight back into battle before he'd had any rest, or come to terms with his own deep sense of guilt for having to choose between one man's life and the morale of the equally exhausted and dispirited soldiers who *hadn't* refused the order to climb out of the trenches and fight again. And three years later, he still had not exorcised that guilt.

It had become too deeply rooted in blood and bone and sinew, like a second self.

Rutledge had tried over and over again to die during the last two years of the War, putting himself in the way of danger, courting the unholy bombardments that splintered the earth, daring the hidden machine-gun nests that raked No Man's Land with lethal fire. Like a lover embracing a bloody mistress he had sought out any peril—and had come through unscathed.

To find himself again and again hailed as a hero, because he seemed to have no fear of dying.

It had been the bitterest irony.

CHAPTER THREE

THE FOLLOWING MORNING, RUTLEDGE FOUND HIS way through the busy streets of Norwich to the address he'd been given by Chief Superintendent Bowles. It was a small house near the new Catholic church, far older than the building in whose shadow it stood, and with a small garden behind it. A gloomy house, upright and Victorian, with sharp eaves that seemed to pierce the low clouds. Rutledge walked up to the door in a misting rain that enveloped the earth like a shroud. On a small wooden board, faded gold letters spelled out *Diocesan Office*. Lifting the door knocker, a great brass ring that fell with a doomsday clamor, he turned to look at the street behind him. A half dozen men were waist-deep in a broken sewer, digging shovels full of stinking mud out of the pit. Urchins gaped down into the hole, fascinated, while passersby held handkerchiefs to their noses against the rank odor. A pair of women huddled together on the corner exchanging news, the hems of their black skirts even blacker with the run-off of the umbrellas they clutched over their hats. A man walking a dog moved swiftly, hurrying it along as it stopped to sniff in the gutters.

No one took notice of the caller at the rectory. Rain was a great separator.

Hamish, whose fierce Covenanter ancestors had taught him well, was skittish about entering this den of popery and idolatry. Rutledge, amused, assured him that his soul was in no danger.

"How can *you* be sae sure, when the Church of England is hardly better than this lot?"

The door was opened by a housekeeper whose hair, graying at the temples, was auburn, and whose face, flecked with freckles, had a touch of Irish in it. The woman looked him up and down as he gave her his name, and asked, "Are you ill, then?"

He smiled. "Official business."

"All the same, you look as if you could do with a cup of tea! And the poor man hasn't had his, either, writing reports all the morning! Come in, then."

She took his hat and coat, clicked her tongue at the dark patches of rain across the coat's shoulders, and spread it carefully over a chair to dry. Then she led the way down a passage to a room at the far end. To Hamish's considerable relief, there were no niches filled with bleeding saints in the passage, nor a pervasive odor of incense. Except for a single small crucifix above the narrow entry, there was no sign that the occupants of this den had designs on anyone's soul.

Opening a door into a gracious room at the back of the house, the housekeeper stood aside to let Rutledge enter. Beyond the windows the rain fell softly on a garden already drab and colorless, and dripped from a small pear tree. A tall secretary desk, the doors in the upper half standing open and the front piled with papers, stood against the far wall, and there was a table and comfortable chairs set to catch the light spilling in the windows. A man in simple priest's garb sat there, staring out at the wet flower beds, a book open in his lap. He looked up as the housekeeper gave Rutledge's name with a flourish.

Hardly a den of iniquity, Rutledge silently pointed out to Hamish. This was more the study of a scholarly man, a place for retreat and thought.

Hamish reserved his opinion.

Setting his book aside and standing, the man crossed the room and held out his hand. "From London, are you? That's a fair journey! Bryony, some tea for the two of us."

She cast a quick, smiling look at Rutledge and said, "The kettle is already on the boil." The door closed silently behind her.

"I'm Monsignor Holston," the tall, thin man continued. He had an aesthetic face and the eyes of a policeman—intent, knowing. The long nose, bearing a pince-nez, was aristocratic and gave the face character if not beauty. But the grip of his calloused hand was firm, strong. He offered Rutledge one of the chairs by the table, and returned to his own to mark his place in the book, close it, and set it aside. "I'm instructed to speak to you on Bishop Cunningham's behalf. He was called away on pressing diocesan business. Scotland Yard. Well, I'm pleased to see you, I must say. This matter of Father James's death has been worrying. What can you tell me?"

Rutledge smiled. "It's more a matter of what you can tell me. I've come to listen."

"Ah. Yes. Well, let's not wait for our tea, then." Monsignor Holston ran his fingers along the edge of the leather corners of the blotter. "It's very straightforward, what the police propose must have happened. The local people took one look at the scene—at the desk broken open, most particularly—and declared that Father James had surprised a man intent on stealing funds collected at the bazaar a fortnight previously. Certainly the money was missing." He realized how formal his words sounded, as if he were quoting directly from the police record, and made an effort to continue in a more natural tone. "Father James was usually in the church at that hour, you see, hearing Confessions, and should have been in the confessional, not his study. It must have been quite a shock to the intruder to hear him coming up the stairs! According to Inspector Blevins, the man panicked, seized the crucifix from Father James's altar, and struck him down before fleeing. That's all the police can tell me with any certainty." The priest stopped, and the blue eyes studied Rutledge's face. There was a wariness in them.

"Straightforward, yes," Rutledge agreed. "But you—or your Bishop—apparently weren't satisfied. Why? Is there more to the story than the police have learned? Or is it something to do with the circumstances in which he was found?"

"Sadly, no, we have no information about the crime itself." Monsignor Holston smiled wryly. "Except that if it was robbery, it was unnecessary. Father James was a very caring priest. He'd have helped the man; he wouldn't have turned him away. Or turned him in, for that

matter. What's frightening is—" He broke off and then added, "I spoke
to the Bishop myself after I'd been summoned to Osterley by the police.
I tried to explain what it was about the crime that troubled me." He adjusted his glasses, as if to see his way more clearly through his own feelings. "I stood looking down at the body, and it's true, the shock
unsettled me. It was such a waste—a terrible, unspeakable waste! But
my reaction went beyond that. I felt something that was *primeval*. Fear,
if you will."

Hamish stirred.

Rutledge said, "If he was a friend, that's a fairly common reaction,
Monsignor. Of a life squandered, and a certain anxiety because death
has struck so near." He paused. "Father James had died unshriven.
Perhaps unconsciously, that weighed heavily. It would be natural for
you to be concerned."

"Yes, I'd take that into account. Of course I would. But it was more
than that. God knows I've attended my share of deathbeds. Like a
physician, I'm able to separate my emotions into tidy cubbyholes, in order to function. But not this time." He looked down at his hands. "I
grant you that to a poor man the sum collected at the bazaar must have
seemed enormous. The blows, Inspector Blevins told me, were struck in
rapid succession. A frenzy, if you will. A terrified man, caught out unexpectedly, might well have reacted in that fashion, hating what he was
doing but driven to shield himself. And yet somehow I can't accept that.
If he had come *openly*—"

"There may have been reasons why the intruder couldn't come
openly. Or perhaps he'd convinced himself that theft was the easier way.
That he couldn't keep his promise to repay—or see that he worked out
the money in time or kind."

"Yes, I grant you that. But consider two things. The intruder must
have known the pattern of Father James's usual movements. Otherwise, why choose that time of day? And he must have known that
the study was upstairs, and that that was where the money was being
kept. He didn't ransack the rest of the house. He went directly to the
study! And surely the first place he'd have searched—the most logical
choice—was a desk drawer. The money *was* in there. Why tear the
room apart, if he'd got what he came for? In my opinion, if the thief
had been more careful opening that drawer and had slipped away before Father James came back from hearing Confession, surely no one

would have been able to say with any certainty just when the money went missing!"

"Logic seldom enters into it. A man robbing a house is usually in a hurry and not eager to be caught. If he'd just killed in a fit of panic, he might have wanted to make it seem he'd expected a better haul. To point a finger away from the fact that he was desperate enough for the little he'd found in the desk."

Hamish said, "Ye ken yon priest's been busy worrying ow'r it. Gnawing at it like a dog with a bone."

Monsignor Holston was shaking his head. "I am trained to think about religious issues. When I apply the same logic to this murder, I find—questions. Not solutions."

"No murder is simple," Rutledge told him. "But if I understand what you are telling me, Father James must have been killed by one of his own parishioners. It's not a pretty possibility, though a likely one. And surely the police have considered it."

A shadow of relief passed over the priest's face. He said, "I'm afraid that several other things point in that direction as well, which I felt the Bishop had to be told. Father James wore an antique gold medal of Saint James on a chain, a gift from his family when he was ordained. The candlesticks from his private altar might have fetched a goodly sum, as would the altar crucifix that was used as the weapon. They were old, at a guess they'd belonged to the priests of St. Anne's since the early 1700s. Why should a thief pass up such tempting opportunities? If he's in desperate need and has already committed murder? What's another minute taken to stuff a crucifix in a pocket or candlesticks under one's coat?" An eyebrow lifted quizzically, as if inviting Rutledge to prove him wrong.

"Perhaps because the thief was afraid they were objects far easier to trace than a small handful of bills or coins."

"Yes, I'd thought of that, too. My answer was, the metal could be melted down, if you knew where to go. The thief might not receive more than a portion of its real value, but it must surely come to a tidy sum. I find myself returning again and again to the fact that if he'd wanted only the money, he could have run out, shoving Father James out of his way, and taken the chance that in such a brief, unexpected encounter in a dark room, he might not be recognized. Better that than the sin of murder on his soul!"

"He's fearful," Hamish interjected, "that he might ken the killer—"

The door opened and Bryony came in with the tea tray, shadowed by a tiger-striped gray cat. Bryony set the tray onto the table close to the priest's elbow, cast an eye over it, then left, the cat following at her heels with a smug air. Rutledge tried not to remember a white cat lying on a pillow in an empty room, looking for its owner to come again.

"The rectory doesn't own Bruce. The cat," Monsignor Holston said in amusement, catching Rutledge's eye on the animal. "He owns the rectory. If I understand his genealogy correctly, his great-great-grandmother was a resident here. That's before the Bishop's time, and mine." He poured a cup of tea for Rutledge and then for himself, passed the pitcher of thick cream and the bowl of sugar. A plate of thin sandwiches and another of thin slices of cake followed.

Rutledge was beginning to see a pattern in the dispassionate account Monsignor Holston had given. His reasoning had been easy to follow—someone who had no connection with the church might have considered the candlesticks and the crucifix an unexpected windfall. This thief hadn't. But he'd known or guessed where to look for the money. As Holston had all but said, the evidence pointed directly to a member of the church. But was that his only deduction?

There were shadows behind the priest's eyes, worry more than mourning. Rutledge decided to bide his time.

As Monsignor Holston settled to his tea, Rutledge asked, "Have the police interviewed members of St. Anne's congregation? Surely they were most likely to know that the bazaar money was still in Father James's hands. As well as where it was being kept."

"Oh, yes, that was done, and done again. There are, as in every parish, Catholic or Protestant, a few . . . er . . . black sheep. These were questioned a third time. But such men aren't likely to commit murder—petty theft, perhaps. Even burglary, if pressed by circumstances. There were at least three needy parishioners who might well have talked their way out of trouble, if Father James caught them in his study. Ill wife in one case, and too many children to feed in another, and a third is known for his taste for the horses. In their straits, any sum might have been tempting. In Inspector Blevins's opinion, none was likely to be a killer. He said not one of them had the stomach for it."

"Perhaps Inspector Blevins should be searching for a man who might have had one of the booths at the fair. Or had come to the fair for the express purpose of finding money somehow. And chosen to come back and try his luck at the rectory, when he had been unsuccessful any-where else."

The cake was heavy with eggs and sultanas. Rutledge thought, *Frances would tell me it's strengthening. . . .*

"Yes, the local authorities have been quite thorough there also. They're still searching for individuals who had set up a booth and any strangers who had drawn attention to themselves. Apparently it isn't easy to trace their movements—this is a popular time of year for harvest fetes and bazaars. They could be in a dozen towns."

Rutledge finished his cake and set aside his plate. The thin man op-posite him had consumed three helpings to his one. Filled with a ner-vous energy that demanded stoking, Monsignor Holston seemed not to notice the richness of the cake.

"Let's return to my earlier suggestion—and yours. What if we turn the tale around, and ask ourselves if the priest was killed—and the pit-tance taken to cover up the crime?" Rutledge asked.

"The police also dismissed that theory. They reported to the Bishop that there is no reason to believe that Father James had enemies." The blue eyes had become watchful.

Policemen often interviewed witnesses and friends of a murder vic-tim who felt a driving need to find explanations, to look for answers. But Rutledge had the strong impression that Monsignor Holston was trying to shape the thinking of this man from London, guiding it care-fully toward an unclear goal.

Rutledge said, "I think it might be time for you to give me the whole of the story."

Monsignor Holston smiled. "Do you usually have so little faith in the things you're told, Inspector?"

"Which is another way of saying, perhaps, that I believe you your-self have not yet come to face the truth."

The priest sighed.

"It isn't a matter of truth," he replied, turning for a moment to look out the window at the rain. "It's a matter of faith. Sometimes there's a feeling one can't shake off. Have you ever experienced such a thing?" When Rutledge nodded, he went on, "Try as hard as I will, I can't ig-nore that primeval response—that sense of danger—of fear for myself, as well as for Father James. I asked the Bishop to send for Scotland Yard because my instincts tell me it was the right thing to do. What if there *is* more here than meets the eye? What if this murder is beyond the experience and training of the local people to investigate fully? What if the killer is able to outwit them, and we see no one brought to justice?" He paused, then said in a strained voice, "It's likely that I'll be sent as the interim pastor at St. Anne's, until a replacement can be found. I don't want to be the next victim!"

CHAPTER FOUR

Rutledge stared at the priest, his mind working swiftly as he weighed what had been said—and what had not.

"You've been afraid from the beginning, haven't you, that Father James was not killed for money? For the sake of argument, what if you're right? What if the theft *was* no more than a cloud of confusion, to mislead the police? If you're worried about being the next victim, the only conclusion I can draw is that you've been told something—"

Monsignor Holston interrupted, his voice earnest. "I was in that room, before they'd taken Father James away. And there was violence in the presence of his body. Violence that went unexplained. And it spilled over on me! Do you understand what I am trying to say? What if this murderer isn't satisfied that it's finished? Or has your profession inured you to death, Inspector? Perhaps it's out of fashion—after the slaughter of thousands in the War—to put the death of any man—even a priest!—down to an unspeakable act?"

"They are both unspeakable acts, murder and war," Rutledge answered grimly. "I haven't become inured to either of them. You're describing the force of the crime, I think, not the motivation."

Monsignor Holston shook his head. "No. It was something in that room. The policemen were about, the lamps lit, the spirit of the man long since departed, the body cold, even—but the lingering sense of violence was frightful." He paused. "As a priest I have no key to unlock the mind of this murderer. But I fear it, and in doing so, I fail the man who has just taken a life. And in failing him, I have failed God." He set his teacup aside.

Rutledge said, "If you've sent for Scotland Yard to restore your faith in your God, we aren't trained for that."

"No, it isn't what I need from you. I need your intelligence and your knowledge of how or why such a crime is committed. I want to be sure that the man the police take into custody this week—next week—next year—is the culprit. It will be easy, I think, to find people who might have been needy enough to steal. And put the blame on them. I want to be absolutely sure it isn't misplaced!"

The priest had failed to answer the question directly.

"He's as slippery as a fish," Hamish warned.

"You're a trained and intelligent man yourself, Monsignor. Surely you've taken the question a step further. If it wasn't something Father James knew—or had told you—then it must be something in that rectory that the killer was searching for. And if he failed to find it, you must feel fairly certain that he'll come back to try again. If you're there, he won't let your presence stand in his way, just as he didn't spare Father James. What in heaven's name could Father James have kept there that would be worth one priest's life, and perhaps two? What could have put him at such risk?"

"If I knew the answer to that," Monsignor Holston said in resignation, "we wouldn't be having this conversation. I'd have told Inspector Blevins at once!"

"Then I'm left with the original police supposition that this was a breaking-and-entering gone wrong. And the people in Osterley can handle that. If I'm to present a case to my superiors that calls for the Yard's intervention, I've got to persuade them that there is very good reason to think the Yard's time is well spent here. Yes, the fact that the victim is a priest naturally weighs with them, or I wouldn't have been sent to Norwich in the first place. But the rule of thumb is that the local constabulary often knows more about the people they need to interview than an outsider could, and are therefore more likely to spot the killer."

"I have given you all the information that it's in my power to give you," Monsignor Holston replied, his austere face clouded with doubt. "I can't tell you more than that—I wish I *knew* more! And I won't lie to you, either. I will say this: Father James was a very good man. Sober and hardworking. A man of faith and deep convictions. I have a duty to him. If his murderer *can* be found, I want him found."

Hamish said, "A priest could be killed for what he knows."

It was true. . . .

Rutledge, finishing his tea, shook his head as he was offered more and set his empty cup on the tray. "There's another avenue we haven't really explored. A clergyman learns to cope with a variety of responsibilities, some of them rather onerous. There's always the chance that what happened to Father James is in some way related to his duties. And in taking them over, you may put yourself at risk as well. Someone may believe you will come to know more than you safely should."

"It's always possible, of course. The truth is, a clergyman can often make quite good guesses about what's going on in his parish. And he's often privy to confidences—never mind what he's told in the confessional. But in that confessional, he may learn the whole story. A husband is unfaithful to his wife, a clerk has cheated his employer, someone has spread a lie that hurt others, a child was not fathered by the man who believes it's his. That's the reason the words uttered in the confessional are a sacred trust. It must be a place where a person tells the truth and unburdens his soul before God. We believe in this sacrament, and we protect it with our silence. Father James wouldn't have broken that vow."

"And if a man or a woman tells the priest something, and later regrets that confidence?"

"He or she may regret having spoken. But God knew long before he or she stepped into the confessional. And the priest is sworn to silence."

"That's not always the practical answer," Rutledge told him.

Monsignor Holston removed his glasses, rubbing the bridge of his nose. "No, it isn't. The practical answer is, that man or that woman may simply move to another parish, leaving behind the priest who knows the truth and finding another one who will accept this newest member of his flock at face value. One doesn't murder the priest for the secrets of the confessional. It would have changed the face of the Church hundreds of years ago if that had become the common practice." He restored his glasses to their proper place, settling them into the deep indentations on either side of his nose, then tried to smile. And failed. "Were you told that Father James was a chaplain in the first two years of the War, until he was sent home with severe dysentery in 1917? Who can be sure that the truth doesn't lie there? In the War?" Monsignor Holston turned his head again to look out at the garden, as if he half expected to find the answer he wanted in the grassy paths and the shrubbery. Or half expected to find someone standing there.

Hamish said, "He fidgets like a man with an uneasy conscience!"

Rutledge answered silently, "Uneasy? Or uncertain?" Aloud he said, "In that event, I see no reason why you should feel that you're in any particular danger."

Monsignor Holston turned from the window to Rutledge. "I have told you. It's primitive—the hair rising on the back of my neck in a dark corner of my church, or coming down the passage here in the house when it's late and I'm alone. Sitting in a lighted room when the windows are dark and the drapes haven't been drawn, and looking up suddenly to see if someone is out there, staring in at me. It isn't real, it's all imagination. And I'm not by nature easily frightened. Now I am."

"Did you serve with the same units that Father James did?"

"I never went to France. I worked among the wounded here in England as they were being sorted out when the ships came in. Most of them were in too much pain to do more than accept a cigarette and a little compassion, some reassurance that God was still watching over them." Monsignor Holston shook his head. "You're probably right, I'm not thinking very logically about any of this. But somewhere in this muddle there must be an explanation for Father James's murder and my own strange sense that something's *wrong*." He took a deep breath. "I'm sorry. You're a very clever man, Inspector Rutledge. You'll sort it out. I am reassured that Scotland Yard has sent us its best."

And that was all that Monsignor Holston was prepared to say.

Leaving the rectory, Rutledge paused to speak to Bryony as she showed him to the door. Around them the house was silent, shutting out the sound of the rain and the echo of shovels scraping against stone out in the street. "I understand that Father James was well thought of."

"Now there was a black day, when Father was killed! I've not got over the shock of it. Well thought of? Of course he was, and well loved, well respected, too!" She took Rutledge's hat and coat from the chair beside the door and held them to her as if they offered comfort. "You can ask anyone."

"People always speak well of the dead," he told her gently. "Even a priest is human, and sometimes frail."

"As to that, I wouldn't know! I'm not one to go around looking for failings. I can tell you Father James was a patient man, and generous. If someone had come to him with a tale of hard luck, he'd have given them the money, they needn't have killed him for it! It'll turn out to be a stranger, mark my words. A cruel and ungodly man with no regard for his own soul." Her eyes remained on his, as if expecting him to make a pronouncement that would set her mind at rest.

"A non-Catholic? Is that what you're saying?"

"Neither Protestant *nor* Catholic, in my view—no churchgoing man would murder a clergyman, would he? I'm saying that whoever it was killed Father James wasn't hungry or in debt. He was calculating and self-serving, with a devil in him. Or *her*. Women can be terrible cruel sometimes. Are there so many of those walking about that it takes all this time for the police to track down the right one? It's been days now since Father's death, and what have the police got to show for it? I call it a crying shame!"

"Surely they've tried."

"Oh, as to trying, now, I'd agree with you there. They've tried. But they're not what I'd call *clever* men." She moved to open the door for him, letting in the damp and the reek of the filthy mud being piled high at the roadside. "Housebreaking and petty theft, fire-setting or assault—they'll find the culprit, because chances are he's done it before. But that's not *clever*, is it? It's only a matter of knowing where to look!"

"And in this case, perhaps only a matter of finding out who has extra money jangling in his pocket, the money he stole from Father James," Rutledge responded reasonably. "Six of one—"

"Is it, now?" She tilted her head to look up at him. "Father James was a family man, did they tell you? This past August his sister presented her husband with three little ones, and Father James was always helping out with the babes. What's she to do now, with winter coming on and no one to come and stay a few days, when one's sick of the croup and she's up all the night? You might speak to Mrs. Wainer. She was Father James's housekeeper, and a more decent woman you'll never meet. Ask her about walking into the study and finding him there stiff and cold, blood all over the place. And for all she knew, the killer lurking in the bedroom, ready to strike her down as well! If you've set Monsignor's mind at rest just now, it would be a kindness to reassure her, too. And only a few hours out of your way, mind!"

"Where will I find her?" He stepped through the doorway as she handed him his coat and hat. He could feel the blowing mist on his face, fine as silk against his skin.

"She's at the rectory still, though I don't know for the life of me how the poor woman can walk through the door. It's her duty to be there, she says. Every day. Just as if Father James was still alive. Osterley is the name of the town. Surely they told you that in London? It's closer to the sea in the north, and easy enough to get to from here." Her eyes were shrewd. "Easier, of course, to go back to London satisfied you've done your duty by us. There's many would do that. Somehow I don't think you're one of them!"

And with that she bade him a good day and closed the door.

Rutledge turned the crank and got into his motorcar, out of the rain. And then he surprised himself by sitting there, considering what Bryony had said, the motor idling under his gloved hands as they rested on the wheel.

He hadn't anticipated being drawn into the life or the death of this man. It wasn't the task that had been set him. . . .

Go to Norfolk to reassure the Bishop that the police are doing their job properly.

And instead he'd been expected, he thought wryly, to perform a small miracle or two. Find a true explanation for the murder of the priest—and then track down the killer.

He didn't envy the local man, Blevins, struggling to conduct an investigation in a climate of disbelief that refused to accept simple murder for what it really was, a commonplace calamity, not the stuff of legends.

But even as he tried to make light of Bryony's forceful plea and Monsignor Holston's fears, Rutledge couldn't escape the fact that their intensity had touched him.

Hamish said, "Aye, but it will pass, with the mood."

Which was probably true. The thing was, Bryony had made it very hard for him to walk away.

Instead, he put the motorcar in gear and turned the bonnet north instead of south toward London, driving on to Osterley.

As a schoolboy, learning to draw the map of Great Britain, Rutledge had been taught that the island resembled a man in a top hat riding a running pig. The top hat was the northern part of Scotland—the Highlands. The man's head and body were the Lowlands and the Midlands of England. The pig's head was Wales, its front feet the Cornish peninsula, its hind feet the downs of Kent. And its rump was East Anglia, the great bulge of Essex, Suffolk, and Norfolk jutting out into the North Sea toward the Low Countries.

It was a picture he and his schoolmates had found diverting, endlessly practicing their drawing of the pig and its rider, unaware that the effort sealed forever in their minds the geography of their country.

Now, as he covered the miles between Norwich and Osterley, Rutledge watched the raindrops collect on his windscreen and resisted Hamish's efforts to draw him into a debate over the interview with Monsignor Holston. He didn't want to delve into the priest's motivations or Bryony's. The earlier mood (as Hamish had predicted) was wearing off, and in its place was a rising doubt about his own judgment. He hadn't been cleared for a return to full duty—and his instructions had been to travel to Norwich. Nothing had been said about continuing north.

Old Bowels would have his liver if he upset the local man on a whim and brought the wrath of the Chief Constable down on both their heads. On the other hand, Rutledge could say with some certainty that he had made precious little progress in "reassuring" the Bishop's representative. The Monsignor wouldn't have settled for less than a full-blown investigation by the Yard, given any choice in the matter. If a visit to Osterley was what it took to satisfy him of the Yard's faith in Inspector Blevins, there would be no official objections to that.

But Hamish wouldn't be put off. "It's no' the body that's standing in your way! Ye havena' put Scotland out of your mind. Ye werena' ready to return to work because you werena' ready to face living!"

"The bandages are off," Rutledge answered flatly. "By the time I'm back in London, the police surgeon will be satisfied that the medical leave can be rescinded."

"Aye, but watching yon fine doctor cut away bits of bandage is no' the same as coming to grips with yoursel'."

"I'll deal with Scotland. When I'm back in London."

"Oh, aye? Then tell me why we're driving north again?"

It was a pretty route, leaving Norwich to follow country lanes through gently rolling hills. Many of them hid small flint or brick villages in pocket-size valleys. And the still-green meadows on the rounded hillsides were sheltered by a line of trees, where fluffy clusters of Norfolk sheep dotted the landscape, their fleece thickening for the winter. So unlike France, with its broken walls and stark chimneys lining the roads from the Front. He could almost pretend that it was 1914, and nothing had changed. But of course it had. There was never any going back.

To Hamish this was "soft country"—peaceful and prosperous, where a living came more easily than in the harsh, often barren landscapes of the Highlands. That very harshness, in Hamish's opinion, had made the Scots formidable fighting men.

Norfolk had produced fine soldiers, too, Rutledge reminded him. But as far as Hamish was concerned, training and blood were two very different factors in the making of an army. One could be taught—the other was in the very bone.

Even in the trenches Hamish had been fond of citing examples—some of them ranging back to the twelfth century—of Scottish prowess in battle. It was, Rutledge thought, a way of life that had seldom brought prosperity or contentment to the Highlands, but in pride and fierce spirit, it had bred a full measure of courage.

The miles rolled away behind them, and then the road Rutledge was driving wound through a cut in a hill and unexpectedly came to an end facing a broad expanse of marshes, as flat as they were striking and bronzed now with the coming winter's palette of red-brown and yellow and old gold. He paused at the junction to stare out across them, thinking to himself that for such a small country, England had its share of beauty.

Here the road went either right toward Cley or left toward Hunstanton, running along the landward edges of the marsh as far as the eye could see. Rutledge turned left, feeling the wind coming in from the northwest, bearing with it the cries of gulls out along the ridge of dunes by the sea. Rounding a curve a few miles farther on, Rutledge found himself in the outskirts of a small, sprawling village, lying under a sky that looked like a great gray bowl, holding in the light from the unseen water beyond the marshes to his right.

This wasn't the famous "Constable sky," those broad horizons that the artist had made his signature: vast banks of clouds filled with delicate color that somehow emphasized the simplicity of the ordinary lives he chose to paint. Farm lads fishing or tired horses drawing a haywain across a tree-shaded stream, each caught in his workaday world—rustic beauty unaware of the grandeur overhead.

Here the sky was self-effacing canopy, accepting its more prosaic role of joining sea and land even when the sea was nowhere to be seen. But it was out there, beyond the marshes that had taken root on the salty, wet silt it had left behind. This part of Norfolk had fought long battles with the forces of wind and water, which had often changed the shape of the coastline. A village might lie on the shore this century and find itself miles away from the sea in the next.

The first scattering of houses led him next into the village of Osterley. To his left a great flint church stood high on a grassy knoll, well above the main road and looking down across it to the houses that marked the waterfront. A church, Rutledge thought, that must have been built by the wool trade and heavy coastal shipping. There were a goodly number of these cathedrals in miniature in Norfolk, which had seen a flourishing economy in its day. If he remembered his history correctly, Osterley had been one of the great ports in the Middle Ages, and some of those riches had gone into the clerestory and the strong soaring towers, creating a sense of light and power at the same time.

Rutledge turned up the lane leading to the church, driving up the hill for a better look. A sign posted by the churchyard gate told him that this was Holy Trinity.

Someone—a woman—walked out the church door, a notebook in her hand, and shielding her eyes, looked up at the clerestory. The way the wind played with her skirts and the long coat she wore, Rutledge got the impression that she was slim, fairly young, and attractive. It was there in the set of her shoulders and the tilt of her head, though her hand and arm hid her features.

"There must be a fine view from yon tower," Hamish said. "It's verra' high."

"A landmark from the sea as well, I should think." The town of Boston in Lincolnshire had used its church tower as a beacon for centuries.

The woman walked back into the church. Frances, Rutledge thought, would have approved of the hat she was wearing. Dark red, with silver and blue feathers on one side that gave it a stylish air. He was tempted to get out and pay a visit to the church, to see her better. Just then a man came up the hill from the village, not by the road but through the churchyard, and went inside. A workman from the look of him, wearing a smock and heavy shoes. She'd been waiting for him, perhaps.

He turned his attention back to the terrain.

Ahead of the motorcar's bonnet, the lane disappeared into a small copse. He thought there must be five or six houses scattered beyond it, but decided not to trust his axles to that twisting, rutted stretch of muddy road. He could just see a few chimneys rising above gabled roofs, and at the far end, what might have been a barn, judging from its bulky silhouette.

Across the lane from the church stood the vicarage, half hidden behind a flint wall, its drive disappearing into old trees that gave some hint of its age.

He turned the motorcar and went back down the lane to the main road. Just on the corner of a street to the right—Water Street, the sign informed him—stood the police station.

Rutledge pulled up in front of it, and got out to pay his courtesy call on Inspector Blevins. But there was a notice posted on the door, dated this morning: *Gone to Swaffham. In the event of an emergency, contact East Sherham police station.* A number was given.

He opened the door and looked inside. The front room was silent, uninviting as a place to wait.

"Aye, and for how long?" Hamish asked querulously. Rutledge closed the door again.

Starting the motorcar, he decided his time would be better spent exploring the village and calling on Mrs. Wainer. That could be viewed as an extension of his original brief—putting Bishop Cunningham's mind at rest—rather than an infringement of the local man's investigation.

Water Street clearly went down to the quay. It ran along there for some distance before turning back to the main road, as if disappointed by what it had found at the harbor. But he passed that turning and stayed on the main road, interested in the size and general layout of Osterley. It appeared to be prosperous enough, no ugly areas of run-down housing or noticeable poverty, but without signs either of money to waste on ostentation.

There were some half a dozen streets running inland to his left, short streets for the most part, although he thought that Sherham Street went on to the next village, for it appeared to vanish over the hill into farming land. Two streets turned to his right, Old Point Road and Marsh Lane. Down Old Point Road he saw the second church in the village, and decided that it must be St. Anne's.

And then as suddenly as he'd come upon Osterley, he was out of it.

A muddy farmyard on the right, a house half glimpsed on a rise to his left, and the main road west dropped sharply down a hill and ran along the marshes that spread to his right as far as the horizon.

Even Hamish was struck by the splendor of the view, and Rutledge turned into a small stony cul-de-sac to look out at the scene. Grasses and marshes covered the land like a rough brown-gold blanket, and a few stunted trees bowed before the wind, on the point of giving up against its force. The grasses moved as if with a will of their own as the wind ran capriciously through them. Here ducks and geese and sea birds owned the silence. A thin line of white at the very fringes of the marshes marked the sea. It was wildly beautiful, and Rutledge thought, *Here is something man hasn't destroyed.*

Hamish said, "Aye, but give him time!"

A small falcon rose from the thick grass to fly some twenty yards, then hover with beating wings above its unsuspecting prey. Rutledge watched it swoop, and then take off again with a dark smudge hanging from one claw. A mouse?

The stillness was broken only by the wind sweeping in from the sea, and he thought he had caught the sound of waves rolling in, a deep roar that was felt as much as it was heard, like a heartbeat. The sense of peace was heavy, and the sense of isolation.

A formation of geese, out over the surf, flew like a black arrow toward Osterley.

Following them with his eyes, Rutledge remembered the lines of poetry from which the words had come. They ran through his mind almost without conscious thought: *"Across the moon the geese flew, pointing my way, / A black arrow on the wing. / But I was afoot and slow, / And stumbled in the dark. By moonset, I was left, / Alone and sad, still far from the sea . . ."*

O. A. Manning had been writing about a man's desperate struggle against despair.

Here in the marshes, watching the wedge of geese, it seemed to be possible to reach the sea after all. . . . He felt his spirits lift.

"Unless," Hamish told him harshly, "it's only an illusion. . . ."

CHAPTER FIVE

IGNORING HAMISH, RUTLEDGE SPENT ANOTHER FIVE or ten minutes there, his eyes scanning the marshes. But now it seemed devoid of
life, the spell it had cast broken.

He got out to crank the motor. Under his feet was a bed of stones,
white round pebbles that, when split, showed their opaque, flinty
core. Many of the towns along the North Sea had been built of such
stone, hard and durable at the center.

As the motor came to life and he turned to walk back to the
driver's side, he found himself thinking about Bryony again. The housekeeper had told him that the police had got nowhere. Why had no one
in Osterley come forward with information about the priest's death? It
was a crime that any community should instantly condemn, the kind of
sudden death that drove people to lock their doors at night and look
askance at their neighbors and remember small events that might be
pieced carefully together until the puzzle was solved.

"*I saw a man . . .*"

"*I overheard such and such while waiting to pay my account at the
greengrocer's . . .*"

"Father James told me one day after Mass . . ."

A village thrived on prying. Privacy was an illusion protected by silence.

Rutledge turned the car once more and went back the way he'd come.

The answer to his question seemed to be that they had no information to give, the residents of Osterley. Or they had closed ranks around the murderer of the priest.

"But that's no' likely," Hamish pointed out.

"Or does it explain why the Bishop called in Scotland Yard?"

Reaching Old Point Road again, Rutledge turned in. The second church was smaller than Holy Trinity, its steeple a slim finger pointing into the gray sky. Built of flint and weathered by the sea winds, it offered a plain face to the world, but seemed to be timeless, after a fashion. A survivor. A black board with gold letters informed him that this was indeed St. Anne's Roman Catholic Church. The churchyard lay behind it, a low stone wall enclosing the gravestones that over time were slowly encroaching on the building. Another hundred years, Rutledge thought, and the stones would reach the apse.

Next to the church was the brick rectory, small and Victorian, but with such a flair for extravagance it might have alighted here one night in a storm and decided to stay. An exotic bird faring well in this northern climate far from its native land. Hardly a setting for bloody murder.

He stopped the motorcar in the yard of the rectory and was on the point of getting out to knock on the door when a woman pushing a pram along the road called to him, "Mrs. Wainer has gone to do her marketing in the town. But I should think she'll be back in an hour at most."

Rutledge thanked her. He turned for a third time, and decided to make his way back to the waterfront. He might even find his lunch there. It had been some time since he'd breakfasted in Norwich.

Osterley was built of local flint with brick facings at windows and doors, the lumpy pebbles seeming to cling to the walls like hungry leeches. And yet there was a quality to the construction that spoke of sturdiness and endurance, and a certain seaworthiness, as if prepared for the onslaught of storms.

He found the street that turned off to the harbor, and it swept him around an unprepossessing bend where houses clung to the edge of the road on either side, then down to the narrow quay, to run along it for some distance before Water Street turned back toward the main road. It was a busy part of the town, people coming and going, carriages and carts standing in front of shop doors, horses with their heads down dozing where they waited. But Rutledge's attention was drawn to the harbor as he drove slowly through the congestion.

Where there had once been the blue wash of water, banks of silt met his eye instead. These grassy hummocks rolled like earthen waves out to the North Sea's edge, and the muddy earth below the stone quay gleamed wetly under the gray sky, a small ghost of its medieval magnificence. A handsome port, suitable for coastal trading, where fishing boats had brought in heavy nets filled with plaice and cod and mackerel, had become a narrow ribbon of water that wandered halfheartedly into view, touched the quay at high tide, and then wandered away again. Two or three small boats had been drawn up behind a line of sheds at the far end of the quay and left to rot. Another pair sat in the black mud, waiting to be pushed into the main stream of the ribbon.

He lifted his gaze to the great arm of sand dunes, covered with shore plants and grasses, which was flung out beyond the marshes on his right, ridged with color—rust and waning green and dull gold. It had once sheltered Osterley from storms, making it a safe haven. But it must also have allowed the sand to find a haven as well, until the water had been lost amid the pits and shallows rising faster than it did. A haunt of waterfowl now, but through the breaks in the ridges one could still glimpse the sea, tantalizing and perhaps close enough to hear when the wind fell off. There must be a fine strand still, out where the headland rose to his left, the kind of place that would have attracted fishermen and bathers had there been easier access.

Small houses, shops, and a single hotel had taken over the waterfront now. Cheek by jowl, they presented a blank face to the sea: few windows and most of the doorways shielded by narrow, rectangular entries that kept out the wind and provided some protection in storms. These were a signature of many seaside towns accustomed to rough weather.

Neither rich nor poor, and mostly unchanged over the past century or more, Osterley offered a middle-class solidity that was the backbone of England, attitudes still firmly fixed in Victorian morality and the responsibility of Empire. Clinging to the edge of the land, the town was no longer a part of the sea.

His was the only motorcar on the street today, although he saw three more standing at angles in the walled yard beside the only hotel.

A fat gray goose, wild, not domestic, picked at the black mud beyond the quay, and its mate stood watch, neck straight and eyes bright. Early winter arrivals. Beyond the town to the right of the harbor the marshes spread east for miles. Rutledge found a small space in which to shift into neutral and look out across them. They held a fascination for him, always had, but he had forgotten their odd beauty.

Just below him in the water, a boat was coming in, the man at the oars handling them well, keeping the bow midstream as if he knew his way, his fair hair dark with sweat as he pulled toward the quay. He wore a good tweed coat, and an English setter sat between the thwarts, tongue lolling as it watched the quay come closer. Rutledge turned off the motor and got out, standing there until the boat had reached the stairs, and then walked forward to catch the rope the man threw up toward him.

"Thanks!"

"My pleasure."

The rower stood up and stepped out onto the lower stair. A man of middle height with a strong face and eyes the color of a winter sea, he was fit and trim. Clicking his tongue, he waited as the dog leaped up the stairs ahead of him, excitement in its movement, waiting for a sign to run.

"Heel, you ragbag!" he said, and looking up at Rutledge added, "He's got more energy than I have! But then he hasn't been working the oars for the past hour or more. I'll have the devil of a time walking home; he'll be there and back twice over before I cover half the distance." It was said with a mixture of impatience and affection. The voice was cultured, without the local accent.

"Can you go out as far as the sea?" Rutledge asked, nodding toward the distant headland.

"Oh, yes. It's quite nice out there. Silent as the grave, except for the waves breaking as they come in, and the birds putting up their usual fuss. I rather like it."

He spoke to the dog and the pair set out up Water Street, the dog matching the man's strides for the first twenty paces and then bouncing ahead like a thrown ball, urging his master on. Then an older woman, coming out of a shop to her horse-drawn carriage, called out, "Edwin? Care for a lift?"

The man waved to her, and whistled the dog to heel. Rutledge watched him swing himself into the carriage and heard his laughter as the woman agreed to allow the wet, wriggling animal to leap up with them.

Returning to his motorcar, Rutledge noticed The Pelican Inn, standing at the far end of the quay, where the road turned up. A barmaid had just finished sweeping the entry and was now shaking out the bit of carpet where customers wiped their feet. She was buxom, fair, and middle-aged, with a good-natured face.

Children rolling hoops ran up the street, shouting to each other, drawing a frown from two well-dressed men conversing under the wrought-iron sign for the baker's shop. A black cat sat in a sheltered corner, licking its fur and ignoring the small terrier that was trotting at the heels of an elderly man with a cane. The man spoke to the barmaid and she laughed.

A pub, Rutledge thought, was one of the best places to test the temperament of a village. He left the car at the end of the quay and walked across to The Pelican.

The barmaid had gone inside and was wiping down the last two tables, her face pink with exertion as she gave them a good scrub. She looked up and smiled at him, saying, "What can I do for you, love?"

"Is it too early for a lunch?"

"The ham's not near done, nor the stew neither, but I can give you a Ploughman's."

"That will be fine," he answered. Bread and good English cheese and a pint.

"Here, sit by the windows where you can enjoy the view." She shrugged plump shoulders and added, "*If* you like the marshes. I find them dreary, myself. Too much wildlife for my taste. Of the crawly kind, if you take my meaning! More of them than there are of us, and that's no lie!"

He sat down by the window that looked out across the marsh and counted a flight of some dozen ducks coming in to what must be a pool hidden somewhere among the tall grasses. The barmaid had disappeared into the kitchen, and he heard the rattle of cutlery and dishes.

As his eyes adjusted to the dimness created by smoke-blackened beams and tables, he realized that he wasn't alone. Another man sat in a corner nook by the bar, his head bent over a newspaper. Rutledge wasn't certain whether he was reading it or using it as a barrier against conversation.

Decoratively, The Pelican contained the flotsam and jetsam of a seafaring port: an iron anchor in one corner, several ships' models suspended from the beams, a handful of blue-and-white Chinese plates resting on shelves nailed to the walls with haphazard artistry, carved seabirds of every shape and size perched on the wide windowsills as if trying to find a way through the glass.

A stuffed greylag goose, enormous and showing signs of moth, occupied one end of the bar, with a sign around his neck advertising a Norfolk ale.

There were even odd bits and pieces from around the world, hung wherever they might fit. A great hammered-copper dish from Morocco or Turkey, set above the hearth, was large enough to serve an entire family without crowding. A small elephant sat in one corner, carved from teak and caparisoned in fraying velvet, with tiny silver bells in the fringe. What appeared to be a water buffalo's horned skull was mounted above the door. And on another wall, curved knives in ornate sheaths shared honors with a hideous mask from somewhere in Africa, leering through shell-rimmed eyes and mouth.

It gave the public house a decidedly eccentric air, as if more than one seaman had settled his account with whatever souvenirs he had in his kit.

Hamish commented, "I canna' say the goose is an encouragement to a man's drinking."

The barmaid came toward the table with Rutledge's lunch—chunks of freshly baked bread and sharp cheddar cheese, a pickle, and a pot of mustard. As she set them before him, she tilted her head to the room at large and said, "We're generally busier than this, but it's market day at East Sherham, and most people won't be back before two o'clock."

She went to draw his pint, and added, friendly gossip that she was, "Here on business, are you?"

He answered that he was, and she continued to chatter for a few minutes longer, telling him that she had been born in Hunstanton and had come to Osterley with her husband, who had since died fighting a house fire, and that she and her two daughters had found a good home here. She seemed to ignore the man in the corner, as if he was another fixture along with the elephant and the mask.

Rutledge said, "I was shocked to hear that a priest was murdered in Osterley a week ago. It doesn't strike me as the sort of town where such a thing could happen."

She shook her head. "I never thought it, either. None of us has got over it, I can tell you. I keep my girls close, and lock the doors at night. If he'd kill a priest, he won't stop at *children*, will he? I shudder to think what sort of devil could do such a thing! I haven't slept deep since it happened."

Rutledge was on the point of asking her another question when a group of men strode in, hailing her with accounts of their success bidding on a pair of rams at the sale in East Sherham and eager to relive it blow by blow. She went off to serve them, and listened with good grace to their rambling story of the day's best bargain. Underlying their enthusiasm was a more somber thread of strain, and they seemed to be intent on ignoring it. Their laughter was a little loud, a little forced. The barmaid—Betsy, they'd called her—soon had them settled with pints to celebrate their success.

Rutledge decided, from the strong noses that marked each weather-beaten face, that they were father and sons. He finished his meal amid the general hilarity and a rash of newcomers bringing their own news of the market. It was, as far as he could tell, the only topic of conversation of interest just now: who was there, what they'd bought or failed to buy, how the prices ran, and any gossip gleaned. For an hour or so, the shadow of the priest's death was being resolutely lifted.

The man at the corner table had not moved, as far as Rutledge could tell, nor had he turned a page in the newspaper. No one encouraged him to join in the good-humored banter or asked him to drink with them.

Settling his account, Rutledge left the pub and went out to start his motorcar.

"It doesna' appear to be a town with dark secrets," Hamish said. "And they didna' stare at you—a stranger—with suspicion."

"Interesting, wasn't it? But then market day generates its own excitement. When the euphoria of a bargain wears off and night begins to fall, people will begin to look over their shoulders again." He'd been to towns where the silence hung heavy as mist, faces shut and unfriendly, where there was no distraction from fear and uncertainty. Here there seemed to be a determined refusal to acknowledge that Osterley had been touched by evil. He wondered why.

Where Water Street turned at harbor's edge to run back up to the main road, there were two horse-drawn carriages outside the greengrocer's shop, and a lad from the butcher's next door was carrying a bulky package out to deposit in a pony cart, accompanying a woman dressed in black with a small touch of cream at her wrists and collar. An elderly woman stepped out of the greengrocer's with a large basket filled with her purchases, and turned to walk up toward the main road. Rutledge thought she might be Mrs. Wainer. But there was no one to ask.

"You can feel the water," Hamish said. "It must be verra' bitter here in winter. Raw with an east wind."

"Sometimes," Rutledge agreed. "When the storms roll in."

Back on the main road, Rutledge braked as he came to the police station, but the sign hadn't been removed from the door. He drove on to St. Anne's and got out of the car, staring up at the rectory. Cupolas and mock turrets and gingerbread gave it a frivolous air that the simpler lines of the Victorian frame seemed half ashamed of. There were carvings at the peak of the gables, and he told himself that if the builder had found a place to add gargoyles, he'd have done it. And yet the whole seemed far more pleasing than any one part.

Next to the rectory was a fair-sized flint house with a small glass conservatory now flecked with moisture from an array of tall plants inside. Most certainly the home of the neighbor who had been away on the night of the priest's murder. The windows on that side of the rectory looked across a narrow stretch of grassy lawn almost into the windows of the larger house.

But the rectory windows also looked down the lawn to the road. Had Father James seen someone there, someone he believed would hear his shout? A laborer walking home from the fields? A constable on patrol?

Hamish said, "Was it luck that the family was no' at home? Or did the killer choose his time because of that?"

"Yes, it's possible," Rutledge answered. "If he'd been watching the house for several days."

The next three houses were more modest in design, curving toward a house closest to the point that must have been part of the port buildings in its heyday. A small hotel? Or a customs house. A placard nailed to a board and neatly lettered in white identified it as a rooming house in its present incarnation. Across the street from where he stood, there were five flint houses, built for comfort more than style.

Rutledge walked up the short path to the rectory door. The knocker, he discovered, was a bit of whimsy as well: a coffin. He let it drop, and the echoing ring of sound startled him, deep as a bell tolling. Hamish, responding to his unspoken thought, said, "It must ha' been the last owner's, an undertaker's."

Rutledge was about to answer him when the door opened and a small white-haired woman dressed in black warily asked his business.

He explained who he was, offering his credentials for her inspection. She glanced at them with relief and then stood aside to allow him to enter a dark hall with two doors on either side of a wide staircase of worn mahogany. A passage ran down beside the stairs to a third door at the back end of the hall. Mrs. Wainer opened the one to her right and invited him into a small parlor, with a gesture offering the sofa as the most comfortable seat. It was a room of surprisingly lovely proportions, with long windows facing the church, a selection of old but well-cared-for furniture, and an oak mantelpiece that rose nearly to the high ceiling. This was ornately carved with ferns and acorns and leaves, and Rutledge wondered if it had come from an even older house.

The scent of lemon wax pervaded even the upholstery and rose to greet him as he sat down. The sheen on every wooden surface spoke of the brisk application of a polishing rag, and there was no dust on the green leaves of the large plant in one corner. Hamish eyed it with dislike. "Yon's the ugliest aspidistra I've ever clapped eyes on."

Rutledge was in agreement. It seemed to thrive without beauty, out of place here, but certainly well fed and watered.

Mrs. Wainer was saying, as she stood before him like a schoolmistress, "Did I understand you rightly? Scotland Yard, you said. That means London."

"Yes, that's correct." Behind her, on the mantel, was a small china clock with a French dial and beveled glass. It ticked with a soft grace.

Her eyes closed for a brief moment, and she said, "I have prayed for answers. And there have been none. Until now."

Rutledge said, not absolutely certain he understood her, "I haven't come to tell you that the murderer has been found."

"No. You've come to look for him. That's what matters!"

"I'm here because Bishop Cunningham was concerned enough to contact the Yard—"

"As he should have been! It was a despicable crime. *Despicable!* I looked at Father James lying there, and I knew straightaway that such a thing hadn't been done by an ordinary man. Inspector Blevins can't seem to grasp that. Or won't. I'm beginning to think he *wants* to believe it was a thief, come for the bazaar money. But it wasn't. Now you're here, something will be done about what happened." There was an intensity in her face that made Rutledge feel uneasy.

"Why are you so certain that the killer wasn't a thief?"

"Because he wasn't! I don't care what they say. You don't knock a man down for such a pitiful sum, then leave behind a medal around his neck worth more than fifty pounds. If you'd kill a priest, you'd feel no compunction stealing his medal. In my opinion, this was *vengeance*. Someone wanted him dead!"

It was an interesting choice of words. Rutledge said, "What had Father James done to bring such wrath down on him?"

"That's what you must find out," she told him earnestly. "I've been Father James's housekeeper since first he came here to Osterley, and that's been well over ten years now. He was a *good* man and a wonderful priest. A *caring* priest. And good people make enemies." She turned her head to look over her shoulder, toward the door and the stairs, as if expecting someone to come down them and call to her. "I don't think I'll ever be free of that horror, him lying there in his own blood, his hand so cold when I touched it that I cried out for the pity of it." Her eyes came back to Rutledge. "A monster did that killing, retribution for Father James standing up against cruelty and evil and sin. Mark my words, that's what you'll find if you search hard enough!"

Hamish said, "She believes what she said, and she willna' be satisfied with any other solution."

Rutledge answered him silently. "She must have loved him, in her own way. And anything less than a monster will make Father James's death seem—senseless—to her." Aloud he said to Mrs. Wainer, "Did you know the money was here? The money from the autumn fair?"

"Of course I did! Father James gave it to me that evening when the fair was over, and said, 'Lock this away in my desk, will you, Ruth? I'll give you the key, and fetch it again as soon as I've cleaned up.' He'd been dressed as a clown, to entertain the children, you see, and the paint was still on his face."

"Did you usually lock money away for him?"

"I did whatever he asked. He trusted me," she said simply.

"Was the desk broken into? To find the money?"

"Yes, it was, damaging the drawer something fierce! But there's only a small lock on the drawer, a flimsy thing at best. It was secure enough from prying eyes, if anyone came into the room. Hardly more than that—and we never had a ha'penny stolen until now! There was no need for safes and bolts on doors. I have told you, he trusted people, Father James did. It wouldn't have occurred to him that this house might be invaded the way it was!"

"Sadly enough, that's often the case," Rutledge answered her. "It's one reason why housebreakers—and the like"— he added hastily—"are often successful. But I have no authority here, Mrs. Wainer. Except to assure the Bishop that everything possible is being done to find Father James's murderer—"

"And how, pray, could you hope to assure the Bishop of that, when you haven't lifted a finger toward setting Inspector Blevins on the right track?" Her eyebrows rose, and she regarded him with a scornful expression.

"The Yard—" Rutledge began.

But she was not interested in the politics of the Yard or its role outside London. Like Bryony in Norwich, she was concerned only with finding a reason for an otherwise incomprehensible crime.

He had disappointed her. And her face let him know it.

Making amends as best he could, Rutledge said, "You tell me that goodness makes enemies. Can you give me the names of anyone who might have had a reason to harm Father James?"

"Don't be daft. If I could have made such a list, I'd have handed it over to Inspector Blevins. And I never heard Father James speak ill of anyone. He had a way with him, listening to what was said to him, considering what was to be done for the best. And, good man that he was, he always looked for the best in people. But he didn't always find it. There are some that are two-faced, smiling and agreeable under your eye, but mean-spirited and venomous behind your back. He knew that, just as any good policeman should."

Her views on the failings of human nature met with approval from Hamish. He said, "Aye, a man owed my grandfather money, and said he couldna' pay it back, his business was sae puir. But it wasna' true. He was hiding the profits."

Rutledge said, "You were in this house every day, going about your duties. How did Father James behave those last weeks? As he always had? Or could you see that he was worried, preoccupied?"

For the first time, he caught a glimpse of fear in her eyes. It was unexpected, as if she had locked it away and didn't want to bring it into the light.

Mrs. Wainer was silent for a moment, then answered, "I'd find his bed not slept in, some mornings. And he'd often be standing at the kitchen window by the back garden, looking out, the tea already made, as if he hadn't been able to rest. That last morning, he turned a surprised face to me when I came in at my usual hour. As if he'd lost track of the time."

"Was there a problem in the parish that kept him awake?"

"If there was, it never reached my ears! But he'd been to the doctor's, several times to my certain knowledge, and I was beginning to wonder if he was ill—a cancer or some such. And it was on his mind."

"A local man?"

"Dr. Stephenson, yes. It's all I could think of, that Father must have been given bad news. I waited for him to confide in me, but he never did. And then he was killed, God rest his soul, and I couldn't help but think as they put him into the ground, he'll not have to worry any more about the cancer."

"Did he show signs of being ill? Coughing—complaining of pain—taking medications you hadn't seen before?"

"No, I'd have come right out and asked him then! It was just—I don't know—just a feeling that he was sorely troubled. I asked him the first time I found him standing in the kitchen if there was anything on his mind, and he said, 'No, Ruth, I'm well.' But there was something *wrong*. He wasn't himself!"

"Something on his conscience, then?"

She gave him a stern and heavy look. "Priests like Father James don't have evil on their conscience! I'd as soon believe that my own son was wicked, and him a respectable bank clerk in London!"

CHAPTER SIX

JUST PAST THE FIRST TURNING FOR Water Street, Rutledge saw the small board indicating Dr. Stephenson's surgery. On impulse he pulled over and stopped, left the car out in front, and rang the bell. It would do no harm to confirm or deny Ruth Wainer's fears.

A woman admitted him, her apron crisp and her hair tightly pulled back into a small knot. It gave her face a severity that was belied by the kind eyes. Rutledge gave his name and asked to speak to the doctor.

"His surgery is closed for the afternoon."

"It isn't a medical matter. It concerns a police investigation." He showed her his identification.

She considered him, uncertain what to do. Finally, as Rutledge smiled at her, she said, doubt heavy in her voice, "He's in his office, writing up a patient's record to send to London. If I let you go in, you won't keep him long, will you? The post won't wait!"

He was taken to Dr. Stephenson's private door down the passage and admitted into the small office, where the doctor sat at his desk, papers spread around him. He looked up, saw Rutledge behind his nurse, and said, "I don't have hours today. Have you told him that, Connie?"

"It isn't a medical matter," Rutledge said. "It's police business. I've been sent down by Scotland Yard."

"The Yard, is it?" Stephenson said, giving his visitor his full attention. "Oh, very well, I can spare you five minutes! No more." He put the cap on his pen and sat back in his chair, locking his fingers together and stretching his arms in front of him.

He was a brisk man, Rutledge thought, but not cold. And he appeared to be competent, for his eyes examined his visitor openly, and behind the short, neat beard, his mouth twitched with interest.

The nurse withdrew, closing the door, and Stephenson said, "You don't look well, you know." He gestured toward a wing chair.

"It isn't surprising. I was shot some weeks ago."

"In the line of duty?" Rutledge nodded. "That explains it, then. You still carry that shoulder a little higher, as if it's stiff. What brings you to Osterley? This business about Father James?"

"I've been asked to reassure Father James's Bishop that everything that can be done has been done in the matter of the priest's death—"

"Then you should be speaking to Inspector Blevins, not to me."

"On the contrary. The questions I have to ask are medical." Rutledge's glance moved from the prints hanging on the blue walls to the bookcase stuffed with medical treatises and texts.

Stephenson pointedly shuffled his papers. "If you are asking me in some roundabout fashion to tell you which of my patients was likely to have committed murder, I can't help you. I'd have gone straight to Blevins if I'd had even the faintest suspicion that one of them could have been responsible."

Rutledge smiled. "The patient I'm inquiring about is Father James himself. You were his physician. And I've been told that he had something on his mind shortly before his death. His housekeeper believes that he might have been seriously ill, and was keeping it from her. If it wasn't his health that troubled him, then we have another avenue to explore. If it was, we can close that door."

"I don't see how his state of mind will help you find the thief who killed him. But I can assure you that Father James was as healthy as a horse, save for a few bouts of sore throat now and again. Bad tonsils, but never serious enough to require more than a box of lozenges for the soreness. They worked well enough, most of the time."

"And yet he came here to see you several times in the weeks before he died."

"There's nothing surprising about that! Religion and medicine walk hand in hand, as often as not. I confer with the priest or the Vicar as frequently as I summon the undertaker. People grieving or in pain or frightened need comforting, and that's the role of the church when medicine has done all it can."

Rutledge let a silence fall. It expressed nothing, but Stevenson seemed to read into it a refusal to accept his offhand remarks. After a moment, the doctor added, "But you're right. The last time or two it wasn't an illness that brought him here—his or a parishioner's. He wanted to ask me about a patient of mine. Man named Baker. Father James had been to see him just before he died. Afterward he began to wonder about Baker's state of mind at the end. Far as I know, it was clear and coherent. I saw no reason to believe otherwise, and I was in attendance."

"One of Father James's flock?"

"Actually, no. I suppose that's what lay behind his questions, although Father James didn't go into the matter. Baker was staunch Church of England, but he wanted to be shriven by a Catholic priest as well as his own Vicar, and his family humored him. Father James, to his credit, attended even though it was one of the nastiest nights I'd seen in a year or more. A few hours later Herbert Baker died of natural causes— I can vouch for that—and his Will was quite straightforward. As a matter of fact, I'd been asked to witness it some years back. None of Baker's children has complained about it, as far as I know. There was no reason to feel any concern, and I told Father James that."

"And yet you tell me he spoke to you again about Baker."

The doctor picked up his pen, indicating that he wanted to get back to his own work. "I just explained what happened. There was some confusion the night this patient was dying. Baker insisted he wanted a priest. The one from St. Anne's. But it was the Vicar who sat beside the old man when he breathed his last, close on to three in the morning. Father James had already gone back to the rectory, having spent no more than half an hour with the patient. I grant you that it wasn't the usual sort of thing, but then I've sat by enough deathbeds myself to know that there's no accounting sometimes. Martin Baker sent for a priest to give his father ease. Rightly so!"

"What do you think was resting so heavily on Herbert Baker's conscience?" Rutledge asked the question conversationally, as if out of simple curiosity.

"I expect it was no more than some youthful indiscretion. Baker had been sexton at Holy Trinity for many years, and he may not have relished spoiling the Vicar's good opinion of him, just at the end. I've known more than one case where a man's wild oats came back to haunt him on his deathbed."

"I shouldn't think that Father James—an experienced priest from all I've heard—would be overly concerned about a young man's wild oats."

"Father James often surprised me with the breadth of his concern for people. There was compassion to spare for any lost sheep. I found it admirable in him." The doctor uncapped his pen. "I've given you far more than your five minutes. This is pressing, the report I'm writing. I have a patient in hospital in London, facing surgery. It can't wait."

"Just two other questions, if you will. Did anyone to your knowledge hold a grudge against Father James?"

"He wasn't that kind of man. His predecessor was autocratic, and while everyone respected him, there was little love for him. Father James on the other hand was a reasonable, clear-thinking individual who took his duties to heart but was never oppressive about it. I wasn't one of his parishioners, but I am told he preached a fine homily in a voice that made the rafters sing."

"I understand Father James was a chaplain at the Front, and was sent home early. With severe dysentery."

"Yes, it was chronic, and the army surgeon was of the opinion he would be dead in a month if he wasn't sent home. Decent water, decent food, and bed rest saw him right enough. Father James wasn't happy to be sent home. He wanted to serve. There was a Father Holston in Norwich who set him right again by telling him that God, not Father James, decided where he could serve best. Which oddly enough came true. In the influenza epidemic he was my right hand. I'd have lost twice the number of patients without his dedication. Seemed to have the constitution of an iron man, I can tell you!"

Rutledge thanked Stephenson and stood up to leave. As he walked to the door, he turned and asked, "When did Baker die? Before or after the Autumn Fete at St. Anne's?"

"A day or two after the bazaar. As I recall, the Vicar said something about the timing of the storm—that it was a blessing it hadn't struck earlier. Now that's all I have to say to you. Good afternoon!"

Hamish grumbled as Rutledge walked out of the surgery, "If it wasna' his health that worried yon priest before his death, and this man Baker didna' weigh unduly on his mind, what kept him awake at night? Was it yon fair at the kirk?"

"Yes, I was wondering about that myself. Sometimes people come a long distance to attend these affairs, if they have any sort of reputation for good food and good entertainment."

"People travel far to funerals as well."

"I think the bazaar is a more likely choice. Father James didn't officiate at Baker's services—the Vicar would have done that."

Looking around him at the town of Osterley, where a watery and inconsistent sunlight was reflected from the flint walls, Rutledge found himself thinking that he would be on his way back to London tomorrow. Back to the letters lying unopened in the desk drawer in his sitting room. Away from the smell of the marshes and the call of gulls overhead. He answered absently, "The local police will know more about such evidence than I do."

But would they? Whatever lay at the core of this murder, whether it was theft or a killing with a purpose, someone appeared to have covered his tracks very well.

Was he clever—or merely lucky?

Hamish said, "For a man who willna' be involved with this death, you ask a good many questions." There was a taunt behind the simple words.

Rutledge said, "No. I've merely tried to be sure that the good Bishop's fears are unfounded. . . ."

But was that really true? In Rutledge's experience, investigations often floundered when the police failed to ask the right question. Or failed to look behind the most obvious evidence at what could have been overshadowed by it. Damning connections grew out of persistence, connections that at first glance were not even visible. Most mistakes were made by the human element—the refusal to be objective.

An old Sergeant at the Yard had told him once, at the start of his own career, "When the police look for guilt, there's always enough to serve their purpose. Nobody is free of guilt. But if you search for the *truth,* now, that's a different tale!"

What was intriguing about this case was the reaction of those who were close to Father James. They ignored the theft and believed that nothing short of a Greek tragedy could explain this murder: The assumption that the death of great men grew out of cataclysmic events. It was implicit in their denial of the facts: Even though a small sum was stolen, it had nothing to do with the actual crime.

But what if it had? A life was not always given its real value. . . .

Hamish said, "Aye, but what if this killer only hunts priests, and there's another one in jeopardy now?"

Neither theft nor Greek tragedy but madness? Rutledge raised his eyes to look up at the church standing high above the road, and wondered how such a killer would choose his next victim. Or if he had already killed before . . .

Since the Osterley police station was no more than a few doors from the doctor's surgery, Rutledge left his motorcar where it was and walked there.

The sign was still up, and he started to turn away, intent on the drive back to Norwich. But there was the sound of a voice somewhere inside, and he hesitated, then reached for the knob, thinking he might find someone with whom he could leave a courtesy message for Inspector Blevins.

He stepped into a scene of chaos.

A huge man had been pushed against his will into a chair that faced the Sergeant's rough, wooden desk, and two constables were attempting to hold him down on the seat while he bellowed at an Inspector listening to his curses with an expression of distaste. A Sergeant stood at the Inspector's shoulder.

The constables turned to see who had come through the door, glanced back at their Inspector, and in that instant of distraction loosened their grip on the massive shoulders.

The Inspector glared at Rutledge, demanding, "What do *you* want?" and then savagely ordered, "Franklin—watch what you're *doing,* damn it!"

"Inspector Rutledge, Scotland Yard—"

The man in the chair surged to his feet like a whale breaching.

Hamish yelled a warning and Rutledge hastily leaped aside.

The enormous man broke away from the constables and lunged toward the door, one shoulder ramming into Rutledge and sending piercing swords of fire through his body. He gasped for breath, the pain nearly doubling him over, but thrust out a foot instinctively, managing to trip up the man and then to dodge his thundering fall.

Everyone was shouting at once: The clamor was deafening.

The constables were on the man like monkeys, and Blevins, breathing hard, swore again. "Don't stand there, Sergeant, give them a hand!" As his Sergeant, an older man, jumped into the fray without much effect, Blevins added at the top of his lungs, "*Hit* him if you have to!"

The wildly struggling man went limp as something struck him on the head with a solid thud of flesh against flesh. A fist.

Rutledge, leaning back against the wall, was trying hard to breathe normally again, dizzy with the effort. The Sergeant, calling angrily to the constables to hold on, leaned over his desk to fumble for handcuffs.

Between them the four men managed to haul their dazed captive to his feet and out of the room, toward the rear of the station. As the prisoner regained his senses, Rutledge could hear his rising bellows and the thumps of his heavy boots as he kicked out at his captors or the walls, whatever was in reach.

Blevins walked back into the room rubbing his thigh with his fist. "Damned ox! Rutledge, did you say? From the Yard? What do they want? Is it about the priest's murder?" As Rutledge nodded, Blevins bent to pick up papers that had fallen from the desk to the floor. He added, "Well, you're just in time." He jerked his head toward the rear of the station, where the protests and curses marked the location of a holding cell. "That's our man. At least there's every likelihood it is. He was the Strong Man at the bazaar. Quite an act, pulling a line of carriages against a team of horses, picking up a bench with two young ladies seated at either end, defying ordinary men to lift his iron weights. Very popular with the young people, engaging personality, they tell me. Name's Walsh."

It had been simple theft after all. "What connects him with the priest?" Rutledge felt like hell, his mind refusing to function, while his lungs burned.

"Circumstantial evidence so far. Mrs. Wainer was quite put out when she found Walsh wandering about in the rectory on the day of the bazaar looking—he said—for water to wash up. She sent him away with a flea in his ear. Fortunately, later on she remembered what had happened and told Sergeant Jennings. And when the police in Swaffham caught up with him at a fair there, he had a new cart for his gear. We've just brought him in, as a matter of fact."

"Nothing suspicious in a new cart, surely?" The fire was subsiding.

"It was paid for two days after the priest was killed. With bits and pieces of bills and coin." Blevins gestured to the chair vacated so abruptly by the Strong Man, then sat himself down behind the Sergeant's desk. There was a cut on the heel of his hand, and he stared at it, then at the bloody stain spreading on his cuff. "Damn the bastard! Teeth like steel traps!"

Rutledge took the chair. His chest was settling into a dull ache now. Gingerly testing, he took a deep breath and felt nothing beyond the usual resistance. But the memory of the pain was still fierce. "The sort of money a bazaar takes in, yes. But surely the kind of thing his act brings in as well."

Blevins glared at him. "Look, we're just at the beginning of this business. I've got men asking questions at the smithy where the new cart was built to see when it was ordered. I've got men asking questions about Walsh's movements the day of the festival here as well as the night Father James was killed. A man that size can't slink around without being noticed. Half the county force has been given to me for the duration to track the killer down. A local lord has even put up a reward for information leading to an arrest. Father James was well liked. We're doing the best we can!"

Rutledge rejoined peaceably, "Yes, I can see that. You seem to have the investigation well in hand. Bishop Cunningham was alarmed enough to ask the Yard to see if there was anything we could do. Monsignor Holston will be glad of the news that someone's in custody."

"I suppose he will." Blevins rubbed his eyes tiredly. "He was a friend of Father James's. Do you want the truth? This is the first reasonable lead we've found. And if he *didn't* kill the priest—Walsh, I mean— why did he put up such a fight? Here and in Swaffham!"

Because, Hamish pointed out, the man might well have other secrets to keep, unrelated to murder.

Rutledge said, "Then you don't want me underfoot. I'll return to London and leave you to it." He had already been planning to do just that, but now there was an unexpected sense that he had somehow failed the people who had turned to him for answers. This arrest wouldn't bring them peace. . . .

Hamish said, "They were wrong—Bryony and Mrs. Wainer and Monsignor Holston. It wasna' a Greek tragedy that brought Walsh here. Only a new cart."

Blevins was staring thoughtfully at Rutledge, debating something on his mind. Then, to Rutledge's surprise, he said, "I'd take it as a favor,

Inspector, if you stayed on. A day or two. At least until we've had an opportunity to look into Matthew Walsh. The Strong Man." He used the words with irony, then meticulously straightened the stained green blotter before adding, "I've felt a good deal of anger over this business. I was one of Father James's parishioners, you see. I'm not certain I'm detached enough to do my job properly. To judge Walsh's innocence as well as his guilt."

"Have you spoken to the Chief Constable—?"

"He tells me that it isn't a question of my feelings," Blevins interrupted. "It's a simple matter of the facts. Well, I ask you, how am I to judge the 'facts' in this murder case when I'd cheerfully watch the bastard who did it hanged?"

"You must have known Father James fairly well. What was he like?"

"Middle-aged, but he went out to France. All through the Somme, he was there, ministering to any man who needed him. Of any faith. Even Hindus, for all I know. You could come and sit down in his tent and talk. I mean—*talk*." He considered Rutledge. "In the War, were you?"

Rutledge nodded.

"I wondered, when I saw you flinch just now. Thought it might be an old wound caught wrong. Well, then, you know what I'm trying to say. Half of us were scared of dying, and the other half knew we were already dead—there was no hope of getting through it. But I never once heard Father James say it was 'duty.' What we owed to England. Or any of that other—" He broke off and grinned sheepishly as he remembered where he was. "He never treated us like fools. Instead he'd help us pray for courage. I was never much of a praying man until the Somme. No more than was required of me, at any rate. Father James taught us to pray for strength to see us through whatever came our way. It was all that saved me sometimes, walking into No Man's Land in a hail of fire. My guts would turn to water, I'd shake so the rifle jerked in my hands. And I'd pray loud enough to hear myself. I wasn't the only one, either."

"No." Rutledge had heard men pray in such straits. An odd mixture of pleading and defiance sometimes, trying to bargain for their lives. He'd done it himself, until the prayer had turned to begging for release.

Blevins shook his head. "Well, that's the kind of man Father James was. And some bloody coward strikes him down for a few pounds. All that good—all that kindness and compassion—wiped out for a bloody *handful* of coins!" He waited for a response, watching Rutledge. There was nothing in his face to show how he felt, but his eyes pleaded.

Hamish observed, "Yon's a worried man . . ."

"I don't see why I shouldn't stay. Until you're satisfied," Rutledge answered slowly. Bowles had, after all, given him a few days in which to carry out his original orders. And the Bishop would never complain of thoroughness. . . .

"There's a hotel here in Osterley. Not up to London standards, perhaps, but it'll suit you well enough. The woman who runs it is pleasant, and the food is good. I'll call round later to see if you need anything. Best to let Walsh calm down before we try to talk to him."

Rutledge heard dismissal in Blevins's voice. The Inspector also needed to calm down, Rutledge thought. Hamish, agreeing, said, "He's no' a bad policeman, if he sees his own weakness."

Standing, Rutledge said, "I left my luggage in Norwich. I'll go back there tonight, and drive up tomorrow. I'd also like to have a look at Father James's study, if you don't mind. Before we talk to Walsh."

"Mrs. Wainer will see to it. I don't think she's opened that door twice since it happened. No doubt pretends the study and the bedroom don't exist anymore. She took it very hard, Father James's death. Blamed herself for not staying on until he'd come back for his dinner. But that's always the way, isn't it?"

"Hindsight. Yes, it's common enough." Rutledge thanked him and left.

He drove back to the outskirts of Norwich, to the hotel there, and left a message with Sergeant Gibson at the Yard that he was staying over. Within half an hour Frances telephoned him to see how he was managing and to pass on the good news that a mutual friend had just given birth to a daughter, mother and child doing well, father recovering.

She had always managed to pry information out of Gibson. The crusty old Sergeant was apparently water in her hands.

There was still an hour before dinner, and Rutledge sat down in the most comfortable chair in his room and shut his eyes against the lamplight.

His chest ached with a vengeance, and he could feel the waves of exhaustion that swept him, too strong to allow him peace. Too much driving, too much strain on the still-healing flesh. But it had been worth it. Away from London, he found he was free of that obsessive need to appear to be unchanged by what had happened to him in Scotland. Here, no one knew his past, or cared about his future.

Rest seemed to elude him, his body tense with pain.

And yet at some point he slept, the quiet in the room giving way to the sound of battle, the distant roar of artillery, the chatter of machine guns cutting down the men struggling across No Man's Land. The rain that beat against the windows in a sudden squall became mud underfoot, slippery, black. He went down, unsure whether he'd been shot or lost his footing. He lay there, unable to find the will to rise again, hoping he was dying. Corporal MacLeod's voice was shouting at him, asking if he'd been hit. He scrambled to his feet, wondering why his chest felt heavy, wondering when there had been time to bandage it. It was hard to breathe as he ran, calling to his men, his eye on the barricaded hole where the Hun gunners lay hidden. He could hear the *thump* of bullets all around him, the screams of the wounded, the prayers and cries of angry, terrified men. His men. He couldn't reach the gunners, he couldn't get within range—the spotters had given him the wrong coordinates, it was a slaughter, *and he couldn't get to the gunners—!*

And then a well-hidden sniper's rifle fired, and somehow he heard it over the din of battle, and it fired again, and at the third shot, for a mercy the machine gun nest fell silent—

CHAPTER SEVEN

RUTLEDGE ATE DINNER IN THE QUIET little restaurant attached to the hotel. Most of the other diners were local people, and he belatedly remembered, thinking about it, that it was Saturday evening. The hats of the ladies lacked style but were worn with pride, and the suits of the younger men were pre-War, ill-fitting, as if the weight lost in whatever theater they'd served hadn't been regained. Couples chatted self-consciously, keeping their voices low and falling silent from time to time as though they had no idea what to say to each other. Four–five years of war left gaps in their lives that would be slow to mend.

He wondered what Jean had to say to her Canadian diplomat. How long, even, she had known him. Not that it mattered . . .

As the door from the lounge bar opened, Rutledge looked up. In that brief instant he thought he recognized the man standing by the hearth drinking down what appeared to be a Scotch and water. But when the door opened again the man was gone.

It was the same man he'd seen bringing in the boat at the Osterley quay, he was nearly sure of it. Edwin, his name was. . . .

The hotel's food was simple but well cooked: carrot soup, roast mutton and potatoes, with a side dish of cabbage and onions, and an apple tart to finish. With only Hamish for company, Rutledge's mind, unbidden, returned to the murder of Father James.

Why is it, he found himself thinking, that there has to be meaning in an unforeseen death? All of nature kills without compunction. Why should Everyman die with a fanfare of trumpets, like another Hamlet? In London he, Rutledge, had seen his share of wanton murder, where life had been snuffed out callously. And yet Father James's friends had searched for purpose in his death, as if this somehow provided a legacy. . . .

Hamish, with relish, reminded him that there was no longer a case. "If yon Strong Man is the murderer, it's no' your duty to finish the investigation."

Rutledge heard him, and even agreed. But he was not satisfied.

If he was guilty, Walsh's motive had been theft. To pay for his new cart. And Father James most certainly would have recognized him. Even in a dark room, the sheer size of the man would have given him away. That alone might have turned Father James toward the window to call for help. On the other side of the coin, if Walsh had been startled to find someone walking into the study, he couldn't have guessed that the priest was not likely to press charges. Cornered, he would have tried to protect himself as best he could, and once the crucifix was in his hand, it was a very small, frantic step to using it. A frightened man, looking for a way out . . .

What would Mrs. Wainer have to say to that? Or Monsignor Holston?

Even Inspector Blevins, with his man apparently safely tucked away in a cell, had asked Rutledge to stay on in Osterley.

Why?

By the time Rutledge had reached his dessert, he had come to realize that each of Father James's defenders had spread over the indignity and degradation of murder a cloak of tragedy. But even their vision of that cloak was different.

What was it about this priest's death that made everyone wary of the simple truth? Or made the simple truth a very odd choice? What had they failed to tell their visitor from Scotland Yard?

Hamish interrupted him to ask why a Protestant in apparently good standing with his own pastor would suddenly demand to see a different one—and one outside his own faith? It was not something that set well with his Covenanter's view of things. Come to that, he persisted, why would Father James feel concerned about that dying Protestant's mental stability?

Rutledge was moving on to the lounge for his tea. In a quiet corner, where the bay window looked out over the dark gardens, he discovered that he was staring at his own reflection in the uneven, two-hundred-year-old glass. It distorted his features, giving him a sinister look. But mercifully, the chair had been set at an angle, the reflection of Rutledge's right shoulder masked by the shadows of the velvet drapes, and there was no way to tell if there was anyone standing behind him— A shiver ran through him and he turned away from the window. Even the teacup in his hands couldn't warm the coldness that had touched him—what if the chair had been placed only another few inches one way or the other, and he had stared without warning into a bloody and accusing face?

Hamish prodded again, the voice just out of Rutledge's line of sight. Still shaken, it took him several minutes to answer.

Confession was a sacrament in the Catholic Church. . . . The stricture on silence was not as strong in the Church of England.

If there had been something on the old man's conscience, something serious enough for confession to ease his dying, he might well have chosen not to tell his own Vicar. As Dr. Stephenson himself had pointed out, Sims knew the family—the wife, if there was one, the children. Instead Baker might have turned to a priest who not only was bound by secrecy but had no close ties with the survivors.

"I canna' see it makes sae great a difference! Unless the truth would prevent Baker from lying in consecrated ground."

That was something Rutledge hadn't considered.

"He wouldna' fash himsel' o'er small sins," Hamish continued. "And I canna' think whatever it was weighed sae heavily on his conscience, if he carried it about wi' him to auld age!"

Rutledge agreed. Nothing so common as infidelity or an unpaid debt would send Father James to the doctor to ask questions about Baker's sanity. And a man confessing to a sin, even to a crime long forgotten by everyone else, would present no question of conscience for the priest. A dying man was past trying in a court of law. Justice, after a fashion, had been done.

Father James had spoken of the dead man's Will . . .

What if one of the inheriting children had no right to the family name?

"Aye. That," Hamish answered his thought, "would be a serious matter."

Or had another name that had been kept hidden for a lifetime—

Was that the secret the dying man wanted to impart to Father James? To leave behind a record of a child's true heritage?

Was it that responsibility that had kept the priest pacing the rectory floor at night? Surely he might have felt he owed some duty there.

If it *was* a Confession, Father James wouldn't have spoken of it to Monsignor Holston. He was bound by his vows not to tell anyone, even another priest. Or even to seek comfort in his own quandary. But Monsignor Holston might have been aware of some distraction, of a heavy burden that was never brought into the open. . . .

It was an interesting dilemma, what to do about a Confessed sin.

And where there was a Will, there was a solicitor who had drawn it up. If there were dark secrets in the Baker family, perhaps he would also have a few of the answers. If there were none to be found . . .

"We're back again to the War," Hamish said without enthusiasm. "You ken, better than most, what secrets soldiers bring home with them. Or what secrets a man might confess before battle, no' expecting to survive it!"

And how to find such a needle in a haystack of returned veterans?

Yet that same needle might have found Father James, nearly a year after the War had ended. . . .

Because he'd come to a bazaar?

The next morning Rutledge left the Norwich hotel and drove back to Osterley, Hamish battering at the back of his mind.

Rutledge hadn't slept deeply the night before, unable to find a comfortable position. His chest had throbbed relentlessly, torn muscle overtired from fighting the wheel (Frances would have had his head if she'd known) and refusing to be eased.

Consequently he'd been subjected to a long and unpleasant interlude every time he'd roused enough to turn over. Hamish, for one reason or another, had taken a dislike to the damp, dreary weather and was in full form.

If he wasn't comparing the rounded green land of this part of Norfolk to the great barren mountains and long glens of Scotland, he was reviewing the circumstances surrounding the death of Father James or mulling over the conversation with Monsignor Holston or Inspector Blevins. Awake, Rutledge was unable to let down his guard. Asleep, pain found him again in an endless, restive circle.

Hamish, Rutledge discovered he was thinking at some point, was a malevolent spirit with no need for sleep.

This morning, fighting a headache from the unpredictable shifts in subjects, some of them seeming to lie in wait for him and aimed with a deadly accuracy, others following the unsettled state of his own thoughts, Rutledge was glad to see a modicum of sunlight sifting through the overcast. It seemed to foretell a lifting of the clouds in his mind.

Hamish seemed to find it more to his liking as well. As the land changed a little, announcing their approach to the sea, Hamish unexpectedly said, "It isna' a verra' pleasant thought, returning to London. I canna' ken why people live in cities, jammed cheek by jowl like so many sheep off to market!"

Rutledge agreed. His cluttered office was claustrophobic when rain ran down the soot-blackened windows, shutting him in with the lamplight and the musty smell of cigar smoke and wet wool. When it rained, Old Bowels's moods were as unpredictable as the shifts in Hamish's trains of thought.

Nor was he eager to return to Frances's watchful care. His sister was a master at concealing her worry behind a light facade of humor, but he knew her too well to be taken in by it. He said aloud, in the silence of the motorcar—a habit he found nearly impossible to break— "I'll be here at least one more day. It will do no harm."

A lorry, bound from King's Lynn to Norwich, sent an arc of muddy water across Rutledge's bonnet as it passed in the southbound lane. He blinked as the spray washed the windscreen and left behind a dark and odiferous residue that slowly vanished in the drizzle that had resumed, swallowing up the sun.

As he drove into the town, Rutledge saw people hurrying toward Holy Trinity, bound for the service. He recognized a few of the faces from his brief visit on Saturday—the farmer and his sons who had successfully purchased the prize ram, the young woman he'd seen earlier in the churchyard, the barmaid at The Pelican, and two of the children who had been playing in Water Street. The familiar habit of Sunday worship comfortably being followed: occasionally greeting a friend, often looking up at the great tower that marked their destination as if already focused on the service. There was something very English about it.

He had the odd feeling that he had come home.

The constable on duty in the police station informed him that Inspector Blevins was at Mass, and had left word that he would expect his London counterpart after lunch.

"If there's a Mass, there's a priest," Hamish told Rutledge as he walked back to the motorcar.

"Yes. I'd like to see who has been sent to conduct it."

He turned the car and drove to St. Anne's. The watery sunlight brightened.

Stopping in the drive beside the rectory, Rutledge sat back in his seat, trying to ease the tense muscles in his chest, massaging his upper arm near the shoulder, commanding it to relax. He'd nearly succeeded by the time the first of the parishioners came out of the service and walked away down the street.

Watching them, he wondered which had been under suspicion before Walsh had been taken into custody. Surely Blevins had considered a good many of them, before the investigation had widened.

In a few moments, Monsignor Holston stepped out of St. Anne's and stood by the door, speaking to each family as they left the service. Rutledge, watching, could see that Monsignor Holston knew a number of them, and found a brief word even for those he didn't. For a scholarly man, the priest had a remarkably affable manner with people. Inspector Blevins, in the middle of a group, stopped to make several remarks, and the priest's face lighted a little. But there was doubt in his expression as he turned his head to follow Blevins and his family as they walked on. A trio of elderly women, dressed in black and very eager to take Monsignor Holston's hand in their turn, brought up the rear of the procession of people. He reassured each woman, bending to hear what the eldest, stooped and leaning on a cane, had to say. But in the end he shook his head.

Hamish said, "He doesna' know who will replace Father James."

"I have a feeling the Bishop may wait until the police have finished their job."

As the women moved off down the path, Monsignor Holston turned to go back into the sanctuary, and then saw Rutledge for the first time, hailing him.

Rutledge got out of the car and strode toward the church.

"Well met," the priest said. "Come and talk to me while I change out of my robes."

Rutledge joined him at the door. "I see you were sent here to conduct the service. Does this mean the Bishop has made no decision about Father James's successor? Or are you taking up residence now?"

"The Bishop's biding his time. I think he prefers to wait until there's some news about the killer. Not wanting to be seen to be filling Father James's shoes with unwarranted haste. But he can't leave it much longer. There are needs here that I can't meet, coming only for a day. And most of all it's a need for continuity, a sense of order having been restored."

They went into the sanctuary together and down an aisle. "This is a very lovely church, you know." Monsignor Holston gestured to the stark simplicity surrounding them. "Father James used to say that it was stripped of all pretension, down to the bare bones of faith. Architecturally, that's quite true. And I think he carried that message through into his pastoring here. But this is a dying parish; there's no work for the young people here along the coast. The Bishop should find a young priest with energy and ideals to fill Father James's shoes. One who might reach them before they wander off to work in Norwich or King's Lynn or Peterborough. You could see for yourself how many of those present this morning were over forty."

"Yes, I had noticed. Is this considered advice? Or an offering to the gods to keep you safely in Norwich?"

Opening the vestry door, Monsignor Holston smiled. "Yes, there's that. I don't mind coming here for the services. I just don't have a fancy for staying."

"I should think with Walsh's capture that much of the strain would begin to dissipate." To soften the remark, Rutledge added, "Although that will take time, I'm sure."

Monsignor Holston shook his head. "There's still something in that house"—he gestured toward the unseen rectory—"that would keep me awake at night!"

"The coffin door knocker, for one?" It was said lightly.

The smile returned. "That was a bit of whimsy on some Victorian priest's part. A reminder that dust to dust is everyone's fate." He took off his robes and laid them carefully in the small black case on the table. After a moment he said, "I was surprised to see you still here, Inspector. I had thought you'd go back to London, duty done."

"I had every intention of going," Rutledge answered. "But Inspector

Blevins has asked me to stay on a day or two. Until they are sure that this man Walsh is the one they want. They only brought him in yesterday, and there's still a great deal to find out about his movements."

Monsignor Holston nodded. "Blevins spoke to the Bishop last night. 'Early days' was what he said, but I think he's very hopeful. Bishop Cunningham asked to be kept informed."

"Blevins would also like to see this ended." Rutledge paused, watching Monsignor Holston as he added the consecrated wafers to his case and closed the lid. As they walked out the vestry door into a spreading patch of sunlight, he said, "I'm just going to the hotel to see about a room. Will you join me for lunch?"

Monsignor Holston sighed. "I'd like that very much. But I have to be back in Norwich for a service tonight. If you're here next Sunday, I'll accept."

"If I'm still here," Rutledge agreed. "Where did you leave your motorcar?"

"Behind the rectory. Look, if you are staying on here, will you keep me apprised of the situation? I'm sure Inspector Blevins will have his hands full. And—I'd appreciate it."

"Yes, I will."

And Monsignor Holston was gone, hurrying around the apse into the churchyard, lifting a hand in farewell as he disappeared in the direction of the rectory.

Hamish said, "He left with indecent haste."

"Yes. I don't know what he's afraid of, but Monsignor Holston is a man looking over his shoulder. He wanted me to come inside with him because he didn't want to be in that church alone. At a guess I'd say he's not sure the evidence against Walsh will stand."

"Aye," Hamish said thoughtfully. "There're ghosts there. But of his making or are they real?"

"I wish I knew!" Rutledge answered, walking back to his own motorcar.

The Osterley Hotel had once been grander, when the town was closer to the sea. Now it offered comfort to what travelers there were and to families and merchants staying for market day. Rutledge thought it might also be the only lodging within several miles where townspeople could put up guests.

The hotel stood on Water Street, where the road ran along the quay, and was built of the ubiquitous flint, three stories with windows looking out over the marshes or onto a courtyard at the side of the building, where carriages and motorcars could be left.

The woman who came to the desk as he entered was nearing fifty, he thought, her graying hair tidily pulled back into a soft knot at the nape of her neck. Clear gray eyes met his when he asked for a room. "For the night?"

"For several days," he said.

She nodded, pleased. "There's a nice view of the sea from number seventeen. If you have keen eyesight," she added with a smile. "What brings you to Osterley? We don't get many holiday-makers this time of year."

"A matter of business," he said pleasantly. "When did the sea recede?"

"Not in my lifetime. The early years of the last century. Though they say that the storms since 1900 are eroding the beaches again, and we might see the water return within the next ten or twenty years. That would be nice!" There was more hope than certainty in her voice. "We serve breakfast at seven, later if you prefer it. And if you'll be in to luncheon, we'd like to know. It's generally served at half past twelve. Dinner is from seven to nine. Then the cook wants to go home. You can also find a meal at The Pelican when we're closed. That's the pub at the end of the quay."

She was leading him up stairs that had been painted a soft green to match the carpet running down the center of the first-floor passage. A line of photographs in gold-trimmed oak frames had been hung along the walls, and he saw that they were early photographs showing Osterley when it still managed to attract a few bathers. Dark and faded, but fascinating as history: Victorian women in black silk gowns and bonnets strolling by the sea with black silk parasols shading their faces from the sun; small boats coming in to the quay in deeper water than existed now; and a fisherman proudly displaying his catch, his cap at a jaunty angle. There was a very early photograph of a coaster unloading freight, boxes and bales and barrels, just beyond The Pelican. And next to that, children forming a ring of curious faces around a pair of seals on the strand, their sleek, wet heads cocked in wary uncertainty. In this one, the marshes were a thickening line of reeds and grasses, more prominent to the east, leaving the western side of the narrowing harbor as a last sacrifice to the encroaching silt.

Noticing Rutledge's interest, she said, "My grandfather took those. Avid photographer with a keen eye for such things. He was lucky with the seals—they don't come this far south very often." She stopped before number seventeen and opened the door.

It was a bright room, flooded with light from a double pair of windows. Large, well furnished with a bedstead of mahogany wood, a dresser with a mirror, and a clothespress that matched. A painted washstand stood in the corner. Two comfortable chairs framed a table under the first pair of windows, and a desk was set under the second.

"The finest room in the house," Hamish murmured.

"I'm Mrs. Barnett," she told Rutledge. "If I'm not in the office, I'm in the kitchen or out to do the marketing. Leave a note if you can't find me."

"I will. Thank you."

"Do you care for luncheon today? As it's Sunday, The Pelican is closed. You'll have to drive inland some distance."

"If that's no trouble."

"We have one other guest at the moment, and she's staying in. Not a very agreeable morning for exploring the countryside! But I think it will clear by afternoon."

She cast one last glance around the room, nodded, and closed the door.

Rutledge went to the windows and looked out. From the first floor he could indeed see the water, a thin line of waves curling in, gleaming dully, and a flight of birds rising from the shingle strand. The hummocky, marshy ground filling the harbor from the headland to his left as far as the great hook of land that served as a natural breakwater on his right appeared to be threaded with foot-wide rivulets of no great depth, as well as the little stream that was all that remained of the harbor.

Having seen the photographs in the passage, he realized that the buildings that had once served the sea—shops selling ship's stores, fish markets, taverns, yards—had long since been turned to other uses. He had noticed one sporting a sign proclaiming a branch of the wildfowl trust. Another had become a smithy-cum-garage.

Hamish said, "I ken the sea taking a man's livelihood. Storms scour the coast of Scotland. Men drown, ships are lost. It's a hard life. But here . . ."

"They turned their hands to other things, I expect. Norfolk is sheep country. Or people simply moved on, those with a skill to offer somewhere else."

For a time he stood there simply enjoying the view, his windows open to the cry of the seagulls and the light breeze that was rapidly clearing the rain out. But the air here was fresh and clean, a tang of salt in it; the houses and shops seemed richly colored in the warming sunlight, their flint and brick walls holding the very character of Norfolk. Many of the streets of this village now looked inland, as if growing accustomed to accommodating the missing sea, but Water Street still ran toward it and then turned when it reached the quay. The pale line of water out beyond the ridges of grass seemed to lack the energy to find a way back, a wan lover with no real passion for a reunion.

Hamish said, "No one remembers when the storms brought the sea inland. I wouldna' hae wanted to live here then!"

Which was, Rutledge thought, a perceptive remark. He noticed an elderly man in a small boat rowing up the stream, heading in to Osterley. He rowed smoothly, back bent, arms moving from long practice in the even, easy strokes of someone brought up on the water. Muscles bulged where the sleeves of his darned sweater had been rolled back to the elbows, and the heavy corduroys he wore were well worn. Watching him pull for the quay, Rutledge realized suddenly that he envied the man, drawn to the water as he himself was.

Though the harbor had vanished—even most of the little boats themselves—the gulls, ever hopeful, could be heard heading toward the lonely rower or wheeling just out of sight above the hotel—as if searching the marshy silt for the next wave. Lacking a boat, he wondered if it was safe to walk down to the distant beach, or if there was a track he could follow.

He straightened, and brought his mind back to the present. His suitcase was in the boot; he would have to fetch it. The tips of the fingers on one hand absently massaged his chest. Too much driving had aggravated the blow he'd received yesterday. Damn the man Walsh! But it hadn't been his fault. Rutledge had been in the wrong place.

Looking at his watch, Rutledge realized that it was nearly twenty-five after twelve. His baggage could wait. He washed his hands in the basin and dried them on a towel embroidered with an OH—Osterley Hotel—

ringed with blue forget-me-nots. The room was scrupulously clean and in good order. Mrs. Barnett was conscientious about her guests' comfort.

Down the passage he heard another door open and then close. The carpet muffled footsteps. The other guest? He wasn't in the mood for conversation. . . .

He waited for a count of twenty, opened then shut his own door, and followed down the passage and the stairs. The French doors to the right of the lobby stood open now, and there was a long dining room with some twenty tables covered in white cloths with green serviettes. But only two by the long windows had been set for the meal. Farther down the room, a woman with a book open in front of her was already spooning her soup. All he could see was the top of her dark head.

Rutledge took his own place, with his back to her, and looked out the windows. Here there was no verandah with white painted chairs, waiting for people to sit in them and watch the water. Those belonged to the south coast of England, where the sun shone with more warmth and regularity. Flowers, nearly withered in the October winds, stood in boxes by the door. A few were still colorful in the brief shelter of the wall.

The dining room with its ornate glass chandeliers was very pleasant. Once it must have been filled with guests, with a large staff to see to them. Now it appeared to be only Mrs. Barnett who served the meals. She came through the swinging doors from the kitchen carrying a tray with his soup on it and a basket of fresh bread.

With a smile she served him and was gone, not lingering to talk. It was excellent soup, a mutton stock with vegetables and barley. He ate with relish, feeling hungry. Hamish, at the back of his mind, was occupied with the street outside.

There were quite a few people about, their shadows barely visible in the pale sunlight. But there was a patch of blue sky to the north, growing steadily larger. Rutledge saw Blevins walk past, lifting his hat to a young woman who held a shy little girl by the hand. A heavy-shouldered man, who looked more like a blacksmith than a farmer or fisherman, his hands gnarled and ingrained permanently with black, was talking to a thin man with the pale face of a schoolmaster. Three laborers, awkward in their Sunday best and deep in conversation, made way for a dray pulled by a farm gray. It passed them in a rumble of wheels, and disappeared around the bend.

A well-dressed man about sixty-five years of age passed through the outer door and opened the inner door to the lobby. His footsteps could be heard approaching the dining room, and he came through the French doors with an air of command that matched the craggy power of his face.

"Susan?" he called.

After a moment Mrs. Barnett appeared in the kitchen doorway, and something in her eyes instantly altered as she saw who had come to dine. She walked forward slowly, her expression a careful blank. Rutledge, keeping his attention fixed on the last of his soup, couldn't avoid hearing the ensuing exchange.

"I'm in town for the afternoon and felt sure you could accommodate me for luncheon today."

"My lord, it isn't possible—there's no table made up."

"Yes, yes, I know, I should have called ahead. But I didn't expect to be delayed beyond an hour. Now I'll be lucky to get away in three." He looked around. "I'll join that gentleman by the window, shall I, and save you the fuss of preparing a place for me." His eyes swept the room again, empty but for the two hotel guests, and then came back to Rutledge. Crossing to the table, he said, "May I join you, sir? It would spare Mrs. Barnett a good deal of inconvenience if you allowed me to share your table."

Behind his broad back, Mrs. Barnett grimaced. Rutledge said, "The question, I think, is whether Mrs. Barnett can manage in the kitchen. If she can, then I shall be happy to have you join me."

"Susan?" She nodded with what grace she could muster. Rutledge wondered if it was her own luncheon that would appear on the extra plate. "That's settled then," the man declared. As she went to fetch plates and cutlery, he pulled out the chair opposite Rutledge and said, "Sedgwick is my name. I live in East Sherham, not far from Osterley. But a long way to drive home for my lunch. A guest here, are you?"

He settled heavily in his chair.

"Rutledge." They shook hands over the silver salt and pepper shakers. "For a few days. On a private matter."

"Yes, that's what brings most of our visitors these days. Business, not pleasure. I understand the town was once quite famous for fish and the fine bathing." He looked up as Mrs. Barnett set his place and then brought his bowl of soup from the tray. "Thank you, my dear! And don't stand on ceremony. Mr. Rutledge has finished his soup; he's ready for the next course."

As she set the bowl in front of Sedgwick, her eyes met Rutledge's.

He had the distinct impression that she would have enjoyed nothing more than pouring the lot over Sedgwick's head.

"I'll wait," Rutledge told her, and she left them.

Sedgwick ate with gusto. "I'm famished," he said between spoonsful. "It has been a long morning and I breakfasted shortly after six. Is that your motorcar I saw in the hotel yard? The four-seater?"

"Yes, it must be."

"My younger son bought one like it a year before the War. Found it an admirable motor. Made the run from London in excellent time and never gave him any trouble." He smiled wryly. "I'm at the mercy of gout, myself. Don't fancy driving when my foot is aching like a fiend in hell."

The conversation moved on from motors to unemployment and then to some discussion of the peace treaty that had been signed. "Is it worth the paper it was written on? I ask you! The French were vindictive as hell, and the Hun is too proud to live long under their heel!" Sedgwick shook his head, answering his own question. "Politicians are the very devil. Foolish idealists, like Wilson in America, or short-sighted and closed-minded, like that lot in Paris."

Mrs. Barnett served them roasted ham and a side dish of carrots and potatoes, seasoned with onions, still steaming from the ovens. As she rearranged the salt and pepper to accommodate the various dishes, she asked Sedgwick if he cared for hot mustard sauce. He smiled and helped himself from the silver bowl she held for him, then sighed. "I don't think anyone can match Mrs. Barnett's mustard sauce. She won't tell me how she makes it. And so I try to remember which days she's likely to serve it. You'll find it excellent!"

As she moved away after serving the sauce to Rutledge, Sedgwick added, "Know the Broads well, do you?"

"I've come here a time or two. A friend kept a boat west of here, but that was before the War. He's not up to sailing these days." Ronald had been gassed at Ypres; the damp ravaged his lungs now.

"Never been much for the sea myself. But one of my sons was fond of boats and took us out a time or two." He smiled sheepishly. "Not the stomach for it, if you want the truth."

Sedgwick was an engaging man, the sort of Englishman who could spend half an hour with a stranger without fear of encroachment on either side. Which told Rutledge, watching the sharp eyes beneath the gray, shaggy brows, that he was not what he seemed.

By the end of the meal, Rutledge had his man pegged. His accent was Oxonian, his voice well modulated, his conversation that of a gentleman, but he still had occasional trouble with his aitches. London roots, and not the West End, in spite of the heavy gold watch fob, the elegant signet ring on the left hand, and apparel that had been made by the best tailors in Oxford Street.

As they finished their flan and Susan Barnett brought the teapot for a second cup, the woman who had been sitting behind Rutledge some tables away rose and walked out of the dining room.

Sedgwick bowed politely, turning his head so that his eyes followed her through the doorway.

"An interesting young woman," he said to Rutledge. "Religious sort, I'm told. She was at a dinner party given by the doctor here, and spoke very well on the subject of medieval brasses."

It was almost condescending.

As if to underline Rutledge's thoughts, Sedgwick added, "Spinster, of course," settling the question of where she stood in his scheme of the world.

"Indeed," Rutledge said, watching her walk across the lobby. The brief flash of a shapely ankle and the glossy dark hair above the straight back seemed at odds with Sedgwick's opinion of her.

Sedgwick excused himself after his second cup of tea and spoke to Mrs. Barnett in the kitchen before leaving the hotel.

Rutledge himself rose from the table, dropping his serviette by his empty cup, and went into the lobby. There was a small sitting room beyond the stairs, the door standing wide. Inside he could just see his fellow guest reading her book. While the room was for any guest's use, the occupant seemed to make it clear that she did not wish for company, her chair set at an angle that discouraged any greeting.

He turned and left the hotel to walk down the street toward the water. A chill wind blew off the North Sea and whipped the saw grass he could just see far out on the dunes. The single boat he'd watched coming in was now beached on the damp strand below the seawall, with wet boot prints coming up the stone steps and leading up into the town. He could follow them, as cakes of gray mud flecked off at each step.

Hamish said, "The priest's killer wore old and worn shoes."

"Yes. I hadn't forgotten. The Strong Man, Walsh, was wearing boots. With hobnails. And his feet are large."

"Aye. It's a thought to bear in mind. . . ."

CHAPTER EIGHT

INSTEAD OF FETCHING HIS LUGGAGE FROM the boot as he'd planned, Rutledge drove to St. Anne's rectory. The mixture of watery sun, clouds, and drizzle that had pursued him all morning had given way to fairer skies. If the sun stayed out, he thought as he pulled into the short drive, the day would soon be pleasantly warm. A light wind riffled his hair as he went up the walk to the door and lifted the coffin knocker. After a time Mrs. Wainer came to answer the clamor, and recognizing the Inspector on the doorstep, greeted him with noticeable relief.

"I thought it might be someone wanting Monsignor Holston!"

"I hope I haven't taken you from your dinner," he said.

"No, I've finished. Do come in!" she said, and was on the point of leading him back to the Victorian parlor when he stopped her.

"I'd like to see Father James's study," Rutledge said gently, "if it wouldn't be too much trouble for you."

She turned her head toward the stairs. "If you don't mind, I'd rather not go up there just now. I still find it hard." She looked at Rutledge again. "It's Sunday, and he was always on time for his dinner, and hungry, having fasted. There's no one to cook for now, though I'd bought a nice bit of ham, hoping Monsignor Holston would stay. . . . I feel at sixes and sevens!" There was a sadness in the words that touched Rutledge. "Well. The Bishop will send a new priest when he's ready."

"It should be reassuring to know that Inspector Blevins has found the man responsible."

The housekeeper answered, "Oh, yes." But her response was polite, with no sense of relief. Only acceptance. "Of course I told the constables the Strong Man had been in the house. But I never dreamed— He seemed—I don't know, apologetic about his size, afraid of bumping into anything. Go on, if you like. There's no harm can be done. And maybe some good. Up the stairs then, and the second door on your right."

"Toward the house next door," Hamish observed.

Rutledge thanked her and started up, becoming aware of how little noise he made on the solid treads—a muffled step, a sound you'd miss if you weren't listening for it.

When he'd reached the landing, he turned. Mrs. Wainer was still standing by the parlor doorway, unwilling to remember what lay at the top of the stairs. There was an expression of deep grief on her face. Then she walked away down the passage, as if turning her back on what he was about to do.

The second door to the right led into a large study, with a bank of long windows covered with heavy velvet draperies that shut out the light. Rutledge was reminded suddenly of what Monsignor Holston had said, that the room had spoken to him of evil. Whether what he sensed now was evil or not, he couldn't say, but the dimly lit room seemed— not empty. Waiting.

Hamish said, "It isna' the corpse, it's been taken away. But the spirit . . ."

"Perhaps." Rutledge hesitated, and then, shutting the study door behind him, crossed the carpet to pull the draperies open, watching the wooden rings move smoothly down the mahogany rod with the familiar *click-clicks*. Brightness poured into the room, and that odd sense of something present there was banished with the light.

He found that his feet were set in a scrubbed and faded portion of the carpet, where someone must have tried to remove the blood that had puddled from Father James's head wound. An onerous duty for the grieving woman downstairs. Rutledge stepped away from it, then looked at it in relation to the windows.

If the victim had been struck down just there and from behind, he must have been *facing* the window. His back to his attacker. Rutledge went to test the latch, and then look out—almost directly into the windows opposite, where he could see an old woman in a chair, knitting.

Everyone described Father James as middle-aged but fit. But Walsh was a very large man. Even if help had come, what could even one of the strapping sons next door have done? It had taken four men at the police station to subdue Walsh. And by the time anyone had reached the study, the priest would have been dead. Yet if he was as capable as all the people who knew him had claimed he was, he would have abandoned any hope of aid, and tried to deal with the intruder in some fashion.

"If he wasna' afraid of the man," Hamish said, "he wouldna' have called for help. If he was afraid, he'd ha' kept an eye on him!"

"Yes, that's what I'd have done," Rutledge answered him. "Even if he knew the intruder, he'd have been wary . . ." Or—too certain of his powers of persuasion?

"Here, if you need the money that badly, take it, and go with my blessing. . . ."

"It's easier to smash the back of a head—when there's no face staring into yours," Hamish pointed out. "With the bayonet, we didna' look into the face." And that was also true. Dead center, twist, withdraw. A belt buckle above the blade, not a pair of human eyes . . .

So why had the priest turned away? Toward the windows, rather than toward the intruder?

Only an exceptionally trusting man would have done that.

"Look, I'll turn my back, and let you walk out of here. Return the money if and when you can; there are others who need it as much as you do. . . ."

Still, to say that, Father James must have had a very good idea who was threatening him. Yet how far could a frightened man trust in return? Had it been a calculated risk, then? To calm whoever stood there, rather than agitate him?

Or had his assailant said, *"Turn your back, and let me go"*—then lost his nerve?

Rutledge listened to his intuition, and heard no reply.

The room, then. He slowly turned to study it. Not only had the drawer been broken open, the room had been ransacked.

If the priest had caught the intruder with the tin box pried open and the money in his hand, and offered him safe passage out the door, when had the room been torn apart? It must have happened *before* Father

James came up the stairs. But why, when the locked desk drawer was the most logical place to begin a search and would have yielded the small tin box straightaway?

If the room had been turned upside down *after* the priest was dead, why not take a few minutes more to search through the rest of the house? The small clock in the parlor—the gold medal around the priest's neck—whatever other easily pocketed windfalls came to hand—these had been left behind.

Why had ten or fifteen pounds satisfied a killer? If Walsh needed that much to finish paying for his cart and would take nothing else—why kill the priest?

Hamish said, "When you came in, your first act was to open yon draperies."

Rutledge looked again at the windows. "Yes. And if Father James had done the same, the killer would then have been presented with his back, before they had even spoken to each other."

He examined the rest of the room. One closed doorway led to the priest's bedroom, as he found by opening it. Simple furnishings—a hard single bed, a wooden crucifix above the headboard, and a much-used prie-dieu against the wall of the study. An armoire between the windows and a low, matching chest at the foot of the bed. A chair stood beside a small bookshelf, and Rutledge crossed to read the titles. Religious texts, for the most part, and a collection of biographies: Pitt the Younger. Disraeli. William Cecil—the great secretary to Elizabeth the First. And a selection of poetry. Tennyson. Browning. Matthew Arnold. O. A. Manning . . .

He turned away and opened the only other door. It led to a bath. Rutledge closed that and went back to the study. Here were the broken desk and a chair, to one side of the passage doorway. A horsehair settee with two straight-backed chairs at angles beside it faced the hearth. In the corner beside the bedroom door stood the private altar. The candlesticks were there, polished to shine like molten sunlight, but the police had taken away the crucifix used as a weapon. A darker spot on the wood marked its dimensions. It would have been heavy. And one blow would have sufficed. Two at most . . .

Hamish said, "A man could stand unseen between that altar and the wall. If the room wasna' lit."

Rutledge was already looking at the space. He wedged himself in it.

A broad man could just fit himself in there. And a thin one . . . But could Walsh?

"Yon priest in Norwich?" Hamish had not liked Monsignor Holston. "Perhaps he canna' return to the scene of his crime."

"If he'd stood in the bedroom, whoever he was," Rutledge speculated, "until the priest had turned his back to attend to the drapes, it would have taken the murderer a half dozen steps to close the distance between them. Even accounting for Walsh's longer strides. And wary, alert, Father James would have sensed he was coming. The first blow wouldn't have hit the back of his head—it would have struck him in the temple."

"Why was Monsignor Holston afraid in the church, as well?" Hamish persisted, but Rutledge was looking again at the shadows between the drapes and the altar's tall back.

"I don't know. That someone would hide in a confessional after the service—enter through the vestry door, and wait for the service to end." He tried to concentrate again. Even if the draperies had been drawn and the lamps were not lit, Father James couldn't have missed the signs of a search. Paper on the floor would have gleamed whitely, even in low light. And what householder would have crossed that scatter of papers and books and furnishings to go to the window? His first act would probably have been to call out, *Who's there?* And to stand on the threshold, waiting.

In that case, the intruder had been in the bedroom and would have had to call to the priest to lure him nearer. Beside the altar, the slightest movement would have drawn the priest's wary eyes immediately. And yet, the crucifix—the weapon—had come from the altar, not the bedroom. Unless the intruder had already armed himself . . .

It was a puzzle. And more than a few of the pieces failed to fit.

Rutledge went to the desk and examined the broken drawer. It was savagely butchered. A shard of wood still hung at an angle, though someone had tried to make it appear tidy by pushing it nearly back into place. He looked at the small lock. Mrs. Wainer was right. Hardly worthy of the effort put in to breaking it so severely.

"Unless," Hamish told him, "it was done in haste, for fear of being caught."

"He shouldn't have been caught. Mrs. Wainer had gone and the priest was usually at the church at that hour. Whoever it was should have had a clear run. . . ."

Twist the evidence another way: the force of the blows that killed Father James.

A man of more than average strength, driven by fear, would have struck with what appeared to be savagery in an ordinary person. And that pointed a finger directly at Walsh. The Strong Man . . .

The thing was, only two people knew exactly what had happened here. One of them was the victim, unable to tell his side of the story. The truth, if it was to be found, had to be dug out of the silence of the killer. And the traces of his presence that could be read in his motive.

It was easy to understand why Blevins was so pleased to have such a likely suspect under lock and key. Walsh had been in the rectory before. Walsh had extraordinary strength. And Walsh was in need of money to pay for his cart.

But how many Inspectors had seen their early proofs slip through their fingers like sand, leaving them with nothing to take before a magistrate?

Rutledge looked around the room one last time, thinking about Monsignor Holston rather than Father James.

Why had Holston wanted the Yard to take over the investigation, or at the very least, to supervise its progress? To find out something he himself couldn't tell the police? Or to protect something he was afraid the local people might discover? A policeman from London had no insight into the residents of Osterley, and could easily miss a small and seemingly insignificant bit of evidence that Inspector Blevins would recognize instantly.

But if Monsignor Holston died next, because he had known—or guessed—too much, how quickly the investigating officers would jump to the conclusion that the connection between the two victims must be their calling—and not shared knowledge. A priest killer—mad, beyond the pale. Kill a third priest, and there would be no shadow of a doubt. Even if the third had been selected at random. Misdirection—the sign of a clever mind.

Hamish said, "But I canna' think that's verra' likely, if there's already someone about to be charged."

"I agree. But it might explain why Monsignor Holston is so afraid."

Surveying the windows again, Rutledge went on. "If it was nearly dark, with no lamps burning, Father James might have drawn the drapes before lighting one. And if the damage was done *after* the murder, there would have been nothing to alarm the priest as he walked in here. The desk drawer would have been out of his line of sight. Which would mean that the *killer* was surprised . . . not the priest."

"There's another way it could ha' happened. If the killer was *waiting* for the priest."

"Which puts an entirely different complexion on it, doesn't it?" Rutledge replied thoughtfully.

Monsignor Holston was right about one thing. There was something odd about this murder scene. It told conflicting stories about the sequence of events. Were the drapes open—or closed? Was the lamp on the desk burning? Where had the killer been standing? And when had the room been torn apart? Had the priest seen his killer? Or had he been struck down before he was aware that he was in danger? Had the murderer come here for the money in the desk—or for something else altogether?

A sieve through which a defense lawyer could walk at will . . .

Rutledge found Mrs. Wainer in the kitchen, staring out the window that looked out onto a stand of lilacs, the back garden, and beyond that, to the churchyard.

She turned as he came in.

He asked her to show him where the footprint had been found, and she pointed to the largest lilac bush on one side of the lawn. Its branches arched and then dipped nearly to a grown man's waist. And there was a bare spot where the grass didn't grow, just by it. The shadows of the bush would have made an excellent place to watch the house. . . .

Rutledge asked the housekeeper if she left the lamp in the study lit when she went home each evening.

"No, not that night, if that's what you're asking me. And I think about it time and again. I wasn't sure, you see, when he might be coming back, and I didn't want to leave it burning untended if he was going to be very late." She hesitated and then said anxiously, "Do you suppose it made any difference?"

"No, I'm sure it didn't. A policeman makes an effort to be thorough, when picturing the scene in his mind. And the draperies. Were they left open or were they shut?"

"They were shut," she replied firmly. "That's what I do when I leave of an evening, except in the summer when there's light well past nine."

"What did Father James generally do when he came in? Did he walk in this way or through the door at the front of the house?"

Rutledge took a moment to look around him. It was a friendly room, painted a very pale green, like early spring leaves, and the curtains at the windows were a rose pink. Feminine, in a way, but not exclusively so. Had Mrs. Wainer had a voice in choosing the colors? Most certainly she had a hand in its care. The great iron stove was polished like rare furniture, the table well scrubbed beneath the hanging lamp, the stone sink empty of unwashed dishes. A small rag rug lay by the door, for wiping feet. It, too, was spotless.

She was saying to him, "Father always came in by the back. He left his bicycle in the shed, then stood his boots there by the door, on the little rug, and hung his coat on a peg if it was wet. I've known him to walk through the house in his stockinged feet, rather than dirty my floors. He was that thoughtful! And then he'd go up to his room, to wash up if he needed to or to leave his coat if it was dry. If the meal wasn't ready, he'd work at his desk, or if there were visitors, he'd come back down to the parlor to speak with them."

"Other people would know this was his habit? To come in through the kitchen door?"

She smiled. "I shouldn't wonder if half the village did the same. Tradesmen come to the kitchen door, and a neighbor bringing over an extra loaf from her baking or a jar of pickles or jam she'd just put up. A man would never think of walking into the front hall with muck on his shoes, or children running in from the rain. I daresay there's not a kitchen door in Osterley that's ever locked, though there's the key on the nail just beside it. There was no need—"

Without warning her face crumpled, the smile dissolving into a grimace of pain. "He was like my own son. I've such grief I don't know how to cope with it." Turning away, she fought to keep her voice steady. "If that's everything, I'll go home now. I shouldn't have stayed this long. . . ."

Rutledge thanked her gently and walked back through the house to let himself out the front door. Halfway down the passage he heard a sob and hesitated. But her grief was private. There was nothing he could do or say to assuage it.

And his place in Osterley was clearly marked out—he came and went a stranger by the door at the front of the house.

CHAPTER NINE

WHEN RUTLEDGE ARRIVED AT THE POLICE station twenty minutes later, after leaving his motorcar at the hotel, he found Inspector Blevins sitting in his cramped office finishing a stack of sandwiches and a steaming thermos of tea. "Missed my lunch," he said, gesturing to the sandwich wrappings. "Someone was reported shooting out in the marshes, and that's not allowed. I spent well over an hour tramping through the bloody reeds looking for the fool. My wife took pity on me and brought me these. Care for one?"

"Thanks, no. I ate at the hotel. Is it safe to walk out to the sea?"

"If you're local, I suppose it's safe enough. I wouldn't recommend it. Too easy to lose yourself, and then I'd be out searching for *you*." It was a friendly warning.

Putting the cap back on the thermos of tea, Blevins looked up at Rutledge and away again. "There's been a complication," he said. He ran his fingers through his hair. "Father James had two sisters—Sarah and Judith. Judith died in the influenza epidemic. Sarah is married and has young children. There was a telephone message here at the station this morning from Sarah's husband, man by the name of Hurst, Philip

Hurst. I've met him a time or two. Steady and reliable. The message was, he'd call back after Mass. And he did, just before the damned shooting started in the marshes."

Blevins stopped fiddling with the thermos and set it aside. "Interesting conversation. Hurst told me that one of Judith's favorite stories as a child was Jack the Giant-Slayer, Father James undoubtedly filling the role of Jack in his sister's eyes. Sarah claims he must have read it to her dozens of times. But that's neither here nor there."

He seemed to be avoiding coming to the point, as if he found it distasteful. Rutledge waited.

"When he was in France, Father James wrote often to both sisters, and Sarah remembers one letter in particular, where he told Judith that he'd finally met the 'Giant.' There was even a line drawing in the margin with Father James dwarfed by this stick figure. And there was some other nonsense about the story, and that was it."

"You're telling me that Walsh is this 'Giant'?"

"God, no! Father James was joking, reminding his sister of their childhood. This Giant could have been anyone he'd seen—a Punjabi for all we know! A good many of the Highlanders were damned tall, for that matter. But now I've got to find someone in the War Office to look up records to see if Walsh *could* have met Father James in France. They won't like that, but if it's true, I need to know about it before I'm made a fool of in the courtroom. It doesn't change anything, even if he did!"

"You'll have to question everyone at the bazaar again. To see if the two men recognized each other that day."

"I don't see how it was possible for Walsh to recognize Father James—he was dressed as a clown to entertain the children, and his face was painted. But of course Father James could well have remembered *him*."

Hamish reminded Rutledge, "Mrs. Wainer spoke of clown's paint. He was still wearing it when he handed her the bills and coins they'd taken in."

So she had. Rutledge regarded Blevins, trying to read his face. "Asking Walsh is the simplest way to find out," he observed.

"You can't ask him anything without being cursed and abused. Better to find out from the War Office than give that clever bastard some way of crawling out of this charge!"

"Does Sarah Hurst still have the letter?"

"It was written to Judith, who showed it to her, and there's no way of knowing if Judith kept it. Much less what's become of it since she died. But Hurst thought we ought to know, and rightly so."

"Could Walsh have been searching for it? Either time he was at the rectory?" It was not uncommon to keep letters after a loved one died.

"Lord, no, how would he have known such a letter even existed? No, it's a false scent, and I'm not going to be sidetracked by it. Besides, if Father James had learned something incriminating about Walsh, he wouldn't have told his sister, would he? Let's leave it! I told you only because I thought you'd agree with me that it's not important."

Hamish reminded Rutledge of an exchange during last night's dinner at the Norwich hotel on the subject of the murder having to do with the War:

And how to find such a needle in a haystack of returned veterans?

Yet that same needle might have found Father James, nearly a year after the War had ended . . .

Because he'd come to a bazaar?

"I see your point." It was enough to satisfy Blevins. Changing the subject, Rutledge told him, "I've been to the rectory to look at the study."

"Doesn't tell you much, does it? Mrs. Wainer scrubbed that carpet nearly through to the nap, trying to get out the blood. Wouldn't hear of having a constable do it for her. It was her place, she insisted, not his." He wolfed down the last sandwich, then began to fold the serviettes in which they had been wrapped. A **B** in Gothic script had been embroidered into one corner, entwined with a sprig of lilac.

"A great deal of force was used to open the desk."

"More than needful. Yes, that's true. But I doubt our blossom of fragility back there in the cells knows his own strength. The same force was used to kill Father James."

"The theory is that he came looking for money to pay for his new cart. But this was some weeks after the bazaar. By that time, the money collected at the fair might well have been already dispersed—to the needy, to pay for a new altar cloth, whatever use it was intended to serve. Why did Walsh believe that the money was still in Father James's hands?"

"I've looked into that myself. More often than not those funds are used as a priest sees fit. The accounts that must be paid by the parish come from another sum that's on deposit in the bank. The Autumn Fete never brings in a large amount. Although this year, the first since the

War ended, we had a better turnout. The men had come home, and the young women who had gone away to do war work were back as well." He paused. "That's been the hardest part for me, you know, accepting that a good many men from Osterley won't be coming home. Whilst you're fighting, you don't think about it all that much. But the butcher's son and Mrs. Barnett's nephew, and so many other faces you'd expect to see about the town didn't make it. Or they're crippled and off somewhere learning how to make baskets or some such that they can sell. The best man we ever had in the marshes is blind. Two of the choirboys are orphans, their mother dead of the influenza and their father killed off Jutland. There's talk of making a small war memorial here to honor the dead of Osterley. I don't see it myself. But those who lost loved ones might find it comforting after a fashion."

Rutledge was reminded of the monument that London was building to the nation's war dead. An enduring memorial to The Great War, the newspapers called it; a place where wreaths could be laid each November and prayers said for the dead who hadn't come home.

He shivered. Many of them had never been found. They still lay in Flanders's Fields, buried so deep in the wrecked earth that not even a farmer's plow would turn them up. Leather boots might last longer than flesh or bone, and helmets as well, but in time, even leather crumbled and metal rusted. After a few years, peas and corn and vineyards would cover their resting place, not a wooden cross or a plinth of marble. Would they even hear the prayers of a grateful nation? And how long would gratitude last?

Blevins was saying to him, "—Father James survived the War, survived the influenza epidemic. A brave man, but never a foolhardy one. Anybody will tell you that. He'd have dealt with the man in his study, given half a chance. But if it was Matthew Walsh, he had no chance at all. I don't know what your experience has been, but in mine a good many men the size of Walsh are of a milder nature. This monster's got a temper. Father James may have made a fatal mistake in judging his adversary."

"There's some truth to that," Rutledge agreed. "But speaking of Walsh's size—I've been thinking about the print of the shoe you found at the rectory near the lilacs."

Brushing aside Rutledge's words, Blevins said impatiently, "Yes, I've already come to the same conclusion. Walsh's foot dwarfs that print. I had a drawing made of it, to match with the shoes of any suspects. You know what this means, don't you?"

This time Rutledge let him have the pleasure of answering his own question.

"It tells me friend Walsh must have had an accomplice."

Hamish, breaking a long silence, warned, "You ken, the sum stolen wouldna' be enough for two. . . ."

"Did Walsh have an assistant at the bazaar?" There had been no mention of anyone else in the Strong Man's act, to Rutledge's knowledge, but that would make sense, if Walsh needed someone he could trust.

"No, no, he worked alone as far as we can discover," Blevins answered. "I doubt he ever made enough to hire an assistant. Some months ago he had a woman with him, but I'm told she wasn't good for business. The young ladies seemed to find her intimidating. Well, that's not surprising! But breaking and entering is a different proposition. There's often another man along to act as lookout. That's why he was standing near the lilac bush. He was out of sight from the churchyard and the neighboring house."

Blevins seemed convinced. For the time being, Rutledge left the subject and moved on.

"What about other towns where Walsh has made an appearance? Were there any crimes that could be traced to him? Is this a pattern?"

"I'd thought of that, too. We're looking into it." After a moment of silence, Blevins said, "We haven't got more than curses out of Walsh so far. Would you like to try your hand at questioning him?"

"It wouldn't do any harm."

"We've put him in irons, to keep him manageable." Blevins reached for a ring of keys and took Rutledge down the passage to the makeshift cells set in behind the offices. "He won't be tried here," the Inspector went on as he unlocked the door. "We're moving him to Norwich by the middle of next week. We're used to drunk and disorderly, petty theft, and the occasional wife-beater who won't learn his lesson. And any murderers we've had to deal with over the years are generally more terrified of what they've done than they are a threat to the peace. But this man is dangerous."

When Blevins unlocked the door of the cell, Walsh was sitting on the iron cot, his face bruised, his eyes defiant. Ankles and wrists were fettered, a heavy chain hanging between them.

Blevins said briskly, "You've met Inspector Rutledge before. Nearly knocked him down. I wouldn't think about trying it again. He's here from London."

Walsh, surprise in his face, said, "Are they taking me to London, then?"

"That could depend on how cooperative you are. The Inspector wants to question you. About the priest's death."

Taking advantage of the man's uncertainty, Rutledge asked almost conversationally, "Ever use an assistant in your act, Walsh?"

Eyebrows raised, Walsh answered, "I used a woman for some weeks. Thought it would make the ladies more willing to let themselves be lifted on the bench, if Iris went first. But she didn't work out. Why do you want to know?"

"I should have thought a man would have been more useful, considering the bench and the weights you must haul about regularly in your cart."

Walsh grinned. "I can lift them and you, too, and I'll show you if you unlock these!" He raised his hands. The chain clanked unmusically, but its weight seemed not to cause him any distress.

Rutledge returned the smile. "Then why did you take someone with you when you killed the priest? Was that more dangerous than pulling a carriage against a team of horses? I'm surprised that you'd choose a woman to stand outside and watch. She couldn't stop the priest from coming home, could she? Or warn you. But what you've done is pitched her into this with you. Accomplice to murder. I should have thought there was barely enough money for one."

The grin had faded. Walsh said angrily, "I didn't kill any man, with or without help! Except in the War, when I was paid to do it. Are all policemen deaf, or is it that you can't do your work properly?"

Rutledge responded quietly. "You bought yourself a new cart." Behind him he could hear Blevins fuming. But the trick with a man like Walsh was to encourage braggadocio. To let him tweak the noses of the police.

"Aye, with the savings from letting Iris go. The old one had got worm in it, sitting in a shed all the time I was away fighting. It had to be replaced. I didn't have any choice!"

"If you didn't kill Father James, who did? You were at the bazaar. Did you see anyone looking for a chance to pick up money?"

"Pickpockets, you mean?" Walsh asked. "There were two, but a constable run them off soon enough. Men in the line of housebreaking don't come to church bazaars. The bloody things are advertised everywhere you look! In shop windows, on pasteboards or lampposts. Invitation to robbery, right out in the streets! All they have to do is watch for a family to leave for the day."

"We'll make a note of that," Rutledge assured him. "Will you tell us where to find Iris now? We'd like to hear what she has to say about killing a priest."

Walsh shrugged. "London, probably. How do I know? She didn't work out, and I let her go. She wasn't what you'd call happy about it, either. But business is business."

"What's her full name?"

"Iris Kenneth is what I knew her by. I'm not saying it was her true name. She's a shill by trade—you know, standing in front of a show like mine and talking it up. Used to work for a Gypsy fortune-teller from Slough, name of Buonotti—Barnaby, he called himself. Italian he was, went home to fight in the War and never come back. So she was at loose ends, and suited me just fine."

Blevins said, "What did you promise her, Walsh? That you'd take her on again if she helped you? Or was there someone else who owed you a favor?"

Walsh's laughter was a deep rumble in his chest that welled up and spilled over into a bass chuckle. "I'd have had to promise to marry her to get her to come in with me again. And I'm not the marrying kind! Not yet, anyway!"

After they'd finished with Walsh, Blevins turned to Rutledge and said, "I don't know. He's hard to read. But I'm ready to put good money down that says he's guilty! Too damned cocky by half!"

"Do you think this Iris Kenneth *was* his accomplice?"

"No. I'd say the shoe's too large for a woman's foot."

"That's probably true. But stuffed with rags, it would be the perfect blind, wouldn't it? A man's shoe. A woman's foot." He let the thought lie there.

Blevins said in resignation, watching his simple case grow to monstrous proportions, "I'll see what London can find out about Iris Kenneth."

The sky was clear now, the deeper blue of a storm passed and finer weather to come, and even the wind had dropped. The sun's warmth was not August's warmth, but it felt good on his face as Rutledge left the police station and walked down toward the hotel. On impulse he continued as far as the quay and stood there looking out across the marshes. He felt tired, deeply tired, and thought about a drink to ease his chest muscles and his arm. But he knew it was better to fight through the pain, if he could.

"You didna' sleep verra' well last night," Hamish pointed out. "Guilty conscience, was it?"

"No." Rutledge was too weary to enter into an argument with his tormentor.

Hamish said, "There's more on your mind than Scotland. This murder—this marshy country—I canna' see what it is that has made you a hollow man."

It wasn't a hollowness, Rutledge thought, that left him empty. It was too much, not too little—conflicting emotions, divided passions, an uncertainty he hadn't felt since June, when he had walked into Warwickshire an exhausted, haunted man with no hope and no expectations, and a great fear of going mad.

It wasn't madness now that he feared—though he knew that his mind teetered on the brink of self-destruction more often than he cared to admit.

But he was damned if he'd let Hamish pry and tear at him like a bird of prey, pulling out his soul to examine it like some rare specimen from the dark corners of the Congo. The question was, how to shut him out. Rutledge had never found a way.

Hamish had the last word—as he so often did. "It isna' a matter of a night's sleep, ye ken that. You willna' sleep until you allow yoursel' to live again!"

Trying to ignore him, Rutledge moved along the quay, to stand so that he could see the little stream where the boats came in to tie up. Wildfowl took off from the reeds and grasses, looking for their night's roost. He watched them for a time, and the long shadows of the late afternoon falling across the marshes. They were golden in this light, or a deep rufous, or pale yellow, and when he stood very still, he thought he could hear breakers coming into the strand out beyond them.

"Tomorrow will be fair," Hamish said, his countryman's instincts strong.

"Yes."

Rutledge turned back, walked to his car in the hotel's walled court-yard next to a stand of late autumn flowers, and retrieved his luggage from the boot.

It was early in the dinner hour when Rutledge came down for the evening meal. Mrs. Barnett greeted him and led him to a table in the middle of the room under the softly lit chandeliers. With a smile she asked if he'd enjoyed his day, and with equal courtesy he agreed that he had.

Where he had eaten his luncheon, a man was dining alone, a heavy cane hooked over the back of the second chair.

Mrs. Barnett turned to hover over him solicitously as he finished his cheese, and Rutledge caught part of the conversation.

The man was saying, ". . . in Osterley. We're a benighted lot here on the north coast."

Mrs. Barnett smiled. "I saw Nurse Davies a time or two in the shops. It was always the rain she . . ."

The glass doors between the dining room and the reception hall had been left open. Sunday night, it appeared, was a popular time for local people to come in for their dinner, and there were already six or eight couples by the windows and two families at the larger tables along the wall beneath the sconces. Their quiet laughter and low-voiced conversation filled the spacious room with warmth and life. A far cry from that noon when it had seemed much too large for its only occupants: Rutledge and the woman guest.

But it appeared that she wasn't dining in this evening.

Waiting for his soup, Rutledge unobtrusively studied the man by the window, the one Mrs. Barnett had spoken with.

There was something in the shape of his head that had caught Rutledge's attention, the way his hair grew thickly from its part, and the line of his chin. He was young—perhaps thirty or thirty-two—but his face was lined with pain, aging it prematurely. A member of Lord Sedgwick's family? The resemblance was there, but softer drawn, as if the bone structure was less formidable.

"I canna' see it mysel'," Hamish said. "He's no' as large framed."

It was true. Unless illness had whittled away the muscle and brawn. And certainly this man appeared to be taller, longer limbed.

Later, as Rutledge finished his soup, he saw the man by the window fold his serviette and set it by his plate, his expression relaxed, as if he'd enjoyed his meal. But he lingered, as if reluctant to push back his chair and retire to the lounge for his tea.

And then Mrs. Barnett came in from the kitchen, as if alert to his needs, and handed the man his cane. He grasped the ivory handle and rose with visible effort, his weight heavy on the thick shaft. He straightened, pausing to catch his breath. Rutledge looked away, but not before he saw the sharp sadness in Mrs. Barnett's face.

After a friendly exchange with Mrs. Barnett, the man walked on toward the lobby with only a slight limp, as if sitting had left him quite stiff and motion improved the ability of his muscles to function. He went on into the lounge to take his tea.

Mrs. Barnett came to remove Rutledge's soup plate and set the roast veal in front of him, and he said quietly, "The man with the cane. Is he related to Lord Sedgwick?"

She nodded. "Arthur. His elder son. His back was so severely injured in the War that they didn't expect him to live. And now he's walking again. It's quite a miracle. But it's hard to keep help. His last nurse was a London girl, not used to the country."

"I should think," Rutledge said lightly, "that the Sedgwick family paid well enough to overcome even that reservation."

Mrs. Barnett smiled but shook her head. "Ordinarily they probably would. But Arthur Sedgwick doesn't live in East Sherham with his father, although when he requires more surgery or physical rehabilitation, he often comes to stay. His home is in Yorkshire, and I'm told that compared to the Dales, Osterley is second only to Paris!"

Rutledge had nearly finished his meal when a woman came striding through the outer doors and walked up to Reception, where Mrs. Barnett was adding up figures. By this time most of the diners had retired to the lounge, and it appeared at first that the newcomer was going to ask if the dining room was still open. Instead she leaned over rather imperiously to touch Mrs. Barnett's arm, interrupting her to ask a question.

Mrs. Barnett's eyebrows went up, and she turned to look at Rutledge through the open doors.

Hamish said, "It appears the news has got around that ye're a policeman."

The woman, turning her head, followed Mrs. Barnett's glance, thanked her, and came through to the dining room.

She stopped in front of Rutledge's table and said, keeping her voice low, "Are you the man from London? Scotland Yard?"

Rutledge, standing now, his serviette in his hand, replied, "Yes. Inspector Rutledge. And you are—?"

"My name is Priscilla Connaught. Please—sit down and finish your meal! But if I may ask you to meet me in the lounge—it's down the passage, beyond the stairs—afterward? I won't keep you long, I promise!" Her voice was almost pleading, as if she feared he'd refuse her.

Hamish said, "She's verra' agitated!"

Rutledge was already answering, "Yes, I shan't be more than a few minutes. Would you prefer to join me—?"

"No! Thank you, no, this is a very—private matter." Glancing around the room at the remaining diners, she shook her head, as if to reinforce her refusal.

"Then I'll join you shortly."

"Thank you!" she said again, and turning, walked swiftly out to the lobby, in the direction of the lounge.

Rutledge resumed his seat as Hamish said, "It's no' a name you ken?"

"No. But if she's already learned that I'm from the Yard, she must live here in Osterley."

Finishing his trifle quickly, Rutledge left the dining room and went down the passage to the lounge.

But it was empty, except for one of the families who had dined at the hotel.

"She hasna' waited," Hamish pointed out. "A woman will change her mind, if she canna' be sure she's doing what's best."

Rutledge turned back to the dining room and met Mrs. Barnett coming through the glass doors. "Oh—there you are! I put Miss Connaught in the small parlor, just there—" She pointed to a closed door beyond the lounge. "There will be other guests having their tea in the lounge. I thought you might prefer a little privacy."

"Yes, thank you," he said. "Could you bring us tea in about five minutes?"

"I'll be happy to, Inspector." Her voice held a cooler note.

Hamish said, "Aye, they know now who you are."

His anonymity—his role as a man with no ties to the problems of Osterley—had been stripped from him. There had been a new reserve in Mrs. Barnett's manner. And it would soon be reflected in that of other people. His questions would be met with reticence.

Rutledge walked on to open the door Mrs. Barnett had indicated.

Priscilla Connaught was sitting by the small hearth, staring at the empty grate. She rose as Rutledge entered the room, facing him as if uncertain whether or not she really wanted to speak to him. Frowning, she gnawed her lip.

She was tall, rather slim, with dark hair showing only the first hints of graying, but her face was that of someone who suffers constant pain. Not lined so much as the planes worn down to bone, giving them a severity that was not unattractive.

Over the dark gray dress she was wearing was a matching coat with a lovely little gold pin at her lapel, stylish but somehow conveying a sense of mourning in the austerity of the cut. Her hat was a softer shade of gray with a small bunch of white feathers where the brim lifted on the left side.

A woman who would stand out wherever she was.

Hamish murmured something, but Rutledge didn't quite catch it, only the words ". . . a fierce pride . . ."

Miss Connaught was saying, "I hope you didn't rush your meal on my account—" Her voice was strained.

"Not at all," he replied with a smile. "I did take the liberty of asking Mrs. Barnett to bring us tea." In an effort to put her more at ease, he asked, "Do you live here in Osterley, Miss Connaught?" He indicated her chair, and after she sat down stiffly, her back ramrod-straight, he took the one on the other side of the hearth.

"Yes—yes, I do. I'm—not a native of Norfolk. My family is from Hampshire."

"I was surprised to find the harbor has all but vanished."

"I—it has been silting up for well over a century, I believe—"

A silence fell. The room, small but comfortably furnished, seemed to stifle her. She looked at the chairs and tables, the magazines on a low stand, the several pieces of Staffordshire porcelain on the mantel—anywhere but at Rutledge's face.

The door opened and Mrs. Barnett came in with their tea. Miss Connaught seemed almost relieved at the interruption, her eyes following the settling of the heavy tray on a table at her elbow.

Rutledge thanked Mrs. Barnett, and when she had gone, he said, "Would you rather I poured?"

Priscilla Connaught looked up at him, startled. "Yes. Would you? I—" She smiled for the first time, giving her face a little color. "I really think I'd drop the pot!"

He filled their cups, asked her her taste in sugar and cream, and handed her one of them.

She sat back, seeming to draw comfort from the warmth between her two hands. After a silence, she said, "I've come to ask you something that matters very much to me. I went to see Inspector Blevins, but the constable on duty tells me he's gone home and I didn't want to disturb him there. I'm not on the best of terms with his wife."

"I don't know that I can help you—" Rutledge began.

"It isn't a state secret!" she said abruptly. "Surely not. I need to know, you see—I need to know if the man they have at the police station is the person who killed Father James. The constable suggested that I speak to you."

Ah! Rutledge thought. Aloud he said, "Inspector Blevins believes that the man is the murderer. Yes."

"And what do you think?"

Parrying the question, he asked, "Do you know Matthew Walsh?"

Surprised, she said, "Is that his name? No, I have no idea who he is."

"He came to the bazaar. He was the Strong Man."

"Oh. I *do* remember seeing him. He was quite a spectacle, actually. Why do they think *he* killed Father James?" She sipped her tea, and he thought for an instant that she was going to spill it—the contents seemed to move in tiny waves, in concert with her nervousness.

"Why are you so concerned for him?" Rutledge asked.

"Concerned?" she repeated, as if bewildered. "For him? No—I

have no interest in him at all. I want to know who killed Father James. It's very important to me to know! That's why I've asked about this man."

"Are you a parishioner at St. Anne's?"

"I attend Mass there. But you're not answering my question directly. Have the police found Father James's murderer or haven't they?"

"We aren't sure," he said. Something in her face shifted. Disappointment? Was that what she felt? He couldn't be certain. "There appear to be very good reasons to believe that this man could have committed the crime. But there are also some unexplained problems. The courts may have to sort it out."

"I need to know!" she said again, her voice harsh with that need. "I can't wait until the courts do their work."

"Why?" he asked bluntly. "Did you care so much for the priest?"

"I hated him!" Priscilla Connaught said roughly.

For an instant Rutledge was reminded of what Mrs. Wainer had told him. That Father James had been killed for revenge.

"That's a very strong word, hate," he told her. "And if you did hate him, why should you care whether his killer is found or not?"

"Because whoever killed Father James has cheated me!" she cried, her voice trembling. "And I want to see him hang for that!"

Looking back on the encounter, Rutledge realized that his face must have reflected his shock. Priscilla Connaught set her cup on the tray with a clatter that sent tea over the lip of the saucer and onto the shining silver surface.

"I shouldn't have come," she said, rising to her feet. "I didn't mean a word of what I've just said. I'm upset, that's all. Everyone in Osterley is upset by this murder. Frightened by it. It's late, I must go—!"

Rutledge stood also. "No, I think you've told me the truth. And in my opinion, you owe me some explanation—"

"I just want the killer found, that's all! That part is true enough. And I wanted to know if that man—what did you say his name was?"

"Walsh. Matthew Walsh."

"Yes. If that man Walsh was likely to be the murderer. And you won't tell me straight out whether you believe he is or not!"

She was flushed, and Rutledge thought she was close to tears. Suddenly he felt a wave of pity.

"We don't have enough proof to charge him yet. It's circumstantial evidence at the moment. But Inspector Blevins is waiting for information that might give us the answer to your question. And as a precaution he's holding Walsh until it arrives."

"Oh, God." Her face seemed to close in on itself, the features tightening as if the muscles were pinched together. "Well, at least that's honest." She glanced around, searching for her purse, found it on the floor by her chair, and stooped to pick it up. "I'm sorry I interrupted your meal, Inspector. But I live alone; there's no one to talk to about this. I sometimes think I've lost my perspective."

"I wish you would be as honest with me," Rutledge answered. "Why did you hate Father James?"

She sighed in resignation, brushing the edge of her hand across her forehead. "It was a very long time ago. Well in the past, and nothing to do with the police. It was before he became a priest. I went to him for advice, and he gave it to me. I followed it because I trusted him. And it ruined my life. It destroyed everything I believed in and loved and cared about. And this man who was so *wise* and *compassionate* and *understanding* became a priest. I have often wondered just how many other lives he ruined in his righteous belief in his own infallibility. But as long as I could hate him, I had something to live for, you see! And now that's been taken away from me. And I really have nothing left. When that man killed Father James, he might as well have killed me, too!"

She swept past him, and out the door. Rutledge, staring at her stiff and uncompromising back, let her go.

Rutledge was halfway up the stairs when he thought about Monsignor Holston. He went down again to the lobby, found the telephone in the little alcove behind the desk, and put in a call to Norwich.

Eventually the priest answered, sounding out of breath. Rutledge identified himself.

"Sorry, I had to make a dash to answer the phone. Is there more news?"

"No, I'm afraid not. But I do have a small mystery on my hands. Tell me, do you know anyone called Priscilla Connaught?"

Monsignor Holston considered the question. "Connaught? No, I can't place her."

"She's a parishioner here at St. Anne's."

"Was she at Mass this morning?"

"I didn't see her. Tall, slim, graying dark hair."

"No. I can't put a face to the name. Does it matter? You could speak to Mrs. Wainer. She'd be able to tell you, surely?"

"Probably not important," Rutledge said lightly. "Apparently Miss Connaught knew Father James a good many years ago. His death seems to have upset her more than most."

"Priests have friendships, like anyone else. That shouldn't surprise you." There was a smile in the voice at the other end of the line.

"No, as a matter of fact, it doesn't," Rutledge responded. And after thanking Monsignor Holston, he hung up the telephone receiver.

Hamish said, "She wasna' the kind of friend yon priest in Norwich would be told about. If she believed that Father James had ruined her life."

"Yes," Rutledge said slowly. "It's an interesting thought, isn't it? I wonder if she came to Confession every week to tell him how much she hated him. The skeleton at the feast, reminding the merrymakers of their fate. Or in this case, the priest of his failure."

The dining room was closed, the French doors shut, and Mrs. Barnett was just coming out of the lounge with a tray laden with the cups and pots of tea that she had collected there.

The contrast with Priscilla Connaught was striking. Mrs. Barnett looked tired, her hands red from dishwater, and her black dress rumpled from the heat of the kitchen.

Rutledge offered to take the heavy tray, but she shook her head. "I'm used to it. But thank you." She rested it on the polished wood of the reception desk, and said thoughtfully, "I didn't know you were a policeman."

"I wasn't here in a strictly official capacity. Not at first," he answered her. "But Inspector Blevins is understandably eager to complete this investigation. I've been asked to stay on until then."

"Yes, I'd heard there was an arrest." She looked around her at the lobby and the stairs to the rooms above. "I was glad it wasn't someone who had stayed *here,* that week. That would have been shocking! We always have a few guests for such an event."

Taking the opportunity presented, Rutledge asked, "Would you mind telling me what you know about Miss Connaught?"

Alarm filled Mrs. Barnett's eyes. "I can't believe *she* has anything to do with Father James's death!"

"She offered some information, that's all. I wondered if it was trustworthy."

"Ah." Mrs. Barnett turned the tray a little, thinking. "It probably is, because she has no particular reason to lie, as far as I know. She keeps to herself." And then as if prompted by his attentive silence, Mrs. Barnett explained, "Which hasn't endeared her to most of the women here in Osterley. Many of them have put her down as a snob. That reserve of hers shuts people out. My late husband always believed she'd been involved in some sort of scandal, and was banished from Society." She tilted her head, in the way women did when amused about the antics of men. "Well, that's the romantic view, anyway."

"What's the general impression?" Rutledge asked, as if merely curious.

"That the only reason she'd be content in Osterley for so many years is that she has nowhere else to go. Occasionally she's invited to dinner, to make up the numbers, and if she accepts, she's pleasant company. But not the sort of woman another woman would sit down and have a good gossip with. Men seem to find her rather attractive and well-informed. But she's not a flirt. I'd always wondered if she was married to someone rather unpleasant and there was a nasty divorce. The woman who cleans for her helps out here at the hotel when we're busy, and according to her, Miss Connaught has no photographs or other personal things in the house, as if there's no past that she cares to remember."

Hamish commented, "Or no future to fill . . ."

Realizing that she had said more than she intended, Mrs. Barnett reached for her tray. Glancing up at Rutledge, she added, "I shouldn't have told you that! It's no more than idle speculation and I'd appreciate it if you didn't pass it on. As owner of the only hotel, my livelihood is dependent on my discretion."

"I see no purpose in passing it on. You've helped me make a personal judgment, that's all."

Lifting the tray again, she smiled. "It must be the fact that you're a policeman. You listen rather well, and before I knew it, I was rattling on. Or perhaps I've missed my dear friend Emily more than I'd realized, since she moved to Devon to be with her daughter!"

He opened the door to the kitchen for her, and said good night.

CHAPTER TEN

STILL MULLING OVER HIS CONVERSATION WITH Priscilla Connaught, Rutledge went out the hotel door into the evening air. The wind had picked up off the sea, cold as night, and he shivered. Turning toward The Pelican Inn, he made his way up Water Street to the main road, stopping for a time to look up at Holy Trinity. The church had beautiful proportions in this light, standing stark against the sky and framed by trees that marched south of it. Whoever had built it had had an eye for setting as well as architecture. Castles usually went up on the highest point in a district, but here it was the church. It must have been built after the Black Plague and the worst of the Wars of the Roses, because there were no defensive aspects in the design. Gracefulness was its hallmark, and the long windows, the high clerestory, the rise of the roof gave the tall tower at the west front and the round beacon tower at the chancel an elegance of their own.

Among the trees in the churchyard, Rutledge's night-accustomed eyes picked out a solitary figure, head bent, standing among the gravestones. Then the figure straightened to stare up at the night sky above the towers. A mourner? Or another lonely soul with no home he wanted to go to?

"Like you?" Hamish asked softly.

Turning, Rutledge walked along the main road, passing the darkened windows of Dr. Stephenson's surgery, the brightly lit ones of the police station, and what appeared to be a small country solicitor's office tucked—with a prosperous air—into the corner where Water Street and the Hunstanton Road met.

His mind kept returning to the different view of Father James that Priscilla Connaught had presented to him, and before he could sleep, he wanted to think it through. Right or wrong, she herself believed it implicitly. Until half an hour ago, he'd believed that everyone had mourned Father James, the man and the priest, in equal measure.

"Relegating the dead to sainthood," Hamish pointed out, "is no' uncommon. No one wants to speak ill of the recent dead."

Unlike Mark Antony's wily promise over Caesar's bloody corpse, Miss Connaught had come to bury Father James in every sense of the word, not to praise him. Which gave the priest human dimensions rather than saintly ones.

"It might have made him a better priest, knowing he'd failed one person," Rutledge argued.

"Aye, it's true. Ye canna' tell without knowing how he'd failed the woman."

But that had been left unspoken. Had Father James failed Miss Connaught personally—choosing the priesthood over marriage—or had he given her advice that a young man devoting his life to the Church might have seen as the only answer, although not necessarily the most compassionate one?

And in spite of her agitation, Rutledge was prepared to believe Priscilla Connaught when she swore she hadn't killed the priest. Haunting him had clearly given her far more personal satisfaction than murder ever could. The reserved woman that Mrs. Barnett had described had been completely distraught.

"Unless Father James had learned to come to grips with it," Hamish pointed out. "It wouldna' satisfy her, then."

Still, this second face of the man was intriguing.

Turning down the other leg of Water Street, Rutledge could see the bowl of sky out beyond the water, dark now but filled with stars, their clarity almost breathtaking. As he reached the quay, he stopped and stood there feeling the distant whisper of the waves, although he wasn't sure he actually heard them. There was a line of luminescence out there as well, as if far beyond his earthbound line of sight, the moon was already rising.

Something prickled along his spine, a warning, and he glanced to his right to discover that he wasn't alone here on the quay. A woman had walked out of the hotel and was standing some twenty yards away. Lost in her own thoughts, she hadn't seen him. Holding her coat about her more as comfort than as a wrap against the wind's chill, she was staring down at the stream that flowed in from the sea.

He stood very still, unwilling to disturb her reverie. She said something, the words whipped away in the wind. Thinking that she must have been speaking to him, he answered, "It's a beautiful night."

But she looked apprehensively in his direction as if only just aware that someone was there.

"Sorry," she said. "I have a most dreadful habit of talking to myself!"

He walked toward her, stopping some ten feet away. She was, he thought, the other guest at the hotel. And, he realized, possibly the woman he'd seen in the churchyard on his first day. It was the set of her shoulders, and the way her skirts moved in the breeze.

"I'm afraid I'm guilty of that as well," he said, then added as one does with a chance-met stranger, "I haven't visited East Anglia in a number of years, and I've never been to Osterley. It's a different world from London."

"Yes."

He thought for a moment that she was not going to continue, that her brevity was a signal to him to walk on.

But then she added, "I've come here before. It was a very long time ago. This trip, I'd planned to continue up the coast toward Cley, but for some reason, I've lingered. I suppose it's because of the marshes. They're beautiful around Osterley."

"... *a very long time ago* ..." He had the feeling that she meant long ago in memory, not in actual years. That she was thinking of someone and unwilling to speak of him to a stranger. A war widow?

Hamish said, "You willna' hear me speak of Fiona—"

"*No!*"

Fiona, who had loved Hamish before the war, and loved him still. . . .
She was a part of Scotland, and Rutledge refused to remember her.

But Hamish did, and the name hung between them like a bad
dream.

The black ribbon of the tidal stream below the quay quivered as a
small fish came to the surface and then vanished again.

The woman was saying pensively, "I don't know why, but the
rivulet there reminds me of something I read once. *'I know a brook /
Where the willow dips long fingers into / Water made sweet with summer. / Where birds come to drink, / And a lone fox lies dozing / In dap-
pled shade . . .'* "

Rutledge finished the lines silently. " '. . . *I know secret places /
Where toads rest, / And a child sits, / Mourning the passing / Of butter-
flies . . .'* " O. A. Manning had written those in a poem called "My
Brother." He knew it well.

Oddly enough, he understood what this woman was trying to say.
That this barren little stream here in the marshes, gone astray and all
that was left of the once-broad harbor, was neither familiar nor safe. As
she, too, had managed to wander from the comfort and safety of a life
she had once lived. But with no offer of surety that either would find a
way back again, the stream or her world.

There was no answer he could make to that. He had no sureties
either. Only of Hamish being there, from waking to sleeping, and unwilling to let him go in peace.

She lifted her head to look up at him, and smiled. There was a wry-
ness in her smile that he found attractive. "How terribly dreary that
sounds! I suppose it's because we've had nothing but rain until yesterday. A rusting of the spirit, perhaps?" As she turned away to walk back
in the direction of the hotel, her profile was outlined by the sky, very pa-
trician, pale as a cameo against the darkness of her hair and her coat.
"Good night."

The farewell was formal, indicating that the brief companionship
here in the dark was happenstance and not at all an invitation to further
acquaintance.

"Good night . . ."

The air seemed to grow colder, and he could hear the lonely
rustlings of the marshes.

Hamish had fallen silent.

Rutledge let her continue to the hotel alone, and stood for a time by the quay, until she had gone up the stairs.

After breakfast the next morning, Rutledge made his way to the vicarage to speak to Mr. Sims. The sun was shining again, catching the sparkle of flint, the dark red of the brick window facings, and the almost Mediterranean warmth of the tile roofs of Osterley.

Water Street was busy, carts and drays maneuvering around each other to make early deliveries—cabbages and turnips for the greengrocer, a brace of ducks and a cage of live hens for the butcher, and lumber for the smith's shop, where a new wagon was in progress. Behind the houses, Monday's wash hung on the lines, blowing in the surprisingly soft breeze.

Climbing the hill toward the vicarage, he could feel the coolness of the copse beyond the church and smell damp wood and wet leaves rotting beside the path. He turned into the vicarage gates, startling a half dozen birds busy at a bush along the drive. They swirled away in a glitter of sound, bright as berries on the wing. Overhead the old trees that sheltered the house spread heavy boughs, reaching out for sunlight and casting an umbrella of shade and shadow across the roof. Thick roots had broken through the earth to form a tangle of enticing places for childhood games—transformed into fortresses for lead soldiers and houses for dolls and sometimes even strong arms in which to curl up and sleep in summer's warmth.

They dredged up memories. Rutledge's grandfather's house had had such places. An ancient oak, which he had thought he would never grow tall enough to reach his arms around, had stood near a pond of garrulous frogs, and just beyond its shade was the swaybacked shed where bicycles and sleds and croquet sets lived. The last time he'd seen it, at the age of seventeen, the back garden had seemed small, like his aging grandfather, and the tree had been toppled in a storm, ripped from rotting roots to sprawl like a drunken giant across the iron fence.

"We worked hard for our bread in the Highlands," Hamish answered his thought, "and didna' play with fine toys on well-trimmed lawns. Instead we washed in the stream that ran through the glen, and watched the sun go down over the mountain, glad to call an end to the day."

Rutledge answered, "It made you what you are, as my childhood made me what I am. I can't say that one or the other is better." But Hamish could.

The vicarage was rather plain, sprawling, built of flint, designed more for a large family than for beauty. But there was a small, graceful porch over the door, and a pot of late-blooming flowers had been set in a patch of sun by the step.

Rutledge lifted the knocker and let it fall.

A man came to answer the door, his shirtsleeves rolled above his elbows and a large paintbrush in one hand. Slim and fairly young, his blond hair awry, he looked more like someone's younger brother than a Vicar.

Rutledge identified himself and Mr. Sims said with some relief, "I'm in the middle of painting. I thought you were someone coming to fetch me. Do you mind if I go on with my work? Before everything dries out? Paint is unforgiving!"

"Not at all." He stepped into the open hall and followed the Vicar up a flight of stairs.

The house appeared to be equally plain inside, with the kind of furnishings found in most vicarages—the outgrown collections of generations of occupants, left to the next man to serve or to be rid of as he wished. The finest piece was on the landing, a small Queen Anne table that must have belonged to Sims. No one would have left that behind intentionally.

"My sister and her three children are coming to keep house for me," Sims said over his shoulder. "She lost her husband in the last year of the War, and I've just persuaded her to move here. The house in Wembley holds too many memories, and there really isn't enough space for a growing brood."

He disappeared into a large room down the passage where new wallpaper had been hung, cabbage roses and forget-me-nots on a cream background. There was a piece of paint-splattered canvas the size of a carpet lying under the windows and along the baseboard. Rutledge, stepping across the threshold, thought how bright and airy it was. Sims said, "This will be Claire's room. I can only hope she'll like it!"

His forehead was furrowed with doubt as he scanned his handiwork.

Rutledge said, "I'm sure she will."

"This is a barn of a place!" Sims added. "I rattle around in it like my own bones. Children's voices and laughter will make a vast difference."

He rubbed one hand over his forehead, leaving a smear of paint, and said with some intensity, "They've got a dog. A big one." He began to paint the sashes. "What can I do for you, Inspector? I take it you're here in regard to Father James's death."

"Yes. I'm trying to cover the same ground Inspector Blevins explored before me. We still have more questions than we have answers."

"I'd heard there was someone in custody. The Strong Man from the bazaar."

"Yes. His name is Walsh. But it will be several days before we can be absolutely certain we have our man. Inspector Blevins knows Osterley, knows the people here. He was one of Father James's congregation. But I'm at a disadvantage. I'd like to know more about the victim, for one thing."

"I thought this was a case of housebreaking gone wrong—" Sims said uneasily, looking over his shoulder at Rutledge as he smoothed the bristles of the brush along the sill.

"We surmise it was. But in murder, I've learned that nothing is certain. For instance, did Walsh know the priest before this autumn? Or had they met for the first time at the bazaar?"

It was a roundabout process, and Rutledge was patient.

"I have no idea," Sims answered. "There's been a bazaar at St. Anne's for as long as anyone can remember. Most of the town attends it, just as the Catholic parishioners come to our Spring Fete. There isn't enough entertainment in Osterley to stand fast on religious lines." He threw a smile at Rutledge as he dipped his brush into the paint can. "As far as I know, this was the first year the bazaar committee decided to allow outsiders to perform. St. John the Lesser had been quite successful with such a program and it was the talk of Norfolk. A number of churches followed suit, and found that this drew attendees from miles around. Many of the villages inland from Osterley aren't large enough to have anything approaching a bazaar, and so this one was—not surprisingly—rather popular. The Strong Man was a last-minute replacement when the wire walkers couldn't come and suggested him instead. At least that's what I'd heard."

"Did Walsh use his own name for his act?"

"Lord, no, he called himself 'Samson the Great.' "

Which suited the man under lock and key—defiant and arrogant.

Changing the direction of the conversation, Rutledge asked, "Was Father James a good priest? As you would judge any man of the Cloth."

Sims turned, studying the amount of paint on his brush. Ruefully he replied, "Probably a better priest than I am. My father was a clergyman— I more or less followed him into the family trade, so to speak. It was expected of me. 'Sims and Son, Clergy.' Like the greengrocer or the ironmonger." He began to paint again, concentrating on the strokes. "My father was terribly proud of me when I was ordained. But I learned soon enough that I never had the deep calling that made him a sincerely committed man. I'll marry one day and raise a family, and serve my congregation faithfully. Holy Trinity is beautiful, and I'll be proud of what I accomplish here." He bent to dip the brush again. "But Father James's church *was* his family, and a more dedicated man you'll never find. And when my sons come to me to ask if they should follow in the footsteps of their grandfather and father, I'll encourage them to ask themselves why they want to be clergymen. If I'm not satisfied with the answer, I'll dissuade them, if I can."

He stopped, appalled, and turned to Rutledge, heedless of the brush in his hand dripping onto his shoes, exclaiming, "I'm sorry! I don't know where that came from! You're not here to listen to me, you're here about Father James."

"You've answered me," Rutledge said, "in your own way."

But Sims shook his head. And with a lightness that was assumed to hide much deeper feelings, he said, "If I had your skill at listening, I'd be a very grateful man!"

"It has haunted you, that skill," Hamish said. For Rutledge remembered clearly every word Hamish had spoken in the trenches, as if each was carved into the depths of the soul, out of reach and never worn away.

After a moment, Sims went on. "Father James had no ambition to rise in the church, even though his Bishop liked him immensely. He was content where he was. He gave himself unstintingly to anyone who needed him, and he was—as far as I could see—a happy man."

"Aye," Hamish agreed, "with promotion a man is thrust into the glare of public notice. Was that what kept him content, anonymity?"

"I've been told," Rutledge said slowly, "that his advice—well meant as it may have been—has sometimes caused great hardship for people."

Sims knelt to work under the sill. "We talked a good deal, he and I. Well, we were both bachelors, and on occasion I'd dine at the rectory or he'd dine here, and we'd spend hours on whatever topic was uppermost in our minds. Sometimes we both feared we hadn't given the best advice. That's an occupational hazard. Are *you* infallible as a policeman? Do you know one who is?" The Vicar glanced up with a wry smile.

"That's a tidy answer for the seminary," Rutledge answered. "Perhaps in the scheme of a man's life—or a woman's—well-meant advice leaves abiding scars and misery."

"We try," Sims said, sadness in his voice. "We pray for solutions, for guidance. For understanding. It isn't always forthcoming. And so we do great harm sometimes." He moved on to the next windowsill.

"Enough harm that a man might turn on a priest and kill him?"

Startled, Sims swung around to face Rutledge. "God—I wouldn't want to think about that!"

"But it isn't impossible."

He put the paintbrush down. "I—no. By the same token, you must understand that when a human being commits a sin, he's well aware of it. He doesn't come to us to be told that; he comes for a solution. A clergyman must address the fact that the cost of paying in full may be heavier or more difficult than the sinner expects. Seeing him through becomes our duty. We can't self-righteously wash our hands of him and leave him to it!"

"But what if the payment for a sin is out of all proportion to what the sinner has done?" Rutledge asked, thinking of Priscilla Connaught's face.

Sims said, "That's where forgiveness comes into the picture. When restitution as such is not possible."

Hamish growled a comment.

Rutledge, who understood better than most what restitution and forgiveness meant, didn't answer. Instead he changed the subject. "Tell me about Herbert Baker."

"Herbert Baker? Good heavens, what has Baker got to do with Father James?" Surprised, Sims stared at him. "Oh—you must be referring to the fact that he sent for a priest! I don't know where you heard *that* story, but it isn't so remarkable. A dying man is likely to worry about his soul in ways that we, with time to make amends still stretching out ahead of us, can't imagine. What would be on *your* conscience that you've never told any other person?"

The question was rhetorical. But Rutledge's face answered him.

"That's what I mean," Sims went on, "when I tell you that a dying man is not like other penitents. Baker asked for Father James, and he came as a kindness. I can't tell you what passed between them. But Father James never gave me any cause to think he was worried about what was said to him that night."

Hamish, judgmental in his own fashion, said, "Aye, but would he? The Vicar is no' a man long on wisdom."

"Did Herbert Baker confess to you?" Rutledge asked Sims.

Sims said uneasily, "Yes. I'm not at liberty—"

But Rutledge interjected, "I'm not asking you to tell me what he said—"

Sims, in his turn, interrupted him. "If you're asking me if there were shocking revelations, no. I will say he was mainly afraid that he had loved his wife too dearly, and God would hold that against him. She's dead, has been for a number of years. Apparently they were quite close."

"And the dead man's Will, what about that?"

"I expect it was in order. There's not a lot of money here in Osterley to squabble over. I daresay the house was left to the elder son, but Martin is a very conscientious man. He'll see his sister and his younger brother right."

Leaving the vicarage, Rutledge crossed the road and walked up the hill to Holy Trinity. When he tried the north door, he found it was unlocked. Lifting the latch, he went inside, his eyes adjusting to the darkness.

Over his head the king-post roof was dark and lovely, and the sun spilled through a great stained-glass window leaving puddles of color on the stone floor. Looking up he saw that it depicted orders of angels— he could recognize the archangels and angels, seraphim and cherubim in rich shades of yellow and blue and blood red. The orders were a very popular theme in East Anglia. In the center was the symbol of the Holy Trinity, and at the bottom were four figures he couldn't identify, although one looked suspiciously like early portraits of Richard II and another was self-proclaimed by the scroll spilling across his lap as the Venerable Bede.

Hamish, to whom stained glass was iconography close to idolatry, was more interested in the construction of the marvelously carved wooden roof. Rutledge walked down the nave past benches capped with ornate poppy-heads, like inhabited fleurs-de-lis, and armrests carved as small animals, from dogs to griffins to ponies.

His intention was to take a closer look at the window above the high altar, but as he entered the small choir he nearly stumbled over a box of charcoal and a knee.

The woman he'd spoken to so briefly the night before was sitting on a hassock making drawings of the odd figures on the misericords—those half-seats on which a monk might rest his posterior without actually sitting down in the choir chair assigned to him.

She looked up, as startled as he was, and said, "Sorry!"

Hamish, remembering Lord Sedgwick's comment, said, "The religious woman."

"Did I hurt you?" Rutledge asked in concern.

"Oh, no. And it's my fault for sprawling across the floor with my kit."

He looked down at the drawing she was making, of a nun with ragged teeth, dramatic and lifelike in bold strokes of charcoal. "That's quite good."

Her expression became defensive. "It's a hobby," she said curtly.

To shift the subject, he gestured around him. "This is a remarkably fine church."

"Yes, it is. I knew someone who was writing a book about old parish churches. He brought it to my attention."

"I shan't distract you, I only intended to look at the glass here." He walked on, examining the window with its fine colors and vividly detailed figures.

To his surprise, she said to his back, "You're the policeman from London, I think?"

"Yes." He didn't turn.

"Perhaps you could tell me—is it true they've caught the man who killed Father James?"

Rutledge turned slowly. "You knew him? Father James?"

"A little. He was interested in work I was doing, and I found him quite knowledgeable about East Anglian church architecture. He was generous with his time and I valued that."

Rutledge walked back to her. Her upturned face was attractive, with intelligent gray eyes and a determined mouth above a very pretty chin. The dress she was wearing, a mossy dark green, was very becoming, but without the drama that was part of Priscilla Connaught's apparel. "We don't know if we have the right man in custody. There's a good deal of work to be done before we can be certain of his movements between the day of the bazaar and the murder. But Inspector Blevins expects to clear that up quickly."

She nodded, as if satisfied.

Yet something in her voice—or the way in which she had waited until his back was to her—had touched that deep well of intuition that Rutledge had always relied on. There had been some deeper interest than mere curiosity in her question, he thought. Probing, his mind still on Priscilla Connaught, he asked, "Were you here in Osterley when the bazaar was held?"

"No, I was in Felbrigg, having dinner with friends."

Rutledge shifted to another direction.

"Did you see Father James the day he was killed?"

"No—"

"Was there anything about his death that worried you?"

He waited, continuing to look down at her. It seemed to make her uneasy.

Reluctantly she tried to explain. "I haven't had much experience with murder investigations. It was probably more my imagination than anything else. But Father James had asked me a question on the last evening I dined with him. It was on my mind for several days, and after he—died—I found myself wondering if it might be important. But if you've arrested your man, then of course I was wrong! It doesn't signify now."

Rutledge replied carefully, "Who can say? Perhaps it still has some bearing on the case. Have you spoken of this to Inspector Blevins?"

She frowned. "No. I thought it best not to say anything. Inspector Blevins seemed convinced that the motive for the murder was theft. Not ancient history."

"Will you tell me what it was? My name's Rutledge. Scotland Yard sent me to Osterley because Father James's Bishop expressed grave concern over the time it has taken to clear up this business. It isn't idle curiosity behind my questions. And I won't repeat what you tell me to anyone else—until or unless I see the need."

The woman picked up her charcoal again and began to put wrinkles into the wimple of the nun, capturing them perfectly. "No, I just— Father James was so kind that I—sometimes one wants to help so badly that one starts to imagine that what one knows is important. I've already explained: The matter he was referring to had happened some time ago, years in fact, and really had nothing to do with Osterley or anyone who lives here. It was only the importance that Father James seemed to attach to it that made me remember it at all."

"Was it a church matter? Or a personal one?"

"I rather thought it was personal. Most certainly the subject was a painful one for me, and he—Father James—was helpful in dealing with that. In return, I tried to answer his question, and failed. A disappointment to him, and a regret for me. But it had nothing to do with Osterley, I give you my word."

She bent her head over the drawing, and Rutledge, looking down at the nape of her neck and the dark sheen of her hair, decided that this was not the time to press her.

"If you change your mind, Mrs. Barnett will see that any message reaches me."

"Yes. Of course." It was said with grave politeness, but he knew she had no intention of doing any such thing.

He waited for a count of ten, but she seemed to be absorbed in her work, as if unaware that he was still there.

Hamish scolded, "You canna' leave it!"

But Rutledge was already walking through the nave, listening to the silences of the shadowy church around him. He was thinking that Mrs. Barnett would give him the name and the direction of this woman, and he could put Sergeant Gibson on to searching for her background, with emphasis on what connection she might have to Osterley or East Anglia. . . .

He had learned early on in his career at the Yard that people who did not want to talk to the police could not be made to do so. But he wanted very much to know what it was that Father James had asked of a comparative stranger that had left behind it such unease.

CHAPTER ELEVEN

THE FIRM OF GIFFORD AND SONS, Solicitors, was a small country practice that had been in business for some time, judging by the brass nameplate by the door. The letters on it were worn almost to smoothness from years of polishing away the sea damp that etched it like freckles.

Rutledge had noticed the location of the firm during his walk the night before. Now as he crossed from Trinity Lane along the Hunstanton Road, he decided to speak to whichever Gifford was available this morning.

The two unusual events in Father James's life shortly before his death had been the bazaar, with its connection to Walsh, and the summons to the bedside of a dying man. Odd though the circumstances had been, there was no indication that out of that deathbed had come, like a phoenix rising, the shadow that had dogged Father James until it killed him.

All the same, it had to be considered. The policeman in Rutledge was too experienced to leave the matter. Nor could he ignore Priscilla

Connaught or the woman he had quite literally stumbled over in the church. They, too, had some sort of personal link with the victim.

"You canna' face London!" Hamish reminded him, with some force. "It's no experience, it's cowardice. You willna' face your own life. Better to delve into another's, and not think about yoursel' and dying and Scotland."

But Rutledge knew he was wrong, that Father James was slowly becoming a puzzle he could not walk away from. Not the priest, but the man . . .

As he came to the corner of the main road and Water Street, Rutledge paused and then opened the heavy door of Gifford and Sons. He stepped into Victorian elegance that had sufficed for two additional reigns and seemed to be in no haste to change. The elderly clerk at the desk might have served through all of them. He was tall and stooped, with the soft, very white hair seldom seen on any head younger than eighty. But the blue eyes that turned Rutledge's way were bright as new paint.

"Good morning, sir," the clerk greeted him. "Do you have an appointment with Mr. Gifford?"

"No, regrettably," Rutledge answered with equal formality, recognizing the game. "However, I hope that he'll spare me a quarter of an hour. My name is Rutledge. Inspector Rutledge, from London."

The observant eyes took him in from head to toe. "Ah. I shall inquire, sir." Rutledge wondered how he had fared in the summing up.

The clerk disappeared through a door into the private sanctum.

Looking about him, Rutledge could see that little had changed here since the first Gifford had begun to practice. The three chairs set against the walls of the spacious room were covered in worn leather, and the velvet-shrouded table in one corner was smothered in photographs in gilt frames, mostly of a man growing older, his son following suit, and then two younger men standing firmly in front of the camera with a look of nervous self-importance. A photograph of one of those men, dressed in uniform, had heavy black ribbon threaded through the openwork of the ornate frame.

"Grandfather, father, and sons," Hamish said. "And one didna' come home fra' the War."

The clerk returned, standing on the threshold. "Mr. Gifford will see you, Inspector."

He led the way down a narrow passage, where two doors on the left were firmly closed, as if with sad finality. All they lacked was the black crepe of mourning. The clerk paused before a third, opened it, and introduced Rutledge with a Victorian flourish.

Rutledge walked into a paneled room bright with racing prints and glass-fronted bookshelves, a fine mahogany desk that was far older than the man seated in the chair behind it, and on the broad windowsills, an array of antique European snuffboxes and Chinese snuff bottles, each a small, exquisite gem, from enameled gold to cinnabar, ivory to painted glass, porcelain to jade. In the indirect light of morning they were quite beautiful.

A miasma of cigar smoke hung in the air.

Gifford rose to greet Rutledge, and Hamish's first comment was "He's small enough to be a jockey!"

He was a foot shorter than Rutledge, with the small features that matched his frame, thin and wiry. His hair was a rich, thick brown, as was his beard.

"I'm Frederick Gifford," he said, gesturing to a chair. "Do sit down and tell me what I can do for you. I assume you've come about the Will?"

Surprised, Rutledge said, "As a matter of fact—"

Gifford nodded. "It seemed unlikely that Inspector Blevins would be interested in its provisions, given the nature of my client's death. I'm told that they've finally caught the killer. It's chilling to think about: Still, I suppose if someone is poor enough, any sum is princely." The words echoed those of Monsignor Holston. Moving the blotter to line up with the pen and inkstand in antique silver gilt, Gifford sighed. "But I must admit that I'm surprised Father James's reputation had reached London. It's a compliment to his memory that Scotland Yard should take an interest in the matter."

"He's fishing," Hamish warned.

Rutledge, accustomed now to offering a placating sentence or two, answered, "Father James's Bishop was concerned enough to speak to the Chief Constable about the case. The Yard, as a courtesy, sent me to reassure him that all that it is possible to do was being done."

"It has most certainly borne fruit!" As if satisfied that Rutledge's credentials were in order, Gifford went on. "Well, as to the Will. There was nothing extraordinary in it. Father James didn't leave a large estate, and what there is goes to his only surviving relative, a sister with a very young family. There's a suitable bequest to Mrs. Wainer, for her years of service as housekeeper, and a small sum for the church fund. Not, I'm sure, as generous as Father James had hoped it might be, in the fullness of time!" His eyes watched Rutledge behind the pedantic mask of solicitor.

"He couldn't have foreseen an early death," Rutledge agreed. He had chosen the words carefully, for there seemed to be something more and the solicitor was bidding his time. Hamish, at the back of Rutledge's mind, was also advocating caution. "Of course it's too soon to be absolutely certain we have the right man. Inspector Blevins strikes me as thorough and experienced. He won't be satisfied until he's found the proof he needs. It does no harm to keep the broader picture in mind, meanwhile."

There was a subtle change in Gifford's manner, as though he had been waiting for a sign that Rutledge, the outsider, was not usurping the local man's position. Villagers looked after their own. . . .

"Yes, well, we don't have many murders in Osterley, thank God! But Blevins is a good man. We went to school together, the three of us— Blevins, my late brother, and I. He followed his father into the constabulary, and we went on to take up law. Two sides of the same coin, in many ways."

Rutledge acknowledged the connection, saying lightly, "Unless you're arguing for the defense."

"True enough." Gifford's smile gave his face an unexpected strength. Reaching into a drawer of his desk, he extricated a sheaf of papers. He looked through them and selected one. "There was a codicil added to Father James's Last Will and Testament some three or four days before he was killed. I haven't been able to carry out his instructions, as the piece of property he'd specified has been mislaid." He stared at the sheet before him, as if refreshing his memory, but Rutledge had the feeling he could have quoted the short paragraph from memory. " 'I leave the framed photograph in the bottom drawer of my desk to Marianna Elizabeth Trent, in the hope that one day she will have the courage to pursue the obligation that I must now entrust to her.' "

"A photograph," Rutledge repeated, as Hamish echoed the words in his head.

"And an obligation. Yes. It was clearly of paramount importance to him, because he had written it out, to be certain I'd got it right." Gifford frowned. "As a rule, a bequest is rather simple: a pair of garnet earrings to a favorite niece, or a collection of books to a cousin. That

sort of thing. People generally want to ensure that a particular possession ends up in proper hands."

"What did you make of this?"

"It isn't my role to question, only to see that everything is regular as
far as the law is concerned."

"You've already contrasted Father James's bequest with that of a
pair of garnet earrings," Rutledge pointed out quietly.

"True enough. When we'd finished, the codicil witnessed properly
and so forth, he told me that it was a debt he owed, and wished to see
paid. If I thought anything—and I'm not admitting that I did—it was
that Father James wished to handle the matter discreetly, whatever it
was. Rather than ask his sister to act for him. Or it may be that it was a
kinder way of returning a photograph he valued, through a mutual
friend."

"Or—unfinished business of some sort," Rutledge said, Priscilla
Connaught coming to mind again. Was Marianna Elizabeth Trent another failure on the priest's conscience? "A task he preferred not to ask
you, as his solicitor, to perform for him. And using Miss Trent as the
intermediary, the gift remains anonymous."

Gifford stirred uneasily. "Perhaps Miss Trent knows this person.
And could be depended on to break the news gently. Or in the right circumstances."

"But this photograph has been mislaid, you said?"

"As Blevins must have told you, the desk was ransacked. Mrs.
Wainer tried to put everything back, poor woman. As far as she remembers, there wasn't a photograph among the contents, at least not a framed
one. I myself looked, and there were no photographs at all in any of the
drawers. It could very well be that Father James simply hadn't gotten
around to putting it in the desk. And Mrs. Wainer can't be sure which
of the photographs on display he had in mind, because apparently he
never spoke to her about the bequest. Needless to say, I've been reluctant to make an issue of it. Nor have I contacted Miss Trent, since it's
rather awkward to admit we can't put our hands on it."

"She might know which it is."

"I'd thought of that. But the Will is under probate, and there's still
time to find it. Early days!" Gifford restored the papers to his drawer.
"A single photograph is not often the subject of a codicil, but there's
nothing wrong in it. And as long as the request is legal and reasonable,
we are required to honor it."

Hamish repeated something Rutledge had said earlier: "He couldna' know he would be killed."

Which was true. It might have been years before the priest's Will was executed.

"Ye ken this photograph might be for a child?" Hamish demanded, following Rutledge's thoughts. "And too young yet to be told who her mother is—or her father."

Rutledge answered him silently, "And that will bear looking into." Aloud he added to Gifford, "Will you leave a message for me at the Osterley Hotel, if you locate the photograph? I don't suppose it will matter to Blevins's investigation, but at this stage, who can say?"

"Yes, I'll be happy to do that," Gifford said, jotting down a few lines in a small leather-bound notebook.

"Did you know Father James well?"

"He was an ordinary man, in many respects. He never made anyone uncomfortably aware of his collar—there was never any fuss about it. I've seen him down on the floor reading a book with half a dozen children. But there was a dignity about him as well that I admired. Quite a good tennis player, and possessed of a wry sense of humor. He had the most persuasive voice." Gifford grinned. "With that gift, I'd have been a barrister! Father James and the Vicar—Mr. Sims—and I sometimes dined together. Not out of deep friendship so much as for the company. I lost my wife in '15. I've learned," he said ruefully, "that a widower with a good law practice is fair game, to make up the numbers at a dinner party. Especially when a maiden sister or cousin has been invited."

Rutledge laughed. He had been introduced to all the sisters of his friends and half their cousins—until he'd become engaged and thus considered off the market. A twinge of memory swept him. Jean had been the first to make it clear that he was not a good prospect now. Even for the most desperate spinster.

Gifford prepared to rise, bringing the interview to a close.

But Rutledge sat where he was. "There's another matter. Did you also serve as solicitor to Herbert Baker and his family?"

It was Gifford's turn to be surprised. "Herbert Baker? Good God, how did you come to know *him*?"

"I didn't. But he died shortly before Father James's death, and I'd like to know how his Will stood."

Bewildered, Gifford said, "I don't believe Father James witnessed it, if that's your point."

"No, but I understand from Dr. Stephenson that he was in attendance just before Mr. Baker's death. What can you tell me regarding the Will's provisions?"

Gifford steepled his fingers. "Very straightforward. There wasn't much in the way of money, although Baker owned the house he lived in. It'd been his wife's family home. Naturally he left that to the elder son, Martin, with the proviso that the other son, Dick, and the daughter, Ellen, live there until they married. Dick just came home from hospital, bad shoulder wound. And Ellen is the youngest. A late child."

Rutledge considered how to put his next question, and decided to be blunt. "Were the three children Herbert Baker's?"

"Good Lord, I should think they were! Ellen looks very much like her mother, and the brothers are the spitting image of Herbert. Same spare frame, and same high forehead, same left-handedness. Why on earth should you suppose they weren't?"

"I don't. I merely wondered if there could be any skeletons in the Baker closet."

The grin reappeared. "Herbert Baker, if you'd known him, was not the man for skeletons. He was sexton at Holy Trinity until his health broke, and while he'd worked hard all his life, he hadn't the money or the time to squander on wine, women, and song. A devoted father, most certainly. And as far as I know, an honest man." The grin broadened into a smile. "If you want the truth, he probably led as boring a life as anyone in Osterley."

"Then there was nothing that might have rested heavily on his conscience at his death?"

"The only thing that ever worried Herbert Baker as far as I know was his wife's illness. It was hopeless from the start, but he sent her to London to be treated. Tuberculosis, and too advanced when Dr. Stephenson caught it to expect a cure." He shrugged. "She was the kind of woman who never complained, never sent for a doctor except in childbirth, used her own remedies for whatever ailed her, and generally died as she'd lived, as self-effacing as possible. But the sanitarium gave her two more years of life, and I don't believe any of the family would have considered it money wasted!"

"Sanitariums are expensive. Where did a poor man find the money?"

"Charity, if you want my honest opinion. It's happened before, actually. Not three years ago there was a woman who needed surgery for her goiter, and a generous contribution from her employer paid the better part of the cost. It was done with circumspection—I handled the paperwork myself, as the donor wished to remain anonymous—and this woman has never learned the truth. She believes she paid the entire fee."

Rutledge said, "You've been very helpful. One final question: Were both of Baker's sons in the Army?"

"Martin was sent home, compassionate leave when his father's health began to fail, and Ellen wasn't up to running the household on her own. Dick was wounded, as I think I mentioned. Both men from all reports did their duty."

But as Rutledge had learned, having used that phrase more times than he cared to remember, the words were a catch all when an officer knew too little—or too much—about a soldier under his command.

"Did their duty" covered a multitude of sins. . . . Had Herbert Baker begged absolution for one of his sons, from Father James?

Rutledge had left the solicitor's office and was walking back toward the Osterley Hotel when a large motorcar with a uniformed driver pulled up beside him. In the rear seat, Lord Sedgwick leaned forward.

"I say, have you had your luncheon yet?"

Rutledge turned. "Good morning. No, it's still fairly early—"

It couldn't have been more than eleven-thirty.

"Well, come and dine with me. And I'll have Evans here bring you back afterward. My son's returned to Yorkshire, and I'm damned if I can stand my own company for another meal. Mrs. Barnett at the hotel"—Sedgwick chuckled—"will turn me out if I appear unannounced a second time within the week. Or have you made a commitment to her?"

Rutledge had not.

"Then come along and bear me company, if you will. We can talk about something other than the price of sheep and what cabbages are currently fetching!"

Hamish warned, "It's no' a very good idea—!"

Rutledge hesitated. Then he opened the door, noting the crest on the panel, and climbed into the car. The interior was beautifully done with velvet cushions and quite fine, polished woodwork. Lord Sedgwick leaned back and spoke to Evans. The motorcar purred into motion, and moved off down Water Street between the carts and people as Evans handled his gears with smooth perfection.

Sedgwick said, "Any progress in your murder investigation?"

"Gossip hasna' been slow in spreading," Hamish told Rutledge. "You'll soon be verra' popular." It was a sour comment.

"We think we may have found our man," Rutledge said noncommittally. "But Inspector Blevins is making certain that he's done his job thoroughly."

"Yes, well, I've posted a sizable reward for information leading to an arrest. I hope I'll have the opportunity to pay it out to someone."

Rutledge recalled that Blevins had spoken of a reward. "Did you, indeed? Were you a parishioner of Father James's? Did you know him well?"

"Good lord, no. Anglican. The East Sherham church is on our estate. Still, I keep a friendly eye on my neighbors. Right thing to do! I rather dislike people killing people, and I know that money can jog memories—or tongues. Father James was a conscientious man, from all reports. A considerable force for good. Over the years, I've applauded that. We can ill-afford to lose men of his caliber. Osterley's best and brightest have already been sacrificed to that bloody War. I saw you coming out of the solicitor's office. Frederick Gifford's brother, Raymond, was one of the finest men I've ever met, and he went down in flames over the German lines. Gifford's two clerks died at Ypres. Anderson at The Pelican lost his boy at Jutland, and Mrs. Barnett's nephew was artillery, shells blew up in his face. Sadly, the list goes on."

They were turning back out of Water Street onto the main road again. On the hill, the flint walls of Holy Trinity seemed to shine with an inner light. "But that's a morbid line of thought. Tell me, what do you do in London, Rutledge?"

"Much the same sort of thing I do here. Ask questions. Collate information. Consider the evidence and try to draw conclusions from it. Search for motives."

Hamish, who'd been silent since Rutledge had entered the motorcar, asked, "Hobnobbing wi' the great willna' give you the answers either."

Sedgwick grunted. "What you do requires patience." Evans had braked to allow a wagon laden with firewood to make the turn into Trinity Lane. Just a few yards beyond it, there was a woman walking along the verge, head down, face hidden by her hat. Rutledge recognized her and apparently so did Sedgwick. Priscilla Connaught, in Wellingtons and a long coat.

Sedgwick spoke to Evans and they slowed. He leaned forward to say, "Good morning, Miss Connaught! I see you are on foot. Anything the matter with your motorcar? I can have Evans take a look this afternoon!"

"Good morning, Lord Sedgwick. No, I'm walking for the exercise. But thank you for your concern."

Something in her face gave Rutledge the impression she was walking off a dark mood. Her eyes flickered in his direction and then came back to Sedgwick.

Sedgwick touched the brim of his hat and Evans put the car into gear once more. "She's had the very devil of a time with her brakes," the former explained to Rutledge. "I told her she'd wind up in the marshes, if someone didn't fix the problem. Evans believes it's in the linkage." Picking up the thread of what Rutledge had been saying earlier, he continued. "I'm not a patient man by nature. Never was. Can't sit confined for long. But then I wasn't trained to it!"

"Few of us are."

They were passing the school now, on Gull Street where it became the Sherham Road. After a time Sedgwick nodded to rolling fields where sheep grazed in the late grass. "I wasn't born to farming. Anyone will tell you, my father made his fortune in the City. He bought the house in East Sherham when the last of the Chastain family died. I spent my summers here. To keep me out of harm's way, I was given into the care of an old sheepman who—God forgive him—thought I was entirely spoiled and woefully ignorant. On the other hand, I believed that anything that allowed me to escape from my tutor was daring and rebellious. Before I quite knew what was happening, I'd learned as much about sheep as old Ned could teach me."

He lifted a hand, deprecatingly. "My father was shocked to discover that I was breeding sheep and had a natural eye for the best rams to improve the flocks. The Chastains hadn't maintained the land or the pasturage, and I was soon badgering him to buy up acreage and extend our holding. He sent me off to Oxford to cure me of such low habits." He chuckled. "That finally made a gentleman of me, but I've always kept my eye on the management of the estate. And it's prospered. Our sheep produce some of the finest wool in the world. Or did, before the War turned everything on its head and all anyone wanted to manufacture was uniforms and blankets."

He turned to Rutledge. "I needn't tell a policeman that life goes on.

But it does, somehow. It must. There's never any turning back to what once was." He fell silent, looking at the window.

Rutledge heard a hidden bitterness in the philosophy, although Sedgwick's tone had been light. But money was not always a guarantee of perfect happiness. . . .

The detective in him intrigued, Rutledge cast about for another subject of interest to the man at his side. "You spoke of a son. I think he must have dined last night at the hotel."

"Arthur? Yes, he's the elder. He went to the Front and came home a broken man. He's still in and out of hospital. Wound in his back. Edwin, the younger of the two, had a gift for languages and was given the task of dealing with prisoners. Or the French. Whoever was most troublesome!"

Rutledge suppressed a smile. The French were not always the most comfortable of allies. And interrogating prisoners never went smoothly.

"Edwin keeps a boat in Osterley," Sedgwick went on. "He and that fool dog of his go hunting in the marshes. Shooting isn't allowed, but the dog's nose stays sharp. Edwin takes him to Scotland for the Season."

Hamish reminded Rutledge of the man rowing into the quay with a dog in the thwarts. The woman who had offered him a lift had called him Edwin. . . . Edwin Sedgwick? Rutledge rather thought it was. The same man had been in the lounge bar in the hotel outside Norwich.

They had reached the outskirts of East Sherham and turned onto a road where tall old trees marched on either side. Overhead, branches arched high to form a cool and shaded canopy, and the undergrowth along the verges was still thick and full here at the end of summer. Ahead Rutledge could see the walled grounds of an estate, with ornate gates marking the entrance to the drive. The crest on the heavy, gilded wrought iron bore the motto "I Will Persevere." Two handsome pillars on either side were surmounted by a griffin. These apparently had belonged to the original owners: Time had etched them, wind and rain had worn them, but they had been carved to last.

A man came out of the lodge to let the car pass through, touching his cap to Sedgwick, who responded with a nod. They wound their way through a finely wooded park, nearly as handsome as that at Hatfield, and turned to the left before sweeping up in front of a lovely old brick manor house. The wings were set back from the main block, and Elizabethan chimney pots soared into the blue of the sky. The lawn, wide and still reasonably green, ran down to a low brick wall, and beyond that the park continued to a line of trees. In the distance, a small Greek temple sat on the rising ground beyond what appeared to be a landscaped stream at the southern edge of the park. There was a feeling of old money here, and a long lineage. Nothing ostentatious, nothing new. An ideal setting, perhaps, for a newcomer to the aristocracy eager to present an appearance of having deep roots in the land.

Evans pulled up and came around to open the door for Lord Sedgwick and Rutledge. Sedgwick thanked him and led the way across the short walk to the house. A housekeeper stood ready to greet them, alerted perhaps by a bell from the gatehouse. She was a trim woman in her late fifties, with a serene face and an air of competence. She nodded calmly when Sedgwick told her there was an unexpected guest, and said, "Luncheon will be ready in ten minutes, my lord. Shall I serve it on the terrace?"

"Yes. That would be fine."

They entered a wide, flagstoned hall. A narrow stair of age-blackened oak on the left led up to the first floor. A massive hearth, which must have been a great comfort in the damp of a Norfolk winter, covered the wall to the right. Above Rutledge's head, the high plastered ceiling was delicately carved with Tudor roses and garlands of fruit.

At the foot of the stairs a Turkey carpet covered the floor, and there were rare Elizabethan chairs on either side of a small Jacobean table. It was quite an attractive room, little changed, Rutledge thought, from the day it was built. They preceded the housekeeper down a passage and through a doorway that led into a drawing room where long French windows looked out onto a sunlit terrace. An ornate stone balustrade reached like arms to embrace the broad, shallow stone steps that gave access to the gardens. Urns shaped like Roman amphora stood at the bottom, and in the center of the garden beyond, an aged mossy fountain spilled water into a bowl shaped like a Tudor rose. The effect was very pretty.

Rutledge found himself thinking of his godfather, David Trevor, in Scotland—and banished the image before it had formed. Trevor was an architect by profession, with a love of buildings that he'd conveyed to his godson through the years. It was hard to see a place such as this without recalling all that had passed between the two men—or, now, remembering what had happened in Scotland just over a month ago.

Rutledge followed Sedgwick out onto the terrace, where comfortable chairs had been set up to take advantage of the garden views. The house-keeper returned with a tray of glasses and decanters while Rutledge was admiring the flower beds. They were showing signs of autumn wear, but they had been designed with an eye for every season. The rare Japanese chrysanthemums were glorious.

"What will you have?" Sedgwick asked, and when told, held out a very good whiskey. As Rutledge turned to accept it, he noticed a re-markable stone rectangle set at an angle in the garden. Larger-than-life apes, four squatting in a row, stared at the house, their eyes unblinking and focused, as if sharing some knowledge that was theirs alone.

They had been carved in bas-relief, with a vividness that was both unusual and riveting. Exotic as the land they'd come from, they rested on their haunches, unperturbed by this English garden, or by the Englishmen who had stepped into view.

Catching the direction of Rutledge's glance, Sedgwick said, "I don't know why my father kept the damned thing. Or, for that matter, why I leave it there. Except that the previous owners of the house felt it brought good luck, and he was superstitious about that. I can't think why it should—it's as ugly as anything I've ever seen."

"It's Egyptian, isn't it?"

"Yes, that's right. Eighteenth Dynasty, I'm told. It once stood in the hall, just by the stairs. Where the Jacobean table is now. God knows how the Chastains came by it! They were magpies, collecting whatever caught their fancy. I couldn't abide looking into those faces every night before I went up to bed. And Arthur swore it gave him nightmares as a child. When my father died, I banished it to the gardens."

Rutledge walked down the steps and went to examine the thick slab of stone. It had been cut from a building's wall, he thought. Longer than it was tall, it was well polished, not rough. The figures of the baboons, it seemed, were meant to catch the morning and afternoon sun in a climate where the light was intense. Slanting rays would give them an almost three-dimensional quality. Here in the much paler light of the English Broads they possessed an almost preternatural air.

Following him, Sedgwick went on, "They're called—so I'm told—'The Watchers of Time.' 'Set the task of witnessing what man and the gods may do. Through all eternity.' That's what the catalog says, at least. We bought the house furnished. Lock, stock, and phantoms." He was smiling, but when Rutledge looked up from the stone, he could see that the smile had not reached Sedgwick's eyes.

Hamish, who had been silent since they entered the house, was saying, "But they canna' speak. The apes. What use are they as witnesses?"

Rutledge answered silently, "They don't judge. They merely observe."

"Aye," Hamish said. "But a man with a guilty conscience wouldna'
find it verra' comfortable, that stare. I wouldna' care for it mysel'!"

CHAPTER TWELVE

LORD SEDGWICK SHOWED HIMSELF TO BE a genial host. He possessed a wry sense of humor, which Rutledge enjoyed, and seldom put his views ahead of those of his guest even when he must have had far more insight into political matters, moving as he did in such vastly different circles.

Rutledge, under no illusions (policemen were not invited to dine with the gentry—indeed, they were seldom welcomed at the front door), took care not to overstep his role. All the same, the hour passed very pleasantly. The luncheon itself was excellent, finishing with a plate of cheeses.

The loneliness of the man under the polish of a titled and privileged life was apparent. Sedgwick's wife had been dead some years, for he spoke of her with an old regret rather than a recent bereavement. Her portrait as a young American bride now hung in the library, he said at one juncture, replacing "a remarkably hideous work of dead rabbits and quail hanging from a nail" that Ralph, the first Lord Sedgwick, had fancied. Ralph had gone shooting with the Prince of Wales in his day, and "bagged enough to show his aim was excellent, but was careful never to exceed his host's count. Quickest way to see yourself off the royal invitation list!"

Arthur, Sedgwick's elder son, had had a taste for racing cars before the War, and had even won a motorcycle race of some note, early on in his career. Sedgwick had traveled to France to watch him compete, and he spoke with wistful enthusiasm for the excitement. "It rained, often as not. I lived in terror that he'd spin out on a curve. Arthur had nerves of steel when he got behind the wheel, and a feeling for the road—and that made him one of the finest drivers I'd ever seen. His wife begged him to give it up, but of course he couldn't. She didn't understand that it was his life, speed and risk."

"Racing is a dangerous sport," Rutledge responded. "And few women are attracted to the prospect of being widowed young."

Sedgwick grunted. "She was the one who died young, before they'd been married five years. Arthur took it hard, of course, but I must admit I was not particularly fond of her. A pretty simpleton."

Edwin, the younger son, appeared to worry Sedgwick. "I see much of my father in him. Strange, isn't it, how a man's nature can jump a generation?" It seemed not to be a compliment. But then the grandfather had made a fortune in the City, and was not, perhaps, a rough diamond in his own son's eyes.

Sedgwick dwelt on none of this, but a word here and there told Rutledge more than perhaps his host had meant to reveal. It was often a failing of lonely men.

"It doesna' signify," Hamish pointed out, "if there's naught to hide."

Certainly in Sedgwick's case, that appeared to be true.

As the table was cleared, Sedgwick looked out beyond the terrace at the expanse of formal beds and cropped lawns, and sighed. "I've a mind to marry again, myself. If only to fill this garden with young voices and bring a spark of life to the house. Damned silly thing to do, but I'm not by nature a man who prefers his own company. Have a wife, do you?"

"No. The War altered any plans I might have made."

"Never too late to start over." He regarded Rutledge for a moment. "It's odd, you know, but you remind me of Arthur. I don't know quite how to put my finger on it. It's there in the way you carry yourself and something in your voice."

"A holdover from the Army," Rutledge said.

"I suppose it must be. You'd like him. A good man. And a deeper thinker than the rest of us—he got that from his mother, not my side. I see it more and more often these days." There was a sudden flash of grief in Sedgwick's face, as if Arthur wasn't the man he'd been before the War, losing that edge that had made him a fast driver and a dashing figure to watch in a race. Wounds changed a man in more ways than the physically apparent damage. Nerve, for one thing, was easily worn down by constant pain.

There had been a man named Seelingham on the boat to France at the start of the War, Rutledge remembered—he tried to dredge up an image of the man's face, and finally brought back a tall, dark, broad-shouldered figure with a taste for books in German. "Never too late," he'd said, "to learn about the enemy. Best way to outwit them, in my view. Otherwise you're tilting in the dark . . ." He'd been a racer, too, but never spoke of his family. Fast boats were his preference. Later Rutledge had heard that Seelingham had lost both legs in a lorry accident near Paris, and was invalided home. He had shot himself a month later.

Was Sedgwick afraid that Arthur's wound would lead him to self destruction because he, too, was shut off from what he loved doing?

Rutledge changed the subject. They spoke only once more of Father James's death, and that in a roundabout way.

"We've had good weather for the most part, this autumn," Sedgwick was saying as he pushed back his chair, favoring his gouty foot a little. "Edwin has been down a time or two, and one morning we went over to Osterley—it was the morning they found the priest's body, actually, although we didn't know it at the time. It had begun to clear, and we left the car up by Holy Trinity Church, then walked as far as Cley, where Evans met us again. We had a look at the dikes and the big wind-mill, ate our luncheon by the marshes, and came home ravenous. Couldn't do that today. Bloody foot!"

Passing through the drawing room later, Sedgwick paused to show Rutledge a watercolor of Osterley in its prime—"One of the Chastains had it painted. It's said to be by Constable, but there's no provenance." Rutledge also noticed a photograph sitting on the windowsill to his right: A man standing by the marshes, shotgun in the crook of his arm, and a setter at his feet looking up adoringly as if eager to run. If Sedgwick saw his straying glance, he made no comment. He didn't have to. Rutledge recognized the face and the dog. Edwin, the younger son, who kept a boat in Osterley's harbor . . .

A short time later he was on his way back to Osterley. The chauffeur had nothing to say, and Rutledge preferred his own thoughts.

Hamish, still mulling over the luncheon conversation, was busy in the back of his mind. Coming around again to the subject of Lord Sedgwick himself, Hamish said, "He's no' a man I'm comfortable with. He's verra' like Sergeant Mullins."

It was an odd comparison. Mullins had replaced Sergeant McIver, shot in the hip and invalided home. Both Sergeants had come up through the ranks, where the heavy attrition of the Battle of the Somme had given men seniority overnight, prepared for it or not. Mullins was a seasoned soldier, careful, gruff, and humorless. He had been a butcher by trade, and could determine at a glance whether a wound was likely to see a man relieved or just patched up at the nearest aid station and returned to the lines. Sentiment seldom played a role.

Lord Sedgwick had that same quality of practical reality that had carried Mullins through the War. He took his world in stride and dealt with it without sentiment.

And yet Rutledge had sensed something else in this man, a wistful desire to be the local squire, as the Chastains had been before him. But he was tainted by his father's roots, and villagers were often greater snobs than their betters. Money could buy some loyalties, but blue blood brought respect.

"That explains," Rutledge answered Hamish's line of thought, "why Sedgwick was eager to put up a reward for Father James's killer. The Chastains would probably have done the same."

Still, the Sedgwicks had, in two generations, gone from the streets of London to an inheritable title and weekends at Sandringham with the royal entourage. The first Lord Sedgwick, Ralph, whose antecedents had probably been of questionable bloodlines, had had to settle for an American bride for his only son. But his grandsons, with any luck, would find themselves wed to daughters of the old aristocracy, and *their* sons fully accepted as titled gentlemen with no lingering odor of trade about them.

Three generations, that was what it took to bridge the social gap. . . .

The future of the dynasty now rested on Arthur's shoulders, and his brother's.

Unless Lord Sedgwick was indeed considering a second—and far more advantageously connected—bride, to better their chances through a stepmother's connections.

It never hurt, in present royal circles, to have a very presentable wife.

Coming into Osterley again, Rutledge turned his thoughts to his own role here.

He was expected not to tread on Blevins's toes. The Inspector had already made that clear. But the more Rutledge learned about the people who lived in Osterley, the better he saw the dead priest—and was finding himself drawn into the theory that the man's life had some bearing on his death.

His fingers gently massaged the scar on his chest, stilling the dull ache.

Still, Walsh was the ideal solution to the bloody crime on Blevins's doorstep. He wasn't a local man—and from the start the Inspector hadn't wanted to discover that his killer was someone he knew. Walsh had a connection with the priest, one that didn't in any way reflect on Father James's memory: The bazaar was a public occasion. Finally, the motive appeared to be simple greed. No seduced wives in St. Anne's congregation, no abused choirboys, no dark secrets that would destroy the man and the office simultaneously.

A very convenient solution indeed. For everyone except Walsh, of course.

But Rutledge was learning that Blevins kneaded his evidence like a loaf of bread, forming it to his own satisfaction.

Whereas his London counterpart was more likely to gather the scattered parts of the human puzzle and look closely at them for bits of knowledge he could string together.

Hamish said, "You'd do better to go back to London, then! You willna' convince yon Inspector that he's made a mistake. And you'll be branded along with him if it all goes wrong!"

Rutledge answered, "Nothing less than a signed confession will serve."

He had meant it lightly, but realized all at once that he had unwittingly defined the course of his own inquiry.

———

At the door of the hotel, Rutledge thanked the chauffeur—and turned to find three local people staring with interest at the sight of a policeman alighting from Lord Sedgwick's motorcar.

The news would be all over Osterley in an hour.

Rutledge walked up Water Street to the police station. There was a constable on duty. He shook his head when asked for any news.

"The new cart was ordered well before the bazaar, half down then and two payments to follow, the last one on delivery, which was *after* the murder. The Inspector is happy about that. But there's a scissors sharpener who's come to light. The man swears he was with Walsh the night the priest was killed."

"What's the likelihood that he's telling the truth?"

"Inspector Blevins has gone to speak to the man himself. The Inspector's not in the best of spirits, I can tell you!"

There was a man sitting on the edge of the quay when Rutledge came back to the hotel. Under his dangling feet a dozen or so ducks padded about in the muddy trickle of water, catching the bits of stale bread that were being thrown down to them. The man's concentration was intense as he fed them. The slump of his shoulders was familiar—Rutledge had seen him bent over a newspaper at a table in the back corner of The Pelican. A gray cat, curious about all the feathery activity, sat some ten feet away, watching the ducks. It seemed to ignore the man, as if he had no reality but was only a part of the quay.

Closer, Rutledge could see the strain on the haggard face, etched by the bright sunlight into deep and defensive lines. The dark hair was threaded with gray. It was an odd time of the afternoon to see a man sitting idle. . . .

Rutledge passed him by, turning toward the hotel.

As he entered the lobby, Mrs. Barnett stuck her head out of the tiny cubicle that served as her office. She smiled and said, "Inspector? There's been a telephone message from London for you. Would you care to return it now?"

It was a message from Sergeant Wilkerson, and after nearly three quarters of an hour of searching for the man, Wilkerson was located and instructed to contact Rutledge again.

Wilkerson's rough voice came down the line with such a roar that Rutledge had to hold the receiver away from his ear. The Sergeant was of the school that believed that shouting compensated for any small insufficiencies in the telephone system.

"Chief Superintendent Bowles asked me to find you, sir. He wants you back in London as soon as may be."

"I'm involved with the investigation here—" Rutledge began defensively.

"Yes, sir, he knows that. But we've found a body. Whether she's connected with your murder or not, we can't say. But the Chief Superintendent wants you to have a look."

Rutledge felt cold. There was no clear reasoning behind his reaction. But he was afraid to ask the name, afraid he might already know what it was. He'd only just heard it himself.

Marianna Elizabeth Trent.

Another dead end . . .

Driving hard and fast, Rutledge reached London in the middle of the next morning. Stopping briefly at his flat to shave and change his clothes, he went in search of Sergeant Wilkerson at the Yard.

They had not worked together very often. Wilkerson was Inspector Joyce's man, and seldom free for other assignments. Joyce, in his mid-fifties, was a plodding but thorough policeman with no expectation of advancement and no desire for any. He had said, often enough, that policework and not paperwork was his pleasure, and the higher one goes, the deeper the tonnage of paper.

Wilkerson greeted Rutledge with some surprise. "You must have driven all the night, sir. Would you care for a spot of tea brought up to your office?"

"I did." Hamish was all that had kept him awake on the road, after Colchester. And even Hamish had lost his edge on the outskirts of London. "Yes, send someone for tea, and then come upstairs."

The tea provided by the Yard was black and strong enough to cope with any man's drowsiness, coating the stomach with an unspeakable sludge that held the body upright for hours.

A few minutes later, Wilkerson stepped into Rutledge's office and took the chair by the door. He waited until the constable on his heels had delivered Rutledge's tea before beginning his report.

The Sergeant was as big as his voice, florid of face with thinning sandy hair and a double chin that overlapped the collar of his uniform, giving the impression he was on the brink of choking to death. A man who had come up through the ranks but bore no malice toward Rutledge, who had come from a very different background.

He began his report diffidently. "About this woman, sir. It was the usual thing. One of the boats on the river found her; can't say whether she went in by accident or design. Bloated but hadn't been there long enough for the fish to get at her. There were some bruises, but nothing to signify anything more than the tossing she'd taken in the water. The problem was identification."

Rutledge, swallowing his tea with a grimace, nodded. Identification of the corpse was the first order of police work.

"She had none on her—no letters or papers or the like—and she didn't match any of our missing persons records. We advertised more than a week for information. Then a woman who keeps a boarding-house walked into a local station and reported that a lodger had skipped without paying her rent, and wanted her found. Right balmy old bitch, I'm told, arrogant and demanding. But the Sergeant on duty remem-bered the description of our lass, and soon enough they had the land-lady down at the morgue. She couldn't have identified the body—she only gave it a glance—but she did say the hair was right. We showed her the clothes the deceased was found in, but she wasn't what you'd call certain what the lodger was wearing the last time she'd gone out. Or whether she could have been provided a new wardrobe by any gentleman she had taken up with. But the landlady did fling another fit about not getting her money, which made Inspector Joyce suspect she must be fairly sure it was the missing woman."

Rutledge asked, before Wilkerson could put a name to the corpse, "Any trouble with her before? The landlady?"

"None, except for the occasional lodger who disappears with back rent owing. Then she's demanding the police earn their keep. She gets a class of women who aren't steadily employed, if you take my meaning."

"Why did Chief Superintendent Bowles think the dead woman might be connected with the murder in Norfolk?"

"Stands to reason, doesn't it? The lass worked as a shill for an Italian bloke who—the landlady claims—died in the War. Then she spent the better part of the summer with a Strong Man's show, called himself

Samson. Your man Walsh, it appears. Landlady remembers when he came to collect her, because of his size. They had a few words, did the landlady and this Iris Kenneth, on parting. But Mrs. Rollings took her back again when the Strong Man was tired of her!"

Iris Kenneth, then. With no connection to Father James . . .

After a visit to the morgue to look at the body and the woman's clothing, Rutledge went with Sergeant Wilkerson to the small boardinghouse on a run-down street where Londoners with thin pockets often took rooms. It was just off Eustace Road, where industry had crowded out anyone who could afford to move on. Mrs. Rollings was plump, with tightly curled black hair, a pinched mouth, and an air of long-suffering. When Wilkerson introduced Rutledge to her, she looked him up and down, then said, bristling, "It doesn't do my establishment any good to have a policeman at the door every other day! This is a *respectable* house."

Rutledge smiled. "I'm sure it is." She thawed visibly as the smile touched his eyes. "We've come to ask if you still have Iris Kenneth's belongings."

"Lord love you, why should I have kept them? Didn't bring in much, I can tell you, not near enough to pay what I was owed. And I needed the room."

She looked up and down the street with the same suspicious air with which she'd regarded Rutledge, and then stepped back from the door. "Do come inside, before I have to explain to half the neighborhood why I'm entertaining the police again!"

They followed her into a musty entry, where a flight of worn stairs ran up into darkness. The windowless entry itself was nearly as dark, for the glass panes in the door didn't cast light beyond the first step, and the lamp was turned so low that it had long since given up trying to illuminate anything but the small circle of brightness on the gray ceiling and the first landing. Mrs. Rollings opened a door on her left, and led them into her sitting room.

It was surprisingly comfortable, if shabby. There were odds and ends of porcelain on the mantelpiece, including a demure shepherdess with a leering satyr at her shoulder. The juxtaposition of the pieces was nearly lewd. Rutledge wondered if it exemplified Mrs. Rollings's sense of humor or the tastes of her guests. Prints on the other two walls were of theatrical productions, one Sarah Bernhardt's *Hamlet* and the other a popular act in the music halls some twenty years ago. Mrs. Rollings herself wore rouge that stood out like two fever spots under the powder, and her hair was dyed. The jeweled rings on her plump fingers were cheap paste, one of them large enough to have poison secreted in it. Rutledge's opinion was that it might have once been a prop in an Italian play.

She offered them the horsehair settle, and the two men sat gingerly side by side on the stiff upholstery. It smelled of dust and old dog. She herself took a very pretty wing chair covered with a faded but handsome brocade. On the table at her elbow was a collection of shells and a number of pottery jugs with the names of seaside towns painted on them. Where her guests had worked?

Hamish, his Covenanter soul offended by anything remotely smacking of the godless theatrical world Mrs. Rollings inhabited, declared, "She's no' going to give you an honest answer! It isna' in her nature."

"We'll see," Rutledge told him. Aloud he asked, "Did you like Miss Kenneth?"

"What has liking got to do with it?" She stared at him, genuinely surprised. "As long as my guests pay me on time and in full, I like them very well."

"Was she a clever girl?"

"She was pretty. She thought that would take her far. But not far enough if she ended up in the river." Mrs. Rollings leaned forward. "Now what was this about Iris's belongings?" There was an avaricious glint in her eyes.

"Do you know if she might have owned a pair of old shoes, a man's, with a worn heel and a tear in the sole?"

Mrs. Rollings's eyebrows rose almost to her hairline. "Old *shoes*? Men's *shoes*?"

"Yes. We'd like very much to know if she possessed such a pair." Realizing that the concept was totally foreign to his hostess, Rutledge added, "Perhaps from some role or other."

Wilkerson, stolid and silent, was looking around the room as if he expected to find something nasty hidden behind the wallpaper.

"Well, I should think not! She wasn't the kind of girl who played in farce—she didn't have the talent for it! It was more in her line to stand there looking respectable and drawing custom. She was quite lovely in green. You'd have thought her a lady, if she didn't open her mouth." Lovely was pronounced as *luuvley*.

Wilkerson said, "Then you are telling us that no such shoes were found in her belongings?"

"None that I know of! And I was fairly careful in searching through them."

"Would another—er—guest have searched them before you did?" the Sergeant continued.

"Here! There's no stealing in my house."

"No, surely not," Rutledge soothed. "But if you come across old shoes like those I've described—even in an unexpected place—will you send a message to Sergeant Wilkerson here?"

"Is there a reward for what you want to know?" she asked sharply.

"No. But it will be in the public interest."

Her expression informed him what she thought of the public interest.

Hamish had been right. Rutledge stood up, and Wilkerson lumbered to his feet as well.

"You've been most helpful, Mrs. Rollings. Thank you for your time."

She regarded them warily, uncertain if it was truly old shoes that had brought the police around. "There's nothing else you wanted to know about her things?"

"Only if she'd pinched any of them," Wilkerson answered.

That silenced Mrs. Rollings. Anything nice enough to have been stolen had already found its way to the next owner or a shop dealing in secondhand goods, no questions asked.

She saw them out with poor grace, and shut the door on their heels.

Sergeant Wilkerson laughed. "She's a right old besom, but there are any number on the street like her." He gestured in either direction at houses no better kept than hers, their paint peeling and roofs showing stains from years of damp. "But they serve a purpose. Many a pretty girl who went out to seek her fame and fortune would be lucky to wind up here, and not selling herself in the stews. There's not been a lot of work for this lot, what with the War and all, but they've managed to survive. Somehow they always do. This Iris Kenneth would have had an eye for the main chance."

"And yet she ended her life in the river."

Rutledge compared the street here with Osterley, where prosperity had slipped away but dignity and resourcefulness had kept up appearances.

"Well," Sergeant Wilkerson added as he turned to walk back to Rutledge's motorcar, "it wasn't much to go on, but you never know."

The epitaph of police work, Rutledge thought.

"Yes," he answered. "But I'd give much to know if Iris Kenneth was pushed, or was desperate enough to throw herself into the water."

"You think that man Walsh might have wanted to be rid of her?"

"It's possible. If she helped him rob the priest's house. Or she may have been working for someone else with a better reason to kill her than Walsh had. The Iris Kenneths of this world seldom live to old age." Although Mrs. Rollings had. It depended, he thought, whether the woman was clever or naive. Whether she could protect herself or was destined to be a victim.

He started the motorcar and stepped up behind the wheel. "I'll be going back to Norfolk," he told Wilkerson. "Will you pass that message to Chief Superintendent Bowles? And if there's any more information about this Iris Kenneth or her death, I want to know about it."

"Aye, I'll see to that," the Sergeant promised. He sighed. "I never fancied drowning, myself. I'd look to a quicker way of dying."

"My first Inspector told me that women preferred drowning because it didn't hurt and it didn't mar the face. When I saw my first corpse from the river, I knew he was wrong. We never identified her. No one could have."

Rutledge went to his flat and slept for two hours, then headed north again. But when he reached Colchester, he pulled into the dark yard of the Rose and Crown and slept until dawn. It was nearly dinnertime when he reached Osterley. The muscles in his chest ached, and his stomach rebelled at the thought of a formal meal at the hotel. After washing up, he walked down to The Pelican.

The cool night air, with its tang of the sea and the earthy scent of the marshes, welcomed him like an old friend.

CHAPTER THIRTEEN

THE PELICAN WAS BUSY WITH THE dinner hour, noisy with voices and laughter and the rattle of dishes, and crowded with local people. The bar had a line of patrons leaning on their elbows and talking to or over each other. One seated on a wooden stool held a little gray-and-white dog in his lap. The tables near the windows were occupied by small groups of diners already served or waiting their turn.

Among them was the woman he had seen at the church two days ago—was it only two?—sitting with several men and another woman, just finishing their soup.

They were deeply immersed in their conversation and no one looked up as Rutledge walked past. He took a small table nearer the bar, where he would feel less confined by the press of people. The tiny island of space around him was a welcomed relief. Hamish, sensing his unease, argued warily for a return to the hotel.

"For it willna' do to make a scene here!"

"I won't," Rutledge answered shortly. But he could feel himself tensing as more custom came in, one group searching for a table, a smaller one heading for the bar, hailed warmly by friends. As he watched them pass, he noticed in the back corner, occupied with a newspaper, the man he'd seen at the quay feeding the ducks and, another time, here alone in the same seat. Crowded as the room was, no one asked to sit with him.

The man had the air of a fixture at The Pelican, as permanent as the bench on which he sat and the table braced and nailed to the wall.

The strained face was bent over the opened paper, and neither Betsy nor the older couple helping her serve took any heed of him. He'd ordered tea, for there was a pot and a cup by his elbow. As if sensing Rutledge's glance, his knuckles seemed to tighten on the page, crimping it.

Hamish said derisively, "He's no' a verra' popular man. No doubt you'll find you have much in common."

"God save him, then!" Rutledge answered silently.

Betsy finally stopped at Rutledge's little table, her manner more formal than it had been the first day he had arrived in the village. "Good evening, Inspector. Are you wishing to dine or could I bring you something from the bar?"

No longer "What would you like, love?" Rutledge smiled. "What would you recommend for dinner?" he asked her.

"You're fortunate tonight," she said. "There's a roast of chicken with dumplings and potatoes, and I can tell you, there's nothing like it this side of London!"

Rutledge felt an unexpected surge of sympathy for the woman in a book he'd once read, who had been branded with an A for Adulteress. Everyone in Osterley knew more of his business than he knew of theirs. He'd been branded with an O for Outsider—no longer the visitor who was benign, no longer the anonymous traveler who could ask questions and expect an honest answer. There was neither coldness nor rudeness in their manner, only a formality that precluded any expectation of breaking through it.

How long, he wondered, did it take a man to reach the status of "one of ours" in this village? For a policeman who hadn't been born here, perhaps never. For a passing stranger there was welcome and courtesy. For an intruder, only suspicion. And yet Father James had come to be one of theirs. . . .

He chose the chicken with dumplings and ordered a pint to go with it.

Although he tried to keep his eyes away from the table by the window and to stop himself from speculating about the relationships of the four people sitting there, Rutledge caught himself glancing that way from time to time. The woman had a quiet vivacity, and seemed to be comfortable with both men. It emphasized the formality she had displayed toward him on the few occasions when they'd spoken.

A stranger even among strangers . . .

He turned slightly to change his line of sight. Indirectly now, he could see the lonely man sitting in the corner. He served only to reflect Rutledge's own isolation. Hamish had struck a chord with his words.

As Rutledge watched, the man's hands began to tremble, and he hastily shoved them out of sight under the table, dropping the newspaper as if it had burned him. Shell shock?

Rutledge shuddered, Hamish suddenly aware and challenging in his mind. He himself had so narrowly escaped from that horror. And the fierce agony of it still haunted him. To be shell-shocked was to be publicly branded a coward—a man unfit to be mentioned in the same breath as the soldier with a missing limb or shot-away jaw. A shame—a disgrace. Not an honorable wound but the mark of failure as a man. He himself had been caged with the screaming, shaking, pathetic remnants of humanity in a clinic that kept them shut firmly away from the public eye. Until Dr. Fleming had rescued him.

He made a point not to look back again. After examining the oddities that decorated the pub, and counting the number of diners, Rutledge set himself the task of cataloging from memory the framed photographs in the priest's house. But none of those he could call to mind seemed important enough to require a codicil to a Will. Certainly most of them would go, along with the rest of his possessions, to Father James's surviving sister, who would cherish those of the family and perhaps pass on a few to Father James's friends. As was right.

Gifford had already indicated that Mrs. Wainer knew nothing about any bequest. But if the photograph wasn't in the desk, it must surely be somewhere. There was no reason why Walsh or anyone else should wish to steal it. However, there might be, perhaps, some way to jog a memory the housekeeper wasn't aware she had.

That would have to wait until tomorrow.

Unwillingly aware of the occasional quiet laughter coming from the table by the window where the dark-haired woman sat, Rutledge felt a sense of depression settle around him and he fought against it, without any help from Hamish.

———

Rutledge was more than halfway through his roast chicken when the woman sitting by the window got up from her table and walked toward him. He thought for an instant she was coming to speak to him and had nearly risen to his feet when he realized that her eyes were fixed on something behind him.

He turned. The man in the corner was shaking like a leaf in the wind, his shoulders jerking with it.

The woman crossed to him and sat on the bench opposite him. Reaching out, she caught his hands before he could hide them again, and began to speak to him. Rutledge, watching, had the feeling it was not the first time she'd done this. Something in her voice—whether the words or simply the sound—had a calming effect, and for a moment Rutledge thought she had actually stemmed the tide of whatever it was that drove the man into such a frenzy of trembling.

He was just turning away again when the man surged abruptly to his feet, with such force that he overturned the bench on which he sat. The unexpected clatter of the wood on the floor stopped conversation in its tracks: every head turned toward the man and the woman. And he stood there, like a hare caught in the headlamps, unable to move. His eyes were shocked, almost beyond seeing.

Rutledge rose and strode forward, reaching the man and taking his shoulder in a firm grip. The man flinched away, and the woman said sharply, but in a voice that didn't carry beyond the three of them, "*Leave him alone!* He's done nothing to you!"

Rutledge ignored her. He said to the trembling man whose face had turned away, toward the wall, "All right, soldier. Let's get some air."

It was the timbre of his voice that got through. An officer's voice. Steady and assured.

For a long moment the tableau was unbroken: the furious woman, the man in the throes of a breakdown, and the outsider who had interfered.

And then it altered, dissolving into movement, the woman stepping aside, lips tightly shut and eyes worried, and Rutledge seeming to walk away, without looking back, his shoulders as ramrod straight as if he still wore a uniform.

An officer expected a soldier to obey. Unquestioned loyalty to rank was the hallmark of training. Rutledge drew on that now.

Hamish said, "He won't follow. He's beyond heeding!"

Rutledge had taken no more than two strides when the man moved away from the fallen bench and, with Rutledge just ahead of him, almost a shield, walked through the gauntlet of staring eyes and through the door, out into the night.

The woman, her face pale with distress, followed.

Outside, Rutledge didn't stop until he was well away from The Pelican's door, nearly to the quay. In the darkness of the waterside, he stood staring out to sea, not looking at the man who had stopped some little distance from him. Then he said, as if addressing a comrade, "There's a wind coming up. But it's a beautiful night, still."

The man just behind him cleared his throat. "Thank you," he said roughly, as if finding it hard to speak. He hesitated. "There were too many *people* in there—"

Claustrophobia. Rutledge knew it all too well. . . .

"Yes."

"Suddenly I couldn't breathe—I thought I was dying. But I never do. Worst luck!"

There was almost a lightness in the words that belied their intensity. But Rutledge felt sure the man meant them. He had himself, on more than one occasion fraught with panic.

"In the War, were you?" It was a common enough question, but the man flinched.

"For a time," he said. And then he walked away, unsteadily but strongly, as if wanting to be alone more than he needed human companionship.

The woman, watching the scene, said, "He *was* in the War. He was a sniper."

She flung out the last word as if daring Rutledge to say anything. Daring him to condemn.

Rutledge said, "Snipers saved my life any number of times. And the lives of my men. Why should I find that so terrible?"

"Everyone else does." Her voice was bitter. He tried to see her face, but it was hidden. The lights from The Pelican barely touched her hair, like a pale halo behind her head.

"Why?"

"He shot from ambush. It wasn't very gallant. It was assassination, if you will. *Not the thing, you know.*" Her voice altered, twisting the words, as if she was quoting someone. He heard an echo, he thought, of Lord Sedgwick in them, but couldn't be sure.

"He killed from ambush, yes, it's true," Rutledge answered her tersely. "Such men took out the machine gunners when we couldn't. They could move in the night as silently as a snake or fox, waiting for their chance, then making their shot. Some of the other men weren't too pleased about what they did. I suppose it must have seemed unsportsmanlike. But I can tell you they were life, when we expected to die."

She said, surprised, "You're a policeman. I expected you to condemn what he'd done as tantamount to murder."

"Was it murder?" He looked out across the dark, silent marshes, listening for the sea. "I suppose it was," he said tiredly. "Those men were deadly; they seldom missed. The German gunners never had a chance. A good many of our snipers were Scots, with years of stalking behind them. Others had a—knack for silence. For stealth. They were brave, very brave, to do what they did. I never judged them."

"His own father judged Peter Henderson. Alfie Henderson was one of Father James's failures. He never forgave his son, not even on his deathbed, even though Father James *begged* him to heal the breach between them. I think Alfie would have been happier if Peter had never come home from France. He believed that being a sniper had brought dishonor to the family name."

Rutledge swore under his breath. It was often that way—people at home, soldiers' families in particular, seldom understood what war was all about. Their gallant men marched away in crisp uniforms, caps at a jaunty angle, flags flying, and went to France to kill the Hun—*how* that was done never seemed quite as clear. Young men in the filthy trenches were not likely to write to their mothers or their young wives and tell the truth: War was neither dashing nor colorful nor honorable. It was, simply, bloody and terrible. Even the government had entered into the conspiracy of silence for as long as it dared.

Wearily he tried to explain. "The Germans actually trained soldiers as snipers. Did you know that? They had schools to teach their best shots. We quite cleverly used whomever we could find."

Hamish was saying something, but Rutledge didn't hear it. The woman in front of him was also speaking. He caught the last of that.

". . . wasn't given his job back after the War. No one else in Osterley will hire him. He's nearly destitute and won't accept help. Father James believed—but now that he's dead, Mrs. Barnett and the Vicar try to see that Peter is fed. But he doesn't want *pity*—" Her voice cracked, and she added, "It's never the evil people, is it, who suffer? It's always the lonely ones who are already afraid!"

She turned on her heel, going back into The Pelican to rejoin her party.

Not hungry any more, Rutledge stood there for a time in the darkness of the October night, and then walked back to the hotel. He would settle his bill in the morning.

When he came into the lobby, Rutledge was greeted by Mrs. Barnett. She gestured toward the small parlor. "You have a visitor, Inspector."

"A visitor?" he repeated, his mind still on the darkness he'd just left. On Peter Henderson and Father James.

"Miss Connaught."

He brought his attention back to the present. "Ah. Thank you, Mrs. Barnett."

With a nod he walked past the stairs and to the small parlor. As he opened the door, Priscilla Connaught got to her feet and faced him, as if facing the hangman.

"I saw you with Lord Sedgwick the other morning. And then I was told you had gone back to London. Is it finished then, the reward paid and the case of Father James's death finally closed?"

She looked as if she hadn't slept, dark rings under her eyes and a nervous tic at the corner of her mouth. The handsome dark blue suit she wore seemed nearly black, emphasizing her pallor.

Rutledge recalled what she had told him—that with Father James dead, she herself had no reason to live. He wondered what she did each day, when not absorbed in her anger. Did she read? Write letters to friends? Or sit and stare out at the marshes, waiting for something that would never come? Peace, perhaps.

He answered with some care, "I went to London on other business. As far as I know, the probe into Matthew Walsh's movements hasn't been completed. There has been no mention of passing out a reward. Not in my hearing."

"Oh." She seemed shaken. As if she had been so very certain that she hadn't thought beyond the need to find out if she was right.

Rutledge, studying her face, thought, *She's in worse straits than Peter Henderson. Father James was an obsession she couldn't live without. Like a drug, only far more deadly.*

Hamish said, "Aye, but there's naught to be done. You canna' stop the investigation."

Rutledge gestured to the chair she had risen from, but she shook her head. And then, as if her legs wouldn't support her any longer, she sank back into the seat.

"Do you know Lord Sedgwick well, Miss Connaught?"

"Lord Sedgwick? Hardly at all. I have met his son Edwin—but that must be close to sixteen or seventeen years ago, now." She sounded distracted, as if only half her mind was on what she was saying.

"Here in Osterley?" Rutledge persisted, keeping to a neutral topic.

"No, Edwin sometimes stayed with a family I knew in London. He was little more than a boy at the time, and I didn't like him very much."

"Why not?"

"He was very easily bored, and more than a little selfish. He'd lost his mother, and everyone rather spoiled him. But I've heard that he turned out rather well—he was on someone's staff at the Peace Conference last spring."

"And Arthur?"

"I know him by sight, of course, but we've never met. Like his father, he was married to an American woman—I did meet her once. At a vicarage tea I'd been persuaded to attend. One of those sweet girls with little to say for herself. And unbelievably pretty. They spent most of the year in Yorkshire and seldom came to Osterley. Later I heard that she'd died."

She was beginning to breathe more regularly now, finding it easier to carry on a polite conversation. The intensity that had held her on the edge of breakdown was draining away, and in its place was a precarious control again.

"Lord Sedgwick was concerned about the brakes on your motorcar."

"He rather enjoys playing lord of the manor. And I've good reason to thank him for that—his chauffeur rescued me once when I'd lost my way and run out of petrol." As if realizing that she was steadier, she asked again, "Are you sure—have you told me the whole truth about Walsh?"

Her eyes begged him for an honest answer.

"Yes," he said gently. "I have no reason to lie to you."

And yet he thought he had. She'd been distraught enough to do something foolish, before she'd reasoned out the consequences.

"Aye," Hamish said, "it wouldna' do to have *her* blood on your hands!"

She stood up again. "I must be on my way—"

"Whatever rumors you hear," Rutledge told her, "come to me and I'll tell you the truth. I give you my word."

Priscilla Connaught took a deep breath and let it out slowly. "I'm not sure I can believe you. I don't know, I can't somehow think straight."

"It might be a good idea to speak to Dr. Stephenson. Someone you trust."

She laughed, a hollow and mirthless sound. "There's not much a medical doctor can do for a shattered life."

"I wish you would tell me what Father James—"

Priscilla Connaught shook her head with finality. "It had nothing to do with his death. Only with his life. And that's finished. Over and done with."

She looked around, saw her purse on the table, and as she picked it up, spoke again. "I've lain awake at night, wondering who could have murdered him. If there was someone else he'd treated as cruelly as he'd treated me. I think I'd be happier believing that than in the story of a thief." Then she turned toward Rutledge again.

"Thank you for your concern, Inspector," she said with great poise, as if they'd spent an evening in pleasant conversation and she was leaving the party. "You've been quite kind."

And with that, she wished him a good night and walked past him out the door.

Another of Father James's failures, he thought, watching the door close behind her. Like Peter Henderson's father . . . How many were there?

Mrs. Barnett was still in the office when Rutledge came back to the lobby and paused by the desk.

"Yes, Inspector?" she said, looking up.

"I'm told that Mr. Sims, Frederick Gifford, and Father James dined together from time to time. Did they come here?"

"Yes, about twice a month, generally. Occasionally it would be just Father James and the Vicar. I've always looked forward to having them come. They were no trouble at all, and I'd enjoy chatting with them when I brought their tea to the lounge." The memory of that caught her for a moment. "It's not easy, running this hotel on my own. I have so little time for anything else. It was almost like having friends drop by, because they would tell me about a book I might enjoy reading or where someone they knew had been traveling or even a bit of news from London that I hadn't heard. My husband knew all of them quite well, you see, and in a small way it brought him back to me for just a little while."

Something to look forward to . . .

It was a gratification Rutledge did not have. And he had, after a fashion, come to terms with the fact that how he lived today, on the edge of breakdown and exhaustion, would be a pattern he could expect in his tomorrows. It was not self-pity, whatever Hamish drummed into his head, but acceptance. The price of living with himself.

Mrs. Barnett hesitated, on the point of wishing him a good night.

Instead he asked, "Would you give me the name of the young woman who is also staying here?"

Something altered in her face. "I'm sorry, Inspector. She's a guest here, and you must ask her yourself."

Hamish said, "It's no' unusual, for a hotel to guard the privacy of a woman traveling alone."

Rutledge, inexplicably angry, as if accused of a breach of manners, said curtly, "It's a matter of police business, Mrs. Barnett, not personal interest."

The words were hardly out of his mouth before he regretted them. But it was too late to recall them.

Mrs. Barnett stared at him, as if she didn't believe him. Then she replied stiffly, "Her name is Trent, Inspector."

He didn't hear what else she was saying, something about Somerset.

"Is her first name Marianna?"

"She's registered as May Trent."

But May was often a diminutive for Mary. The Queen, Mary, was called May by her family.

Had Gifford known Marianna Trent was staying in Osterley? He'd chosen not to tell Rutledge that.

Or was he trying to make sure that Rutledge didn't go in search of the woman?

"You didna' ask," Hamish informed him.

The next morning, Rutledge found Inspector Blevins already in his office at the station. A letter lay open on the blotter in front of him.

He looked up as a constable ushered Rutledge into the room, and nodded.

"I hope your morning has been fairer than mine."

Rutledge said, "The scissors sharpener?"

"Yes, a man named Bolton. He swears Walsh was with him the night the priest was murdered. It won't be easy to pry the truth out of him. If there is any truth to be had."

"I have another bit of bad news. The London police believe they've found the body of Iris Kenneth in the Thames. The woman who kept the lodgings where Iris Kenneth lived was satisfied enough to sell her belongings for whatever they might bring."

Blevins was staring at him. "When was she found?"

"A week ago. Two days before you picked up Walsh."

"Damn!" Blevins leaned back in his chair. "It's like dealing with a will-o'-the-wisp—you no sooner think you have your hands on the truth when it evaporates like morning fog! Do you think Walsh might have killed her? To shut her up?"

"God knows. There's no real evidence to support murder. She may have killed herself. Or someone else may have put her into the water. I did ask Mrs. Rollings about an old pair of men's shoes. She couldn't believe that Iris Kenneth had ever owned anything of the kind."

Blevins reached for the letter he'd tossed aside. "Read this."

It was a statement from the cart maker. One Matthew Walsh had contracted with him for a new cart on 31 August, 1919, and had paid on account until the agreed-upon sum had been reached. The last payment, four days after Father James's death, was in small notes and coins. The problem was, the other three payments had been as well.

"It's a conspiracy, that's what it is," Blevins went on sourly. "Standing by each other—the cart maker, the scissors sharpener, Walsh . . . I don't know what to believe."

"It's odd, isn't it, for a scissors sharpener to be friendly with a Strong Man who frequents bazaars and small fairs? They aren't of the same class. One is an itinerant peddler, the other a showman of sorts."

"Yes, I'd thought about that. But there's a connection, in fact. The two men were in the same unit in the War. War changes things."

It did. You learned to trust a man not because of what he had been in civilian life but for what kind of soldier he made. Whether your life was safe in his hands when you went over the top or whether he was likely to get you killed . . .

"Which could matter enough for this man Bolton to lie for him," Hamish was saying.

Or—Bolton might have been standing watch the night of the murder.

"It might well have been Bolton's shoe print out by the lilac bushes," Rutledge said aloud.

"I'd considered that. I don't think I could prove it, not without the shoe he was wearing at the time. But there's a possibility, all the same. Witnesses saw Bolton any number of times that day, but no one saw Walsh. Bolton claims he came in just after dusk. Could be the truth."

"What does Walsh say?"

"What you'd expect. He was happy to claim it was true and he demanded to be released at once." Inspector Blevins's lips twisted in a bitter smile. "As for helping us with our inquiries, I've pried more information from a razor clam!"

Rutledge asked, "If Walsh isn't your man—for whatever reason—where will you look next?"

Blevins said grimly, "I bloody well don't know! I'd already looked at the good people of Osterley, before Walsh turned up as a likely suspect. And there was nothing I could find that made any sense, nothing that pointed to someone wanting to murder Father James. Theft was the most likely reason for what happened, and Walsh was the most likely thief. But it's early days yet! I've yet to hear from the War Office, we're still tracking Walsh's movements, and I am going to crack Bolton's alibi, if I can. Early days!" he said again, as if to convince himself.

"Do you know a Priscilla Connaught?"

"Yes. She lives alone out by the marshes and seldom mixes with anyone in Osterley, as far as I know."

"She's a member of St. Anne's."

"So are fifty other people. Sixty." Blevins leaned forward, his elbows on the blotter. "My money is still on Walsh. Until I'm satisfied that there's no earthly chance he's guilty."

He looked at Rutledge, pain in his face. "I've told you before, I *want* the killer to be a stranger. I don't want it to be anyone I know. I don't want to think that any member of St. Anne's parish, any friend of mine, any neighbor—any enemy for that matter—could murder a priest!"

"And yet," Hamish said, "he was killed!"

Rutledge said, "It would be easier to watch a stranger hang."

Blevins shook his head. "I'll watch the murderer hang. It won't matter to me if I know his face or not. It isn't the hanging that I can't live with. It's the thought that someone I have seen every day in Osterley is capable of such a crime." He regarded Rutledge for a moment. "You're not a Catholic. You may not see this the way I do."

"I don't see that being a Catholic has anything to do with it." He refused to be drawn beyond that.

The Inspector looked away, his eyes moving on to the high, soot-streaked ceiling, as if searching for answers there. "Murder isn't finished by killing, that's what I've learned in this business. It's just the beginning. A death opens doors that are better left shut. I'm a very good policeman. I do my duty and I mind my town like a bitch watching her pups. I see that people live in safety and in peace, if not in harmony. And the harmony is gone now."

Against his will, Rutledge said, "What do you know about Peter Henderson?"

Blevins's eyes came back to him. "Peter? I don't think he's capable of killing anyone ever again." There was a pause. "But his shoes are old and worn. And Father James did his best to heal the breach with Peter's father. When he couldn't, he tried to make Peter swallow his pride and go to the old man and beg forgiveness, if only to be accepted back into the family at the end. They—Father James and Peter—quarreled about that. Publicly. Down on the quay. You could probably make a good case for Peter Henderson. But I don't want to. The poor devil's suffered enough."

Rutledge retrieved his motorcar from the hotel and drove to Old Point Road, his destination the rectory.

Mrs. Wainer, surprised to see him, opened the door wide and said, "Come in, sir. Has there been any news?"

"No, I'm afraid not. I wanted to ask you—"

From the kitchen came an old voice, saying, " 'Oo is it, Ruth? Is it Tommy?"

"It's the policeman from London, dear." She turned back to Rutledge, apologetic. "It's Mrs. Beeling. She's come for a cup of tea and a gossip. In the kitchen . . ."

"I won't keep you—" Rutledge began, but the housekeeper shook her head.

"No. Come along back, if you don't mind—she's not well, and I don't like leaving her alone too long!"

He followed Mrs. Wainer down the passage to the kitchen. The woman at the table was swathed in shawls, as if she felt cold, her gnarled fingers closed around a cup of tea, and her clouded eyes turned toward the door. "That's not Tommy," she stated, regarding Rutledge with obvious suspicion.

"Tommy Beeling is her grandson," Mrs Wainer said in explanation to Rutledge. "No, Martha, it's the policeman from London. Inspector Rutledge."

The old eyes sharpened. "Oh, aye." Mrs. Beeling nodded her head almost regally, as if welcoming Rutledge to her own house. "The one come to find out who killed our priest."

Feeling as if he weren't there, Rutledge bade her a good morning and then turned back to Mrs. Wainer.

She was saying, "Tommy—that's her grandson—drops her off here for a little visit, on his way to market. Martha used to speak to Father James for ten minutes or so, and then we'd have our tea here in the kitchen." She gestured toward the kettle on the stove. "The water's still hot, sir, if you'd care to have a cup. I could bring it to you in the parlor."

"Thank you, no. I do need to ask you a question, and then I'll be on my way. If Mrs. Beeling doesn't mind?"

Martha Beeling didn't. In point of fact, she was delighted to be a witness.

Rutledge asked, "The photographs that Father James kept about the house. Do you recognize the people in all of them?"

"As to *recognizing*," Mrs. Wainer said doubtfully, "no, I can't say that. But I knew who most of them were. His parents, of course—his sister and her husband—the brother and sister that died—Monsignor Holston—friends from seminary. He'd point them out sometimes when I was dusting and say to me, 'Ruth, I've just had a letter from John, there, and he's taking up a church in Gloucestershire.' Or he'd heard that one or another had gone to Rome or to Ireland. It was like family, you know, the way they kept up with each other."

"Was there a photograph of anyone whose name he never gave you? Someone he never identified for you?"

"I wasn't one to pry, sir! He told me what he wished to tell me, I never asked." She bristled a little, as if he had questioned her integrity. "If you're meaning that photograph that Mr. Gifford was looking for, I don't know which it could be."

Hamish said, "You must tread wi' care, yon lawyer willna' wish for you to make too much of the bequest."

And not in front of the inquisitive Mrs. Beeling!

Rutledge patiently explained, "I'm looking for information, you see. About Father James, about the people he knew—and trusted—and cared about. Not only the seminary and his family, but individuals as well. A soldier he'd befriended at the Front. A woman he'd known long before he became a priest. Nothing suspicious or doubtful, only a personal memory that he'd kept to himself."

"You're welcome to see for yourself. The truth is, after Mr. Gifford left, I've thought about it a good bit, and there's nothing out of the ordinary."

He tried another possibility.

"Do you know a Miss Trent?"

"The lady at the hotel. Oh, yes, sir, she's called on Father James a time or two. The man she was to marry, he was killed in the War, and she's finishing the book he'd begun. As a memorial, so to speak. It's all about what's to be found in old churches—misericords, brasses, pew ends, baptismal panels, that sort of thing. Before he went off to France, her young man had written all the book except the chapter on Norfolk. As you'd expect, Father James knew the history of any number of the churches up here in the north, and was helping her."

Suddenly enlightened, Rutledge remembered that Lord Sedgwick had referred to May Trent as having a religious bent. He could understand why such a mistake had been made, if she spent so much of her time visiting churches.

Mrs. Beeling spoke up. "You're speaking of that pretty lady who was here to tea once when I came? Very kind she was, asking after my Tommy." To Rutledge she said, "Tommy nearly lost a leg in the War. He still limps something fierce. The bones not knitting right." And that carried her to a new train of thought. "You was the policeman in the motorcar t'other day, with Lord Sedgwick. Tommy was taking me to the doctor, and he said he saw the Inspector with His Lordship, but I took it to mean Inspector Blevins. And that made no sense at all!"

"Why not?" Rutledge asked.

"His Lordship's far above taking up Inspector Blevins. Proud man, like his father. And *he* was as mean as they come! My grandmother was parlor maid to the Chastains, that lived in the hall before the first Lord Sedgwick took it over. When she married the coachman, they was given a grace-and-favor cottage in the village, for life. No such thing when I married my Ted. Head gardener, Ted was, and the old lord—Ralph, this 'un's father—he knew the gatehouse cottage was coming open, and he never said a word. But this 'un's wife, she tried to make up for it, and was kind enough to give me a brooch to wear on my wedding day." The old woman fumbled in her shawls, and held out a lovely little enameled brooch, a hunting scene of hounds and horsemen over a fence after the fox. "That's an *American* hunt, that is. Not one of ours. See the fence? Wood railings! You can tell by the fence!" She had remembered exactly what she'd been told about the little brooch, and it was a prized possession, one she wore when calling on friends.

Rutledge admired it, and she beamed with pleasure. Then, as class-conscious in her own way as any member of the aristocracy, she added spitefully, "They both married Americans, you know. The present lord and his son Arthur. Couldn't find no titled English lady that would have them, smelling as they did of London trade. It wasn't *old* money, you see." She glanced at Mrs. Wainer's pursed lips. "Well, I should say the present lord found himself a well-born bride over there, and she was very kind. Died of her appendix, she did. Mr. Arthur's was a love match, they tell me. He went one summer to visit his cousins on his mother's side and fell in love with one of them." She ended triumphantly, "*And* I met that one, too. A pretty little thing, shy as a violet. But Ralph's wife—Charlotte, I think her name was—was long dead when he was given the title. Just as well; they say she was no better than she ought to be. A Londoner, *she* was."

Mrs. Wainer threw an apologetic glance at Rutledge, and said, "Now, then, Martha, let me warm up your tea!" She rinsed the pot and turned to lift the kettle, pouring the steaming water over fresh leaves.

But Mrs. Beeling was delighted with a new audience. "Arthur's wife is the one that drowned. On that ship that went down. She ran off from Arthur, they say, though no one knows quite why, except that he was away in France racing whenever he could and she must have been lonely, out in the middle of nowhere like she was!"

"Here, in East Sherham?" Rutledge asked, encouraging her.

"Lord love you, not *here*. They lived over to Yorkshire, where Arthur had bought a house after the marriage. He never got along with his brother, Edwin. I wondered if Edwin didn't care for his sister-in-law more than he should. The story was, he'd head to Yorkshire on that motorcycle of his, as soon as Arthur set out for France. Both were motorcycle mad one time or another. Noisy, smelly machines, to my mind. Edwin still has one; I've seen it."

Mrs. Wainer brought the fresh pot of tea and added more small cakes to a plate. "Now, you help yourself, Martha, and I'll just see the Inspector out."

Mrs. Beeling was still enjoying herself. "I don't quite know why he took you up in his car," she added, returning to more recent events, perplexed. "Unless it was to hand over the reward money he put up for Father James's murderer."

"As far as I know, there's been no reward given to anyone," Rutledge said.

She nodded sagely. "I'm of two minds about yon Strong Man. I was at the bazaar, and he never exchanged more than a word with Father James, and him decorated like a clown—"

"But he was in this house in the afternoon," Mrs. Wainer said earnestly. "I found the Strong Man wandering about inside this *house*!" She cast a resigned glance in Rutledge's direction. "That's what alerted Inspector Blevins to look for him."

"Yes, and a dozen other people were in here as well. I saw Lord Sedgwick's son come to have a lie-down, when his back was paining him. I asked him if I might bring him a glass of water, and he said thank you but no. There was also the doctor's wife, to put a plaster on Mrs. Cullen's cut finger, and—"

"The Sedgwicks were at the bazaar?" Rutledge asked, although he knew they were. But Mrs. Beeling seemed to have perfect recall.

"Osterley doesn't have a lord, you see," Mrs. Beeling explained graciously, "though there's always been good blood here. The Cullens and the Giffords and so on. But there's no title. Still, the family does try to make an appearance on special days, and that's as it should be." She nodded. The Sedgwicks were not old money, but they were still money. "As for Arthur, he's in terrible pain, they say, but he can get about. He'd come down for the fete and stayed on for that Herbert Baker's funeral."

"He was at Herbert Baker's funeral?" The garrulous old woman had given Rutledge more information in a quarter of an hour than anyone else had done in several days of asking questions.

"Of course he was. Herbert Baker had been his father's coachman, and then driven Arthur's wife about in the motorcar until her death."

Rutledge turned to Mrs. Wainer and said, "If you don't mind, I'll take you up on the offer of a cup of tea."

She wasn't pleased to serve him in the kitchen. And as it turned out, he wasted the next quarter of an hour.

Whatever her sources were for the gossip she had freely dispensed, Rutledge discovered that Mrs. Beeling had nothing more of interest to tell him, except that she most certainly had her own opinion on why Herbert Baker had seen two priests shortly before he died.

"When you're old, things begin to prey on your mind," she told him affably, as if from personal knowledge. "You wake up in the night, dwelling on what was done or left undone. And it seems far worse in the darkness than it ever was in the light, until you take to brooding on it, more often than's good for you. You take to worrying that it's too late to make amends. I know myself, sometimes it weighs heavily on me, the things I've said and done. There's nights when my bones are aching and I can't sleep, and I'd even bow down to those heathen idols that His Lordship has in his garden, if I thought it might clear my mind!"

The Watchers of Time.

Rutledge said, "But what had Herbert Baker done, that made him send for the Vicar and the priest?"

"Who's to say? But I heard he's the one who let Arthur's wife step out of the motorcar in King's Lynn, and then went off to get himself drunk while she was speaking with the shopkeepers about a birthday party. Only she never visited the shops. She went instead to the station and took the next train to London, and disappeared. Until the ship went down, and they discovered the poor lady had been aboard!"

It made sense. Hamish, listening to the nuances behind the words, agreed. Guilt might have tormented Herbert Baker—who had the gift of loyalty. Not a sin of commission, but instead failure to do one's duty for a single hour. His drinking couldn't have set in motion any of the events that had followed. All the same, he might have bitterly blamed himself for them.

If—if—if. If I had been there—if I hadn't been drinking—if I had minded my duty . . .

Was that what lay on a dying man's conscience, driving him to try to buy himself absolution in two faiths?

CHAPTER FOURTEEN

RUTLEDGE, DRIVING BACK TO THE HOTEL, told himself that Herbert Baker was proving to be a dead end. But the bequeathed photograph was still elusive . . .

He braked to a slow pace behind a wain piled high with hay.

Rutledge was beginning to wonder if the killer hadn't taken it with him. Did that explain the ransacking of the desk? But what would Walsh—or his accomplice, for that matter—want with a photograph? How would they have known it even existed, and what earthly value did it have? And if it did have value, why had Father James made a sudden decision to leave it to May Trent?

Why—when he could have given it to her on the same day he'd brought that carefully crafted paragraph into the solicitor's office and asked to add a codicil to his Will?

The wain reached the turning for Gull Street and the Sherham Road and began to swing wide to plod around the sharp corner. Abruptly—without any warning—Rutledge found himself locked in an angry exchange with Hamish.

It had nothing to do with the discussion in the rectory kitchen. Not directly. It was instead an accusing and angry personal indictment.

"I canna' ken why ye're sae keen on proving yon Inspector wrong! Are you sae certain the Strong Man is innocent? When you walk away fra' this town, you'll leave behind raw wounds that willna' heal as swiftly as yon hole in your chest! It's a cruel thing, to stir up secrets to no purpose! Ye were sae set on Herbert Baker's Confession as the key to this death, and now the auld woman has explained why it wasna' any sich thing!"

"There are too many questions about Walsh. If he killed the priest, it had nothing to do with the bazaar money. I'd wager a month's pay on that! And I can't go over Blevins's head and ask the War Office for information about where Walsh served. But that will have to be dealt with one way or another, before we can discuss guilt or innocence."

"I canna' see how a *photograph* is important."

"It may not be. That's a part of police work, too—to eliminate the variables."

"And when the photograph also turns into a wild-goose chase, ye'll go back to London?"

Rutledge said nothing. The wain lumbered into the turn, top-heavy and awkward. Two young boys along the road shouted at the driver, and began to run after him, as if trying to overtake the wain, their laughter spilling out like silver threads. The team of great Norfolk horses pulling the wain ignored the rowdy pair, heads down and shoulders into their harness. Rutledge watched them, concentrating on shutting out the voice in his head.

But Hamish was not to be put off.

"You willna' see it, but ye're running from yoursel'. You couldna' find peace in your sister's house, you couldna' find peace in your flat, and then you couldna' find peace at the Yard. And ye willna' leave Norfolk, because there's nowhere else to go. You're afraid because in hospital you discovered a fierce will to *live*—"

Rutledge answered grimly, "I've been shot before—"

"Aye, that's as may be! Piddling wounds that didna' require more than bandaging at the aid station or a dram of whiskey! This was verra' different. It left its mark. *Why are ye sae afraid of living?*"

Rutledge realized that the motorcar had not moved, and the wain was nearly out of sight down the Sherham Road. He drove on past the intersection and pulled into a tiny lane that ran between two houses.

There he put the gears in neutral, set the brake, and leaned back to rub his hands over his face as if to erase the emotion there.

It was something he had tried to shut out from Hamish. But the Scot, used to burrowing deep into his secrets, had ferreted it out.

In truth, it had little to do with Scotland. . . .

On the night of his second surgery, he had heard the doctors telling Frances that the odds were against him; he might not survive going under the knife. "Too close to be sure," one of them had said, and he had listened to Frances's voice in his drugged state halfway between consciousness and sleep.

"He won't leave me alone," she said fiercely. "He won't."

And then someone had leaned over his bed, hovering in what appeared to be a mist but was only the anesthetic taking hold. At the time it had given the white hair and the kind face an insubstantial air, as if half dreamed.

"There's nothing to fear, son. Whatever happens. But if you want to live—He'll listen. Be sure of it." The South Country voice speaking softly in Rutledge's ear was confident, serene.

After that, the darkness had come down, and there had been no pain, only peace. It was not until many hours later that Rutledge had come back, in worse pain, to wakefulness.

It had startled him, to find himself alive. And he had been terrified that he'd begged to live, when he had no right . . . no right at all.

Much later, Frances had brought the corpulent little clergyman in to meet him. The doctors, Rutledge learned, had sent for the man to offer comfort to her if her brother died. In the light of day, Mr. Crosson was neither insubstantial nor half dreamed, but a practical and straightforward rector who regarded the patient with sharp blue eyes and said, "Well, then, Mr. Rutledge. I'm glad to see you know your own mind!"

It was far from the solace that Mr. Crosson had intended. Instead it had shaken Rutledge as deeply as the lines of sleeplessness on Frances's face. And it confused him as well; all his energies for so very long had been concentrated on dying and to live was something he wasn't—couldn't be—prepared for.

"Oh, aye, was that it, then?" Hamish asked derisively. "Most men would ha' been glad to live to see an end to the case. You went to hospital and buried your head in sand! You went back to work to bury your head in sand. And you stay here in Norfolk to bury it again."

"What do you want from me?" Rutledge said tiredly. Listening to gulls call from the direction of the harbor, he tried to defend his answer. But their wild laughter distracted him. "You know that Blevins needs to sort out this murder."

"Oh, aye, a training program for the local constabulary, is it?"

Rutledge nearly lost his temper, but Hamish got there before him.

"Ye're the man with a fine understanding of people, they say. Can ye no' understand yoursel'? D'ye think I wanted ye to die? No, like yon Connaught woman, I havena' any wish for you to die. No' until I'm ready! In France God wouldna' have you, and He doesna' want you now. But I do!"

Had he wanted to live? Rutledge asked himself, as he put the motorcar into gear once more and took off the brake.

There was no honest answer to that.

There hadn't been for three weeks.

And Hamish fell ominously silent as they passed the turning for Water Street and slowed for Trinity Lane.

Rutledge made the turn into Trinity Lane, and pulled the motorcar into the web of shadows cast by a tree just by the churchyard wall. Switching off the motor, he sat back against his seat for a moment before stepping out into the light breeze that tempered the sun's warmth.

From the churchyard where he walked, deep in thought, he could just catch the glimmer of the sea, struck by the sun and bright enough to hurt the eyes. Seagulls were wheeling above the tower, like white rooks, their hoarse cries almost human. He found he was listening to them instead, not wanting to think, not wanting to feel.

And then a woman called to him from the north porch of the church. "There you are, Inspector," she said, as if she had waited there for half an hour or more for him to arrive. "I thought you'd forgotten!"

He turned toward the church, where May Trent was crossing the grassy churchyard toward him. "You had said something this morning about wanting to speak with me—"

Rutledge had said nothing of the sort. But as she moved away from the north porch, a man followed her out of the church. It was Edwin Sedgwick.

Her face was toward Rutledge, and there was a pleading smile on it. It made her look young and vulnerable.

"Yes, I have to apologize for being late," Rutledge said immediately, removing his hat and standing there by the first row of gravestones, penitent.

Edwin Sedgwick moved gracefully in Miss Trent's wake and she turned slightly to introduce the two men.

They shook hands. Sedgwick was saying, "I'd heard that you're assisting Inspector Blevins. Any luck with the investigation into Walsh's background? I had to drive my brother to London yesterday; I haven't heard the latest news."

"We've come up with a few pieces of information that seem to point in his direction," Rutledge responded. "You knew Father James, I think?"

"We weren't congregants at St. Anne's, but of course everyone came to the bazaar. My father was offering a prize in the children's games. Looking back on it, it seems to me that Walsh was affable enough, minding his own business and something of a success with the ladies. Hard to believe he was the sort to come back later and murder anyone, much less Father James."

The sun was in his face, the cold gray eyes warmed by concern.

"Was there anyone else there that day who might have had words with the priest? Or showed any signs of unusual interest in the rectory?"

"On the contrary, as far as I could tell it was an orderly crowd, and the amusements seemed to keep them entertained. The afternoon appeared to be very busy, and I think Father James was pleased." He frowned as he tried to remember. "There was one skinned knee, as I recall, when some boys ran out to play among the graves. My father quickly put a stop to that, and Mrs. Wainer bound up the wound. My brother was in some pain because of his back, and shortly after that, he asked my father to drive him home. I left with them." He turned to May Trent. "The famous bidding war began just after that."

She laughed. "Oh, yes, Mrs. Gardiner and Mrs. Cullen saw a pitcher at the White Elephant Booth at exactly the same time. Father James finally had to ask them to draw lots. I thought it was clever of him."

Sedgwick looked at his watch. "I must be going. Evans is waiting for me at the hotel. Inspector." He smiled at Miss Trent. "I'll speak to you another time."

"Yes, indeed." She watched him stride briskly down the walk and turn toward Osterley as he went through the gates. Then she quietly apologized to Rutledge. "I'm so sorry! I was nearly *desperate,* and you came along just when I needed rescue!"

"What happened?"

"He came looking for me in the church and asked me to have dinner with him in King's Lynn. I told him I had other plans for this evening, and he was just about to ask me about tomorrow night, when I saw you out here. He's an attractive man, and probably not used to rejection, but I'm—I'd rather not establish a precedent by accepting his invitations. It was *such* a relief to see you! Do you mind very much?"

"Not at all. But surely you could have managed, if I hadn't come along."

With a lift of her chin, she said, "Yes, of course. But you see, Peter Henderson wasn't feeling well, and he was resting in one of the pews down by the altar screen, where it was cool. Wrapped in a blanket that the Vicar keeps there for him. I didn't want Edwin Sedgwick to jump to conclusions—" Her face turned a becoming shade of pink.

Rutledge smiled, and it lighted his eyes. "I understand. Is there anything I can do for Henderson?"

"If you could drop me at Dr. Stephenson's surgery, I'd be grateful. A headache powder would probably help him. He doesn't eat regularly, I'm afraid, in spite of our efforts to see that he does, and I suspect that's the root of the problem."

"I'll take you and then bring you back."

"No, please. Peter sometimes uses the church as sanctuary, when it's cold or wet. He knows I go there often; it doesn't seem to bother him. But if you came in—"

"Whatever seems best," he told her.

They walked together toward the motorcar, and she said, apropos of nothing, "You don't believe Matthew Walsh killed Father James, do you? I wonder why."

He studied her face. "Why should you think that?"

"A woman's intuition, I suppose. And the way you go on asking questions. As if you seem to be waiting for something. A mistake. A false step. I don't know. I have this rather uncomfortable feeling that one day quite soon, you'll pounce!"

It was a very different attitude from Hamish's.

And it made Rutledge feel ashamed.

How did one touch the spirit to test *its* scars? The reasons a man did things, the unconscious pressures behind ordinary decisions . . .

As he opened the door for her and went to crank the engine, Rutledge realized that he'd missed his chance to ask her about the photograph.

Outside Dr. Stephenson's surgery, Rutledge stopped long enough for Miss Trent to thank him again and then disappear through the waiting room door.

He pulled out again in the wake of a milk wagon, and was halfway down Water Street when he saw Blevins walking in the same direction.

Blevins turned at the sound of a motor and recognized Rutledge at the wheel. He called out curtly, "You're a hard man to find when wanted!"

"I've been to speak to Mrs. Wainer again."

A greengrocer's cart came up behind the motorcar, the horse snorting uneasily at the smell and noise of the vehicle. Blevins said, "Don't clog traffic. I'll meet you on the quay."

Rutledge nodded. He left the motorcar in the hotel yard and walked out to the quay. Inspector Blevins was already standing there, staring down at the water. Sun streaked it as the tide trickled in. It was moving the narrow stream sluggishly now, but would do so with more method later.

Blevins's shoulders were stiff, angry.

Rutledge said, coming up to the other man, "What's happened?"

The Inspector turned, looking around to see if they could be overheard.

"I hear you've been hobnobbing with the gentry." There was cold fury behind the words.

"Lord Sedgwick? He invited me to lunch. I was interested in knowing why."

"Did you find out?"

"No. At least—I'm not sure," Rutledge answered truthfully.

"What's that supposed to mean?"

Rutledge held on to his temper. "Look, I don't know these people the way you do. I couldn't. I haven't lived here all my life. I have to depend on instinct to hear what lies *behind* their words. You never warned me off Sedgwick. Or anyone else."

"Sedgwick put up the reward for Father James's killer. Did he tell you?"

"Yes. He did. What difference does that make? Does it remove him from suspicion?"

Blevins turned back to look at the marshes. His profile was set, hard. "I had asked the Chief Constable to speak to the Yard about keeping you on here, and a Chief Superintendent by the name of Bowles agreed to it. Now I'm not sure I did the right thing."

Suddenly Rutledge could see through Blevins's fury. He resented the fact that the man from London, with his polished airs, had been treated with noticeable favoritism by the local gentry when he himself never had. . . .

"Sedgwick won't make any friends for you. I can tell you that," Blevins went on. "And if you have ambitions in London, he won't do you any good. He's not *old* money."

"I never believed he was," Rutledge answered coldly. "And as for any favors he might do me, I choose my own friends and pick my own enemies." He let the words lie there, a challenge.

Blevins looked at him again. "There was a rumor. The Chief Constable had heard that you came back from the War a broken man. Half the policeman you were. If that."

Unspoken was the rest of what Blevins wanted to say. "You might be in need of patronage . . ." But the words hung in the very air between the two men, accusatory and damning.

Hamish was saying something, but Rutledge was intent on fighting his own battle.

"I came back from the War broken by the waste of it," he told Blevins, his voice harsh. "It *was* a bloody waste of lives and we brought home nothing—*nothing!*—to show for four years of dying in trenches not fit for swine. I asked no favors from anyone, and I received none. I did my job as well as I knew how, just as every other man back from the Front tried to do his. No one gave me back my past, and no one will hand me my future. Whatever your grievance is with me now, it has nothing to do with the War, and nothing to do with my skills as a *policeman!*"

Blevins stared at him, and then looked away, surprise in his eyes. Behind the thin face and the polite manner was a will stronger than he'd believed. "All right. I apologize." He took a deep breath. "I'm at my wits' end, that's what it is. Look, I have to put together—and damned soon!—a sound enough case against Walsh that I can take to trial. Otherwise I have to let him go. We can't hold him forever on suspicion. And right now, *that's all I've got!*" Blevins took two quick steps away, and then turned back to Rutledge. "It's like chasing wraiths, nothing can be nailed *down*!"

"Have you told him about Iris Kenneth's death?"

"No. I find I can't stand the sight of the man. He's taken to sitting there smirking, like a damned gargoyle. One of my constables swears he'll choke Walsh into confessing." A twisted smile crossed his face. "Damned fool is half Walsh's weight!"

"Let me be the one to break the news."

Blevins considered the offer. "All right. Come and talk to him, then. Nothing else is working. This is worth trying."

They walked in silence back to the police station. There, Blevins gave the key to Rutledge and gestured in the direction of the small cell.

When Rutledge unlocked the door, Walsh was sitting on the bed, a smile pinned to his face. That changed when he saw that it was not Blevins or one of his constables. A shadow of concern took its place.

"What are you doing, standing there in the doorway, like the Trumpet of God?" Bravado in a deep voice.

Hamish said, "He thinks you've come to take him to Norwich. Or London."

It was a sharp observation.

Rutledge said, "There's been an interesting development in your case."

Walsh shoved himself to his feet, a big man with hands twice the size of Rutledge's. "And what might that be?"

"Iris Kenneth."

Surprise swept over Walsh's face. "What's she got to do with anything?"

"We thought she might have been the person you left on watch under the lilacs. That clump of bushes is out of sight of the neighbors' windows. A clever place to stand and watch, in my opinion."

"She never stood there! Because *I* wasn't there. And if she told you she was, it's out of malice. She's a *bitch*! She's got it in for me because I didn't keep her on, that's what it is! I could wring her neck!"

Rutledge waited to a count of ten, watching the man's face. It was a thinking face, but not a cunning one. The Strong Man wasn't just muscle and brawn; he was capable of working out the ramifications of his position and dealing with the reality it represented. But he didn't appear to have that extra measure of slyness that sometimes cropped up in people of his ilk.

As if in agreement, Hamish observed, "He's no' one to lurk about in the shadows. He's been larger than most men, all his life." And it was true. Walsh had probably never feared anyone or anything. Unlike a small man, whose wits were all that stood between him and a bullying, Walsh had never needed to bluster or bargain. His arrogance grew out of his certainty about himself in the scheme of things.

Rutledge let his silence draw attention to itself. When something changed in Walsh's manner, less belligerent and more wary, he finally said, "Iris Kenneth is dead. Did you kill her, too?"

The shock was real. Walsh sucked in his breath, and there was a sudden tightness around his mouth, an incredulity that left him shaken with a realization that he might have fallen into a trap.

"You're lying to me!" he said, the deep bass voice rolling around the walls of the small cell like thunder overhead.

"Why should I lie? I can take you to London tonight and show you her corpse. If it hasn't already been turned into a pauper's grave."

"She's *not* dead! Iris had a way about her, a lively way. But she kept her wits about her, and she *never*—I don't believe you!"

With a shrug, Rutledge turned to leave. "I don't really care whether you believe me or not. I'm not lying to you. She's dead."

"How? By what means!" Walsh asked quickly, taking a step forward as if to stop Rutledge from leaving.

"Drowning," Rutledge said coldly. "Not a pleasant way to go, surely?"

And he walked out of the cell, shutting the door behind him.

Walsh was there as he turned the key in the lock. His fists pounded furiously against the door. "Damn you! *Come back here—!*"

But Rutledge walked away down the passage to Blevins's office, to the drumbeat of Walsh's fists battering on the door.

As Rutledge walked into the office and dropped the key on the desk, Blevins said, "What's that in aid of?" He inclined his head toward the savage pounding. "I don't see you've gained much of anything!"

Rutledge sat down in the chair across the cluttered desk from Blevins. "I don't know who killed Iris Kenneth," he said. "But I'd give you heavy odds that it wasn't Walsh." He could feel the weariness building up in him, the strain across his shoulders that came from depression and stress. "Not that it matters. We're far from proving she was on the scene, the night of the priest's murder."

"He had the opportunity, surely? We didn't pick him up until after the woman went into the river, from what you've told me of the timing. He had a reason to want her silenced. He could have taken a train to London, finished her off, and taken the next one back to Norfolk!"

"And left his cart and his equipment with the scissors sharpener?"

"That's possible! We should look into the trains. A man the size of Walsh would stand out. Other passengers might remember seeing him."

"It's best to be thorough," Rutledge agreed. Then he added, choosing his words, "Something was said earlier about having to release Walsh, if you didn't have incontrovertible proof. Perhaps—as a precaution— we might be well advised to look at other suspects."

Warily, Blevins asked, "Starting where?"

"I was about to ask you that."

"I've told you, no one in Osterley had a reason to murder Father James!"

"We won't know that with any certainty until Walsh is found guilty."

Disconcerted, Blevins studied the Londoner. "Do you really believe I'm wrong about Walsh?"

Rutledge answered indirectly. "If you're forced to let Walsh walk out of here, will you still be convinced he was guilty?"

Blevins looked away, a long sigh expressing his frustration and uncertainty. His fingers toyed with the edge of the blotter, worrying a small tear in the corner. He was reluctant to give up any part of his authority—and equally reluctant to exercise it. This was his village, his people. To be seen rigorously investigating the private lives of those he lived with on a daily basis would bring their wrath down on his head. To let Rutledge usurp his position was an admission that he was not prepared to do it himself. For whatever reasons.

Finally he told Rutledge, "I don't want to know what you're doing. Not at first. But when you think you've got something I should hear, then I want to hear it. However unpleasant it might be. Do you understand me?"

Rutledge agreed with grace, knowing that Blevins had crossed a line that would come back to haunt him. Hamish, in the back of Rutledge's mind, added silently, "If the killer is no' the Strong Man, you've made an enemy."

And that was equally true.

Down the passage the pounding had stopped, and Rutledge found the silence disturbed him.

Blevins waited until Rutledge had reached the door to the street before asking, "Where will you begin?"

After a moment, Rutledge answered, "Where death begins. With the doctor who examined the body."

As Rutledge stepped out into the hazy sunshine of the October morning, he heard Hamish clearly, as if the voice had just walked out of the police station at his heels, no more than two steps behind his left shoulder.

"There's no turning back," Hamish warned. "If you're wrong, he willna' let you live it down!"

But Rutledge answered, unaware that he'd spoken aloud, "So be it."

CHAPTER FIFTEEN

RUTLEDGE WAITED NEARLY TWENTY MINUTES IN Dr. Stephenson's surgery before the nurse, Connie, summoned him and led the way to the small private office in the rear.

Stephenson, looking at Rutledge over the tops of his glasses, said, "I'd heard you went back to London." He collected the sheets of paper he'd been reading and set them in a folder. "Blevins is a capable man. I can't quite see the need of someone from London looking over his shoulder. Most of the town feels satisfied that Walsh killed Father James, and if there's been any evidence to the contrary, I haven't heard about it."

"When a man travels the country as frequently as Matthew Walsh did, his movements aren't always easy to follow. And the timing on a given date can be critical," Rutledge answered without rancor, waiting to be offered the chair on his side of the desk.

Stephenson nodded toward it, and Rutledge sat down. "Then what brings you here today?"

"Walk lightly!" Hamish warned.

"I wasn't present when the body was found. I'd like to hear what you saw and noted at the scene."

"I wrote everything down for Blevins. The next morning, in fact."

"That's the official report. Well-considered medical opinions designed to stand up in court. What I'd like is your personal opinion—whatever you felt and saw and thought, whether you could support it with fact or not."

Stephenson leaned back in his chair. "I can't think why! It was a clear-cut case of violent death. No question about that."

Rutledge rejoined mildly, "Still, you might provide a small piece of the puzzle that's been overlooked."

Stephenson, a man used to judging people and tracking down the site of illness from small signs, considered Rutledge more sharply, his mind working swiftly behind the shield of his glasses. "You aren't suggesting that someone in Osterley—"

Rutledge cut across what he was about to say. "For instance, Monsignor Holston tells me he was disturbed by the presence of something malignant and evil in that room. Mrs. Wainer on the other hand believes that the murder was motivated by revenge. But neither of them would write such impressions in an official report. Nor would you."

Hamish was saying something, but Rutledge listened to the silence instead.

Stephenson scratched his jaw, a rasping sound in the quiet of the room. "I can't say that I had an initial reaction. Unless it was disbelief. The constable who came to fetch me told me that Father James was dead. I was short with him, saying that it was my business, not his, to make that determination. After we got to the rectory, I remember thinking that this vigorous, intelligent man seemed smaller in death than he was in life. But we were standing over Father James rather than looking him in the eye as we usually did, which probably explained why he seemed—diminished. There were half a dozen people in the room and I could hear a woman sobbing somewhere down the passage. Mrs. Wainer, that was. After that I was too busy to do more than note the circumstances." He stopped, looking back at the scene imprinted on his memory.

Rutledge said, "Go on."

"He was lying by the window, facing it and partly on his left side, his left hand outflung and open, and I remember thinking that he couldn't have seen the attack coming. But Blevins was pointing out the destruction in the study—chairs overturned, papers and books scattered about—and suggesting that Father James had walked in on this confusion and then gone to the window to call for help. That's an old house, but the sashes work smoothly; I tested them myself. Still, even if Father James had been successful in attracting attention, it would have been too late. The bastard had found the opportunity he was looking for and struck hard. Nevertheless, the victim *was* facing the windows, and Blevins knows his business better than I do. Mine was to examine the body."

Hamish said, "It wasna' proper, surely, to influence the doctor's view!"

"It's done often enough. Setting the scene, as it were," Rutledge silently responded. "Human nature to pay heed to it."

Stephenson took a deep breath and studied the ceiling. "There had been an emergency on one of the farms around five that same morning—I was tired. And Blevins was taking it hard—he was one of Father James's flock, as you probably know. I saw no reason to doubt what he was telling me."

"How did Blevins look to you?"

"He was extremely angry, but his face was pale, his hands shaking. I thought it likely that he'd just vomited from the shock. He said two or three times, 'I can't understand killing a priest for a few pounds—I didn't think we held life as cheaply here as in London.' Or words to that effect."

"Tell me about the room."

"It'd been ransacked. You must know that. I could hardly set a foot down without tramping on papers or books and the like. I looked for evidence of a struggle, but didn't find any. I said something to Blevins about that, as I remember. I'd always had the feeling that Father James could look after himself. I'd see him on the road on that bicycle of his at any hour of the day or night, and in any weather. I was surprised that he hadn't made any effort to defend himself. Of course, that was before Blevins brought in Walsh."

"Aye," Hamish reminded Rutledge, "it's a question you raised, yoursel'."

Stephenson looked at the pen on his blotter. "I couldn't find any scratches on the hands, nothing under the nails. No marks on the face. Rigor was present, and I was fairly sure he'd been dead for more than twelve hours."

His eyes came back to Rutledge's face, as if the medical details were more comfortable than speculation. "The back of his skull was crushed and that large crucifix lay on the floor near the body. I could see hair and blood on it quite clearly. I knelt on my handkerchief and someone held a lamp for me, so that I might examine the wound better. There had been at least three blows—I could identify the shape of the square base at three different points. I would say that the first blow stunned him, the second one killed him, and the third would most certainly have made it impossible to survive. Each blow was delivered with consider-able force, judging from the compression of the skull."

"Which confirms," Rutledge said, "that the priest was standing, his back to the killer?"

"That's true. I was told later that there were no fingerprints on the crucifix where it must have been gripped for leverage—either it was wiped clean or the killer wore gloves."

"Women wear gloves," Rutledge said thoughtfully, thinking of Priscilla Connaught, who was tall for a woman.

"I won't tell you that it couldn't have been a woman," Stephenson answered, "but I find it hard to believe a woman would have struck more than twice." He shrugged. "Still, it would depend on her state of mind. This was a bloody wound, and in my experience, few women are willing to splatter themselves with bone and blood and brain tissue, no matter how angry or brave they are. It's not medical opinion, of course, but as a rule, women avoid that sort of unpleasantness. I pronounced him dead, and called it what it was: murder."

Rutledge mused, "I come back to the question, what would I do if I walked in on a thief?"

"I've never faced an intruder in my house, Inspector. I'd feel violated, walking in on such wanton destruction—I know that—and damned an-gry as well. If I recognized the person, I'd tell him to stop making an ass of himself and get the hell out of my house, if he wanted to escape charges. I'd be in no mood to be charitable. And probably get myself killed for it. I'd be more wary of a stranger, not knowing what he was capable of, but I'd still go after him. But then I'm not trained as a priest. It would make a difference."

Hamish said, "He was in the War, Father James. Would he turn the other cheek?"

As if he had heard Hamish's comment as clearly as Rutledge did, Stephenson straightened the folder on his desk to march with the right margin of the blotter and added with an odd tension in his face, "If there was no thief—if it wasn't Walsh—then Father James was con-fronted by an enemy."

Rutledge said nothing.

Stephenson moved uneasily in his chair. "No, disregard that, if you will. Blevins is a good policeman—he wouldn't have got it wrong!"

Again Rutledge let the comment stand. Instead he asked, "Did you know much about Father James's past?"

"That's the trouble with you people from London! You don't live here, you don't understand the people here. You look for complexity, and these are not complex people." Rutledge started to speak, but Stephenson said, "No, let me finish! Some twenty years ago, we had discussions to see if anything could be done to bring back the port. Experts from London preferred to keep the marshes as a sanctuary for birds. We said, What about the needs of the families who had to scratch a living here? But nobody listened. This was a good place for marshes, and marshes we would keep," he said with growing heat. "Well, I'm the man who sees the cost of the struggle to make a living out here. I knew that Romney Marsh had been drained to make it fit for sheep grazing, and we could do the same here, along with dredging the port, making it safe for small boats and a holiday place for people who haven't the resources to travel to the southern beaches. The experts would have none of it. You're the expert here; you want to find something to blame Father James for, something to excuse the time and money the Yard has spent in sending you here. Well, it won't wash. I knew the man. You didn't."

"He's avoiding the question, ye ken," Hamish pointed out.

Rutledge said without rancor, "I'm not suggesting that Blevins is wrong. Or that Father James was guilty of some unspeakable crime. But none of us is perfect—and people will kill for reasons that you and I couldn't comprehend. One of the worst murders I've ever seen had to do with a simple boundary dispute, where a hedge ran over the line. Hardly a case for violence, but it ended in one man taking the shears to the other."

Dr. Stephenson looked at him for a long moment. Then, as if against his will, growing out of some inner need he couldn't silence, he said, "In all my personal and professional encounters with Father James, I never felt any doubt about his integrity or his honor."

A *but* hung in the air between them, like a shout that couldn't be ignored. Rutledge waited, silent.

And as if goaded by that, the doctor said, "Damn you! I don't know why I'm telling you this. But there was something years ago that puzzled me, and I suppose that's why I couldn't put it out of my mind. It had to do with the sinking of *Titanic*. Once when I walked in on him—this was several months afterward—there was a great pile of articles spread out across Father James's desk. A hundred or more cuttings, with notes in ink in the margins, and even photographs of passengers and recovered bodies. He saw me looking down at them, and before I could say a word, he'd gathered up the lot and swept it out of sight into a drawer, as if it were somehow . . . obscene material. I made some remark about the disaster, and his interest, and he said, 'No, that's nothing to do with me.' It was odd, to hear a priest lie, and about something so—*ordinary*." Dr. Stephenson frowned. "He never spoke of it again, and nor did I. But the lie never set well with me. I— In some fashion it altered my view of the man."

He studied Rutledge's face.

Rutledge said. "Perhaps he knew someone who had sailed on her."

"I wondered about that, but people in Osterley seldom travel beyond Norwich or King's Lynn. They most certainly don't have the money for passage on a ship like that. I myself know of only one person who sailed on *Titanic,* and she didn't live here at all. I can't believe that Father James had more than a passing acquaintance with her."

"Who was she?"

Stephenson answered testily, "Lord Sedgwick's daughter-in-law. His son Arthur's wife. An American. It was hushed up at the time—she'd left her husband and sailed for New York without a by-your-leave. Sedgwick and young Arthur had searched everywhere, they'd no idea where she went or why. She simply vanished. Until the ship went down, and someone found her maiden name in the passenger list. Terrible shock to the family."

"Was her body retrieved?"

"I believe it was. The family held a private service on the estate. Look, I should never have spoken of this. For all I know, Father James had dreamed of running away to sea as a boy! *Titanic* was a marvel; she caught the fancy of the entire country. He was probably embarrassed to admit to sharing that excitement." Stephenson took out his watch. "I've three more patients to see before I can go home for my dinner. Is there anything else you want to know?"

He made it sound as if Rutledge had been prying, vulgar curiosity driving him.

Rutledge rose and thanked him for his time.

He reached the door and was just putting his hand on the knob when the doctor said swiftly, for a second time, "Look, forget what I just told you." There was a harsh expression on Stephenson's face, a fierce desire to recall his words, and a strong dislike of the man who'd heard them.

As Rutledge walked down Water Street, he found himself wondering if indeed Father James had lied to the doctor. It was a small lie, of no great importance. Unless it was nested in a pattern of lies? This was perhaps what lay at the center of the doctor's unease.

In the hotel lobby, Monsignor Holston rose from one of the chairs there and said, "I've come for lunch. Will you join me?"

It was an unexpected invitation. Rutledge said, "Yes. Let me wash up first, if you don't mind."

"Of course."

Rutledge took the stairs two at a time, wondering what had brought the priest here from Norwich.

"He canna' stay away, for a man who doesna' wish to stay here," Hamish commented dryly.

Busy with that question, Rutledge reached the head of the stairs, turned toward his room, and in the narrow passage nearly collided with his fellow guest coming the other way.

"I beg your pardon!" he said, catching her arm to steady her. "I was in too much of a hurry."

Startled by his sudden appearance, May Trent said hesitantly, "It was my fault as well. I had just knocked at your door. Today in the churchyard I should have apologized for last evening. You were trying to help, and I turned on you like a termagant. It was rude and ungrateful of me!" There was a rueful smile in her eyes.

"Not at all," he said lightly. "You had no reason to believe my methods would work."

"I had no cause not to believe in them. But I have a way of collecting lost sheep, and then defending them from imaginary wolves. When I returned to my table, my friends had a few pithy comments to make. You may consider me chastised and properly chastened."

Rutledge laughed, and received a deeper smile in return. He noticed a flicker of a dimple in one cheek, and on the spur of the moment said, "I have a friend who has come to take lunch with me. He's a priest, and should know more than most about the old churches in this part of Norfolk. If Mrs. Barnett can accommodate us, would you care to join us?"

Hamish grumbled that it was unwise.

For an instant Rutledge could see that she was tempted, but she shook her head. "That's kind of you. My friends are leaving for London tonight, and asked me to come with them as far as King's Lynn. I've promised."

She started past him, to the top of the stairs, but he put out a hand to stop her. "Miss Trent, I need to ask—it's a matter of police business. Are you aware that Father James has left a bequest to you in his Will?"

"Bequest? There must be some mistake."

"His solicitor has had some difficulty carrying out Father James's wishes, because neither he nor the housekeeper has been able to find the item—"

Miss Trent shook her head. "I don't know what you're talking about. I've heard nothing of this—and I know of nothing that Father James might wish me to have." She was clearly mystified, and a little apprehensive.

"It was a photograph. It was kept in the drawer of his desk, but apparently it isn't there any longer. Did he by any chance give it to you himself?" And perhaps hadn't got around to rescinding the codicil. . . .

She said, "No. He gave me nothing, and he said nothing about a bequest. Are you quite certain—why should he leave me a photograph?"

"Perhaps you should speak to the solicitor about it. The name in the Will is Marianna Trent, of London."

"But I haven't used Marianna since I was a child. Everyone calls me May. Marianna was also my aunt's name, you see, and perhaps he meant her? Although he never said anything to me about knowing her—" The confusion in her face seemed genuine.

"Did he ever show you a particular photograph? Of himself, of his family, possibly of someone who was in some fashion dear to him? Someone he discovered you had known as well?"

The confusion cleared, but a frown took its place, as if the reminder was not welcome. "I think—it's possible I know what you mean. But I haven't the time to discuss it now. I'm already late; my friends will be waiting. When I come back to Osterley tomorrow? Will that do?"

He wanted to tell her that it wouldn't. But she was eager to be gone, and he had no choice but to step aside and let her pass. She went quickly down the stairs, her heels clicking softly in the carpeting, and he heard the door to the street open and close behind her.

Hamish said, "It doesna' seem to be of importance to her, this photograph."

"On the contrary," Rutledge answered thoughtfully. "I believe she would much prefer not to talk about it at all."

Mrs. Barnett had already seated Monsignor Holston, and was chatting with him at the table. She looked up as Rutledge came striding through the French doors, and smiled. "Here he is now," she said. "I'll just go and fetch the soup."

Except for the two men the dining room was empty, no other tables set, no other guests expected.

The scent of warm bread rose from a basket on the table as Rutledge took his chair next to the window.

"I have it on the best authority," Monsignor Holston was saying. "This is one of the tallest loaves ever to come out of her ovens."

"I've had no complaint about the food here," Rutledge agreed. "I don't see how she manages the hotel without more help. I've seen a maid upstairs a time or two, and there's someone in the kitchens to do the scullery work. But Mrs. Barnett appears to do most everything else. She's a widow, I think?"

"Her husband was quite a gifted man. He could turn his hand to anything and it would flourish. But Barnett died just before the War, of a gangrenous wound. A horse stepped on his foot, and infection set in. They amputated the foot, then the leg, and in the end couldn't do anything to save him. She watched him die by inches, and nursed him herself."

"Did you know him?"

"As a matter of fact, I did. He'd been hired by Father James for work on the rectory, and I'd approved the cost at the Bishop's request. Barnett was working there when he was injured."

"You seem to know the parish here rather well. Are you equally knowledgeable about all of them?"

"No more than most. Old churches and rectories require an enormous level of upkeep, and while the local priest does as much as he can, the diocese has to fund many of the major repairs. Which means that I inspect and report, approve agreements, and pay the workmen." He grimaced. "A far cry from the office of priesthood I prefer. That's why I'm under consideration for St. Anne's, because I've asked to serve a church again."

Dishes of hot soup arrived on the tray Mrs. Barnett held aloft, and she set them before the two men with an unobtrusive grace. Vegetable, Rutledge decided, in a rich beef broth. He realized he was ravenous.

Cutting through the crisp crust of the loaf of bread, Rutledge said, "Did Father James find his parish troublesome? That's to say, the kinds of problems he had to deal with here? I should think it would vary from church to church."

"Human nature is human nature, everywhere. Still, this was once a rich parish, and now it's not. The kinds of problems shift with the economic balance."

"Give me an example."

Monsignor Holston was suddenly uneasy. After some seconds, he began slowly, "A priest counsels broken marriages and intercedes in disputes. Sometimes he has to take sides, and that's never simple. He tries to set the moral character of his parish; he keeps an eye on wayward children. God knows there are enough of *those,* thanks to the War."

"Which tells me he knows the secrets of dozens of people."

Monsignor Holston shook his head. "We're not speaking of the confessional."

"Neither am I. Only of secrets that might be more important to someone than we realized."

"The Vicar at Holy Trinity can tell you much the same story, if you ask. Hardly the stuff of revenge, if that's what you're getting at. For instance, there was a youngster here in Osterley. Wild and heading for trouble. We discussed what to do about him. How best to redirect his energies. Father James discovered that the boy was interested in motorcars and aeroplanes, and was all for becoming a mechanic. His father was set on making him a farmer, like his forebears. It took some persuasion, but the father finally relented and let the lad learn a trade." He smiled wryly. "It isn't always quite that easy. But that's more or less typical, all the same."

"Not as typical as telling a straying husband that he has to confess to his wife that there's a child out of wedlock. Or telling a man angry with his neighbor that he has to apologize and make restitution for whatever he's done. That's more the stuff of revenge." Leaving the thought lying there, Rutledge changed the subject. "Tell me about Father James's interest in *Titanic.*"

Surprised, Monsignor Holston stopped with his spoon in midair, staring at Rutledge. Then he said slowly, "I suppose he was overwhelmed by it, like the rest of us. And of course *Lusitania* as well. There's great loss of life when a ship goes down. It's almost incomprehensible."

Hamish said, "He willna' gie ye a straight answer!"

"There was a particular photograph Father James wished to bequeath to someone. The solicitor can't find it. It wasn't in his desk, where he'd indicated it would be found." Rutledge broke off a piece of bread.

Monsignor Holston put down his spoon. "Let me see. There were the usual photographs from seminary, quite a few of his family, that sort of thing. He liked Wales, he'd walked there a number of times on holiday. As I remember, he'd had a number of those framed, and of course a few from the Lake District, too. Speak to Ruth Wainer. She will know."

"I have. She doesn't," Rutledge said baldly, and paused, to let Monsignor Holston finish his soup. When the plates had been removed, he went on. "What did you know about Father James that frightens you so much? Did he have another side that we haven't stumbled across? A secret life, perhaps."

An angry flush rose under the priest's fair skin. "That's ridiculous! You know it is!" He considered Rutledge for a moment and added more calmly, "I thought the matter was settled. That it was Walsh who'd done the murder!"

"I have a feeling you aren't satisfied with Walsh as the killer either. You wouldn't still be afraid of that rectory, if you were. And it's true—there are holes in the evidence against him. Even Inspector Blevins is aware of that. The question is where to look if Walsh is shown to be innocent. I have no allegiances here in Osterley, you see. Or to the church that Father James served. I'm not afraid to turn over stones and see what's there. . . . I think the time has come for you to tell me what's behind your fear."

Monsignor Holston said earnestly, "Look. I'm in no position to tell you whether Walsh is guilty or not. What I *can* tell you is that Father James had no secret life—"

"He was—apparently—fascinated by the *Titanic* disaster—"

"So you say!" Monsignor Holston interrupted. "But he never told me the disaster fascinated him. For God's sake, even priests have a life of their own. I know one who has written quite knowledgeably about butterflies. Another who collects front-edge paintings, and one who prides himself on having grown the finest marrows in Suffolk. I have an interest in grafting fruit trees. I can't say that I talk about it very often. But it's a way of relaxing, when I have the time."

Hamish said, "He's a bloody master at shifting your questions. . . ."

"Mrs. Wainer believes Father James was killed for revenge. Why would she tell me that, if he had no enemies?"

"You'll have to ask her!"

"And there's a Priscilla Connaught, who said that Father James ruined her life, and she hated him. It must have been true. I watched her eyes as she said the words. There's a man called Peter Henderson, whose father disowned him, and Father James did his best to heal the breach, to the anger, apparently, of both parties. Failures, both of them! Potential murderers? Who knows?"

Mrs. Barnett came with another tray laden with dishes. She took one look at Monsignor Holston's stormy face, and at the coldness in Rutledge's, and made no effort to talk to them as she deftly arranged the dishes of vegetables and roasted potatoes, then set in front of them the heavy platters of baked fish.

When she had gone, Monsignor Holston tried to recover his equilibrium. Struggling with something he himself found it difficult to express, he made an effort to explain. "The boy who wanted to be a mechanic had secret dreams he couldn't tell his own father. But he told Father James. People do confide in priests: their dearest hopes, darkest fears. But we aren't perfect, and we aren't always going to get it right. Failure means the person wasn't ready to come to terms with a problem."

"Perhaps a comfortable conclusion to draw as an excuse to walk away."

"We can't work miracles where none is wanted. And sometimes we can't stand up in a court of law and tell the secrets of others—" The words had slipped out, and the priest's eyes told Rutledge that he was instantly regretting them.

"Are you trying to say that one of the secrets Father James kept had to do with breaking the law?"

Monsignor Holston lifted his serviette to his mouth, giving him time to find the words he wanted. "I'm telling you that Father James never led a double life. I would swear to that. In your courtroom. As for what his parishioners confided in him, Father James took his knowledge of that to the grave. I was never a party to it, unless there was some way in which I could help. Which is as it should be. What I don't understand, if we're getting down to bitter truth, is why you're still asking *me* questions when there is already a man in a cell. If as you say, I have a feeling of dissatisfaction, how do you define your own persistence?" Monsignor Holston let that lie between them for a moment, then added, "You haven't been exactly open with me, either, have you?"

Hamish, who had been listening carefully, said to Rutledge, "He doesna' want you to stop searching!"

Rutledge didn't answer, his eyes on Monsignor Holston's face.

"Did Father James ever speak of Matthew Walsh to you? During the War or after it?"

"That's the name of the man Blevins brought in, isn't it? No. Should he have?"

"Just closing a circle." And then Rutledge changed the subject entirely to something more pleasant. But he'd learned what he wanted to know. Not even for the deep friendship that had existed between the two priests was Monsignor Holston willing to break whatever rules bound him. Or it could be that he suspected that something had disturbed Father James over the same period during which Mrs. Wainer had noticed a similar uneasiness, and was afraid to speculate aloud on the reason for it, because if he was wrong, he might reveal matters best left hidden.

"Aye, he canna' tell you the lot, and let you sort through them!" Hamish agreed.

If the murderer was afraid that what one priest knew, he might pass on to another, surely that pointed away from a parishioner at St. Anne's? And toward someone who wasn't clear on how the priesthood worked.

It was an interesting avenue to explore. Rutledge had a sudden feeling that Blevins was right about one thing—that it wasn't the collar that had made Father James a victim.

For the remainder of the meal, Monsignor Holston appeared to be distracted, as if behind the now ordinary conversation he was conducting with Rutledge, he was weighing what he had said earlier—and what conclusions the man from London would have drawn from his words.

As they rose to leave the dining room, the Monsignor paused on the threshold to the lobby, his eyes heavy with a personal guilt. "I'm a clever man when it comes to the faith I uphold. I understand the nuances of Church Law, and the responsibilities I've undertaken. Father

James was a man who carried that a step further. He was deeply involved with the needs of people. That's why he was still a parish priest, while I had moved higher in the Church hierarchy. If he hadn't been a priest, I think he would have been a teacher. Please keep that in mind as you go digging through his life. You could do a great deal of harm, without ever intending to do it."

Rutledge understood what he was trying to say—that it was important to exercise discretion in what was brought out into the open.

Monsignor Holston went on wearily, "I'm not sure what I believe anymore. Whether there was a sense of evil in that study or not. I could have imagined it, just as you suggested the first day we talked. I could have been searching for a way to explain the death of a friend. I don't even know how I feel about Walsh, whether I have compassion for him or not. In the days just after the murder, I was haunted by the need for action, for answers, for proof that this death mattered to the authorities, that out of the shame of it would come some meaning, a memorial to a good man."

Rutledge said, "I don't believe you were necessarily wrong about the sense of evil there in the study. My only question from the beginning has been, why should evil reach out to touch a parish priest in a small town, hardly more than a village, on a bleak and marshy stretch of coast? That's the answer I have to find."

Monsignor Holston started to say something, then bit back the words. Instead he reached out and clapped a hand on Rutledge's shoulder. "I'll make a bargain with you—with the devil, as it were. If you come to me with the truth, and I recognize it, I'll tell you so."

And with that he was gone, leaving behind an air of contradiction that was the closest this Norwich priest could come to openness.

CHAPTER SIXTEEN

NEEDING AIR TO CLEAR HIS MIND, Rutledge walked as far as the quay. He was trying to pin down what it was that disturbed him about Monsignor Holston's vehement defense of his dead colleague and friend.

It was the subtle way in which the investigation was being manipulated.

Don't look here—don't look there. He didn't do anything wrong, you needn't explore that. Like a puppet master trying to untangle the strings of an obstreperous character who wouldn't play his role properly.

If it wasn't the church—if it wasn't the man—if it wasn't the parish—if it was not a fall from moral grace—then the only explanation left was a theft.

Or another crime that had been committed and that had never been exposed . . .

Hamish said, "Whatever it was that worried Father James, it couldna' ha' been a murder—there hasna' been one!"

"Yes," Rutledge said slowly. "All right, what if it's true that the priest knew of a crime?" He remembered the Egyptian bas-relief at East Sherham Manor. The Watchers of Time. The baboons who saw all that men and the gods did, witnesses—but without the power to condemn or judge.

What if the priest had become just such a witness? What if he had heard something that, bit by bit, had led him to knowledge that was dangerous? Like a bobby who walked the London streets, a priest knew his parishioners by name and face and nature. He knew the good in each person; he knew the temptations they faced. The needs and passions and hungers, the envy that drove some and the greed that drove others. He knew what they confessed to him, and what by observation he had grown to understand about them.

It was an intriguing possibility—and for the first time, it brought together a good many of the seemingly disparate facts.

Father James's noticeable uneasiness before the murder, the unexplained sequence of actions in the priest's study, and the seeming difficulty in finding a connection with anyone who might have a personal reason for killing him.

"If he didna' have any proof of what had been done, whatever the crime was, then he couldna' go to the Inspector with suspicion. But someone might ha' *feared* he would."

"Yes. Especially since Blevins was a member of his church. Secrets have more than one kind of power . . ."

A very clever piecing together of a puzzle—that had destroyed Father James, in the end.

The only question was: What crime had Father James stumbled over, and if the evidence of it had died with him, then where were the small signs of his knowledge that must surely have existed somewhere?

Or had the killer found them when he overturned the study, and taken them away along with the bazaar funds that were kept in the desk?

A few pounds that provided an apparent motive—but were just an opportune shield for the real motive.

Hamish reminded him: The theft had sent Inspector Blevins off on a wild-goose chase that had yielded a suspect.

"And Walsh could still be the man we're after . . ."

That would be irony, if he was.

But how long had it taken Father James to weave together the strands of truth that had turned into knowledge?

Begin with the bazaar, Hamish advised.

"No, I'm going back to the study," Rutledge told him.

He set out for the police station to ask permission of Inspector Blevins.

As before, Mrs. Wainer had no wish to accompany Rutledge upstairs.

"I've come to believe that Inspector Blevins has found the man who did this terrible murder. He told me himself that the proof was clear, and I've had time now to think about it a little. I ought to admit that I was wrong about the revenge; it's just prolonging the pain, and taking me nowhere. And so I've begun to box up Father James's belongings, to send to his sister. If the Bishop names a new priest soon, the rectory should be ready for him. It's my duty!"

Rutledge glanced around the parlor. It seemed unchanged from his last visit. "What have you removed?"

She looked down at her hands, her face torn. "I started with his old things in the garden shed, and then the kitchen entry. I find it hard to think about touching this parlor—or facing the upstairs—but I'll manage. It's the last task I'll ever perform for him, you know. And I want to do it right."

"I do understand, Mrs. Wainer. I shan't keep you long. I'd like to have a look at the framed photographs if I may, and I need to ask you if Father James stored any of his private papers in some other room of the house."

"I shouldn't think so," she answered doubtfully. "There's the study and the bedroom, and a room just down the passage that's always been used to hold parish books and the like. Accounts, for one thing, and the church records—baptisms, deaths, marriages. There's a grand number of them now; the books fill two shelves." It was said with pride.

But these would be passed on to the incoming man. The public duty, and not the private life. "I'm sure they do. Can we begin with the parlor, perhaps? Show me, if you will, what belonged to Father James personally."

She began by the windows, picking up each photograph. "That's the little house in Cumberland, over near Keswick, where he spent an entire week just before the War. It poured cats and ducks, and he couldn't set foot out the door without a thorough drenching. He played backgammon until he was blind, he said. And here's the young priest who was ordained with him. Father Austin. He died of the gassing in the War, poor soul . . ."

Each of the photographs had a story, but none of them appeared to have special significance. Mrs. Wainer moved on to the small treasures.

"He liked pipes, although he never smoked, and he collected more than a dozen," she reminisced as she touched each one. "And over there is the walking stick, in that Chinese umbrella stand, that he carried with him to Wales and the Lake District. Westmorland. The stand belonged to a great-aunt, it was a wedding gift to her, and I'll be shipping that along to his sister. And the clock on the mantel there—"

There were books on the shelves that were Father James's, his name inscribed in a fine copperplate hand, mixed among others that belonged in the rectory. Rutledge turned the pages briefly, but found nothing of interest tucked between the leaves.

"Hardly secret vices and dark crimes," Hamish mocked.

When Rutledge turned to the stairs, the housekeeper said, as she had before, "Go on then. I'll have a cup of tea ready, when you've done your work." She had returned to the kitchen before he had reached the top step.

He went first to the small room where the ledgers of church and rectory business transactions were kept, and where the heavy, bound books with *Church Records* on their spines stood on a separate pair of shelves.

Looking through the ledgers first, Rutledge found, in various hands, the long list of repairs and improvements, wages and offerings that represented decades of activity. The roof of the rectory had been repaired after a storm in 1903, and there was a faded receipt in the rough, untutored hand of the man who had done the work. You could, Rutledge thought, identify with certainty every expenditure: when it was made, to whom, and for what purpose. And the name of the priest incumbent at the time. Every penny of income was noted, every payment of wages due. He found the entry, scrupulously made in Father James's hand, of the sum earned at the bazaar: eleven pounds, three shillings, six pence. The last entry was wages paid to Mrs. Wainer, two days before the priest had died.

The great volumes of church records listed the names of priests and sextons, altar boys and gravediggers over the years; a compendium of who had served God and in what capacity. Later pages recorded baptisms by date, with the name given the child, the sponsoring godparents, and the parents. By accident Rutledge came across the name "Blevins," and found the Inspector's own baptism: pages later, that of his first child. Among the marriages were Blevins's, Mrs. Wainer's, and others whose names Rutledge recognized.

The deaths were more somber: *George Peters, Aged Forty-seven Years, Three Months, and Four Days, died this Day of Grace, Sunday, Twenty-four August, in the year of Our Lord, Eighteen Hundred and Forty-Eight, of a fall down a well shaft in Hunstanton on Saturday the twenty-third.* And later on: *Infant son of Mary and Henry Cuthbert, stillborn, this Fourteenth Day of March, Eighteen Hundred and Sixty-Two, laid to rest beside seven brothers and sisters. May God have Mercy on His Soul.*

It was the chronicle of life and death in a small village, perhaps the only mark many of these people had made in their short span on earth. He found it sad to read. *Jocelyn Mercer, Aged Three Days short of Her Fourteenth Year, of Diphtheria . . . Roger Benning, Aged Five Years, Two Months, and Seven Days, of Cholera . . .* The last volume ended with Seven July, Nineteen Twelve. The latest must, he thought, be kept in the church vestry.

The room yielded nothing more of interest—it was, as he'd thought, a public room, where the church officers had as much right of access as the priest.

Rutledge moved on to the study. From what Blevins had told him, Rutledge knew that Mrs. Wainer had restored the scattered papers and books and other belongings to their proper places. She wouldn't allow the police to touch them.

Rutledge thumbed through the books, studied the photographs on the table by the hearth and on the mantel. They were a record of friends and family over the years, of journeys to Wales, of the great Fells in the Lake District. He even lifted the cushions of the settle.

This room was in some respects another public place, where Father James counseled his parish or talked to young couples on the brink of marriage or heard the grieving words of widows and parents and children. Where the deacons came and discussed church affairs. Where any person might wait, and with natural curiosity, look around him. Hence even the flimsy lock on the desk, perhaps . . .

Hamish said, "But the *Titanic* cuttings were *here,* on the desk, when the doctor saw them."

"Yes, that's true. He walked in while Father James was examining them, most likely." Rutledge searched through the desk with care. Nothing of interest. And no photographs, framed or otherwise. Just as the solicitor had said.

Moving on to the bedroom, Rutledge felt his usual sense of distaste. He disliked what he was about to do, hating the need to violate the privacy of the dead. But murder victims lost not only their lives and their dignity but their innermost thoughts and secrets, secrets they would have preferred to deal with, if they'd been warned they were about to die.

He himself was careful not to preserve any record of the voice in his head. There was no diary entry, no letter, not even a conversation with a friend that would distress his sister, Frances, after he was gone. Only the private files in Dr. Fleming's office, and Fleming could be depended upon to leave them sealed.

"Was that what fashed Baker?" Hamish asked. "He couldna' rise from his bed, and he couldna' ask the Vicar to look into a drawer or burn a letter."

It was something to consider. It would, indeed, explain why Father James had wanted to be so certain of Baker's state of mind before he carried out whatever instructions he may have been given. For instance, burning an old love letter . . .

Rutledge searched through the priest's meager belongings, the clothing in the wardrobe and the church robes folded in the chest at the foot of the bed. Relieved to find nothing of consequence there, he stood in the middle of the room, thinking.

Hamish said, "It was no' a verra' guid idea after all—"

Rutledge replied absently, "The frustrating part of the search is not knowing what I'm after. Or if it exists in any recognizable fashion."

Monsignor Holston's words came back to him: *If you come to me with the truth, and I recognize it, I'll tell you so.*"

There were other rooms on the first floor. But opening the doors confirmed what Rutledge expected: bedchambers made up for guests, with nothing in them of a personal nature and all of them scrupulously clean.

"You couldna' hide a wee mouse in here," Hamish commented as Rutledge closed the last of the doors.

He climbed the narrow, uncarpeted flight of stairs to the top floor. Rooms here had been designed for servants—small and without character, unfurnished for the most part, or cluttered with the collected debris of several generations. Lamps, iron bedsteads, rusted coal scuttles, a wardrobe with one door warped on its hinges, chairs with caned seats that had never been mended, chipped mirrors, and the like. Even a broken window sash leaned against an inside wall next to two rakes whose bamboo handles had splintered.

A few of the odds and ends appeared to have been used year after year for bazaars, including a small cart, half a dozen umbrellas and long wooden tables, boxes of signs and ribbons, and the kit of clown's makeup that Father James must have favored for entertaining the children.

There was also, near the top of the steps, where Rutledge would have expected to find such things, a small traveling trunk and a valise that bore the priest's name on the labels. Cheap, conservative, and well worn.

Running probing fingers through the jumble of belongings stored in the trunk, he came across the corners of an envelope, fairly large and rather thick, but unevenly so, as if there were several things stuffed inside. Lifting out the assortment of hats and gloves and hiking boots that lay on top, he picked up the packet, testing its weight in his hands. It had been neither hidden away nor in plain sight.

Letters from Father James's dead sister Judith? Or the ones he had written to her, with that enigmatic reference to the Giant?

Inspector Blevins would be pleased if they were!

Rutledge sat down on the dusty floorboards, his elbows resting on his bent knees, and held the envelope upright between his spread feet.

There were no identifying marks—it hadn't been mailed and there was no name on the outside.

As he opened the flap and looked in, Rutledge said "Ah!" in almost a sigh. A fat collection of cuttings met his eye. Drawing them out, careful not to lose one, he could already see that they were newspaper and magazine accounts of the sinking of a ship that was unsinkable.

Sorting through them at random, he noted that certain developments had been clipped together—the publicity over departure, the tragedy, the search for bodies, reports from Ireland, editorial reflections on the tragic loss of life, lists of the dead and missing, accounts of the ensuing inquiry—as if Father James had carefully cataloged each new addition to his accumulating data. In the margins were handwritten notes, referring the reader from one article to another.

Dr. Stephenson was right—this had all the hallmarks of an obsession, not a passing fancy. Too much work had been done to coordinate all the information. Photographs from news accounts ranged from smiling Society figures boarding the great liner to pitiable corpses lying in plain wooden coffins in Ireland, eyes half shut and faces flaccid.

It was, in all conscience, Rutledge thought, a gruesome collection.

He looked down into the trunk to see what else might have been

stored there, then ran his fingers again through the oddments of belongings that had formed the bottom layer. A frame came to light, one edge
caught in a knitted scarf. Rutledge retrieved it and turned it over.

A young woman standing beside a horse, her face bright in the sun,
smiled up at him, her hair shiningly fair. Judging from the lovely hat
in one hand and the stylishness of the dress she wore, she was well-
to-do.

But who was she? Was this the photograph that Father James had
left to May Trent? There was no resemblance between the two women.
Nor was there any to Priscilla Connaught. Rutledge hadn't met most of
the other women in Osterley. Frederick Gifford's dead wife? The doctor's daughter? Someone from the priest's youth?

"Look on the reverse," Hamish suggested. And Rutledge took
the back out of the frame to remove the photograph. There was a date:
10 July, 1911. And the words, lightly inscribed, so as not to mar the face.
Gratefully, V.

V. Victoria sprang to mind. It had been a popular girls' name
throughout the late Queen's reign. As Mary was now, in honor of the
present Queen. Vera? Vivian. Veronica. Virginia. Verity. Violet?

He ran out of possibilities.

Still, Blevins could perhaps help him there. Or Mrs. Wainer.

On the other hand—

Hamish said it for him. "I wouldna' be in haste to show it."

Getting to his feet, Rutledge found a flat leather case lying in a corner of the room, a coating of dust covering it, and a cobweb linking it
to the frame of the bottomless chair beside it. The grip was broken at
one end, but it would do.

Rutledge looked around him a last time at the "waste not, want
not" philosophy of householders who store in their upper floors and at-
tics the ruined furnishings and venerable treasures they couldn't quite
bring themselves to throw away. *In the event it's ever needed.* And most
of it lay there still, forgotten and unwanted, from generation to generation. Judging by the dust and cobwebs, even Mrs. Wainer seldom ven-
tured up here. . . .

He wondered if Father James had kept that in mind when he stored
the clippings and the photograph in his trunk. Or if that was where they
were generally kept.

Rutledge shook the dust from the leather case, sneezing heavily, and
discovered that there was a mouse hole in one corner of the leather.

Human flotsam and jetsam, Hamish pointed out, sometimes served other creatures well.

Smiling at that, Rutledge set the cuttings and the photograph inside, closed the flap, and looked into the small trunk a last time—even stretching his fingers inside the torn corner of the lining on the right side—before deciding that he had the lot. He carefully repacked the clothing before going down the attic stairs.

When Rutledge walked through to the kitchen, the housekeeper was standing at the back door, in the midst of a lively conversation with the coal man. His apron, black with coal dust, matched the color of his eyes, and the bulbous nose matched the heavy chest that spread out from wide, muscular shoulders.

Rutledge's tea was ready on a tray, the kettle steaming gently on top of the stove. An ironed, white serviette over a plate kept sliced sandwiches moist.

Hamish said, "If you didna' stay, chances are, he will—"

And in the same instant, the coal man looked up with disappointment on his face as Rutledge stepped into the kitchen.

Rutledge said, "Mrs. Wainer, I've finished for the moment. I have a few papers here that I shall need to look over and return to you—"

"Papers?" She turned with some alarm, her eyes flying to the case he was carrying.

"Old cuttings, for the most part. Dated well before the War. I'll just look through them before you box them up with the rest of Father James's possessions. But you never know, do you, where something useful might turn up?"

She hesitated, clearly uncertain where her responsibility lay. Rutledge added, "They're to do with shipping, not church business. Perhaps you've seen them on his desk. A hobby of his, was it? To study maritime affairs?" It was as far as he was willing to go, with the coal man unashamedly listening to every word.

"There was nothing like that in his desk," she protested, but before she could ask to have a look at them the coal man stepped forward.

"Begging pardon, sir. Shipping, you said? Not that ship that sank back in '12, was it?" His heavy hands, with coal dust thick in the cracks and creases, worked at his apron, as if not accustomed to speaking to his betters before spoken to.

"As I remember there was a reference to *Titanic,*" Rutledge replied guardedly. "Yes."

"Then if I might offer a word, sir?" There was a diffident smile on his face. "My daughter, she's got herself a fine situation in London. Father James—God rest his soul!—asked if she might do him a small favor, and he sent her twenty pounds to buy up all the London papers and cut out whatever there was about the ship's sinking and the inquiry. He wanted every word she could find. And she must have sent him dozens of cuttings, sir, by post every week."

Rutledge opened the case and pulled out the cuttings, laying them on the table and spreading them with one finger. "Like these?"

The coal man came closer, peering down his nose as if shortsighted. "Aye, I shouldn't be at all surprised, though I never saw 'em. Jessie sent them straight to the rectory." He paused, and when Rutledge didn't move the cuttings, he added, "When t'other ship was torpedoed, that *Lusitania,* my daughter wrote him to ask if he wanted her to do the same again. But he thanked her and said he'd seen enough of tragedy. His very words."

"And so it would be your guess, would it, that this was a passing fancy?"

"He never spoke to me about that ship!" Mrs. Wainer seemed hurt that she'd been left out of his confidence. "It was the talk of England, and I don't remember he ever said anything more than what a pity it was."

"But do you recall seeing the letters coming from London?"

"As a rule, Father James collected the post," she explained. "But you'd have thought, if they were that important, he might have asked me to be on the lookout for them." She peered down at the cuttings again. "I'd have put them in a scrapbook for him if he'd wanted me to. It's just not like him not to say a word!"

"And no' like him to lie to the doctor," Hamish added, an echo of Rutledge's own thought.

Turning to the coal man, Rutledge asked, "Did you ever tell anyone about the favor your daughter was doing for the priest?"

The jowly face flushed. "No, sir!"

"It would be natural—a matter of pride!"

"My work takes me into any number of houses, sir," the coal man said with a certain dignity, "and I never gossip about one to t'other. Ask Mrs. Wainer if she's ever heard me gossip!"

Mrs. Wainer shook her head. "No, he never does."

Rutledge collected the cuttings once more and put them back in the case. "Thank you, Mrs. Wainer. You'll have these papers back within the week. I shan't have time for tea after all. Do you mind?"

She was still more than a little concerned about the papers, but said doubtfully, "If they'll help in any way, sir, then by all means . . ."

Rutledge spent the next hour in his room, going through the yellowing cuttings. They were dated in an untrained hand, with the name of the newspaper or magazine written underneath. The coal man's daughter? Another—the priest's?—had underlined names of passengers, marking each with an *S* noting survivors, an *X* noting the recovered and identified dead, and an *M* for known missing. This was a sad and depressing list, but those who had not been recovered were sometimes mentioned by name—the wealthy, the powerful, the famous. There were hundreds with no grave but the sea and no one to ask about them—or grieve for them. Whole families lost together.

Which was, in a sense, more haunting, but at the same time perhaps, kinder.

Rutledge put the cuttings aside for a moment and stood by his windows looking out at the marshes. He glimpsed Peter Henderson walking along the quay, head down, shoulders hunched, and wondered if the man had a home to go to. And then recalled that his family had cut him off. Where then did he live?

His mind on the clippings again, Rutledge felt a sadness that came from touching the tragedy of others. One could claim that it was fate, the invincible weight of the iceberg and the unsinkable ship colliding on a cold night in the North Atlantic, where there should have been no such danger at that time of the year. Who chose those who would live, and who would die? Was that what disturbed the priest? That so many could simply be left to freeze and drown in the sea by an omniscient and all-powerful God? There were 1,513 known to be dead. . . .

Or was it far more personal than an exercise in the definition of God?

He went back to work, rubbing his shoulders as he concentrated on the cuttings, looking for a clue.

And in the end, he found not what he was looking for, but what he had not expected to see in these articles.

The name of Marianna Trent . . .

She had been dragged into one of the lifeboats, unconscious from a blow to the head. A blessing perhaps, with fractured ribs and a broken leg. Speculation was that she'd been struck by another boat while floating in the water. A sensation at first, for she had no name, and later of no interest to journalists hungry for fresh news. She must have remained in hospital in Ireland for some time, because there was a small cutting dated three weeks after the disaster, relating that this woman had been released and was returning to England, her leg still in a cast but healed sufficiently to travel. The article also contained a small and telling final paragraph.

"Miss Trent, whom the doctors have pronounced fully recovered, has no memory of the tragedy, but says that she dreams at night about falling into black water. When interviewed by the shipping authorities, she could provide no new information about the collision or the subsequent actions of officers or passengers to save the doomed ship."

How well, Hamish asked with interest, did Father James know this woman before she came to Osterley? *Titanic* went down in April 1912—

It was, Rutledge thought, a question to pursue.

In the end, Rutledge went not to Inspector Blevins but to the Vicar of Holy Trinity as the most likely person to give him the truth.

Mr. Sims had been sitting in his study, working on his sermon for the coming Sunday service, and he led Rutledge to the cluttered, book-filled room with the air of a man just released from prison.

"You'd think," he said ruefully, "that for a man of the Cloth, divine inspiration would pour forth like water from a holy spring. I've agonized over this week's message for hours and still have no idea what I'm trying to say."

He looked tired, as if he hadn't slept, shadows emphasizing the blueness of his eyes.

"How is the painting coming?" Rutledge asked, for the smell of wet paint was still pervasive.

"With greater speed than my persuasive powers. My sister is wary about changing schools this far into the year. Her children are sad to leave their friends. Her own friends are asking her if she'd be happy here in the Broads. I have run out of words for *her*, too." The last was said on a sigh.

When they were seated in the study, with its dark paneling and almost grimly Victorian austerity, Hamish said, "This is no' a place of inspiration!"

Rutledge had to agree. The gargoyles that surmounted the hearth, and the agony-stricken caryatids that supported it, two well-muscled monsters with their mouths twisted open with effort, were depressingly vivid.

Catching his expression as he glanced at them, Sims smiled. "I find this room most useful when I'm discussing appropriate behavior in church with small boys. They can't take their eyes off the figures, and it drives home my message quite well."

"I think I'd find it more comfortable writing with my back to them." Rutledge's voice was light. "Unless the subject was Judgment and Damnation."

Sims laughed outright. "It never occurred to me. This was the study of the Vicar before me, and I've tried to follow his example."

"Better, surely, to follow your own? There must be any number of rooms in this house that are more cheerful."

Sims nodded. "Actually, there is a small office I'm fond of. Now, tell me how I can help you with your problems? Any news on the man Blevins is holding?"

"The police are still tracing his movements." Rutledge gave the stock answer. He waited for a moment, and then asked, "You were there, when Father James left the bedside at Herbert Baker's house?"

"Yes. He came into the parlor and the Bakers offered him a cup of tea. He was tired, but he sat down and—in my opinion—made the family feel a little more comfortable about what Baker had done, in sending for a priest."

"Did he bring anything with him, that Baker might have given him? An envelope, a small package—" He left the sentence unfinished.

"No. He had his small case with him. With consecrated wafers and wine. If there was something Baker had wanted him to have, it was small enough to fit in there. Or his pocket. Why? Does the family think anything is missing? I can't believe—"

"Nothing is missing," Rutledge replied quickly. "I found myself wondering if perhaps Baker had given him a letter to post. It's as likely an explanation as any for Baker's whim." He shrugged, as if it wasn't important. "Put it down to curiosity—the besetting sin of a policeman's mind. No, what actually brought me are these."

He had folded a half dozen of the cuttings to fit into his breast pocket, and now he took them out to hand to the Vicar. "Tell me what you make of these."

The Vicar unfolded them and began to sift through the cuttings. "They appear to be news articles of the ship that sank back in '12." He looked up, a question on his face, as if uncertain what Rutledge wanted from him. "Were they Baker's?"

"I shouldn't think they have anything to do with Baker. No, I found them among Father James's papers. And this—" He took the photograph from his pocket and passed it across the desk.

Something changed in Sims's expression. "How did you come by this?" His voice was carefully neutral.

"Do you recognize the woman?"

"No, I think you must tell me first how you came to have this!"

"It was also in Father James's possession. From what I've learned, just before his death he chose to add a codicil to his Will, leaving what I believe to be this photograph to someone—"

The Vicar's face had paled, as if the blood had rushed to his heart and left his skin without its natural ruddy color. "Not to me! *He would never have bequeathed it to me!*" His voice was constricted by a tight throat. But he couldn't take his eyes from what he held in both hands, as if it were a treasure—or a dangerous thing.

Rutledge, watching him, said, "Why not? If you know the woman?"

"I know—*knew*—her."

"Can you tell me her name?" He moved gently, carefully, keenly aware that he was trodding on very emotional ground.

"She's dead! Let her rest in peace. She had nothing to do with Father James—"

"He never met her?" Rutledge deliberately took the words literally.

"Of course he'd met her—but she wasn't a member of his parish, she didn't live in Osterley—" His words were disjointed, as if he spoke without thinking, responding to the tone of voice and not the sense of Rutledge's questions.

"Then she was a member of your parish."

"No. Not at all."

With an effort, the young Vicar handed the framed photograph back to Rutledge. It was an act of denial. As if by giving it back, he was absolved of any more questions about it.

"You haven't given me her name," Rutledge reminded him.

"Look," Sims said, his eyes wretched with pain, "this is a personal matter. She had nothing to do with the priest or his church or his death. How could she have? She had nothing to do with me, not really. Not in the true sense. It's been seven years—she's been *dead* for seven years! Just—leave it, will you?"

"I can't. Until I'm satisfied that something Father James kept seven years and then felt was important enough to bequeath to someone in his Will, shortly before his murder, is not a matter of grave concern." He chose the word purposefully. Not death. Murder. Violent and intentional murder.

It brought Sims out of his shock. His face seemed to collapse, as if Rutledge had so completely broken down his defenses that he had nowhere left to turn. He had never been a forceful man, he had never had the strength of a Father James, and yet in his own fashion he did have the ability to face the truth.

"For God's sake—" he asked, "—*did* he leave it to me?" When Rutledge said nothing, he went on, "All right. If I tell you what you want to know, will you leave us both in peace? Just—leave us in peace!" He stopped, as if afraid he might say too much.

"What was she to you, if you weren't her priest?"

Sims's eyes went to the caryatids, the anguished figures howling in pain as they supported the heavy weight of the mantel. Rutledge thought, *He knows how they feel—his burden is as heavy.*

Hamish said, "He was in love wi' her. Let it be!"

But Rutledge waited, forcing Sims to say what he did not want to say.

"I—I cared about her, because she was in trouble. But there was nothing I could do to help. With all the might of the Church behind me, *there was nothing I could do to help her!*"

CHAPTER SEVENTEEN

IN THE SILENCE THAT FOLLOWED, RUTLEDGE gave Sims a space in which to collect himself.

Then he asked, "What was her name? Victoria? Vera? Ver—"

"I won't give you her name," the Vicar broke in wearily. "For God's sake, man, have a little sense! She's long dead, and you'll only stir up what's best forgotten. I gave that photograph to Father James my-self, for safekeeping. It was—it was part of a promise. And I kept it, that promise. I did what was asked of me while she was alive, and I tried to close the door once she was dead. I don't know why he wished me to have it again. I thought perhaps he'd burned it years ago. But I never quite had the courage to ask. Who knows about this? Gifford? I'll have to speak to him—"

"Father James didn't leave it to you," Rutledge said finally. "But he did wish someone else to have it."

The impact of the Londoner's words left Sims stunned. "Not to *me*? Merciful God!" He tried to absorb that, and then asked, "If not to me—then to whom?" When Rutledge didn't answer immediately, Sims continued. "Look, you've got to tell me! That photograph could do unimaginable harm."

Rutledge said, "If that's true—that a dead woman's photograph could do such harm—I can't imagine that Father James would have kept it, much less passed it on. He wasn't, from all I've learned about him, either cruel or callous."

"But don't you see? It was given to *me*. Out of simple fondness—a gesture that was meant in all innocence. That's the trouble, it could be misconstrued—interpreted in another light. It would sully her memory, to no purpose. If you won't tell me, I'll go to Gifford myself—"

Relenting, and at the same time testing the waters, Rutledge answered, "I can't tell you. But if it matters, this was bequeathed to a woman, not a man."

Sims leaned back in his chair, a man emptied of all feelings. "Yes, that makes a kind of sense. Thank God!" And then he repeated silently, *Thank God!,* his lips moving without his knowledge, as if they uttered a prayer.

Hamish's first question came when the motorcar was turning through the vicarage gates into Trinity Lane. "He didna' ask you who the woman was. He didna' care."

"I think he cared—but he felt it was right—just—that she should have it."

"Which means he already kens the name of the woman."

"Or—thinks he does. Interesting, isn't it?"

Mrs. Barnett was crossing the lobby when Rutledge came into the hotel. He stopped her, and left a message for May Trent to give him a time and place where they could meet. He included the words Official Business.

She was still out, Mrs. Barnett informed him as she took the folded sheet of notepaper and put it safely in the drawer of the reception desk. And might be staying the night with her friends.

He didn't think that was likely. May Trent was avoiding him.

———

Rutledge went over the cuttings again, looking for any connection between May Trent and any other passenger on the ship and for anyone with a name beginning with V.

But he found no guidance in the reports of the sinking, the survivors, the missing, or the dead. Nothing that leaped out at him as the answer he sought.

He was on his way down the stairs to put in a call to the Yard, to ask Sergeant Gibson—who had an absolute gift for ferreting out information—to look into the shipping files at Lloyds and the White Star Line for women passengers whose Christian name began with a V. The first words out of the crusty old Sergeant's mouth were likely to be "And are there any other miracles, sir, that you might require of me?"

Instead he met Mrs. Barnett coming up to find him. "There's a telephone call from the Yard, Inspector. It's urgent."

He thanked her and followed her back to the narrow little office. "Rutledge here," he said into the phone.

Sergeant Wilkerson's voice came down the line with the force of a foghorn. "That you, sir? I've got a bit of bad news. Or it might be good news, depending on one's point of view!"

"What is it, Sergeant?"

"That Iris Kenneth we found dead in the river, sir. Well, it isn't her after all. Iris Kenneth just walked in her landlady's front door and like to've given the old biddy apoplexy on the spot. Thought she'd seen a ghost, she did. But it was a very angry ghost, who was soon threatening to have her up for theft for disposing of her personal property. Which the landlady, if you recall, sir, had already sold."

"Are you quite sure," Rutledge said, "that the woman is truly Iris Kenneth? This time?"

"Oh, yes, sir. There was quite a row, and the local station sent a pair of constables along to see what it was about. All the roomers living there swear that it's Iris, but of course Mrs. Rollings is fit to be tied, claiming *she* never clapped eyes on this woman in her life! Well, stands to reason," he added, suppressing a gleeful note in his voice. "She's likely to be taken up on charges."

Rutledge thought, *It must have been quite an entertaining scene.* "Where has Iris been, did she tell you?"

"By the time I arrived, there was some semblance of peace, and she confessed she's been staying with friends in Cardiff, hoping for a part in some production there. In my opinion, she was short of money and ruralizing until something came up. At any rate, I took the liberty of contacting the Cardiff police, and they just sent word she's telling the truth."

If she was Iris Kenneth—who was the woman in the river? And what did the corpse have to do with Matthew Walsh?

Hamish answered him. "Nothing at all."

Rutledge asked Wilkerson if he'd questioned Iris Kenneth about Walsh.

"That I did, sir! And she tells me he's a devious bastard who would strangle his own mother." Wilkerson's laughter boomed down the line, nearly deafening Rutledge. "She hasn't had any decent work since he let her go, and if she could point to him being Jack the Ripper, she'd be happy to do it. It's anger talking, in my view. Revenge. She doesn't sound afraid of him, only furious with him. I asked her if he'd threatened her or hurt her in any way—showing his violent nature, so to speak. She swore he never touched her—she'd had a little knife to use on him if he had—but he's a brute and a niggardly bastard, and selfish to boot."

A woman scorned.

"If you learn anything about the other woman, let me know."

"She's gone into a pauper's grave," Wilkerson replied. "There won't be any more interest in that one. More's the pity, but still, she won't be the last. If something does come up, I'll make sure you hear of it."

Rutledge asked for Sergeant Gibson, but was told that he was giving evidence in court for the next two days.

Blevins took Rutledge's news with a shrug. "We're not making much headway, ourselves. An old Gypsy who scratches his living sharpening scissors and tinkering is not likely to hold the police in high regard. They've moved him along too many times, and treated him like a pariah. He won't forgive that. And he'll lie like a sailor to get his own back! It won't matter to him whether Matthew Walsh killed a priest or not."

"Has this scissor sharpener—Bolton—ever been charged by the police? Other than rousting him as a public nuisance?"

"Nothing that could be proved against him." In frustration Blevins added, "They're worthless, that lot." Deserved or not, it was the general view of Gypsies: thieves and liars and heathen, filthy and secretive vagabonds. "Inspector Arnold, who first interviewed this man, is of the opinion that he's probably up to his neck in this, which means he'll stay with his story for his own sake, not Walsh's."

Rutledge said nothing.

Blevins smiled ruefully. "Well, I'm glad of course for Iris Kenneth's sake that she's alive and safe, but it would have helped our case against Walsh if we could have charged him with her murder as well. Your Sergeant Wilkerson is sure, is he?"

"The other roomers in that boardinghouse had no reason to lie."

"No." He moved papers around on his desk and then said, "It has to be Walsh! There's no one else it could have been." His eyes, looking up suddenly, dared Rutledge to refute it.

"He has the best motive for murder that we've found so far," Rutledge answered neutrally. "That has to count for something. Will you tell Walsh, or shall I? That Iris Kenneth is alive?"

"I'll tell him." There was resignation in Blevins's voice. "We can't charge him for the real drowning victim's death, can we?" It wasn't meant to be answered; it was no more than a reflection of his mood.

"Ever hear Father James speak of an interest in ships?"

"Ships? He was interested in the small boats around here. Handled the oars like a man used to the water. We've been out fishing a time or two, but he never said anything to me about ships. Why?"

"I wondered, that's all. I found some cuttings among his papers. They had to do with *Titanic* sinking."

"I'm not surprised. Shocking, the loss of life. We all felt it."

"Yes." Rutledge let the silence lengthen before adding, "And *Lusitania*. Did he ever speak of her?"

"I'm sure he was horrified, everyone was. What's this in aid of?"

"I don't know," Rutledge answered. "At the moment, very little."

Blevins grinned without humor. "You're reaching, man!"

At the dinner hour Rutledge found his place at the only table set. Mrs. Barnett said, "I'm afraid it's rather lonely tonight. Thursdays often are."

Later, as she brought his main course, she informed him, "I've had no word from Miss Trent. Were you expecting her to join you for dinner?"

"No. Yes. I've some questions to ask her."

Her gaze sharpened. "Oh?"

Rutledge smiled. "I wanted to ask her about a photograph I found. I thought it might be of interest to her."

"I can't imagine how. She isn't local. Perhaps I could help you?"

"It's in my room. I'll bring it down after dinner—"

The front door opened, and someone came into the lobby. Both Rutledge and Mrs. Barnett looked up.

It was May Trent.

She found them staring at her, and it seemed to startle her, but she said nothing, going directly to the stairs and starting up them. Leaving his meal to follow her, Rutledge caught up with her on the landing.

"I need to speak to you," he said.

"I'm tired—"

"No, I don't want excuses. If you don't mind coming to my room, it will take no more than five minutes." When she seemed on the point of arguing, Rutledge said, "My food is getting cold. Will you come with me or not?"

She looked back down the stairs, as if hoping to see Mrs. Barnett staring up at them. But she found no help there. The innkeeper was in the kitchens.

"All right. Five minutes."

She went ahead of him, and he opened the door of his room for her, leaving it standing wide. There was no one to overhear their conversation.

May Trent looked about her with interest, as if mentally comparing his accommodations with her own.

He went to the desk drawer, and on a sudden whim, took out the photograph first.

Handing it to her, Rutledge said, "Can you identify this woman?"

It was a natural question. He had no intention of upsetting her and was completely unprepared for her reaction. Her face crumpled, as if she was on the verge of tears. But none came. Her eyes were dry and furious.

Jerking the photograph from his hand, she turned it on its face and dropped it on the bed, as if it had burned her fingers. "No. I won't talk to you! I won't!" She moved to go, and he stopped her, his hand on her arm. "Let go of me!" she cried, color flaring in her face.

"You can talk to me here, or you can talk to me at the police station," he said angrily. "Your choice!"

"I'm leaving Osterley. I've only come to pack my bags and go. My friends are waiting—"

"They've gone to London," he told her, guessing. "And I can put you under arrest if I have to, to keep you here. There's an empty cell next to Walsh."

She rounded on him, anguish in her eyes. "I won't talk about it, do you hear! I couldn't tell you anything if I had to, don't you understand? I don't *know* anything! *I can't remember anything!*"

Hamish cautioned, "Someone is coming."

There was the sound of someone walking down the passage, a soft footfall. It was Mrs. Barnett. She stopped in the doorway, horrified by the sight of Rutledge clutching May Trent's arm as she tried to fight free of his grip.

"Inspector Rutledge!" Mrs. Barnett exclaimed, moving toward them.

He looked up, speaking with the cold air of command that had served him on the battlefield when his mind had been too tired and too worn to think. "Mrs. Barnett. Sit down. Now."

She opened her mouth, stared at them, and sat.

"There's a photograph on the bed. The one I spoke of earlier." He kept his grip on May Trent's arm as he spoke. The skin was warm through the cloth of the sweater she was wearing over her long skirt. "Pick it up, and tell me if you will, whether you recognize the woman in it."

She reached for it, turning it over, frowning at the face looking back at her. "I think—well, I know it's a photograph of Virginia Sedgwick. Lord Sedgwick's late daughter-in-law."

May Trent had begun to cry, her face averted, half shielded by her shoulder.

"She was the wife of his elder son? Arthur?"

"Yes. That's right. But why should you be harassing Miss Trent with it? She never even met this woman, as far as I know!"

"How did Virginia Sedgwick die?"

"She disappeared. No one knew where she had gone. It was whispered that she'd run away from her husband, but I know that couldn't have been true! She just wasn't the sort."

Hamish said, "It's been said of many a wife. That she wasna' the sort. But who can be certain?"

"I don't understand, what is this about?" Mrs. Barnett was still wearing her apron, and she wiped a smudge from the glass over the photograph. "Please, will you not let Miss Trent go?"

"Did her husband ever find Mrs. Sedgwick?"

"No. That is to say, not alive. She went down on that ship, you see. *Titanic*. She wasn't using her married name, and no one thought to look under any other, until Lord Sedgwick hired someone to do what the police apparently couldn't—" She stopped, biting her lip in embarrassment.

"How do you know all this?" he asked.

"My husband told me—he'd met Edwin on the train, coming back from London. Edwin was quite upset. He said his father and Arthur had gone to Ireland to bring back the body."

"I'd read that most of the dead were buried in unmarked graves?"

"So they were. But Lord Sedgwick was convinced he could find her. For Arthur's sake. And he must have been successful; I heard there was a service in the little church on the Sedgwick estate. The Queen sent flowers, I was told."

Rutledge released May Trent.

Hamish rasped, "Ask her—!"

He said to her, "Does the Vicar know you were on *Titanic*? That you may have met Virginia Sedgwick, and seen her drown? Or that Father James was trying to awaken your memories?"

"No! I have never told anyone here! Father James—he had clippings—he'd seen my name among the survivors, and he wanted—" She stopped, unable to go on.

"And you can't remember what happened the night of the sinking."

She shook her head, her dark hair spilling over her face, hiding it.

But Father James had bequeathed her the photograph. And asked that she do something about it—find the courage, as he'd put it.

The priest hadn't believed that her memory of that night had never been regained. Or else he had hoped that given time—and over the years he thought he still had to live—she might yet remember. Still, it was a strange way to go about it—to leave a message in a Will. Once he was dead, what difference would it make?

The cuttings. The photograph. The bequest.

But why was it so important to Father James?

It went through Rutledge's mind before he could stop himself from thinking the unthinkable. That perhaps May Trent had killed the priest, to prevent him from prying into memories that she could not face. And never wanted to face.

Some eight months ago, he himself had tried to kill the doctor who had forced the secret of his own ghosts out of the silence he had wrapped around himself like a dark and protective cloak.

May Trent had suddenly found herself in the running, with a better reason than Walsh for committing murder. . . .

Abruptly realizing that both May Trent and Mrs. Barnett were watching him, he made an effort to meet the younger woman's eyes.

They flickered, as she read his thoughts.

"I didn't kill him," she said quietly, numbness washing all expression out of her face. *"Truly . . ."*

But what, Hamish was demanding, if the worried priest had backed away from confrontation, and written the codicil to his Will instead, hoping that in time May Trent might relent and do whatever it was that mattered so much to him? Only to learn that it was already too late; he'd set in motion a chain of events that couldn't be reversed. . . .

Something that need never reach the light of day, if he lived to old age.

Rutledge said harshly, to the two women in his room and to the voice in his head, "I don't know the answer. I wish to God I did!"

CHAPTER EIGHTEEN

THERE WAS ABSOLUTE SILENCE FOR A long, disturbing moment.

Mrs. Barnett's eyes were wide with distress. The emotionally charged atmosphere had left her speechless, unprepared to take up either side.

May Trent, who had borne the brunt of Rutledge's intensity, found the inner resources to stare back at him, a remarkable strength in her face. "You don't mean that," she told him. "You *can't.*" But there were tears on her lashes.

The room seemed to shrink in on him, the walls squeezing out the air, the two women between him and the door a trap he couldn't escape from. Taking a deep breath to shake off the sense of smothering, Rutledge fell back on the one thing that had always brought him through: His ability to command.

In a voice that sounded absolutely normal, despite the turmoil that racked him, Rutledge said, "Mrs. Barnett. Can you serve Miss Trent her dinner tonight? I think she needs food, and she's not in any condition to go elsewhere."

"In her room?" Mrs. Barnett asked doubtfully, rising.

"No. In the dining room. Miss Trent, go and wash your face, then come downstairs with me." He added as she started to protest, "I promise you I won't bring up Mrs. Sedgwick or—or your own experiences. But I need to hear about Father James's interest in *Titanic* and her death. And if you will tell me that, I shall stay out of your way after tonight."

A fierce pride touched her. "I don't want your pity!"

"I'm not offering you pity. I'm searching for answers. If you can help me, I'll take that help with gratitude." Then he added with a surprising and unexpected gentleness, "Go on. It's for the best."

May Trent studied him. He could almost read what was going through her mind—that she didn't want to be alone with her thoughts—but neither was she up to enduring public scrutiny at The Pelican, if her emotional state showed as she must have felt it did. "Give me five minutes."

She walked out of the room and toward her own. Mrs. Barnett, watching her go, said to Rutledge, "That was *inexcusable.*"

"No, murder is inexcusable," he told her flatly. "I can probably understand her feelings better than most. But I won't walk away from my investigation when there are answers to be had."

"But she *couldn't* have known Mrs. Sedgwick! Even if somehow they'd met on shipboard, it wouldn't have anything to do with Father James, would it? As for accusing her of *killing* him—!"

"She accused herself," Rutledge replied, weariness in his voice. "It got out of hand, Mrs. Barnett—it sometimes does, when people are being questioned. I'm not sure why you came up here, but once you were here, I had no choice except to ignore you."

Still rattled, she said, "Inspector Blevins would *never*—"

"I'm not Inspector Blevins." He turned to shove the photograph safely away again in the desk.

"No," Hamish pointed out, "and more's the pity!"

Rutledge ushered Mrs. Barnett out of the room. As he shut the door behind them, he said, "Forget what happened just now. You can't change it, for one thing, and for another, you don't really understand all the reasons behind it. Meanwhile, since you've heard everything that has been said, I'd like to ask you what sort of woman Mrs. Sedgwick was."

Mrs. Barnett seemed to have trouble concentrating on his question. They had reached the stairs before she began tentatively, "I—I can't really tell you. I hardly knew her. She was always with one or another of the family—I seldom had an opportunity to say more than half a dozen words to her alone—"

Then she faced him. "I don't know why this *matters*—!"

"Because in one way or another, she mattered to Father James. And even though we have Walsh in custody, we aren't absolved from considering all the other avenues the victim's life opens to us."

Doubtful still, she answered, "I didn't know her! But she seemed nice enough. Well born. I've heard she came from a very fine American family, a niece or cousin to the present Lord Sedgwick's American wife. Quite pretty, as you could see for yourself. Rather shy and quiet, with a lovely smile."

"Did she attend church here in Osterley?"

"Here? No, not very often. There's a charming little church on the estate in East Sherham. But the Sedgwicks would come to Osterley around once a month, and the Vicar tried to interest Mrs. Sedgwick in good works. She was too shy, and always sent excuses for not showing up."

"Did she have many friends in Osterley?" Rutledge asked as he walked with Mrs. Barnett through the French doors into the dining room. He saw her glance quickly over her shoulder as if she would like nothing more than to escape from him to her kitchen.

"I don't suppose there was anyone here quite suitable. People generally appeared to like her—I never heard anyone say anything unkind about her. Men found her quite attractive. That soft American accent for one thing, and she seemed—I don't know—my husband said that she brought out a man's protective instincts."

Mrs. Barnett clucked her tongue at the congealed food on his plate, and added quickly, "I'll just warm this up."

"Did women like her?"

"I suppose they did. But women of her class are often—you either fit into their circle or you don't." She paused, pensive. "It's odd, I've just remembered something. The Sedgwick family came here occasionally for luncheon on market day. My husband's mother, who is gone now, always called Mrs. Sedgwick the 'little rabbit.' Almost as if she imagined her huddled in the midst of the dogs, trying to vanish." She shook her head. "I never saw that, myself."

She took up the plate and started for the kitchen. Then she turned and forced herself to ask, "You won't upset Miss Trent again, will you? I should hate to lose her as a guest just because you've badgered her.

There aren't that many weekly guests this time of year. And it isn't right that you should use your office to upset her!"

"She'll be safe enough, I promise you," he said, and she walked through the swinging doors to the kitchen without looking back.

Miss Trent came in reluctantly to join Rutledge. Her face was exceedingly pale, and she seemed uneasy when she realized that they had the vast room to themselves.

Rutledge said immediately, "I ought to apologize. But I have a job to do, and I try to do it well."

It was a more effective apology than an abject capitulation, and she accepted it.

"I don't particularly care to take a meal with you," she said in return. "But it's probably more comfortable here than at the police station, with everyone staring!" A quirk of sudden humor in her eyes told him she was giving him his own back.

He laughed. "Yes, I suppose it is. But I promise to talk about Father James, not you."

"I didn't know him well—"

"You told me once before that he'd wanted something from you that you couldn't give him. Was it to do with Mrs. Sedgwick?"

"Yes." Like a swimmer plunging into cold water, she shivered. "I don't know how he discovered that I'd—that there was a connection with the ship. But one day as we were having tea, he asked me if I remembered meeting her. I told him I couldn't even remember sailing. It's all blacked out, like amnesia, only it was shock that did it."

"Do the doctors feel you might eventually remember?"

"They persuaded me not to try," she said uncomfortably. "They told me it was better if I didn't. I've had dreams—but they were always terrifying, and I'd make certain not to think about them afterward."

"Do you still have those dreams?" He stopped and said, "Sorry. I meant it from the point of view of understanding what you've suffered."

"Sometimes. Usually. I don't know. I don't want to know."

"And Father James felt that perhaps you could recall some of the voyage. If you tried. Or—given time."

"Yes. He was convinced it was important to try. To put it behind me instead of running from it. But I didn't want to open that door. I thought he was wrong to suggest it. There were other survivors. But he was—wary—about approaching them without some authority."

"What was his interest in the Sedgwick woman?"

May Trent frowned. "I'm not sure. When she disappeared, it was very trying for her family and everyone who knew her. Why this sudden whim, this need to run away? Apparently there wasn't an answer. And I suppose if Father James found someone like me who might be able to define her state of mind when she took passage, he would have been comforted. No, that's the wrong word! Satisfied?" Shaking her head, she went on. "I suppose what he really wanted to hear was that she was safe and happy. It was almost as if he needed to know that, to have any peace himself."

"What if she hadn't been on board—what if she'd bought her passage and then changed her mind?"

"Oh, I can't believe that—Father James never once suggested that she hadn't been on *Titanic*!"

"After all," Hamish pointed out sensibly, "the remains were brought back to Norfolk. The proof of death was there."

"A coffin was brought back to Norfolk," Rutledge contradicted the voice in his head. "No one would have opened it to have a look at the contents."

"Father James seemed to be uncertain whether this was a planned 'escape' or if she just took an opportunity that presented itself. She'd been on her way to East Sherham from Yorkshire, and she decided to spend an hour in the shops in King's Lynn, because she was planning a party. When she failed to meet the chauffeur at the appointed time, he was patient, he didn't raise an alarm for several more hours. And later someone remembered seeing her at the railway station. She was seen again in Colchester, on the train to London. She'd taken nothing with her, which I found odd, but of course she could have bought whatever she needed in London shops."

"Did Father James tell you the chauffeur's name?" Rutledge asked.

"If he did, I can't recall it."

"What I can't fathom is the relationship between a priest and one of the Sedgwick family," Rutledge said. "It doesn't fit into any explanation I can think of."

"Actually it was probably nothing more complicated than the fact that Virginia Sedgwick had a grandmother who was Catholic. Father James mentioned that in passing. Mrs. Dabney had been terribly fond of her. If Virginia was homesick, I expect she'd be drawn to something familiar. And Father James had a very practical faith. If she'd come to him, troubled or lonely or just needing comfort, he'd have tried to help her without proselytizing."

"The Vicar would have been closer to her age," Rutledge speculated.

But Miss Trent was saying, "I wasn't very attentive, I'm afraid, although Father James did his best to bring her alive for me." She had the grace to flush. "I didn't want to be interested in her. I didn't want to find myself thinking about her, and then starting to dig into the blackness—I couldn't face it!"

Her eyes pleaded with him for understanding. "It sounds quite selfish and callous to say that. Especially now that he's dead. But there was nothing I could do for Virginia Sedgwick, was there? And the thing was, I couldn't bear to go back. And I couldn't explain *why* I couldn't go back. It's such a simple question, isn't it? 'Do you remember?' "

"I think he must have believed that, given time, you would remember—otherwise he wouldn't have chosen to leave you that photograph."

May Trent said, "Knowing that—now that he's dead—puts a tremendous burden on me. I don't quite see how to cope with it. I wish he *hadn't*—!"

"But then he hadn't expected to die within a matter of days."

The shock of that left her silent for a moment. "Yes. I see your way of putting all this together. If he harried me, I must have killed him, just for a little peace. But he *didn't*. I know he was the sort of man who believed that good would triumph. That one morning I'd sit up in bed and suddenly remember meeting this woman on the deck or in the dining rooms, the card rooms. Somewhere. After all, women traveling alone tend to gravitate toward each other—it wouldn't have been so amazing if our paths had crossed."

Mrs. Barnett came in with a tray bearing hot platters and trailing an aroma of beef in a wine sauce. She set their plates down with care, studying the faces at the table. "I'm so sorry, Miss Trent, but there isn't any more soup."

"I'm not really hungry. But thank you." When she had gone, May Trent said, "I don't think I can swallow a mouthful—what am I going to do . . . !"

"At least make a show of trying," Rutledge told her bracingly. "You'll feel better having eaten."

"You don't understand," she said irritably. "It's not something I relish, this black hole in my life. It takes a revenge of its own!"

"I think I do," he answered her.

Their eyes locked. Hers widened in surprise, as if reading the depths of his, and turning away from what she found there. He felt a spreading hurt.

Her voice trembling, she replied, "Yes. Well, is there anything else you want to know?"

"Tell me about yourself. What you do, where you've been. Why you have stayed so long in Osterley."

She grimaced as she tried a forkful of beef, but she persevered. He gave her credit for courage.

"The last is easy to answer. I've been looking at old churches, and I found Osterley to my liking. I prefer to stay here rather than pack my bag every few days and move to another hotel. I like the marshes. They appeal to me. The desolation, perhaps. Or their strange beauty. I've never quite decided which it is."

"Do you live in London?"

"Somerset. I grew up there, and I feel at home there."

"What took you to America? Is that a safe question to ask?"

She turned away. "I had the care of an elderly lady who was the aunt of a friend. She was going to New York to visit her son, and I was asked if I'd like to make the journey with her. As a companion, actually. But she was perfectly capable of looking after herself—"

She broke off and fought to regain her composure, clearing her throat with the effort.

He knew then that her charge had not survived. Which must have added enormously to the ordeal May Trent herself had suffered. Rutledge said, "Then you'd have come back to England in a few months?"

"Yes, that was the plan. I'd never been abroad, except to France a time or two, and once to Germany. I saw it as an adventure—" The words caught in her throat. "Can we talk of something else?"

She soldiered on valiantly through the rest of the meal. He thought perhaps she'd stayed at the table to prove to him that she could. Or because she didn't want to go upstairs alone.

Where the ghosts in the night lay waiting for her.

It was something that they shared, this fear of being alone. . . .

After a long silence, May Trent put down her fork and considered Rutledge. "How can you bear to question people the way you do? Prying and digging into lives as if none of us possessed a shred of privacy. I should think it would be very wearing, after a time. It's worse than gossiping or—or eavesdropping."

Hamish said, "It's true, it's no' a gentleman's way."

Rutledge winced but said, "If people told the truth the first time they were questioned, we'd have less need to pry. But lying shrouds what people say in layers of darkness. These have to be peeled away, and sifted, and verified, and even set aside as intentional misdirection."

Playing with the bread beside her plate, she said, "I can't believe that! Most people are honest enough, aren't they?" She had rolled two small marbles of the bread before she realized what she was doing.

"Were you honest with me, earlier this evening?"

She flushed and said, "I was protecting my own secrets, not those of Father James."

He hesitated. "If I come to you tomorrow and ask you if you killed Father James, will you tell me the truth?"

"Of course! Why should I not? I'm innocent."

"Would you tell me the truth if you had—for reasons I couldn't fathom—struck him down and left him to die on the floor in his own blood?"

Something stirred at the back of her eyes. "I'm not mad. I know you'd hang me, if I told you that. But that isn't the same as prying! It isn't the same as demanding the name of the woman in that photograph, when—when speaking of that ship digs into my shadows, not hers."

She held up a hand to stop him from answering her. "How would *you* respond if I asked you about the War? You were in the fighting, weren't you? You did see bodies blown apart and bones protruding from flesh, your friends cut in half by machine-gun fire, and nothing but blood where their chests used to be? You did kill people, didn't you? How does it feel to watch a man die as you shoot him—?"

With a sharp intake of breath, Rutledge got up from the table, and went to the window. The street was dark, the last of the light gone, and the quay empty, save for a small marmalade cat, trotting along sniffing the air.

"I'm sorry, I didn't mean—" she began, startled by his reaction.

And then she lifted her chin, a little trick she had when she was defiant. "No, that's not true! I *did* mean to hurt. I wanted you to know how your wretched questions tormented *me*!"

"Touché," Rutledge told her quietly.

May Trent did not take her tea in the parlor with Rutledge. She went up the stairs without looking back.

But something in the set of her shoulders suggested that she was crying.

Unable to sleep, Rutledge walked out to the quay, to look up at the stars. A whiff of pipe smoke made him turn in time to see Dr. Stephenson coming in his direction.

"Well met," Stephenson said, but without sincerity. "I had an emergency delivery, and I'm still too excited to go to bed. Touch and go, but mother and son are going to be all right. What's your excuse?"

Rutledge thought, *I could tell you I've been tormenting two women—at least they feel I have.* Instead he answered, "I have a liking for the marshes, I suppose."

Stephenson grunted. "What's the news about Walsh?"

"Among other issues, Inspector Blevins has been trying to find out if Walsh had encountered Father James in France."

"Oh, I shouldn't think that was likely. Besides, what difference would it make? The fact that they'd met wouldn't change what happened in the rectory, or why."

"Blevins has learned that Father James had written a letter from France to his sister Judith. He made some remark in passing about a story she'd liked as a child. About Jack and the Giant. But Judith is dead, and the letter hasn't survived."

Stephenson began to chuckle, deep in his throat. "Sometimes I don't pretend to understand the policeman's mind! Jack the Giant, you say?"

"We can't leave anything to chance—"

But Stephenson cut him short. "You're fools, the lot of you! It wasn't Jack, it was Jacques. And he was tall and thin as a rail, looked like a beanpole—but he was hardly a giant! Father James told me about this man—felt that I'd be interested in the way he treated wounds. Jacques Lamieux was his name, and he was a French Canadian medical man. He came to France for firsthand experience, and he got his fill of it. We still correspond. He has a practice in Quebec, and a reputation for being the best there is at amputations—a very high percentage of his patients live."

Still chuckling, Dr. Stephenson walked away. Then over his shoulder, he said, "You can tell Blevins for me that I can produce letters from Lamieux dated this month. Hard to bash a man's brains in, from that distance!"

Rutledge lay awake for hours, staring at the ceiling, his eyes following the pale ripples of light that clouds threw across the beautifully plastered finish as they moved in front of the half-moon.

Hamish talked about the War, about the men they'd lived with for days at a time in the trenches and in the holding areas, waiting for their turn. Most read, talked, played cards, wrote letters home, anything to while away the hours of boredom before the wild wash of fear when they were ordered to fall in. No one spoke of the dead, then. It was not superstition as much as dread that this time their own names would be added to the long rolls of missing, wounded, and killed. This time, *they* wouldn't come back. The chances were never good. Luck—sometimes skill—sometimes mere instinct—could change the odds in your favor. But there were so many dead, so many. As if the War were a monstrous beast, hungry for flesh and impatient for bodies.

No man who had fought in battle remembered it afterward without the rich coloring of his own fears. Scenes replayed themselves in slow motion, unwinding like a ribbon of terror, and a soldier's greatest fear was that his own gut-wrenching cowardice would let his mates down. And so he was brave in spite of himself, but never brave enough, never able to save them all, and he dragged the unlucky ones back to the trenches while they screamed to him to leave them, it hurt too much, and he held them as they died, and all the while furtively thanked God that he himself was whole. Only to lie awake at night, drowning in guilt because he had lived somehow.

Was that the fear that May Trent carried with her? That she had let the elderly woman in her care die? That somehow in darkness and terror and confusion, she had let go of a hand, to save herself—hurried too fast, to save herself—been blind, when she should have seen—

Guilt was what scoured the soul after it was over. And she would protect the darkness because it was comforting. Or because she feared the truth about herself.

Was that enough to drive her to murder, when Father James pushed her to remember—? He'd have turned his back on *her* . . . unwitting. Perhaps walk to the window and look out at the night while she found her handkerchief and pretended to wipe away tears. And she would have found it easy to silence the voice that was, somehow, reaching into the depths of her mind and hurting.

What had Dr. Stephenson said? That Father James had had such a beautiful voice and knew how to use it as a tool of his work.

Hamish growled, "Yon Inspector wouldna' care whether it was Walsh or this woman he hanged. Ye ken, it doesna' matter as long as it isna' someone from Osterley."

Drifting into sleep, Rutledge heard himself answer. "Virginia Sedgwick wasn't from Osterley, either. . . ."

CHAPTER NINETEEN

RUTLEDGE AWOKE FROM A DEEP SLEEP to the sound of thunder. *The guns,* he thought, as he tried to shake off the dullness that weighed so heavily on his body, like a mattress, muffling and distorting the noise. *They've started firing again—*

He could hear one of the Sergeants calling his name, and cleared his throat to answer, but couldn't.

And then sleep fell away and he realized there was a pounding on his door, and the voice calling him wasn't one he knew.

Rising swiftly, he went to open the door and found a young constable standing there, blood on his cheek and shoulder, his face white. Rutledge struggled to recall his name. Franklin—

"Inspector Blevins asks, sir, if you'll come straightaway."

Rutledge opened the door wider. "Yes, all right. Tell me what's happened." He crossed to the chair by the window and began to dress, adding a sweater under his coat.

The constable was saying, "All hell's broke loose, sir!" His voice was still high-pitched from shock, but steady enough. "That man Walsh has escaped—he struck me over the head and was gone before I could do anything. When I got my senses back, I ran to wake up Inspector Blevins, and on the way back to the station, we saw Mr. Sims, coming from the vicarage. There was someone trying to break into the house. It *had* to be Walsh, sir!"

Rutledge found his shoes and stockings, pulling them on hastily, then ran his fingers through his tousled hair. "All right, let's be on our way."

Hamish was saying, "I canna' believe he'd run. It's sure proof against him!"

May Trent, in a dressing gown, her hair in a dark plait over one shoulder, was at her door as he strode into the passage. The words found their way into the jumble of thoughts in his mind: *She's damned attractive—*

"What's wrong?" she asked. "Is there something amiss?"

The constable started to answer her, but Rutledge said, "No, it's a problem at the station. I've been sent for. Go back to sleep, there's nothing to worry about."

There was doubt in her face, but she nodded and went back into her room, shutting the door. As he turned toward the stairs, he heard the *click!* of the lock behind him. Just as well, he told himself. But Walsh had no reason to come here. . . .

They let themselves out quietly, and Mrs. Barnett, in dressing gown and slippers, shut and locked the door behind them.

As the two men walked fast up Water Street to the station, Rutledge said, "You were on duty, then?"

"Yes. Walsh was asleep when I checked at midnight, snoring like the wrath of God. He always does—you can hardly hear yourself think!"

"And?"

"Close on to two o'clock, I heard him making an odd sound. As if he was choking. I went back to the cell, wary because Inspector Blevins had warned me he might try something. But there he was, hanging from the top bars, choking his life out, kicking like a mad horse. I opened the door, to get him down from there, but he was tangled in a shirt, and I had to struggle to make any headway. Then his fist came down on my face as I managed to lower him, and I hit the back of my head on the door. That's all I can tell you."

"And he made a run for it. All right, what else?"

"For the life of me I don't understand why he didn't kill me! He could have done, easily enough, and there'd be nobody to raise the alarm. As it was, it took me all of a minute to shake off the blow, I was that dazed, and half sick. But I got to my feet and went after him, running out of the station and looking in both directions. I couldn't think he would go to the quay; there's nowhere to escape there. I went up Water Street and looked up and down the main road. I couldn't see anything, or hear anything. I went on to Inspector Blevins's house. It took him nearly five minutes to come down and open the door, and then he was accusing me of rousing the children with my clamor!"

Excitement had loosened the young constable's tongue, and he was finding it hard to conceal his reaction to Blevins's rebuke when he'd been trying to carry out his duty. Stumbling on the cobbles, he caught Rutledge's arm to steady himself.

"You should see the doctor," Rutledge told him as they walked through the open door of the station. All the lights were lit, and another constable was waiting for the two men.

"You're to stay here, Harry, and wait," he said to Franklin. "If you'll come with me, sir, I'm to take you to the vicarage."

"Give me two minutes," Rutledge said, and he walked back to the cell. Looking in, he could see that by standing on his toes, Walsh could have reached high above his own head to an exposed pipe coming out of one wall and crossing to the other side, wrapping his twisted shirt around it like a rope, and giving every appearance of a man hanging there.

After all, as Hamish was pointing out, the man was used to entertaining crowds. He would have put on a good show.

Long enough, at least, to lure the gullible young constable into the room.

Hamish said, "Blevins will have his hide!"

Rutledge silently agreed. He turned on his heel and followed the second constable—Taylor, was that his name?—out to the street.

By the time they had reached the vicarage, they could already see that all the lights had been turned on, giving it a strangely festive air, as if Sims was about to hold a party there.

The front door stood wide, and Rutledge could hear the station Sergeant moving about in the bushes near it, his torch flicking first this way and that. They found Sims and Blevins sitting in the study, like two wary bulldogs distrustful of each other.

Blevins said, "What took you so long?" His voice was querulous, tired.

Sims seemed to be happier to see Rutledge. He nodded, and then looked over his shoulder out the black window, as if he could probe the darkness in the tree-shadowed garden.

"I stopped by the station. To see how Walsh had played his trick. Quite clever."

"Clever, hell. A child of six could have seen through it!" Blevins swore. "No, that's not fair to Franklin. What matters, when you come down to it, is that the man's got away."

"There was a prowler here?" Rutledge asked the Vicar.

"I thought there was," Sims said uneasily. "I awoke with a start to hear something downstairs. A banging. I thought it was a summons to a deathbed. I found my slippers and came down as quickly as I could. But there was no one at the door. I called out, to see if whoever it was had given up and was walking away. And I could have sworn I heard *laughter*—distant laughter!" He shivered involuntarily. "I stepped into the sitting room and picked up a poker by the hearth there, and went out to see if rowdy youngsters were having fun at my expense. But there was nothing. No one." His voice changed on the last words, as if still unsure that there had been no one on the grounds. "I decided to fetch Blevins, here, to see if there was anything amiss in the church. It's too large and dark to search on my own."

Hamish said, "It wasna' youngsters he feared—"

Rutledge said, "Do you often have problems with vandalism?"

"We're more likely to find boys scaring themselves to death in the churchyard, daring each other to raise spirits. But before I could reach Blevins's house, I ran into him on the road."

Rutledge turned to the Inspector. "Do you think it was Walsh? Here at the vicarage?"

"I don't know. He might have thought he could find something to sell, to get himself out of Norfolk as fast as possible. It appeared that one of the shed doors has been opened. He could have looked there for tools to strike off his chains."

"That's far more likely," Rutledge agreed. "Did you search the church?"

"Not yet. Do you have another torch, Vicar?"

"Yes—there's one in the kitchen." He went to fetch it.

"Brave man," Rutledge commented, "to tackle these grounds alone, and in the middle of the night!"

"He was terrified for his life, if you ask me," Blevins said sourly. "I would have been, the surviving clergyman in the village."

"Sims hadn't been told about the escape. And Walsh would have no reason to kill Sims."

"So you say. Who knows what he's capable of?"

Sims returned with the torch, and Rutledge followed Blevins out of the vicarage, down the drive, and up the hill to the church. They walked in silence, their path just visible in the light of the half moon, but it was sinking fast.

The churchyard was empty, the white stones ghostly in the pale light, their shapes stark against the dark shadows of hummocky grass.

"If there was anyone here, he's gone now," Blevins said softly.

They walked on toward the north porch door. It screeched like the imps of hell as Blevins pushed it open, and he swore from the start it gave him.

Hamish said, "At least yon Strong Man canna' slip away fra' ye!"

"Walsh? Are you here?" the Inspector called. "The church is surrounded, man, you haven't a chance of getting out of here! Might as well surrender now, and save yourself a rough time of it if you try to run!"

Blevins's voice echoed in the stillness, bouncing from the rafters and around the stone walls, giving it a strangely unnatural sound.

There was no answer.

"Walsh? You didn't hurt the constable. You can go back quietly to the station, and nothing will happen to you. Do you hear me? But if we have to winkle you out of this church, and you do any damage here, I'll have your hide for garters. Big as you are, I'm not afraid of you!"

Nothing but his own words came back at him.

The moonlight seeping through the stained glass of the windows cast awkward patterns around the pews, gray here, black there, and the shape of a poppyhead outlined against a pane.

Rutledge thought, *He'll be impossible to find before daylight, if he's here.*

Blevins turned on the torch, blinding them and spoiling their night vision. Flashing it around the stone floor, across the backs of the pews, toward the choir screen in sweeps that raked the great nave with cross-bars of light, he covered as much of the darkness as possible.

Rutledge said, "He has the advantage now. We'll have to guard the doors until morning."

"No, I intend to finish this now. You go toward the tower. I'll move toward the choir." He turned among the pews, his heels scraping on the stone flags. A man determined to get what he wanted.

Rutledge went on toward the tower, letting his eyes readjust to the darkness, using the great window there as his mark. Hamish, whose hearing had always been keen on night watches, said, "There isna' anyone here—"

Blevins blundered into something. He grunted heavily and then called, "I'm all right."

Rutledge made his way along one wall, reached the tower, and started into the opening.

His foot caught something on the floor, and the rattle of chain startled him. Leaping back out of reach, he knelt and began to sweep the floor with his hands. Nothing. Neither flesh nor cold iron. He moved six inches forward and repeated his sweep.

His fingers touched iron this time, and fumbled across thick links of chain.

"Blevins," he called, not raising his voice. "I've found something. Bring your torch."

Blevins turned and came toward Rutledge, the silvery light shining on his face.

"Down here, man!" Rutledge snarled. "Not into my eyes!"

The torch reached Rutledge's knees and moved ahead.

On the stone floor lay a chisel, a great hammer, and the chains that had been around Walsh's wrists and ankles.

But there was no sign of Blevins's prisoner.

CHAPTER TWENTY

RUTLEDGE DROVE EAST ON THE MAIN road out of Osterley, a ruddy-faced, yawning farmer beside him in the motorcar.

In the rear seat, Hamish stirred uneasily, and Rutledge felt every shift and movement as if it were real.

Blevins had acted swiftly, sending constables and any able-bodied man they could rouse to knock on doors, recruiting more men as the search for the Strong Man widened.

One party went out into the marshes to look for missing boats. The greengrocer and the barman at The Pelican accompanied Dr. Stephenson in his motorcar driving out on the western road toward Wells Next The Sea and Hunstanton.

Six men set out on the road toward East Sherham, while others fanned out through Osterley, looking behind fences, opening the doors of sheds, waking householders to ask if they'd heard anything, seen anyone. Bobbing lanterns marked their progress through the darkness like a great Chinese dragon, and wives watched from windows, shushing children who were unsettled by the night's noises.

The road east toward Cley was the least likely direction to search, but it had to be covered. There was nothing here but the North Sea and a dead end—a man on the run would quickly find himself in a box, with nowhere to turn but south. Still, several roads that led down toward Norwich branched off from the Cley Road, and these were Rutledge's goals.

The farmer, a man of few words, roused himself to remark, " 'Course *he* might be clever enough to come this way, on purpose to throw the hunt off."

Driving slowly, his headlamps scouring the road ahead while the farmer watched the verges, Rutledge could feel nothing—no sense of a fugitive hiding in the edges of the marsh or ducking behind trees and garden gates. He'd mastered that instinct during the War, where German snipers were skilled at picking off the unwary, and machine gunners hidden in cleverly disguised trenches and shell holes and up-rooted trees waited for the onslaught of troops, holding fire until the unsuspecting were well within range. Hamish, behind him, seemed to keep watch as well, softly noting a high growth of shrub or a clump of wind-twisted trees that provided a likely covert for the human fox they were hunting.

The one factor on their side, Rutledge found himself thinking, was that Walsh was too big to hide himself in smaller and harder-to-see coverts. But in the dark, out in the marshes with their sluices and dikes, shadows could play deadly tricks. . . .

The farmer cleared his throat. "Ain't likely, is it, that we're going to find him in the dark? It'ud take an army searching in daylight—"

He broke off as a dog turned out of a field and trotted down the road, caught brilliantly in the headlamps. "That's old Tom Randal's dog—blessed beast got out again. I never saw such a one for wandering off every chance that comes. You'd think he'd be grateful for a good home!"

They were nearly past the dog when the farmer sat up and added, "On second thoughts, mayhap we should look in on Randal. Can you turn this thing around?"

Rutledge saw a drive ahead next to a high wall. He reversed into it and went back down the dark, empty road, the way he'd come. The dog had already disappeared into a patch of thick reeds and grasses.

"Just there!" the farmer finally said, pointing to a turning. A small cottage was set back from the road on the inland side, half lost among trees and a wild tangle of shrubbery. "Not much now, but once it was a pretty enough place. My wife treasured the plant cuttings Mrs. Randal offered her. She's gone now, Mrs. Randal, some six or seven years back. Tom's let her gardens run to seed."

Rutledge drew up in the rutted, overgrown drive. The house was dark, hunching in on itself, vines running up the porch and struggling to hide the windows on the first floor.

Hamish said, "If ye believed in witches—"

Rutledge smothered a chuckle. The house needed only a cauldron smoking in the yard.

They walked to the door and with his fist the farmer pounded on the panels as hard as he could. "Deaf as a post," he explained. "When he wants to be. My wife always claimed he'd rather be left alone."

After a time, someone threw up the sash of the window just above the porch. It squealed with a shriek like a night bird's. As Rutledge winced, a gray head appeared in the opening and called down, "Who's there?"

"It's Sam Hadley, Tom. We need to talk to you. Come down to the door."

"It's past midnight," Randal growled. "Go home to bed!"

Rutledge called, "It's a police matter, Mr. Randal. Please come down."

"Police?" There was a pause and then mumbled curses. The window went down with a bang, and after a long wait, the door opened.

The tall, thin man in a heavy robe tied at the waist like a sack peered out at them. He turned to Hadley and said, "That's not Blevins!" It was accusing, as if he'd been lied to. "*Nor* one of his constables!"

"Inspector Rutledge, from Scotland Yard in London, Mr. Randal. A man suspected of murder escaped from custody tonight in Osterley, a man named Walsh. We're searching for him."

Randal watched his lips closely as he spoke, then looked up at his eyes. "Walsh. That the one killed the priest?"

"He could be dangerous. He's larger than most, with wide shoulders and noticeable strength." He went on to describe the fugitive. This time, as Randal listened, he forgot to watch Rutledge's lips.

"Nobody's been here. I'd have known—"

"That yellow dog of yours is out in the fields," Hadley said. "I saw him myself. We thought we ought to come and find out if you're all right." He had pitched his voice between a shout and a yell.

"Dog's out, you say?" Randal frowned. "I penned him up before I went to bed! We'd better have a look at the outbuildings, then. Wait here." He closed the door, and came back shortly with heavy shoes on his feet and a heavy staff in his hands, solid oak and thick enough to kill a man. "That a torch you have, Hadley?"

Hadley flicked it on and they made their way toward the back of the house, where a barn and several sheds showed signs of age, but were in better condition than the front garden. Randal, Rutledge thought, had his priorities right.

The sheds were empty. Hadley shone his light around each in turn, while Randal peered intently at the contents—farm tools, old gear and wheels, tubs and barrows, often rusted and broken. From time to time he poked the heavy staff viciously into the shadows behind them. "No. Nothing taken," he said as they finished the outbuildings and turned toward the barn. "And not likely to be," he muttered. "Damn fool waste of time."

But it was a different story in the barn. The stalls where Randal's horses were stabled lay on the far end, past the heavy wagon and the plows. There were four stalls, two of them occupied with great gray horses, staring back at the light with luminous eyes and pricked ears. The warmth of their bodies and their breath filled the night air, a homey scent of horse and straw and barn dust, and the heavier odor of manure and urine.

"God damn it to hell!" Randal swore. "Where's Honey?"

He broke into a shambling run to throw open a stall door and lean to look inside. Hadley, right behind him, shone his light into the dark rectangle. But the horse that occupied the space was not there. Trampled straw reflected the yellow beam, and a clump of droppings.

Randal, beside himself, cried, "She's my best mare—if he's *hurt* her—"

Rutledge looked at the size of the other horses. Norfolk bred, they were very large, heavy-boned, and tall.

Hamish spoke, startling him. "One of those would bear Walsh's weight."

Randal was nearly dancing with anger now, clutching his staff in a white-knuckled grip, pounding it against the flagstone floor with every other word as he demanded to know what had become of his mare. A string of profanity indicated what he was prepared to do with the thief when he caught up with him.

Rutledge said, "Was—er—Honey the same size as these two?"

"Of course she is! That's her son, the darker one. And t'other is her daughter."

They hurried out of the barn, and searched the yard. But there was no sign of the horse, and it was too dark to be sure whether there were other footprints in the dust besides theirs.

"Where would she go, if she got loose?" Rutledge asked.

"She wouldn't leave the barn." Randal spoke with ill-concealed impatience, as if Rutledge were daft. "She'd never leave the barn, unless someone came in and took her."

"The dog," Rutledge said. "Do you think he could track her?"

"That old fool? He's not worth a farthing! I keep him for his bark, not his common sense!"

Randal was staring around the yard, fuming, as if expecting Honey to come toward them, head down sheepishly, to snuffle his robe for apples.

But the mare was gone, and Rutledge thought the odds were very good that Walsh had taken her. The farm wasn't, as the crow flew, all that far from Osterley and Holy Trinity.

He turned to Hadley. "Where would he go? If he'd taken the horse?"

Hadley shrugged heavy shoulders. "Through the meadow there, and the trees beyond. After that, who knows? He could travel some distance without being seen, if he kept his wits about him and didn't stir up dogs."

"We'll have to come back in the morning. We can't follow him now. Not across the fields on foot."

But Randal was adamant that they go after the fugitive immediately. "Honey's got a soft mouth, but he won't know that, will he? Bastard'll ride her until she drops, most like. I want her back, and I won't wait for morning!"

By Rutledge's reckoning, Walsh had a head start of at least two hours. The first part of it on foot, as Hamish was pointing out, but with the horse under him now, he could have covered miles in any direction. South to Norwich?

It was possible. . . . But Rutledge had the feeling that Walsh wouldn't box himself in for long—he'd leave East Anglia as swiftly as possible, and lose himself in the crowded Midlands or the outskirts of London, Liverpool, Manchester.

When Rutledge explained this to Randal, the farmer swore again, went stumping back into the barn, and began to saddle one of the remaining horses. Rutledge tried to persuade him to wait until dawn, but Tom Randal had made up his mind. He threw himself into the saddle with an agility that belied his years, and said with cold determination, "If I find him, I'll get my horse back. If you wait until dawn, he'll have ridden her into the ground, and she'd not be fit for anything but the knacker's yard!"

He brandished his staff at them as he touched his heel to the flank of the big gelding, and clicked his tongue. The horse, snorting, went placidly out the barn doors and trotted off toward the meadow. For all its bulk, it moved quietly on the thick sod.

Hadley shook his head. "He's always been an ornery old devil, Randal has. But he's right. On horse he has a chance, and I can't say I blame him." Farmer understanding farmer. Ingrained for centuries, this caring for livestock was survival.

"Walsh won't let Randal anywhere near him. He'll be tired, frightened—and dangerous." Rutledge looked around the barn at the scythes and rakes and pitchforks hanging from pegs along the walls, and a barrow with a tumble of trowels, hammers, short-handled mallets, and other implements. "God knows what he's armed with now. There're enough tools here to fit out a small army!"

"Randal's no fool. He wants that mare back in the worst way, and he'll be canny. And that staff of his is no mean advantage." Hadley sighed. "We'd best tell Inspector Blevins what's happened."

Blevins was pacing the floor at the station, trying to coordinate all aspects of the search, but clearly wishing himself out in the field. He looked up as Rutledge walked through the door.

"You're back soon enough. Anything?"

Rutledge made his report, with Hadley's commentary to support it.

Blevins scowled. "The mare could be anywhere. And who's to say that Walsh is on her? Still, precious little else has turned up."

He had an old map spread out across his desk and he bent to run his finger down the road toward Cley, stopping at the square marking the Randal farm, with its pastures and fields fanning out to the south. It backed up to a much larger holding, an expanse of pasturage that slanted toward East and West Sherham. Toward the Norwich Road, there was an unbroken chain of farms and estates, miles of what ap-peared to be fairly uninhabited land.

A man on horseback could make good time, even in the dark, where only sheep would hear his passage.

Rutledge leaned over the desk with Blevins, eyes scanning beyond the now-still finger. There was a maze of lanes and footpaths that led in every direction. They were like small streams draining a basin, converg-ing at one or another village. People in Norfolk looked inland from the sea to market towns, where goods and produce could be sold, a more trustworthy livelihood than the shifting coastline in the north.

Blevins was saying as his finger moved to draw a circle south of the farm, "I'll get word to the villages in that district, tell them to be on the lookout for a Norfolk Gray carrying a large man. If the bastard's ahead of us, better to let someone else cut him off. And we'll get on with the search in the town."

Pointing to land that marched behind the Randal farm, Rutledge asked, "Who owns that property?"

"It was the old Millingham estate. The present Lord Sedgwick's fa-ther bought the lion's share of it, and the Cullens and the Henleys own the rest. Good sheep country."

He turned to issue an order to the harassed schoolmaster standing behind him, filling in for the constables, and then went on to Rutledge, "If you'll have a word with the Vicar, that we think our man is well away from here, he'd appreciate it. Hadley, I want you to join the searchers down the lane past Holy Trinity. I've yet to hear a word from them—tell them to send a report! The Inspector here can drive you as far as the vicarage. And, Rutledge, after you've spoken with Sims, go di-rectly to Miss Connaught's house, if you will. Hadley can give you the direction. She has a motorcar—see if you can persuade her to let us bor-row it for the next few hours."

Rutledge said, "By stealing the mare, Walsh marked his direction. There's still a possibility that he'll double back, working his way west until he can find help."

"If I were in his shoes, I'd keep going, counting on the head start to see me safe." Blevins's eyes met Rutledge's across the desk. Without words—without the need for words—the message was clear: *Walsh wouldn't have run, if he wasn't guilty as hell!*

As far as Blevins was concerned, out of the night's disaster had come one comforting certainty.

As Rutledge followed Hadley back into the street, he found himself thinking about what Blevins had said—that Walsh would be counting on the miles between himself and Osterley to see him safe.

Was that true? His mind reviewed the road system he'd scanned on the map. Walsh was no fool. He might well lay a false trail. He'd planned his escape, and while it was a matter of luck that he'd stumbled on Randal's farm, where a horse could be taken without arousing the household or sending the dogs into frenzies of barking, there must be a dozen farms where the barn was far enough from the house to allow Walsh to break in.

And the yellow dog must have been an unwitting accomplice, delighted to be set free and not questioning the manner of it.

Sims was grateful for the news. He looked haggard. "I'm not afraid of Walsh," he said, and oddly enough Rutledge believed him. "Although Blevins seems to think I was quaking in my shoes for fear I'd be the next victim! And I'm not convinced, somehow, that Walsh is guilty of murder."

"Why do you say that? Have you seen him, met him?"

"No. Which is why I've kept my mouth shut. But I've had long nights to think about Father James and his death. It seems to me that Walsh took a chance coming back here weeks after the bazaar, expecting to find money at the rectory. Most churches live hand to mouth. It would have been easier to break into a house if he was desperate. Besides, if he was wandering about in the rectory the day of the fair, as Mrs. Wainer claims he was, he'd have seen for himself that there was very little to steal."

"He must have assumed," Rutledge said, echoing Hamish in his head, "that no one would connect his presence at the fair with a theft a good two weeks later." That was Blevins's opinion. "Someone at the fair could have calculated, roughly, how much money had been taken in. And there was a last payment to be made on the new cart, before it would be handed over to Walsh." He was playing devil's advocate, to give Sims an opportunity to get to the bottom of what he wanted to say.

Sims took a deep breath. "That's a tidy assumption. On the other hand—was Walsh that clever? If so, you'll play merry hell catching him now!"

"Then who killed the priest?"

There was a long silence. "I don't know," Sims finally answered. "But I have the oddest feeling sometimes. Of being watched. Our festival is in the spring. June. Why would anyone take an interest in the vicarage, if money was all they were after? Look around you—"

Monsignor Holston had also had the feeling that he was watched. . . .

Sims was saying, "You're fairly certain, are you, that what I heard was Walsh chiseling off his shackles?"

"Certain enough. We found the chains in the church. You identified the tools as yours, and the latch on the shed door was broken," Rutledge reminded him. "It seems clear that Walsh came looking for a shed or outbuilding he could break into. And the church was a perfect place to hammer off the chains. No one lives close enough to hear the racket. Except perhaps for you."

"Yes, well, from what you say, he's running now and not likely to hang about in Osterley." He rubbed tired eyes. "All right, thanks. Tell Blevins if he needs me, I'm available. I won't sleep anyway after all this excitement."

"I must be going. I'm to make sure Miss Connaught is safe. Blevins has been trying to see that all the people living alone are warned."

A wry smile crossed Sims's face. "Yes, go by all means. I'll be fine."

But as Rutledge walked out the door to the car, he heard the bolt shot home behind him.

Hamish said, "Was the laughter real—or his imagination, yon Vicar?"

Rutledge answered silently. "I don't know. Shock can play strange games with the mind. On the other hand, it's easy to hear what you expect to hear."

"Aye. Well. He heard something."

Priscilla Connaught lived in the house at the edge of the marshes, lonely and isolated, where the wind bent the trees and shrubs into Gothic shapes and the grasses rustled like whispers. The walk to the front door was dark, flowers leaning dry seed heads and wilting blossoms over the path. Rutledge could hear the seeds crunching underfoot. Out on the marshes, a bird called, low and forlorn, like a desolate soul looking for solace.

Hamish said, "This is no' a place for a woman alone!"

But Rutledge thought that it must have appealed to Priscilla Connaught, who carried secrets with her and preferred to use her life as a weapon against a man she hated.

He knocked loudly on the wooden panels, and then pitching his voice to carry, he called, "Miss Connaught? It's Ian Rutledge. From Scotland Yard. Will you come down, please? I'd like to pass on a message."

A light came on in a window on the first floor, and he stepped back so that it would fall on his upturned face. A curtain twitched, and he could feel her eyes. Hat in hand, he stood there and said again, "It's Ian Rutledge."

After a time another lamp was turned up, and another, tracing her progress through the house. The front door opened a crack. "What do you want?"

There was something in her voice that struck him. A resistance, as if she was prepared to turn him away. He thought for an instant that there was someone else in the house with her, and then realized all at once that she was braced against his next words.

He said, warily, "Inspector Blevins asked me to come and see that you were safe. Walsh has escaped, and we're trying to make certain that he's not still hiding in Osterley—"

"Escaped? How? *When?*" Her surprise seemed genuine.

"In the middle of the night. We've tracked him east of town, but it's as well for you to be aware of the danger."

"But you said he'd killed the priest!" she cried. "*How could you let him go?*"

"We didn't offer him the key, Miss Connaught. He escaped." Rutledge was tired, and in no mood to mince words. "Have you seen or heard anything—"

She cut across his words, saying quickly, "I can't stand here in the night air—I must go—"

"Are you all right?" he asked again. "Would you like me to search the house, or the grounds, to be sure?"

"I don't care what you choose to search. Where did you say he was last seen, this man Walsh?"

"We've found evidence that he was moving east of Osterley. Toward Cley, or possibly south in the direction of Norwich. There's a horse missing from Tom Randal's farm out on the east road. Inspector Blevins would be—"

"Where is this farm, for God's sake?" she demanded impatiently.

He told her, adding, "Inspector Blevins has asked—"

But she was gone, the door slamming shut in his face. He could hear her behind the door, a scream of outrage, as if Walsh's escape had been designed to torment her. And then silence.

He stood for a time on the walk in front of the house. He saw the lights turn off, and then the twitch of the curtain in what must be her bedroom. He turned, knowing that she must be watching, and walked back to the car. Winding the crank, he found himself debating with Hamish what to do.

In the end, he drove off, then left his car down the road, out of sight in a bank of thick shrubbery. On foot, now, he had barely reached her road when he heard the sound of a motorcar coming from the direction of the marshes. There were no lights.

Standing in deep shadow, he waited. The motorcar was small and there was only a driver to be seen, silhouetted against the clouds out to sea. A woman's profile, stiff beneath a cloche hat. He watched as she came to the intersection with the main road. Without hesitation she turned out into it, gunning the motor with angry force. The tires screeched in the grit of the road, and then the car was gone, speeding east—toward Cley.

Rutledge thought, *If she finds him before Blevins does, she'll kill him if she can. For taking away her vengeance.*

Hamish answered, "Aye, she drives yon motorcar like a spear!"

But there was little chance of her overtaking Walsh. She'd exhaust herself first, and go home. Still, it was his duty to stop her, bring her back to Osterley, and ask Mrs. Barnett to keep an eye on her.

Time was running out, and time just now was very precious.

"It's a gamble, either way," Hamish agreed. "If she runs afoul of Walsh, there's trouble. For her and for you. If Blevins canna' stop the Strong Man, and Walsh kills again while you're distracted by this woman, it's on your head."

It *was* a gamble.

Rutledge made his choice. The most certain outcome of a night of turmoil was losing Walsh. Once the man was safely out of East Anglia, he had every prospect of staying free. He must have laid plans—

Striding through the darkness back to his own car, Rutledge's mind outpaced his feet. *What would he himself do, in the Strong Man's shoes? How would he use this one carefully crafted opportunity?*

Hamish answered, "Aye, it was well done, his escape. I canna' be-lieve he'd leave the rest to chance."

"No."

Walsh had apparently been a friendly and popular showman, what-ever darker shades of his nature lurked beneath the smiling surface. The success of his act had depended on pleasing the public. "Step up, ladies, and test the Strong Man for yourselves. . . . See, here's a bench, and all you have to do is seat yourselves at either end. . . . Don't be afraid, you're as safe as a babe in arms, I won't drop you. . . . Who'll wager a bob to see if the Strong Man can pull this carriage as well as any horse. . . . All right, lads, who among you wants to lift the Strong Man's Iron Hammer. . . ."

There must be colleagues he could turn to, someone who would of-fer him temporary shelter, money to move on—and silence. It was, by necessity, a closed fraternity, this showman's world. People who trav-eled from place to place to earn their living put down no roots, and counted on the goodwill of their own in place of family. Many of them had had scrapes with the law, and they'd believe Walsh when he claimed he was innocent. The police were a common enemy.

A closed fraternity also meant that not even the redoubtable Sergeant Gibson at the Yard had a ghost of a chance to trace him once Walsh disappeared into it. Big as he was, he could still vanish. The key was to stop him before he reached that safety.

Rutledge bent to turn the crank and then got behind the wheel of his motorcar. But if the object of this exercise was to block Walsh's es-cape, the question became *How?* Cutting across country as he was, he could be anywhere.

Hamish said, "What precipitated his escape?"

"At a guess, he chose tonight because Franklin was on duty—young enough and naive enough to be gulled. Innocent or guilty, men of Walsh's ilk don't rely on justice to set them free. Blevins and his people made no secret of the fact that they were eager to see Walsh hang. Or—perhaps he wanted to find out for himself that Iris Kenneth was alive."

"No man would choose to die by the rope," Hamish reminded him.

Rutledge turned west. It was instinct and not reason that guided him now. Somewhere before Hunstanton on the north coast, Walsh must pick up the road to King's Lynn. Key to the rest of England.

Inland from the coast road were a hundred hills and meadows that would provide better cover. But on the other side of the coin, estates like

Lord Sedgwick's and villages like East Sherham would block Walsh's path, forcing him slightly north . . . toward the road.

Hamish was swift to remind Rutledge that he was counting on unadulterated luck.

Yet Rutledge had the strongest feeling that if he drove as far west as the turning for Burnham Market, and then began to follow the tangle of roads that led back to the east from there, he might just have that stroke of luck. . . .

The sky was lighter now; he could no longer see his face reflected in the dark windscreen. And—thank God—never Hamish's.

He scanned the horizons, eyes only half on the road.

A horseman silhouetted against the horizon wouldn't attract much attention. But Walsh would be no ordinary horseman. He was a huge man on a large, heavy mount, blundering through fields and across plowed land, depending on his sense of direction to keep him heading west. He risked stirring up sheep and their guardian dogs—and eventually someone was bound to see him.

The marshes on Rutledge's right were dark expanses of grass and shadow now, caught for an instant in his headlamps and then gone. A badger ambled along the road, picked out by the light, and scuttled into the underbrush around a small clump of trees. A night bird swooped across his path, and eyes followed his passage, gleaming for the space of a heartbeat, and then vanishing in the grasses. This was no place for a man . . . and Walsh hadn't been bred to the marshes. They would be a barrier.

He would avoid them.

Another seaside town ghosted into view, straggling along the main road, rising out of the marshes before turning toward the vanished sea.

A uniformed constable stood at the turning, watchful and alert. The message from Blevins, then, had traveled this far west. Rutledge raised a hand, slowing so that the man could see he had no one else in the vehicle. Except Hamish . . .

The constable saluted as Rutledge passed.

The early morning was cool, but he was grateful for the freshness of it, keeping him awake. The tires bumped on the uneven surface of the roadbed and clattered over a small bridge. Buildings loomed and then were gone, trees spread heavy branches over the road, casting deep shadow. From time to time he saw other constables walking the streets or, a straggle of men with them, cutting across country toward outlying farms, poking into hay bales, searching outbuildings, scanning the ground with torches for tracks.

Ahead was the turning Rutledge was watching for. A church marked it, stark against the sky, malevolent and dark and secretive, huddled beside the road.

Hamish said, "Yon church is no' a comfort in this light. Small wonder that half the world is superstitious! The night changes shapes and conjures specters in the shadows."

Rutledge thought, *Better them than you . . .* He could drive past the rest of them, secure in the knowledge that they wouldn't follow—

He headed south now, then turned a little east, passing through village after village, his eyes scanning the fields and peering into the light mist that was rising in the shallow valleys.

A horseman could pass unseen in its folds. He stopped and scanned the white sea. Later, wishing for his field glasses, he studied one valley with care, but there was only a cluster of thornbushes along a stream, in the haze bent like the backs of hiding men. From time to time there were other constables stationed at crossroads, or climbing through the sheep toward an outbuilding on the side of a hill.

Wending his way from road to road, still following his instincts, Rutledge traveled in a zigzag back in the direction of Osterley. Down this road—turning here—only to turn back again—all the while searching, making the connection and deciding as he ran through sleeping villages where that war-honed intuition might carry him next.

It required patience, and a mind focused and determined. Tiring, he stopped once and rubbed his eyes with cold fingers, wishing for a pot of tea and twenty minutes of rest. His nerves, tautly stretched to their limit, kept him awake at the same time they drained his reserves of energy.

And all the while, Hamish doubted Rutledge's intuition and his decisions.

If Rutledge was wrong—if Walsh *had* gone directly south—then Blevins's counterparts would be in need of every man available to widen their own search. But *were* they having any better luck?

And when full daylight came, what were Walsh's chances then? How close would he be to Norwich, if that was his goal?

Thinking of Norwich brought Monsignor Holston to Rutledge's mind. A priest who searched for shadows outside his window as night drew on, and listened to the creaking of his house, afraid of something he couldn't identify.

Like Sims . . .

What would Monsignor Holston feel if he knew that the man accused of killing Father James was on his way to Norwich? Fear? Or acceptance—

But there were no horsemen riding out in the dawn in this part of the county, save for a farm boy kicking the sides of a horse twice his size as he made his way across a stream.

By breakfast, Rutledge had circled back as far as the Sherhams—now all too aware that he'd wasted the hours, wasted his energy, and for what? Nothing.

Had Walsh passed him just over the crest of a hill or behind a screen of trees, or lost in the shadows that collected in the mists along small streams bisecting the land?

A bitter thought. And Hamish, as tired and grim as Rutledge was, seconded this honest indictment of his abilities.

"You arena' the man you once were. You havena' come to terms with yoursel', nor wi' Scotland—"

And yet Rutledge would have sworn, if asked, that he'd been right in his decision to work back from the west.

Another thought struck him—had Walsh already been captured?

No. Rutledge had seen constables still guarding the roads west, and at the junctions running through villages. He'd seen men searching—

And Walsh would have seen them, too. As the day brightened, he might even go to ground.

The intuition he prized so highly was failing him. Rutledge accepted the truth: One man alone in a motorcar bound by the roads had no chance to work a miracle when Walsh had the flexibility of so much space.

And today luck was favoring a fleeing man who must be as weary as his pursuers, and as determined, but with Fortune—or Fate—on his side.

CHAPTER TWENTY-ONE

BETWEEN THE SHERHAMS AND OSTERLEY, RUTLEDGE'S fatigue swept over him like a heavy blanket.

It was Hamish who shouted the warning, barely in time to prevent the motorcar from heading straight off the road into a ditch that ran with black water.

Rutledge pulled carefully to the verge and rubbed his face. The autumn dawn had broken, drawing long golden shadows across the road and among the trees, and the flickering of light and dark had mesmerized him before he had even realized it.

He took out his watch and looked at it. Most of Osterley would be at breakfast now, and the searchers straggling in like lost sheep, ready to sleep before going out again.

But it would be useless. Blevins had been stubborn—and wrong.

Walsh wasn't in Osterley. The man was well away, on the road to Norwich, watching his back and praying that the next dip in the land didn't bring a police blockade into view, choosing their spot where the twisting road allowed no escape, even for a man on horseback. If he had ridden the mare hard, as her owner, Randal, had feared, he would have made good time. If he'd handled her with some care, she could take him a long way in the morning light. Hunched on the saddle, his head drooping in weariness, his profile would be different. . . .

Rutledge put the car into gear again and drove several yards farther, where he could stop safely and sleep for ten—twenty—minutes. He thought of trying for Osterley and his bed, but the exhaustion went too deep.

Hamish was saying something about duty, but Rutledge didn't hear him, wasn't paying any heed. He slumped between the door and the seat, where his head would be cradled, and was already falling heavily into merciful sleep.

A horn blew loudly—once—twice—a third time. Rutledge came up out of waves of blackness, confused and unable for an instant to remember where he was or why.

Another car was coming up behind him, slowing, voices shouting at him.

Fighting off the last dregs of sleep, he sat up and tried to focus on what they were saying.

It was Blevins, who pulled alongside. "For God's sake, wake up, man! What are you doing out here? Where have you been? I've had half of Osterley searching for you!"

Rutledge cleared his throat. "I was driving back to Osterley when I nearly ran off the road. What's happened? Have you found Walsh?"

"A report came in just half an hour ago, and I wasted fifteen minutes hunting for you. Get in, and I'll tell you on the road. Constable, take the Inspector's car, will you, and follow us."

The constable got out and started toward Rutledge's motorcar. In an instant of absolute panic, Rutledge found himself saying, "No! I'll follow you—"

He couldn't leave Hamish in the rear passenger seat, with a stranger driving the car—

"Don't be bloody-minded! Constable, do as I say."

But Rutledge was wide awake now, well aware that where he himself went, Hamish would follow. Yet in that wild half-world between waking and sleeping, he had responded out of habit—*Hamish always occupied the rear seat. . . .*

As Blevins took over the wheel, Rutledge turned his own motorcar over to the grinning constable. Coming around the boot, he noted the bicycle lashed to the back of the motorcar Blevins was driving. The Inspector snapped, "Hurry, man!" and barely waited for Rutledge to close his door before the car was off down the road at speed.

"That's Jeffers, from Hurley. It's a town southeast of the Sherhams. He was sent to bring me back to where they've found a body. Some fool thinks it could be Walsh, but I can't for the life of me see how he came to be *there*."

Rutledge felt the hairs on the back of his neck rise. "Body, you said?"

"That's right. A body. Constable Jeffers doesn't have any information. The other constable, Tanner, who was out on foot searching the area, stopped a woman on her way in to the Hurley shops, and asked her to send Jeffers on to Osterley. Jeffers couldn't find a motorcar and had to bicycle in. Took the devil's own time doing it, too!"

"And the horse?"

"They didn't say anything about a horse. That's why I'm willing to wager this is a wild-goose chase. If Walsh has already run the mare into the ground, he wouldn't be shy about finding himself another mount. Why would he be on foot?"

Because he had started on foot—

Hamish's voice rang through Rutledge's head.

They were silent the rest of the way. Carts were on the road at this early hour, and people walking to their fields or leading out the cows. Small boys on their way to school were trotting behind a pair of squawking geese, laughing as the geese darted at first one boy and then another and they dodged the attack. Blevins shouted at them to mind what they were about, and they dropped back sullenly.

"You wouldn't have seen that sort of behavior before the War," he told Rutledge. "There's a generation growing up wild. Mark my words."

It was a frequent refrain in rural England these days.

When they reached the outskirts of Hurley, there was a farmer in boots and brown corduroy trousers standing by the road. An old hat was jammed on his head and he wore a heavy green sweater with a ragged hem straggling down one hip.

"Inspector Blevins?" he called as the motorcar slowed. "The doctor's been and gone. Take the road just there, to your left, before you get into the village proper. Follow it near half a mile, and you'll see the farm gate."

Blevins found the road, and it soon dwindled into a lane, hardly worthy of the name. A farmhouse faced a sloping hill of pasturage, where the white backs of sheep caught the morning spears of light. The lane continued, little more than a wagon wide now, last summer's wild-flowers brushing dry heads against the coachwork on either side. Within a few minutes they came to an open gate, where a muddy and well-rutted farm track began. "Here, I should think," Blevins said, turning in.

The track climbed a hill for some distance, angling toward the shoulder and a cluster of young trees. Blevins followed it for some fifty yards, and then pulled in where bruised grass indicated that the doctor had stopped as well. Beyond that, the track's ruts offered a challenge. Blevins said shortly, "I'd not like to find myself bogged down up there."

Rutledge got out and Hamish said, at his shoulder, "Walsh could ha' made it this far."

It was true. They trudged in silence toward the copse of trees, and a constable stepped out of it, standing there waiting. Blevins was finding it hard to get his breath, and Rutledge glanced at him.

The Inspector's face was nearly gray with strain, his jaw set and his body tense. With each stride he began to swear softly, trying to contain the pressure that was building in his mind. Rutledge's longer legs made easy work of the hill, but his chest burned from the night of driving.

The constable, hunched against the morning chill, touched his hat to Blevins, and nodded to Rutledge. "Constable Tanner, sir. I thought you'd want to see this. The doctor says he's dead, and they're sending up a cart from the farm, to bring him in."

"Who the hell is it, man?" Blevins halted as if unable to walk another ten yards. But it was his fear of the answer that had stopped him.

"It's Walsh, sir. Just beyond the trees." Tanner turned to lead the way, and Rutledge followed. Blevins moved slowly in their wake, as if unwilling to confirm the truth.

Tanner continued his report to Rutledge. "I can't say how long he's been dead—just before dawn, I'd guess, or not long after. His clothes are damp."

Just beyond the trees, the land sloped again, this time to the south. And about ten feet beyond the crest lay the sprawled body of a man.

Rutledge could see at once that it was Walsh—the size of the shoulders, the length of the awkwardly bent legs defined him before they had reached the head.

Rutledge looked down at the bloody dent in the temple, and had no need to squat on his heels and feel the hand nearest him for warmth or touch the throat for a pulse. But he did it anyway to give Blevins time to recover.

The hand was cold, damp. There was no pulse in the equally cold bare flesh beneath Walsh's collar. The giant-sized Matthew Walsh seemed shrunken, a bundle of discarded clothes, lying here on the wet grass, his trousers soggy with dew, and Rutledge found himself remembering what Dr. Stephenson had said about Father James. When the power of the personality had gone . . .

By that time Blevins had stopped just at Rutledge's back, and Rutledge could feel his gaze running over the corpse of his prisoner.

He rose slowly to his feet, not turning. Hamish said, "He died quickly. How do you think it was?"

But Rutledge was silent. Tanner, watching Blevins's face, shifted from one foot to the other, waiting for his superior to speak to him.

And then Blevins said harshly, anger and grief thickening his voice until it was unrecognizable, *"I wanted to see him hang!"*

No one spoke for what seemed minutes. Then Blevins said, "All right, Tanner, tell me what happened."

Tanner flinched, as if he'd been accused of murdering the man himself. He was young and all elbows and knees, but he said with a confidence that belied his years, "If you'll look just over here, sir—"

He led them some six feet from the body and pointed down at the iron half-circle lying in the grass. "See here, there's a shoe. And I backtracked the horse some distance. He cast it perhaps a quarter of a mile back—I found a muddy patch where you could see clearly that the off hind hoof was bare."

Blevins grunted, then squatted by the shoe. "All right. Go on."

"It's my thinking, sir, that the rider didn't want to do anything about it, exposed as he was. It's fairly open on the hill; with the farmers out early, he'd have been wary of being seen. But he brought it along with him, and here, with the trees to screen him from the farm, looked to see what the damage was, and if he could continue with this mount, or if he needed to find himself another."

"It makes sense," Blevins said, nodding.

"And when he lifted the off hind, the horse didn't care for it, backed away, and when Walsh bent to try again, kicked him in the head with the shod hoof."

"How do you read that?"

"The grass is trampled a bit, just below where he fell, sir. See, it's bruised and the ground is torn in one place. As if he might have been trying to make the horse stand still for him. Everywhere else you look, there's no sign of that."

Blevins went over to look at the grass. "Are you certain the doctor didn't do this? Or you, even."

Tanner's face was earnest. "No, sir, the doctor came in from the head. He said it was a heavy blow, caught Walsh just right, crushing the bone at the temple and killing him outright. An inch lower, and he'd have had a cracked jaw but lived to tell about it. An inch higher, and he'd have suffered a severe concussion." He was clearly quoting the doctor. "The wound itself supports the possibility of it being the shoe." He half turned, looking around them. "There's really no other clear explanation."

"Yes. I suppose that's true." Blevins's voice was flat. He wasn't interested in how Walsh had died. He felt cheated and was already trying to come to terms with that.

"The doctor says when he has the man in his surgery, he'll be able to tell if there're any grass bits in the wound, but he'd be surprised if his first opinion changes," Tanner finished diffidently. He had grown used to the corpse, guarding it. But the Inspector from Osterley seemed to be dazed, like a grieving relative.

Blevins got heavily to his feet, as if he'd aged ten years in the last ten hours. Looking around him at the empty hillsides and the long twist of the lane below, smoke rising from the farmhouse where a man in boots was hitching two horses to a long cart, he was silent.

"I hadn't counted on it ending like this," he said.

"There's no other way it could have happened," Tanner answered, as if Blevins had challenged his account. "If the horse wasn't his, it might have taken exception to Walsh's handling. Especially if he was angry about the shoe, and rough."

Rutledge walked back to the body.

It made sense. He sat on his heels and studied Walsh's face. The expression was one of faint surprise, as if he had died even as he saw the blow coming. But was the shape of the wound right?

Hamish said, "It's deep. The rim of the shoe must ha' caught him. I canna' think what else would have struck such a blow. But it's tae bluidy to be sure."

"She'd have lashed out blindly, and put some force behind it. Catching him before he could leap away." Behind him, he could hear Tanner and Blevins talking quietly. "He isn't the first or the last to die this way. And he was close to giving us the slip. Still—if he'd stayed on this route, with luck I'd have crossed his path somewhere near East Sherham."

Hamish said, "Ye ken, horses pulled Walsh's cart. He'd have known how to handle the mare. He saddled her and got her out of the barn without fuss."

Below the hill, the farmer was bringing the cart through the gate, to fetch the body.

Rutledge put out his hand and roughly measured the wound without touching it. As the sun's light began to brighten the clouds, he could see a blade of grass in the bloody edge. The doctor was here—what, a good half an hour earlier? While it was still dark enough to make such small details nearly invisible. . . .

He got to his feet as Blevins came to stand once more at Walsh's head.

"I've let him down. Father James," the Inspector said with a heavy sigh. "I swore I'd find out who killed him. And I did! This was an easy way for the bastard to die!"

Rutledge's motorcar arrived, pulling up at the gate just as the farm cart reached the trees. Blevins went to meet the farmer, calling, "Leave the cart there. Better to carry him across to it than to muck up the ground."

"I'll just lower the tail, then." The farmer, red-faced from years in the wind, took out a handkerchief and wiped his glasses. "Doctor says he was kicked by a horse. The dead man. Not one of *mine*. They never left their stalls last night."

"No. Not yours." Blevins answered curtly.

The other constable was climbing toward them now, the smooth movements of a countryman in his stride.

With the farmer holding the horses' heads to steady the cart, the four men lifted Walsh, grunting under his weight. The body shifted awkwardly in their grip, mocking them in death as it had in life. They tried to move in step over the uneven ground, until one of the constables slipped, barely regaining his balance in time to prevent pulling the others down with him. It was as if Walsh were still struggling to stay free, fighting their efforts, and they were breathing hard by the time they got him to the wagon.

Heaving the corpse into its bed, they misjudged the weight again, and the head brushed along the wooden bottom, leaving a smear of drying blood.

Blevins swore. "You'll do the doctor's work for him, if you damage that wound!"

Then they stood back, as if by unspoken command, and stared mutely at Walsh. It was an unexpected ending to the night, the adrenaline that had energized them through the long hours of searching beginning to fade and leaving them with an odd sort of feeling—of having lost, not won. Keyed to action, there was nothing to do now but go home.

The dead man's eyes seemed to gaze at the side of the cart as if distracted by the rough pattern. The horses stirred uneasily, troubled by the smell of blood and sweat and death. One stamped its hoof, and the harness jingled.

Rutledge thought of the corpses he had seen in France, loaded like cords of wood onto wagons, stiff in the cold air that did nothing to stop the heavy odor of maggot-infested wounds and rotting flesh from choking the men handling the dead. There was no honor in death, whatever the poets claimed.

O. A. Manning, the poet who had never seen the Western Front, had said it best: *"The bodies lie like lumber, / Obscene, without grace, / Like a house uninhabited and not yet ready / For ghosts . . ."*

As the sun reached over the hill behind them, Rutledge could see the wound more clearly now.

It reminded him of something, and he was too weary to bring it to the fore of his mind. Something he'd seen, as a young policeman—

Hamish said, "What? Think, man!"

But it had escaped him. . . . It didn't matter. And he was too tired to care.

At his elbow, Blevins was saying to Rutledge as the farmer raised the tailgate and turned his horses, "You'll be wanting to start back for London, I daresay."

"What? Yes, I suppose so." Rutledge looked back at the trees, as the cart began its rumbling descent down the hill, the farmer talking to his team as if they were old friends. There was no reason to stay. . . .

"Easy as you go, Nell. There's no haste, lass—"

Rutledge turned to Blevins and said, "Where's the mare?"

"The mare? What mare?"

"Honey. She isn't here. There's no sign of her."

"At a guess she's halfway home by now!"

They started down in the wake of the cart. Rutledge said, "I'm surprised Walsh hadn't made better time than this. I'd have put him farther west by first light." He rubbed his hand along his chin, feeling the roughness of his beard against the skin of his fingers.

In the quiet morning air, the clump of their boots on the muddy hillside and the harsh breathing of men and horses was a counterpoint to the creaking of the cart's wheels echoing across the valley.

Blevins was still finding it hard to manage what he regarded as failure. "She cast her shoe, and it slowed him. What difference does it make?" he continued impatiently. "I'm not in the mood to speculate on the late Matthew Walsh's last hours. I'm cold and tired, I've not had my breakfast, and he's dead. It's finished. I'll write my report and officially close the case, and that's the end of it." He stared hard at Rutledge. "Unless you've got a more likely suspect to hand me, from all those questions you've been badgering people with. Oh, yes, it's my town, I hear what's been said! Right now, to tell you the truth, I feel like stringing up the bloody corpse! A live one would be a hell of a lot more to my liking!"

May Trent's name came unbidden into Rutledge's mind.

CHAPTER TWENTY-TWO

THE LONG ORDEAL WASN'T OVER FOR Rutledge.

Someone had telephoned the Osterley Hotel and left a message for the man from London. A farmer's dairyman had come across Priscilla Connaught in her wrecked car, weeping hysterically, on a road a little east from where Matthew Walsh had been found dead.

Rutledge had forgotten her––she had left her house in a rush, looking for Walsh, and he had forgotten her.

The sleepless night showed in the dark circles under Mrs. Barnett's eyes, and in the faded color of her face. He couldn't ask more of her. Instead he said, "Will you go up to Miss Trent's room, and ask if she'd mind accompanying me when I fetch Miss Connaught and her car? I think it best to have a woman with me."

Mrs. Barnett raised her eyebrows in surprise. "But she left last night shortly after you did. Miss Trent. I thought you knew!"

"She hasn't come back?"

"No. I'd locked the outer door, you see. Until a quarter of an hour ago. Of course I'd have heard the bell, she'd have no other way of getting in. And I've been awake since the telephone rang."

"Never mind, then. Er—do you think I could have a cup of tea before I leave?" He couldn't worry about May Trent now. . . .

She looked at him, must have seen the weariness eating into the bones of his face. "Must you go out again? Surely Miss Connaught is better off where she is, while they're still searching!"

"Blevins has called it off. The search. Walsh was found."

"Well, that's a great relief, isn't it? It means we're all safe. I've just put the kettle on. And I think there's some cold bacon and a little cheese, if you want me to make up a sandwich."

"Please!"

As Rutledge climbed the stairs, Hamish said, "The woman's right. Sleep for an hour—there isna' any need for haste."

He answered, "She gave someone my name—the farmer or the dairyman—and sent him out to find a telephone. I should have stopped her rather than drive half the night on a fool's quest. In a way, whatever has happened is my fault."

When he opened the door of his room it seemed to open its arms to him, welcoming and silent and still dark, with the shades drawn. But he ignored the temptation of the waiting bed and walked across the carpet to run his fingers again over the bristles of his chin. He felt grimy, unkempt. Shaving and a clean shirt would help.

The face staring back at him from his mirror as he worked up a lather in his mug and applied the brush to his cheeks and throat was gaunt, with the dark growth of beard lending it a sinister look. Hamish reminded him that he could pass more easily as a murderer than the dead Walsh.

Rutledge could still see the big hands lying limp, without force, on the grass, and the flaccid muscles that had once given the impression of great power to the Strong Man's shoulders. In his mind's eye, as he shaved, he reexamined the wound. An irony—a horseshoe spelling the end of the road for an escaping murderer.

What were the lines he'd found so fascinating as a boy? Something about for want of a shoe, a horse was lost—for want of a horse, a rider was lost—and it went on in that vein until a battle was lost. . . .

Certainly for Blevins, the battle had been lost.

Ten minutes to shave, wash up, and change, and then Rutledge was calling to Mrs. Barnett as he crossed the lobby.

She was just coming through the kitchen doorway, carrying a thermos of tea, a basket of sandwiches, and two cups. She said, "Don't break the cups, will you? I need them back."

"I'll be careful. Why did Miss Trent leave? Orders were for every-one to stay indoors until Walsh was caught."

Suddenly anxious, Mrs. Barnett asked, "You *did* say you'd found him, didn't you? I'm afraid I'm beyond thinking just now."

"We found him. He's dead." It was terse, and he hadn't meant for the words to sound that way.

"Dead—"

"Why did Miss Trent leave?" he repeated.

"She was rather worried about Peter Henderson—all that search-ing, people moving about—and if he didn't know why, it'd be upsetting. I expect Peter could take care of himself; he's quite at home in the night. I mean, from the War and all that. I've seen him wandering about at all hours, just—wandering. Sometimes he stands on the quay and stares up at the hotel. Not in a threatening way, you understand. I think the light comforts him somehow. I don't know how many times I've asked him to come in out of the rain, but he always shook his head and thanked me and walked on. I leave him alone, now. I'm sure he'd hear the search parties long before they saw him!"

Or hear Walsh, blundering through the dark?

Hamish reminded him, "Ye wondered, once, where he slept at night. . . ."

So he had. Rutledge thanked her and went out into the brisk wind that had arisen, thinking he ought to have brought his coat. But he didn't have the energy to go back for it. Hamish warned him that he was in no shape to drive, either, and Rutledge said curtly, "I don't have much choice!"

"You willna' die. I'll no' let you die. Still—what if you kill someone else?"

It was not a pleasant thought.

He carried with him the directions that Mrs. Barnett had taken down from the man telephoning the hotel on behalf of Priscilla Connaught. The most direct route would have sent him back through Hurley, where Walsh had been found, but he chose instead to turn left out of Water Street and head east, then south and west again. He found himself wondering if this had—roughly—been the path Walsh had followed, too. It would explain to some degree why the man hadn't got as far as Rutledge had expected. And on such an erratic course, it would have taken luck, a phenomenal amount of luck, for Priscilla Connaught to have caught up with him. . . .

Hamish said, "It wouldna' do any harm to stop and see if the mare's at the barn."

Rutledge thought, "Let Blevins attend to it," but as he neared the cottage he slowed and turned into the drive, bumping down the ruts to the barn.

The instinct that had served him so well in the past had been erratic since the War, as if deserting him and then finding him again. He tried not to turn his back on it when it stirred and woke.

A dog barked furiously at him, the yellow dog he'd seen the night before. It ran out of the barn, stiff-legged, its upper lip curled back from teeth that seemed to gleam in the pale light.

Rutledge stopped the motorcar some twenty feet from the barn, set the brake, and opened his door.

Hamish said something, but he ignored it.

Speaking to the animal quietly, his voice firm and ordinary, Rutledge said, "Good dog—good dog. There's a good dog. Come here. That's it, easy, my friend, no one means you any harm." Matching his movements to the cadence of his speech, he got out to stand beside the car, slowly sinking to his haunches.

"Here, now, there's a good dog. I won't harm your master. Is he at home?"

Fierce and staccato at first, the barking changed to a loud and lengthy statement of duty, the black nose rising into the air, and the tail no longer rigid but dipping in the middle. In another thirty seconds, the dog came forward, nose outstretched, eyes wary, the bark more for show than for attack. Soon Rutledge was rubbing the rough head and tweaking the ears as he dug his fingers into the thick fur behind them. Tongue lolling, the dog would have licked Rutledge's face if he hadn't moved in the nick of time. Laughing, he stood and said, "All right, then, show me the barn. Will you do that?"

Hamish said, "You ken, if *you* tamed him, someone else could have. Walsh."

"Yes. That's what I wanted to find out." He moved casually toward the barn, the yellow dog prancing at his heels, licking his hand in an invitation to play. But Rutledge was intent on his own business.

He paused as he reached the barn door, and then stepped inside. The dog followed happily, and Rutledge turned toward the stalls.

In the dim light of the barn, there was only one head raised to stare back at him with ear-twitching interest. The doors of the empty stalls stood wide.

Randal had not come home. And neither had the mare that he'd gone to find.

Satisfied, Rutledge prepared to leave, and the dog, sensing a lessening of tension, brought an old rag to him, offering it with a sloppy grin. Rutledge took it from the wet mouth and tossed it toward a bale of hay that stood beside a harrow.

The rag hit the back of the harrow, and something fell with a clatter, dislodged by the pull of the cloth. The dog went after his new toy, but looked back at Rutledge with an air that all but said, "It's out of reach—not fair."

Rutledge crossed to the harrow and leaned forward to retrieve the rag. It was entangled with something, and he brought both objects up together, tossing the balled rag toward the barn door before setting a hammer on the hay.

The dog raced off.

And a memory suddenly clicked. Rutledge stood still.

He was a young policeman again, walking into a house where a shirtless middle-aged man was in tears, begging him over and over to believe that he'd meant no harm—no harm. But in the kitchen at the back of the house lay the much younger wife, a bowl of eggs shattered on the floor around her, the shells broken and the whites as slippery as glass. From the muddy earth on her boots, she'd just collected the eggs from the hens in the back garden.

Her temple had been crushed by a carpenter's hammer, a single blow with the weight of the husband's heavy shoulders behind it. The weapon lay on the floor where he had dropped it, bright blood on its head. He had, he said, been using it to mend the cellar stairs.

Rutledge couldn't recall now what the pair had quarreled about. Only that he'd felt like picking up the hammer and using it himself on the man. He'd been young, idealistic still, unused to murder. The man was on his knees by the quiet body of his wife, begging her to get up, to clean up the mess on the floor. To pull down her skirts before the policeman, and Rutledge had felt the upsurge of a fearsome anger.

And the wound—the wound was a bloody gouge on the temple. Not like—and yet somehow very like—the bloody hole in Walsh's temple.

Why had he associated the two cases?

Because he was tired enough for his mind to play tricks. . . .

The dog came back with the rag, tail waggling, asking for another toss. But Rutledge was lost in the past, his eyes turned inward, his fingers moving involuntarily over the head of the hammer as he tried to bring back the images in his mind, to observe them more clearly. *What was it that had stirred his memory? Not the shape of the wound— Not the kitchen floor, where the broken egg yolks ran into the thicker stickiness of the blood . . . Nor the man whimpering at his side.*

He took the wet rag and threw it once more, and realized that it had left a smear of saliva across his fingers. He looked down at them as Hamish said something, and was on the point of wiping them on the loose hay when he stopped.

Rutledge stared at the tool in his hand, another thought rising among the confused images that exhaustion was fusing, like drug-induced dreams in hospital, into a semblance of reality.

The mare hadn't been at the scene when the doctor arrived—he wouldn't have been able to examine her shoe for signs of blood and hair. And by the time she was found, any useful traces on the shoe would have been worn away. A pity. It would have been clearer evidence in the chain of events Blevins had to sort out. Indeed, someone ought to wait here until the mare was brought in.

He himself should be on his way to Priscilla Connaught. . . .

His mind fragmented by multiple lines of thought, Rutledge tried to find coherence. And the fatigue riding him refused to let him.

How many hammers were there in Osterley—in a twenty-mile radius of Osterley?

It didn't matter. The bodies of the dead often told their own stories of how they died. But not always why. It was the why that mattered now.

He realized what Hamish had just said to him. ". . . a needle in a haystack . . ."

Rutledge turned and walked toward the stalls that had held three Norfolk Grays only last night, thinking that the hammer had been in the barrow with its brothers only last night. He'd seen them there when he'd gone through the barn with the farmer Hadley and Tom Randal.

But he hadn't been searching for hammers, only for Walsh—

The luminous brown eyes of the remaining horse met his and as Rutledge neared the stall, the animal blew softly, interested in the mixed smell of dog and motorcar that he carried with him. The yellow dog walked patiently at his heels, panting and grinning, a willing conspirator if Rutledge took it into his head to steal this last mount.

Rutledge approached the horse with care, concentrating on speaking quietly, reassuringly, before reaching out to the nose stretched toward him. "Where are your stablemates? Hmmm? And what's keeping your master—"

Hamish said something, fast and unintelligible.

There was heaving movement in the shadows at his shoulder, hardly visible, more a sudden blend of sounds and shapes so startlingly close that there was no defense against it. Rutledge ducked, prepared for a wild attack.

A second gray horse, awakened by a voice next to where she'd been dozing head down in her stall, swung it high and stretched forward to nuzzle him.

The mare.

She was home.

Once his breathing had settled back into the range of speech, Rutledge stepped into the stall, calling her name softly as he ran his hand down her neck and then along her flank, before moving toward her hindquarters. The mare quivered, her coat rippling with the movement of the nerves under it, but she stood still. He kept one hand on her back and bent to lift the heavy hoof on the near side. In the poor light of the barn, he couldn't see well enough to examine it.

Turning her head to stare at him, she let him work with her without protest. He put down that hoof, and then moved to lift the other.

For an instant he thought she was going to kick out, and he could see himself caught in the head just as Walsh had been, his back too near the stall's high side wall to let him escape the blow. But she simply moved a step forward, as if to give him more room.

The shoe was missing.

He put down the heavy hoof, keeping his hand gently on the mare's rump. Her coat was rough with the lather of sweat, briars and leaves tangled in the thick hair. She had been ridden very hard, and she was tired. . . .

He lifted the hoof again. She turned her head, the great brown eyes watching him.

But she did not kick. She was safe in her own stall now, and not likely to object, in her present state. He let the hoof down, and moved around toward the big head.

"Clever girl, to find your own way home." He slapped the neck just below the ears twitching with interest as if wondering what it was he wanted.

Hamish said, "Left to hersel', it's no' a great surprise."

Where was Randal?

IIad he come back yet? There was no sign of the gelding. This time Rutledge moved on to the last stall to peer inside. It stood empty.

Randal was still searching for his lost mare.

Rutledge laid the hammer by the harrow, where he'd found it, and walked out of the barn. He could hear ravens calling in the woods, and somewhere the sharp whistle of a pheasant.

Priscilla Connaught was waiting. He had to go.

It was almost a surprise when he heard Hamish's voice saying, "The woman willna' go away. Stay until yon farmer comes back."

Rutledge thought, "I'll finish what I've begun." But in Hurley, the doctor would be ready to examine Walsh's body. Hamish was right. He ought to be there, too. No matter what he did, he was off track—last night, this morning—and there seemed to be nothing he could do about it.

Besides, it was Blevins's case. The Inspector would have to be present.

He absently fondled the dog's ears. Walsh was dead. Whatever Hamish thought, one had always to remember the living.

CHAPTER TWENTY-THREE

THE FARMHOUSE WHERE PRISCILLA CONNAUGHT HAD been
taken after wrecking her motorcar was set, like so many others, back
from the road down a winding lane that led up a slight rise and then
into the farmyard. It was muddy, the warm smell of manure coming
from a cart by the far wall where the milking shed had been cleaned.
The cows themselves, some dozen of them, were already plodding
steadily out to pasture, following a routine so well established in their
lives that they needed no human direction.

A walk of paving stones led across to the house, and one branch of
it disappeared through a hedge around to the front. Rutledge left his car
by a stack of bricks covered with a tarpaulin and picked his way across
the yard to the walk. There was a door at this end of it, what he assumed to be the kitchen door into the yard. It opened before he got
there.

An anxious woman peered out at him. She wore her graying hair in
a bun at the back of her neck, and a heavy sweater over her dark dress.
"Inspector Rutledge?" she asked, her voice rising.

"Mrs. Danning? I met your husband along the main road. He's

brought the team down to pull Miss Connaught's motorcar out of the ditch."

She said, disapprovingly, "I shouldn't wonder he'll have his hands full. She shouldn't have been driving so fast just there. It's a miracle she didn't do serious harm to herself!"

It was, he thought from her expression, more a condemnation of a woman at the wheel of a motorcar than it was of speed. Priscilla Connaught would have little in common with Mrs. Danning. They were brought up in very different worlds. The farmer's wife had work-reddened hands and dressed much as her own mother must have done a generation ago. Youth had deserted her, her life given over to chores and cooking and raising children. To her, Priscilla Connaught was a city-bred peacock suddenly and inexplicably set down in a farmyard.

Holding the door for him, she walked ahead down a flagged passage, past the dairy room and a larder, then opened another door into the warm, lamplit kitchen. "She's just in here," Mrs. Danning added over her shoulder, and he stepped into the large room, his hat in his hand. Although sparsely furnished, there was a good round table, handsome chairs, the work sink, and two oak dressers. One of them held jugs and plates, cups and bowls, the glaze shining in the lamp's glow.

Priscilla Connaught, her hair pinned up haphazardly, her coat dirty and torn, a long scrape across her cheek from her ear to her nose, was sitting hunched in a chair by the coal stove, though the room was warm. Someone had given her a shawl to wrap around her shoulders. It was handmade, thick, and appeared to have been knitted of whatever oddments of wool had been in the basket. There was almost a frivolous air about it, as if the juxtaposition of blues and grays and a very pretty rose had not been thought out as a pattern. A child's first efforts, perhaps, for the stitches were sometimes too tight.

He said, "Miss Connaught?"

She looked up, her face streaked with tears and blood from the scrape. The misery in her eyes shocked him.

"Thank you for coming," she said. "I didn't know who else to ask. These people have been very kind—but I'd like very much to go home, now."

He crossed the room to pull out a chair from the table, to set it next to hers. "Are you hurt?"

"Hurt?" She stared at him, as if the word was foreign to her. "I don't *think* I am."

He'd seen the car in the ditch. She'd have taken some punishment.

Rutledge reached out and gently lifted the hair from her face. His intent had been to make her more comfortable, but she flinched as he touched it, and he saw that there was a bloody cut at the very edge of her forehead.

Turning to Mrs. Danning, Rutledge said, "Could you bring me a wet cloth, please?"

She went to the sink and pumped up water into a small bowl. "It'll be cold. Shall I set it on the stove for a spell?"

"No, that will do." She brought him the bowl and a clean towel from a drawer. Rutledge got to his feet, dipped the towel into the bowl, and moving the hair aside, began to clean blood from the wound.

Priscilla Connaught's breath caught at the coldness of the water, her eyes fluttering, but she held her head still like a good child, and let him work. Mrs. Danning, standing just behind him, was saying, "My dear lord, I never saw that! And she didn't say anything—"

It was deep, and the blood welled up, in spite of his efforts to stem the flow. Rutledge said, "I don't mean to hurt you—" And then he added, to distract her, "How did you come by this?"

"I don't know," she said faintly. "I don't remember anything, except wanting to die . . . lying there in the ditch, wanting to die."

She began to cry, silently at first, moving her face away from his fingers, and then the sobs shook her body, and she hunched away from his ministrations, into herself.

Mrs. Danning took the bowl from his hands. Her voice was troubled as she said, "She was this way when Michael brought her in. He's the dairyman. He'd gone out with the milk cans, and the dogs found her first—dark as it still was, the motorcar was that hard to see in the ditch. He discovered she was alive, and ran back for my husband, to help get her out of the vehicle—her door was jammed, they said, and she couldn't walk. They thought she'd broke her ankle or worse."

Rutledge looked down. One ankle appeared to be swollen, the stocking sagging around it torn and filthy. A strap on the shoe was torn as well.

"Could you make us some tea?" Rutledge asked, to keep Mrs. Danning occupied. "I think it might help. I could use a cup myself."

"It won't take a minute. The kettle's still hot."

As she busied herself with the tea preparations, Rutledge sat down again and reached out to put his hand on Priscilla Connaught's shoulder.

"You're safe," he told her. "It's all right now. Come, look at me." He took out his handkerchief and pressed it into her hands, but she just clenched her fingers around it, like a lifeline, and couldn't seem to stop the wrenching sobs that enveloped her.

If she'd been a man, if she hadn't had the head wound, he would have slapped her lightly, to snap her out of the hysteria. Instead he said harshly, "That's enough!"

She took two or three gulping breaths, startled into obeying, her eyes lifting in surprise to his face. Rutledge took the handkerchief from her fingers, and began to press it against her wet cheeks.

As if the words bottled inside had finally been unstopped, she said shakily, "I tried to kill him. I saw him there in the dark, bent over in his saddle, and I *wanted* to kill him. I drove into the hedge instead— because I couldn't bear to hit the horse—"

He waited, letting her talk. "I *shrieked* at him, blowing the horn, screaming, heading straight at him, and the horse threw him then, and I drove directly over him. I wanted him dead, and then I wanted to kill myself. I tried to point the bonnet at a tree, but the wheels slipped in the grass, and I missed it and went into the ditch instead, and was terrified that I wouldn't die—and it went black, and I—" She started to cry again. *"I'm still alive!"* Her eyes were on his, begging. "I wanted it to be swift, painless, over within an instant . . ."

Beyond the table, he saw Mrs. Danning standing with the teapot in one hand, the lid in another, staring at her unexpected guest, horror on her face.

She clearly hadn't heard this part of the story, she knew only that there had been an accident. "Is there someone dead? Michael didn't say anything about that!"

Rutledge, his mind working swiftly through what Priscilla Connaught had said, heard Hamish ask, "It couldna' be Walsh she ran down—"

"How do you know he's dead, Miss Connaught? Did you see him after you hit him?"

Hamish said, "There'll have to be a search."

Priscilla Connaught frowned. "I drove straight over him. He must be dead!" She brushed her hair back again, and looked at the blood on her fingers. "Is that his blood?" she asked, confused. She took the handkerchief from him and scrubbed the spot. "I don't know. I can't—I can't remember any more. Except that it's finished. That's all. Finished." She made a faint gesture and after a moment added, as if bewildered, "It's easier said than done, trying to kill yourself—" She stared at him, as if this was a new discovery, something she hadn't foreseen.

She began to weep again. Mrs. Danning set down the pot, lifted the teakettle from the black stove, and poured in steaming water. "It'll only take a bit to steep," she said.

"How do you kill yourself?" Priscilla Connaught asked weakly through her tears. "I thought of slashing my wrists, but I didn't have anything sharp—only the tools in the boot, and they wouldn't do the job. *I wish I was dead!*"

Hamish said, "She needs a doctor's care. She canna' be trusted."

It was true. Rutledge took a deep breath and said, "This isn't the place to talk of dying. Or the time. You mustn't upset Mrs. Danning!"

Priscilla Connaught looked up at the sturdy farmer's wife. "I'm sorry," she said, and then repeated it. But he thought the apology was more a response to his tone of voice than to his words.

Rutledge coaxed a cup of sugared tea into Priscilla Connaught, which warmed her, but failed to make any headway in bringing her out of her depression and exhaustion. Instead she lapsed into a silence that seemed almost a blankness. Setting aside his own tea, he said, "Let me drive you back to Osterley. My car's just outside. We'll fetch yours when you've rested. The Dannings will see to it, meanwhile. It will be safe enough here."

With visible effort, Priscilla Connaught roused herself from her silent misery. "Yes. I can't stay here. I've caused these kind people enough distress already. But I don't know that I can walk. My foot still hurts."

"I'll help you, then—"

Her eyes were red-rimmed and dark with pain. "I just want to go home. Will you take me home? Please?"

"Yes. If that's what you want." It would probably be best to summon the doctor to her, rather than bring her into a reception room full of staring people.

With the help of Mrs. Danning at the doors, Rutledge managed to half-carry Miss Connaught out of the house and set her in his motorcar. Mrs. Danning provided a pillow for her injured foot, and stepped back, as if glad to wash her hands of her troublesome guest. He went back to the house with Mrs. Danning, promising to see that both the shawl and the pillow were returned and making arrangements for the car to be retrieved later.

The farmer's wife began to collect the cups and spoons from her kitchen table, her face creased with worry. "Who is it that's dead? I couldn't make head nor tail of her story! Should we ought to summon the police? She wouldn't hear of a doctor for herself, and we didn't know about anyone else being in the car!"

Rutledge said, "I'm not certain exactly what happened. Dr. Stephenson will give her something to make her rest. Then we'll be able to sort it out."

He was on the point of saying more, but Mrs. Danning's face cleared and she nodded. "I've heard he's a good man. He'll see her right." Then she added, "When my husband pulled her out of that car, she begged him to look for a horse. She thought she'd struck it. But there *was* no horse. Nor any other injured party! He searched for near on to a quarter of an hour, to satisfy her, and never saw any sign of a horse!"

"A Norfolk Gray mare was stolen from a stable outside of Osterley last night. If you should find her, please send word to me as soon as possible." But he'd already seen the mare. And she showed no sign of injury.

Rutledge turned the crank and climbed into his seat. Priscilla Connaught pulled the gaudy shawl closer as he circled the yard and began the long, rough descent down the drive to the main road. "I'm sorry," he said, glancing at her. "I'll make the journey as comfortable as I can."

"It doesn't matter," she answered tonelessly, shrugging deeper into the folds of the shawl, her chin invisible. They rode in silence for a very long time. She hardly noticed when they passed her car and the farmer with his team, though Rutledge waved to him. And then she seemed to throw off some of the lethargy that wrapped her in bleak despair, as if the tea had finally helped.

He thought she might be recovering a little of her usual strength, and was encouraged. When she turned to stare at him, he offered her a brief smile.

She didn't appear to see it.

"You were in the War!" she said fiercely. *"Tell me how to die!"*

He thought of all the men he'd watched die. And tried to shake off the dark cloud that settled over his spirits.

"There's no easy way," he said bitterly. "Trust me. I know."

When they had reached the marshes, turning toward Osterley, Rutledge said in a neutral tone, as if discussing the weather, "What happened to the horse?"

She turned to look at him. "What horse?" she asked, frowning. "I don't remember a horse. . . ."

Dr. Stephenson came at once in answer to Rutledge's summons, and listened with concern as the Inspector explained what had happened to Priscilla Connaught. Then the doctor took the stairs up to her bedroom, where she lay with the shades down, her face turned to the wall.

When he came down half an hour later, drying his hands on a pale yellow towel embroidered with white violets, he walked into the sun-bright parlor and took the chair by the window. The room was pretty, with walls of a very soft cream, accented by the deep blues of the uphol-stery and carpets, and a pale climbing rose entwined in the matching drapes. A woman's room, and yet empty of the small treasures that usu-ally adorned such an ornate mantelpiece or filled the polished tabletops. In a way it seemed to reflect Priscilla Connaught's empty life. She had, over the years, collected nothing but misery.

"That's a nasty cut on her head. It could be serious—I'd not be sur-prised if there's some concussion. Bruises," Stephenson told Rutledge. "And a good many more will likely show up. She's already sporting deep bruising on the shoulder and hip. But nothing appears to be bro-ken. The ankle has been sprained, and I've taped that to reduce the swelling."

"The head injury. Serious enough to confuse her memory?"

"I can't say. The woman is suffering from more than the effects of the car running into the ditch—agitation and emotional collapse, to head the list. The sedative I've administered will keep her quiet for some hours, and we'll see whether she's calmer then." He paused. "The right eye is turning black now. She won't want to look into her mirror for awhile. And I took a stitch or two in another cut on her scalp. Bit of glass lifted a flap of skin and hair. I daresay she'll have a headache for a day or so. I'll find someone to sit with her. Ellen Baker should do, she's gentle and has a way with her. High-strung women like Miss Connaught aren't always the best of patients."

Rutledge said, "You may want to make another choice. She was looking for ways to kill herself. She ran into that ditch on purpose, from what I could learn, and she believes she's killed a man."

Stephenson's eyebrows rose. "Does she now! I could tell she'd been weeping. I didn't know the rest of it, and she didn't volunteer anything. Why does she want to kill herself? Because of this man Walsh? Doesn't make any sense! Didn't realize she even knew him!"

Rutledge felt the fatigue burrowing deep into his very bones. "It has nothing to do with Walsh. Not directly. But there's a strong sense of guilt. Real or fancied, I don't know. I think she ought to be—watched."

"In that case, I'll send for Mrs. Nutley. She's had seven sons, all of whom have battled their way through life, and she's nursed everything from broken bones to depression to drunken stupors. She'll manage well enough." He crossed the room to stand at the window, looking out at the marshes. "It'll rain before dinner." He turned back to Rutledge. "There's a narrow line between love and hate sometimes, you know. And it can be crossed unwittingly."

"I can't tell you what's behind it. She's—a very private person." And he wasn't prepared to break her confidences. Not yet.

"That isn't much help. I'd need to know what signs to look for!"

Rutledge rubbed his face with his hands. "All I can tell you is that she went out last night"—was it only last night?—"to look for Walsh. She was—one of Father James's flock, and afraid the man would escape justice. And somewhere between that time and dawn this morning, she believes she killed someone and she tried to kill herself."

"Went out on her own? I can't see Blevins allowing that!"

Rutledge was too close to exhaustion to fight a battle of wits with this very sharp man. "He didn't know. Ask him yourself, if you like." Whatever secrets Priscilla Connaught possessed, if the good doctor hadn't stumbled over them in ten or twelve years, it was a salute to her deep and abiding need for privacy.

But Dr. Stephenson's curiosity was, quite frankly, aroused.

"Then what did she say when you walked into the farmhouse?"

"That someone was dead. And she'd tried to miss the horse. But later on she was confused about the horse, whether it was there at all."

It was a bald account. Rutledge left it at that.

Dr. Stephenson grunted. "Well, the accident itself could have caused confusion between what she intended to do and what she did do." He took out his watch and looked at it, sighing. "I've a long day ahead of me. I've had two men brought in with broken bones, and a woman hysterical enough to deliver prematurely. And that doesn't count the scrapes and cuts and sprains from people wandering around in the dark most of the night! I'll send my nurse to find Mrs. Nutley and see that Miss Connaught is cared for. If you'll wait here for half an hour?"

"How long do you think it will be before her mind is clear?"

"Hard to say," Stephenson replied, considering. "Wait until tomorrow before questioning her again. She may be making more sense by then."

When he was gone, Rutledge looked in on Priscilla Connaught and then sat in a chair in the room across the passage from hers. He intended to watch; instead, he fell heavily asleep.

When Mrs. Nutley arrived, letting herself in quietly, he forced himself back to wakefulness. But it was hardly more than that. She clicked her tongue when she saw him. A motherly woman with a strong face and an awesome air of competence, she said, "If you know what's best for you, you'll get yourself in that spare bed over there and go back to sleep."

But there was still too much to be done.

Blevins was working in his office when Rutledge walked through his door. He looked up with a sour expression and said, "I thought you'd be asleep by now. I wish to God I was."

"If I look as weary as you do, we're both a fine pair of sleepwalkers."

"Matched set." Blevins leaned back in his chair. "The doctor in Hurley tells me Walsh was probably kicked by the horse and died where he stood. The loose shoe fits rather roughly into the wound in his skull, even though it wasn't the one that did the damage. The doctor's not sure what the angle was, of course, when the kick was delivered. What matters was a luck of the strike. Delivered just exactly at the wrong place for any chance of survival. Death by misadventure."

Rutledge said easily, "Any sign of other injuries? A fall—running into something in the dark?"

Blevins laughed. "You don't give up, do you? London told me that, when I asked for you. All right, just for the hell of it, why should there be?"

"The searchers seemed to have had a rough night of it," Rutledge answered, taking the other chair and sitting down. He hadn't had breakfast, he remembered. Only the sandwiches that Mrs. Barnett had put up for him when he'd gone to find Priscilla Connaught. "Does Walsh have any family? Have you notified anyone that he's dead?"

"There's the scissor sharpener. I doubt he'd walk to the corner to help Walsh, now that he's dead. What's in it for him? With no real proof that he was the lookout while Walsh riffled the study, he's home free."

"There's Iris Kenneth. She might know if Walsh had any family."

"Yes. Well, do you want the task of going to London to fetch her? She's not likely to come north on her own!"

"I suppose you're right. Still—"

"If you're on your way there," Blevins said, watching Rutledge's face, "you might do me the courtesy of calling on her yourself."

After a moment, Rutledge made a last effort to break through the emotional barriers that Inspector Blevins had set up.

"Put aside your personal feelings about Walsh—and about the death of Father James. If you'd walked into the study of a stranger that morning, how would you have described the body lying by the window?"

"The same way. An intruder had struck hard and fast, out of fear of being recognized. Matthew Walsh won't be giving us the answer to *why* he did it—but I don't suppose, in the scheme of things, it makes much difference. He ran. That's guilt."

Rutledge said quietly, thinking it through, "The killer—Walsh, if you like—didn't strike once, looking to buy time for an escape. He *meant* to kill."

"Yes. It was deliberate. Makes me sick to think about it!"

"On the other hand, if there hadn't been any money in the tin box in the desk—if it had been spent or given away by that time—how would you have decided on the motive for murder?"

Blevins said impatiently, "The same way."

"No, you couldn't have looked at it the same way! There was no money in the desk, nothing to draw a thief to the study. Nothing for Walsh or anyone like him to slip into the rectory to steal."

"You're setting up a scene that didn't exist! Walsh couldn't know that, could he? See it my way for once! Walsh was desperate—this was his last hope of finding the sum he needed to finish paying for that bloody cart. He may have killed in a fury when he discovered the box *was* empty!"

"If this had happened before the bazaar—" Rutledge began.

"All right! Let's take your position and examine it. A dead man and no tin box would tell me there was another reason, a personal reason, to kill that priest. But I knew Father James too well—and in all your questioning, *you* still haven't answered that one, either!"

Blevins, tired as he was, couldn't make the leap of imagination. Hamish said, "You canna' expect it from him. He was too close to the victim."

Rutledge took a deep breath, thinking, *Hamish is right.*

"If Father James knew something that worried him—possibly involving a police matter—would he come to you with it?"

"Of course he would! I'd be the first person he'd turn to," Blevins answered with a lift of pride.

But he hadn't—and for the same reason: Father James, too, had known the Inspector's limitations as a man and as a policeman.

Rutledge said, "I hear there's a chance that Monsignor Holston will replace Father James until a suitable choice can be made. I'm driving to Norwich later. Shall I tell him that Walsh has died?"

"Suit yourself. I expect half the county has heard that by now. What's taking you to Norwich?"

Rutledge smiled. "A personal matter. By the way—who'll be given the reward that Lord Sedgwick put up?"

"Not the police," Blevins said wryly. "And Lord Sedgwick ought to make that decision himself."

"I expect he will." Rutledge rose from his chair. "Have you by any chance seen Miss Trent? I'd like to speak to her before I leave for Norwich."

"She went out last night, found herself badly frightened in the woods north of the church, and spent what was left of it at the vicarage. I stopped there to tell the Vicar that Walsh had been found. He thought she was still asleep."

"What frightened her?"

"God knows. An owl probably, or a badger. Women have no business out in the middle of the night on their own."

"You've heard, I'm sure, that Priscilla Connaught was out looking for Walsh? Ran her car into a ditch and was lucky to survive with only a concussion."

"Yes, well, rather proves my point, doesn't it?"

Rutledge reached across the desk to shake Blevins's hand. "If you'd like a last piece of advice, I'd wire Iris Kenneth if I were you. Save the ratepayers from burying Walsh in a pauper's grave!"

"I might, at that." He thought about it. "Yes, I will!"

Rutledge left, glad to step out into the sunshine. It had a grayness to it now that forecast rain later, as the doctor had suggested. After the early morning, it had never been a clear day. But even in this light the marshes seemed rich with color, and the wind moved through the grasses like a wraith.

The walk from the police station to the vicarage seemed to stretch before Rutledge like the Great Wall of China, miles upon miles to travel on foot. His body rebelled at the thought. Hamish ridiculed him for his weakness.

Ignoring his tormentor, he went back to the hotel and started the car.

CHAPTER TWENTY-FOUR

Mr. Sims opened the vicarage door warily, peering out at Rutledge shrouded in the heavy shadows cast by the trees along the drive.

"What brings you here? Half the town is sound asleep after the long night. I understand Walsh has been found, and is dead."

"Yes, that's true. On both counts." Rutledge said it pleasantly. "I came to ask if Miss Trent is awake."

Sims said, "I expect she's still asleep. But if you care to leave her a message?"

"Would you mind looking in on her? It's rather urgent." His voice was still quite pleasant, but the edge of command had crept into its timbre.

Sims was on the point of arguing when a door opened at the top of the stairs. May Trent stood there above them in a dressing gown far too large for her, her hair unbound and hanging in a dark stream down her back. She didn't look as if she'd been asleep. The smudges under her eyes were as deep as Rutledge's own.

"I'm awake, Vicar," she said. And then to Rutledge, "But hardly dressed to receive callers."

"A policeman isn't ranked as a caller, Miss Trent. I understand you were frightened last night. What did you see or think you heard in the woods that brought you here in some haste? We're trying to track Walsh's movements."

"How did you know—" she began, and then realized that he'd tricked her. "Yes, all right," she said after a moment. "If you'll give me a little time to dress?"

He agreed, and the Vicar led him into the kitchen at the back of the house. The curtains were still drawn. A dresser taller than he was stood against one wall. Dishes were piled in a pan of soapy water on a small table by the windows, and the remnants of breakfast were still on the stove—toast and sausages with fried eggs. A jar of marmalade and a dish of butter sat on the main table, next to three used teacups.

"I was making fresh tea," Sims told Rutledge, nodding to the kettle on the stove. "My guess is that you could use a cup! I've drunk my share this night."

Remembering what Hamish had said earlier that morning as he'd finished Mrs. Barnett's provisions, Rutledge asked, "With a little whiskey, if you've got it."

"Yes, indeed," Sims answered, opening a cupboard and taking out a fresh cup. "I'll just go and fetch it."

"First, I'd like to hear how Miss Trent arrived last night."

"Nothing much to tell." Sims peered into the sugar bowl. "I heard a knocking at the door, and I called down from a window to see who it was. Miss Trent said she'd got separated from her search party, and was uncomfortable about walking back to the hotel on her own. I let her in, telling her I'd just dress and then see to it that she got back to the hotel. But she asked for tea to warm her, and by the time I'd made it, she was sound asleep in her chair. I left her there with a blanket over her, and sent her upstairs around six, when she woke up disoriented and still half asleep."

It was told smoothly, with enough detail to give it the air of truth.

But even Hamish growled his disapproval.

"Yes, that's a fine tale for the gossips of Osterley!" Rutledge replied, taking the cup that Sims poured him.

"It's the truth—!" There was outrage in the Vicar's voice.

"Yes, I'm sure it is. But May Trent doesn't strike me as the sort of woman easily frightened by noises in the woods, if she was out with a search party, and she came down that dark drive of yours when it would have been far wiser to hurry down the hill to the comparative safety of Water Street." He paused. "After all, Walsh had been *here* just hours before. As far as she knew, he might still be hidden in the grounds, waiting until the hue and cry faded. No one thought to search the church tower, did they? Or all the rooms of the vicarage?"

Hamish said, "It's no' an impossibility. . . ."

"You'd have got her out of here, fast as you could, if you'd had any sense," Rutledge said. "But what she came to tell you made you both decide to stay here."

Sims murmured, "I'll just find the whiskey."

But before he could move, the kitchen door opened and May Trent came in. "You said it was urgent?" She wore her clothes, wrinkled from sleeping in the chair, like a badge of honor. Her eyes strayed to the teapot. Sims was already searching for another clean cup.

She sat, accepted the tea he poured for her, added sugar, and sipped it as if it was warming her, her fingers around the bowl of the cup.

They were, Rutledge thought sourly, as companionable as a long-married pair, while he had only a matter of hours to finish what he'd set out to do.

"Get your coats, if you will. We're driving to Norwich in five minutes."

May Trent regarded him suspiciously. "I'm exhausted. I'm not going to Norwich or anywhere else—only to bed. And quite frankly, so should you, Inspector. You don't look as if you're rested enough to undertake—"

"You'd have done it for Father James."

"What has this drive to Norwich to do with Father James?" she demanded.

"I think he began by trying to solve a problem, and found himself pitched headlong into something far more horrifying than he was trained to deal with. He did what he could. The man who may have killed him is dead now—there won't be a trial, no clear judgment of his guilt, or for that matter, his innocence. Blevins is satisfied that the case is closed. But I'm left with an uneasy feeling that it isn't. It's *convenient* to blame Matthew Walsh. And shut our eyes. But I should think someone owes it to Father James to get to the bottom of what troubled him. I'm willing to try, but I can't do it alone."

Both Sims and May Trent were silent, absorbing what he'd said. She was the first to recover. "Then let that someone drive to Norwich with you."

But something made her look away from him.

"Walsh is dead," Sims put in. "I can't believe that Walsh would have tried to escape, if he was innocent! If the facts, once they're collected, would exonerate him, why not wait to be cleared?"

"Because he was a poor man and terrified that justice wouldn't care if he went to the hangman. Which reminds me—if you're convinced of his guilt, tell me why the two of you spent the night in this empty barn of a house, and wouldn't leave it or go for help?"

May Trent stared down at her cup. "I'm a silly woman. The Vicar asked me again and again if I'd walk with him as far as the hotel. But I couldn't go back outside and feel safe. You said yourself—a murderer was on the loose."

"I think he was," Rutledge replied slowly. "But perhaps it wasn't Walsh."

She spilled tea into the saucer and clicked her tongue in annoyance. "I wish you would tell us what's wrong! What it is you want from us."

Sims took the saucer from her, poured out the spilled tea, and wiped it with a serviette. He said, "I have work to do here. I can't abandon my parish on a whim. Miss Trent is justified in asking what it is you want."

Rutledge said quietly, "I'm a policeman. Have you forgotten? I don't have to ask. I can require you to accompany me. Now, if you've finished your tea, we'll be on our way."

Listening to Hamish battering at the back of his mind, Rutledge made one detour on his way to the road south.

He pulled once more into the rutted drive by Randal's farm.

But the gelding and the farmer had not come home.

Rutledge was beginning to feel uneasy.

The motorcar was silent as they drove south. Rutledge, uncomfortable because the Vicar was sitting in Hamish's usual place, was not the best of companions, and May Trent kept her face turned away from him, looking out the window.

Hamish, on the other hand, was conducting a long and skeptical conversation with Rutledge.

"It isna' the best way! Go to London, and speak to yon Chief Superintendent, tell him what it is you suspect! Let him reopen the inquiry."

"Bowles won't be any more receptive than Blevins was. And the case will be closed. I have at best twenty-four hours to solve the mystery that surrounded Father James's last days. *But it was there.*" Rutledge paused. "And there's a secret binding these people together. Each seems to know only a part of it. What I don't understand—yet—is whether the mystery and the secret are one and the same. I'm willing to bet my career that they are!"

"Aye, it could be so. But the days of the rack are over—you canna' force them to tell you. Or be certain in the end you've got the truth."

Rutledge concentrated on the road for a time and then picked up the thread of his silent conversation with Hamish. If nothing else, it kept him awake. But it failed to satisfy either one of the participants.

Hamish's last salvo was telling.

"They willna' like it in London."

"No. But we're a long way from London." Rutledge shut out the voice in his aching head and tried to concentrate on the busy road south.

It was close to teatime when Rutledge pulled the motorcar into a small space between a cart full of cabbages and the deep hole that still reeked like a cesspool.

He got out, stretched aching shoulders, and went around the boot to open the door for May Trent. But the Vicar was already there before him, saying, "Why didn't you tell us that it was Monsignor Holston you were coming to see!" His voice was cross. "There was no need to be so damned mysterious!"

He and May Trent stood waiting by the road while Rutledge went to knock on the door of the rectory.

Bryony opened it, beamed at Rutledge, and asked after greeting him, "Will you be staying for tea? I've got such a lovely bit of French cake for Himself, and—" She broke off as she saw the two people behind him, looking up at her from the street. "Ah, this'll be business, then!"

"I still wouldn't say no to tea," Rutledge assured her, smiling. On their way south, by mutual agreement, the three travelers had agreed not to stop for lunch.

May Trent closed her eyes, as if shutting out the watery sun that had been threatening rain for two hours or more. Bryony saw it, and called to her, "Come inside, madam, and let me take you upstairs for a bit. You look like you could do with a rest."

She only smiled and shook her head. "No. But thank you!"

They were ushered into the study, where Monsignor Holston looked up from his book in surprise.

"I didn't remember visitors were expected!" he said to Bryony, setting the cat, Bruce, on the floor.

"The Inspector has come again, Monsignor, and brought guests with him." She quietly closed the door as he greeted Rutledge warmly. Then he smiled at the Vicar and shook his hand, before the introduction to Miss Trent was made. Their host seated her with courtesy and said, "Father James spoke to me a number of times about the manuscript you're completing. It's quite an undertaking. If I may be of any assistance, you need only ask. Norfolk has a good deal of material to draw from."

"As I've discovered!" She thanked him, managing to smile. "Memorials, even so, are often an excuse to go on mourning. He tried to tell me that as well."

"I expect time will take care of that, too."

Rutledge said, "We're here about Father James, as it happens. Walsh is dead. He—died—last night, trying to escape."

"Killed?" Holston asked. "By the police?"

"He was kicked by a horse. At least that's what the evidence suggests. There'll be an official inquiry, as a matter of course."

"God rest his soul!"

Sims said, "Altogether, it was a harrowing night for everyone."

"Walsh appeared to have the best motive," Rutledge said. "There was a certain amount of evidence against him, but not all of it was conclusive—or satisfactory. On the other hand, I've been exploring Father James's movements during the fortnight between the bazaar and his death." His eyes turned toward Holston. "And I need to learn from you, Monsignor, what Father James told you about the Confession of Herbert Baker."

Completely unprepared for the question, Holston said, "I couldn't, even if I—"

"I'm not asking for a revelation of Herbert Baker's last words. What I want to know is what *Father James* told you about this man."

"He never spoke to me about Baker or his family—"

"I'm sure that's true. But he came here one day shortly before he died and told you that he had just been given information that had upset him, and that the person who had passed on this information had had no idea of its importance to Father James personally."

It was an arrow shot into the air. But the sudden tightness of Monsignor Holston's face told Rutledge that it had come very close to its mark. "No, it wasn't that—"

"Did he also tell you that he was helpless to do anything about it?" Rutledge kept his voice at a conversational level, as if he was continuing to confirm knowledge he already possessed.

"There was nothing he *could*—" Monsignor Holston stopped. Then he said, "Look, he didn't confide in me. Or confess to me. He didn't tell me the circumstances. But I could see he'd come for comfort—from a friend, not a fellow priest."

"How could you see that?"

"He walked in that door and paced the floor for over an hour. I didn't ask him why—we've all been through that kind of personal despair. To tell you the truth, there was one family in particular that he was deeply concerned about. I thought his visit had to do with them. When he sat down in that chair, where you're sitting now, I made some comment to that effect. He raised his head and looked at me. 'No, they're doing well enough just now.' Then he added simply, 'God works in mysterious ways. I've been given an answer to a question that has troubled me for *years*. But I can't make use of it to set things right. It came unexpectedly, and in such a way that my choices are very limited.' He put his face in his hands and I could see that he was under a great strain. I asked, 'Would it help to speak to the Bishop?' and he said, 'That door is shut, but there may be another that will open.' And so I went back to the report I was writing, to give him a little space. Half an hour later he was gone, and that was the end of it."

"But you guessed—did you not—what he was referring to."

"Not then."

Rutledge waited.

Monsignor Holston said, "It wasn't until the funeral Mass for Father James that I first heard the name Baker."

"During the service?" Rutledge was surprised.

"Actually, a young woman came up to me afterward to say that she didn't know Father James well, but that she had attended the Mass from a sense of duty. He'd given her father comfort as he lay dying, even though Herbert Baker wasn't a Catholic. She felt she was returning a kindness, in her own fashion. She was quite shy, stammering out the story, but I thanked her for coming and told her that Father James would have appreciated her thoughtfulness. And it was true. Later on I asked Sims, here, about her. Dr. Stephenson overheard and added that Father James had come in to the surgery to inquire about Baker—whether his mind was clear at the end. His point was that Father James had been a conscientious priest, but I read more into the conversation than Stephenson realized. Because I knew the one other bit of information that mattered."

"That Herbert Baker had been coachman—and sometimes chauffeur—to Lord Sedgwick's family," Rutledge said.

"Everyone in Osterley could have told you that, if you'd asked. No, that it was Herbert Baker who drove Virginia Sedgwick to King's Lynn, the day she disappeared. At her particular request."

The Vicar, listening apprehensively, sat back with a sigh. But Monsignor Holston had no more to say.

Rutledge turned to May Trent. She had kept her composure, a woman with hidden strengths, learned from her personal suffering. He chose a different course with her.

"The other door Father James mentioned—it was you. He wanted to know if Mrs. Sedgwick had been on board ship, if you'd actually seen her, spoken with her. If you had, then he no longer had to rely on Baker's confession, whatever it was, to fill in the details of Mrs. Sedgwick's disappearance."

"No, it wasn't like that! He was trying to help *me*. To stop the nightmares. He said." Her voice was odd, a tremor behind it. She seemed on the point of adding more, but stopped.

"And when you refused to remember, the priest went to his solicitor and added a codicil to his Will. Father James left you a photograph of Virginia Sedgwick"—there was a sharp intake of breath from the listening Vicar—"but not the cuttings that he'd collected so painstakingly. He wanted only your own memories, and he wished you the courage to write down what had happened—to you and to her. Why would he have believed so strongly that you—of all the survivors—had met her on shipboard?"

"I didn't *refuse* to remember, as you put it. And he didn't believe any such thing!" She was flushed, her chin high and her eyes bright. "I can't understand why you keep harping on it. He just felt that the nightmares would stop if I could face them once and for all. And I couldn't; I wasn't ready. He never forced me to go back to that night—he was careful. We tried to discuss less frightening experiences, who had the cabins next to mine, the people I sat with at meals, what I wore the first evening out—and I couldn't even remember that!"

Hamish scolded, "The lass is tired. Let it go."

Rutledge heard him. He said to May Trent, trying to make amends, "I'm not hounding you—"

"You are!" she said angrily. "You're worse than Father James ever was. *You don't know what it is like to be haunted, you've never sat up screaming in bed in the middle of the night, hearing the dying cry out for help and knowing that you will live and they won't—!*"

Exhausted as he himself was, the strength of her emotions touched him on the raw. His own anger flared with unwitting heat.

"Don't I? *I live it with every breath I take*—"

Hamish's voice was sharp. "You *mustna'* betray yoursel'!"

Rutledge's iron will shut off the flow of words even as he heard the warning. His face had grown so white and so strained that May Trent reached out a hand to him, as if to stop him, too. And then she dropped it.

They stared at each other in horrified silence.

Rutledge thought, *I've never come so close*—

Hamish was still yelling at him, dinning in his head like the German guns, until he could barely function. *"Ye're vulnerable because she's the first woman who's been through the same horror*—"

But Rutledge didn't care. How far had she seen inside his own grief? As far as he'd seen into the depths of hers? He didn't know. It was not something he wanted to think about. It didn't bear thinking about. . . .

Sims and Father Holston, watching the two of them, immobilized by the sudden silence after the fierce intensity of their exchange, were unwilling witnesses.

And into the electrical atmosphere that no one knew quite how to cope with, the door opened and the housekeeper, Bryony, wheeled in the ornate walnut cart with the heavy Victorian tea service gleaming in the lamplight.

CHAPTER TWENTY-FIVE

THE VICAR GOT TO HIS FEET. "Monsignor Holston, if you'll have your housekeeper summon a cab for us, I'll see Miss Trent safely on the next train—"

Monsignor Holston, rising as well, cut across his words. "I expect that Inspector Rutledge can explain—"

But it was May Trent who collected herself with an effort and said, "No. We need to finish this." She turned to Bryony and thanked her for the tea, adding, "I'll pour."

As the housekeeper left, she busied herself with the cups, her head turned away from the men in the room. But her hands were shaking, and her eyes were haunted in her drawn face.

Rutledge, his own face still as pale as his shirt, stood where he was, lost in the emotional storm that had swept him. Hamish, his voice harsh, was saying, "You canna' be so foolish!"

Miss Trent handed a cup to the Vicar, who awkwardly looked around for a table to set it on, his eyes avoiding Rutledge's. Monsignor Holston took his and sat down again behind the desk, rearranging papers lying on the blotter as if giving everyone a little time to recover. She brought a cup to Rutledge and said, "Drink it. Now, while it's hot and sweet."

He accepted the tea like a man sleepwalking, and seemed not to know what to do with it. After a moment, he drank it, hot as it was, and seemed to draw strength from it.

May Trent set aside her own cup and silently passed the slices of cake and the thin sandwiches—egg and ham and cheese—each a small white triangle of bread that seemed likely to choke them all.

It was ritual—and in ritual lay some normalcy. Each of the uncomfortable occupants in the quiet room accepted his role in this charade. And in the end, the tension in the air began to subside a little.

Monsignor Holston bit into an egg sandwich and swallowed it in a gulp.

Bruce the cat, who had slipped into the room with the housekeeper, came out from under the desk and stared impassively at the ham sandwich between Sims's fingers, and the Vicar seemed to consider offering it to the animal. He couldn't think why he'd accepted one in the first place, except out of politeness. His stomach was a twisted knot of despair. He didn't want to hear any more; he'd had enough.

Miss Trent drank her tea in silence, and then said, "I can't tell you whether or not Virginia Sedgwick was on the ship. I remember sailing, I vaguely recall dressing for the evening, although I can't tell you what I chose to wear. I remember going to dinner, and faces and people speaking to me. A hodgepodge of images, unconnected in any way with me personally. It's as if I don't want to remember who lived and—and who died. It is such a terrible thing, to drown. I nearly did—someone hauled me into a boat, like a bundle of wet rags, and I was coughing and sick and so frightened I couldn't speak. There were others in the water—" She gulped for air, as if drowning again, and said quickly, "No, *I won't go back there!*" She stopped and looked at the hearth, as if to find something new to pin her attention on. After a moment she continued, her voice uncertain. "Father James had worked with the wounded during the War. He told me that talking might help stop the pain and the dreams. But I'd buried it for so many long, difficult years. I'd reached a plateau of sorts, where I was someone else. People no longer remembered that I'd been on *Titanic*. When the War came, I was planning to be married and looking ahead to a future that would be happier than the past. But it was—I never told Roger about what had happened to me, I thought that if he *didn't* know, I'd not see the reminder of my pain in his eyes, and be forced to look back. Someone else told him. A friend, who believed that Roger would want to know the truth and be better able to comfort me when the dreams were—worse than usual. That's why I'm finishing his work. I had already decided to break the engagement, once he was safely home. But he never came home. And I carry that guilt, too."

She looked from one to the other of the three men. "I didn't know Father James had his own nightmare. I wasn't much help to him, I'm afraid." There was a faint quality of the child in her voice, begging forgiveness. "I didn't understand how great his need *was*!"

Rutledge sat down heavily, trying to bring himself back to the task at hand. He wished that the Vicar and May Trent had taken the train, and he could drive back to Osterley—or anywhere—all alone. Except for Hamish, who never left him alone.

The Vicar said, into the silence, picking his words, "Virginia Sedgwick was a woman hungry for affection. I watched her—I was invited to several of the parties at Sedgwick Hall after she married Arthur. She believed her husband loved her. She most certainly loved him. But he was mad for racing; he lived in a world of fast machines and dangerous sport. As far as I could tell, he was oblivious to her dislike of living alone out in the middle of Yorkshire, where she had few neighbors and fewer friends. He expected her to find pleasure in running the house, as his mother had done—she was a well-known hostess, and quite clever at smoothing over her husband's connections with trade. It never worked, their marriage. When I heard Virginia had left him and gone back to America, I was—glad it was over. I couldn't bear to watch her suffer."

Rutledge, grateful for the change in subject, asked, "You spoke of friends. Were there any close friends she confided in?"

"No." As if to soften the harsh negative, Sims added. "She found it hard to find common ground with women of her own class, and was too friendly with the servants. They took advantage of her. That's why she came to the vicarage to talk with me, using whatever flimsy excuse she could think of. Father James and I were safe, you see. Clergymen, not likely to take advantage. In any sense."

Intrigued, Rutledge asked, "What did she talk about?"

"The flowers. The music. She liked music. Services for the family were usually held at the church on the grounds of the estate. She preferred Holy Trinity because it was so beautiful. She'd spend hours sitting in the nave polishing the benches or mending the cushions. I found her one day on a ladder, cleaning out the cobwebs around the stained-glass windows. Impeccably dressed, her gloves filthy—" He stopped. "They closed the house in East Sherham when Sedgwick went to London, and she was sent back to Yorkshire, then."

Monsignor Holston said, "Father James met her in London, just after she'd come to England. They served on some committee or other together. He said she was the happiest woman he'd ever seen. And he was the man she turned to when the marriage soured. She was a woman of strong faith, and he tried to bolster that. That's one reason he wasn't prepared to believe that she could turn her back on her husband and leave England. He always defended her, and it's my feeling that he always hoped she might try to get in touch with him."

The Vicar said unexpectedly, "I thought it was better for her just to go. Father James and I quarreled over that. He wanted to find her, and I told him I'd have no part in it."

Hamish said, "Aye, it's the difference in age between the two men. Both wanted to play knight, but no' in the same fashion."

Rutledge silently agreed. It was that male vulnerability to their own protective instincts. To save the damsel from the dragon—the dragon, in this case, Arthur Sedgwick's seeming indifference to his beautiful young wife—and somehow make her life better. Priest or layman, it didn't matter. Each man had responded to Virginia Sedgwick.

Monsignor Holston pushed his plate away. "There's a more practical side, you know. It's my understanding that she had a considerable inheritance, from a grandmother who had heavily invested in railroads among other things. What was the disposition of that, if she died? Or—if she just disappeared? And another question—why didn't her family in America raise a hue and cry, when she went missing?"

"No one could foresee that her ship would sink!" the Vicar said.

"Father James told me in late 1912 that she wasn't listed among the passengers," Monsignor Holston replied. "That is, not until *after* the inquiry. Sedgwick hired someone to look into the matter for him, and he finally found her name. This would explain why Father James was so interested in what Miss Trent could tell him."

Rutledge said, "Why was there a problem?"

"There was a record of her purchasing her fare, but none of her boarding the ship. Apparently there was some confusion over names."

May Trent said unexpectedly, "If I had wanted to get away, and money wasn't an issue, I'd have paid my fare, and then taken another ship. Or no ship at all. Virginia Sedgwick could very well be alive and still in England."

Hamish said quietly, "Or dead, having never left England."

Rutledge, pursuing that thought, asked, "In which case, if Herbert Baker changed his mind on his deathbed, and told Father James the truth about that journey from Yorkshire to King's Lynn—or even what happened in King's Lynn itself—it must have been very difficult for Father James to hold his tongue. And it's quite possible, isn't it, that someone doesn't want the truth about Virginia Sedgwick to come out?"

Monsignor Holston replied slowly, "I hadn't considered that. But it explains why I've been uneasy since I saw Father James dead. If you are not a Catholic—if you don't understand the sanctity of Confession—it would be natural to believe that Father James told me or even the Vicar here whatever he'd learned from Baker . . ."

Sims spoke up suddenly, his face unhappy, eyes torn.

"There's another part of the story."

"Virginia Sedgwick was—a lovely child. I don't think Arthur Sedgwick realized that when he met her in Richmond. She told me she was always surrounded by cousins, brothers, sisters—they seldom had the opportunity to be alone, she and Arthur. And in company, she was shy, she spoke softly, and she had the gift of listening. What's more, her grandmother, worried about her future, had left her a fortune. Rich, beautiful—and not—not truly *whole*."

They stared at him. In his mind, Rutledge heard Lord Sedgwick's dismissive words: *"Attractive simpleton, that's what she was."* Rutledge had taken it as hyperbole—but it was the truth.

"They brought her to England for the wedding, you know," Sims said wearily. "Her family. A very fashionable affair in London. I don't think Arthur ever realized that she was—simple. Until they went away on their wedding journey. Her family had made certain they were never alone together."

May Trent asked, "How do you mean? Simple?"

"Virginia—she'd had a fever as a small child. The family blamed it on that. They *swore* it wasn't hereditary. But by that time Arthur was married to her, and he discovered that this very pretty, very sweet, very young bride was not simply modest and shy. Her mental development was retarded."

Rutledge said, "And he didn't like the feeling of being cheated."

Sims agreed. "It may explain why he spent so much time in France, racing with his friends. Why he left Virginia behind in Yorkshire, isolated from his friends and from London Society. Reading between the lines, I gathered that this was the reason behind his brother Edwin's frequent visits when Arthur was away. He was making damned sure that the simpleton didn't fornicate with the servants or the stable-boys, and produce a half-wit bastard who would inherit the family title!"

Monsignor Holston, after much persuasion, agreed to return to Osterley with them and speak to Inspector Blevins.

It had been a heated argument

"I can't see that it will do much good. So much of it is speculation," the priest protested. "Father James is dead, Baker is dead—for all we know, Mrs. Sedgwick is dead. All we may succeed in proving is that the chauffeur, Baker, was cajoled into letting his passenger flee her husband, there in King's Lynn. And there's no *crime* in that."

Rutledge argued, "It isn't a question of convincing Blevins. It's a matter of strategy. If there is sufficient doubt, he must reopen his investigation."

"How will you begin?" May Trent asked.

Turning to the Vicar, Rutledge asked him, "Think back. Herbert Baker was your sexton. Can you recall when Mrs. Baker was ill-enough to be placed in a sanitarium for her tuberculosis? You must have visited her then!"

Sims rubbed his eyes. "She was very ill in November 1911, I think, and they didn't expect her to live through the winter. With sanitarium care, she did."

"By the spring of 1912 then—when Mrs. Sedgwick went missing—Baker could see that continued care was essential to keeping his own wife alive?"

"He never expected miracles," Sims corrected Rutledge. "She *was* dying."

"Yes. She'd have been dead in November without that care. She survived *two years* with it. That mattered to a man who loved his wife very deeply."

Sims responded, "Herbert Baker was a decent man—loyal."

"How did he define loyalty?" Rutledge persisted. "If someone convinced him he was acting in Virginia Sedgwick's best interests, would he shut his eyes?"

Sims said, "He'd never *harm* her!"

"But would Arthur Sedgwick feel the same way?"

The argument had ended there.

It was crowded in the car, and Hamish, in the rear seat with the two men, was restless and not in the best of moods.

Rutledge drove like an automaton, beyond exhaustion. May Trent sat in the seat beside him, head bowed, lost in her own thoughts. Once she turned to him and asked, "If Virginia Sedgwick was—simple—how did she manage to elude Baker, find her way to London, and arrange to sail on the next ship leaving for America?"

Sims answered, leaning forward with one hand on the back of her seat. "It's what worried Father James. Why he feared she might be dead. God knows, Arthur received plenty of sympathy. He could have married again any time, an eligible young widower with more money than he knew what to do with, and no children to share in it? But he'd been burned once. He stayed clear of any entanglements."

"And what did you think?" Rutledge asked him.

There was a long silence. "I thought perhaps Edwin Sedgwick had engineered her flight. I was jealous. I had wanted her to turn to me. I wanted to be the shining knight on the white horse who rescued her. I sat there alone in the vicarage and told myself that she'd been more clever than I knew. And I asked myself what she'd given Edwin in return. I'm not very proud of it. But it's the truth."

Monsignor Holston added unexpectedly, "She's never been declared dead, you know. It was all kept very quiet. Father James wrote to her family in America. They swore Virginia hadn't come home. They'd agreed with Lord Sedgwick's decision to hire people to look for her and were satisfied that it was very possible she had been lost at sea. But Father James was convinced early on that if she *had* arrived safely, they would have sent her back."

Hamish added, "It doesna' seem that her ain family cares o'wer much what happened. They were eager enough to palm her off on an unsuspecting suitor."

Sims swore. "To hurt *her* would be like hurting a child!"

May Trent said, "I shudder to think—it was so wild that night, when we went down. She'd have had no idea, what to do—" She stopped, waited until her voice was steady again, and went on. "But there had been a great deal of talk about the ship. She might have been attracted to the idea of sailing home on a famous ship. It would have made it easier for her to plan. . . ."

"Then what did Herbert Baker Confess?" Rutledge asked. "If he'd only helped her to find a train to London, he didn't share in the guilt of her death."

Hamish said morosely, "We're back to who paid for the care of his ill wife?"

Baker had even asked the Vicar if it was possible to love someone too much—

The question was, if one of the Sedgwicks had plotted Virginia's disappearance, which one had it been? Arthur? Edwin? Or Lord Sedgwick himself?

Rutledge could feel the weariness that dragged at him like an anchor.

When the story got out that Herbert Baker had sent for a priest as well as the Vicar, had someone been terrified that the past would come back to life if the priest delved too deeply in it?

It was a strong enough motive for murder. If you'd killed before.

When they neared Osterley, a low mist hung over the marshes and the dips and twists of the road, the verges vanishing and reappearing like links in a chain. The dampness in the air sometimes produced a passing squall.

Rutledge stopped again at the Randal farm, unwilling to leave that loose end unraveled. Over the protests of his weary passengers, he got out and went to hammer on the door.

A ragged and battered figure came stomping around the corner of the house, yelling obscenities.

Rutledge stared.

Randal was bloody from a dozen cuts and scratches on his face and hands. Bruises marked his jawline and his left arm was held close to his body.

"The mare's run into the ground, damn you, and that bitch done her best to kill *me*! I'm flipping lucky to be able to walk!" The farmer's anger was a live thing, too long pent up. He kicked out at the corner of the house, then kicked again. "I'll be seeing that solicitor in the town. I'll be wanting somebody to pay for last night's piece of work!"

Rutledge said, "Walsh is dead. The mare killed him."

"Good on her! So the constable told me when I rode home by way of West Sherham. It serves the bastard right, and I hope he rots in hell where he belongs, the son—"

He looked up and saw the woman in the car in the drive. "Is that the bitch—" He started forward.

Rutledge in three long strides caught Tom Randal's arm and held him back. "No. It's someone else. The Vicar is with her."

Randal peered at the motorcar. "That 'ee, Vicar?" he called.

"Yes, hello, Tom. What's happened to you, man!"

Randal shook his head. "I was run down by a crazed woman in a motorcar, that's what happened! Damned near killed me, she did, and of a purpose, too! Drove straight over me, after frightening the gelding half to death! It took me a quarter of an hour to catch him!"

He turned back to Rutledge, still furious. "I'm in no fit state to ride into Osterley. I'd take it as a favor if you'd see that a constable pays me a call out here. You owe me that. I've a claim to lay against the police and against that bitch. And I'll be calling on the solicitor in the morning!"

"You ought to see Dr. Stephenson—"

"I'll live. And you can tell that damned fool Blevins if he'd been better at *his* job, I wouldn't have two horses in my stable that aren't fit for work and won't be for another week! Who's going to help me do mine, I ask you!"

He turned and kicked savagely at the house a third time before stalking around the corner, muttering imprecations under his breath.

It was hard to feel sorry for the old curmudgeon, but Rutledge could sympathize. Tom Randal had been caught up in something over which he had no control, and Priscilla Connaught had shown him no mercy.

He walked back to the car. It would be just as well to send Dr.

Stephenson out to make a call, he thought. When the fury and the sense of being wronged faded, Randal would be hurting rather badly.

At least, he thought, bending to turn the crank, Priscilla Connaught hadn't killed the man.

Rutledge left the Vicar at his front door. Sims looked up at the dark shadows of his house, and turned, as if half afraid to go in. Then, with resolution, he unlocked the door and closed it behind him.

Holston, on the other hand, refused to spend the night in St. Anne's rectory. "It's bad enough by daylight, but with the mists swirling about it and the churchyard, I'd just as soon be in a well-lighted hotel!" he said wryly.

And so Rutledge pulled into the hotel yard and delivered the remainder of his passengers into the care of Mrs. Barnett, who welcomed them with the news that dinner could be warmed if they cared to dine.

Rutledge, standing in the dark outside the door, could feel the fatigue moving through him like a sluggish stream. But he turned and went instead to The Pelican for his meal.

Betsy, the barmaid, who came to ask what he'd have as Rutledge took the last seat in the crowded common room, was buoyant. "We're doing a fine business tonight," she informed him. "Everyone slept away the day, and now they're eager for company and gossip." She looked around her, pleased, then remembered what the cause of her good fortune was. Her mood shifted. "They tell me, though, that the man is dead. Still, it's a swifter way to go than a hanging, any day!"

"What are people saying about Walsh? Do they believe he killed Father James?" Rutledge asked, curious.

"Well, of course, he must have done! He escaped, didn't he? Inspector Blevins was here no more than half an hour ago, and saying that he'd spoken to the Chief Constable in Norwich. Everyone's relieved that the police have done their best. Even though there's to be no trial."

Looking around her once more, she waited expectantly for his order.

The death of Walsh, he thought, had been papered over. Justice had been served. Perhaps it was true. He was beyond caring. He ordered an ale and a serving of the stew, and Betsy brought him a covered dish of warmed bread from this morning's baking and a slab of butter.

Hamish said, "Ye ken, you'll no' make any headway against what Blevins has been saying. And they're eager to believe him. There's the sticking point. It was no' one of his friends or neighbors who killed the priest, and no' one of theirs. That's what matters. They can go to bed this night and no' be worried about being murdered in their sleep."

There was an outburst of laughter from a group by the window. Every head turned to look. Rutledge could see the general mood was relief, and it bordered on the hysterical.

Hamish was right. Order had been restored, their own sturdy faith that no one from Osterley could be guilty of such a heinous crime had been upheld. But a stubborn refusal to go against his own better judgment made Rutledge argue with his nemesis.

"The priest kept working toward a solution to Virginia Sedgwick's disappearance. The story about two priests at one deathbed was bound to get out, and someone began to worry. I don't think Father James expected to be attacked. Perhaps his visit to Norwich was the last straw. Even the *appearance* of having confided in his fellow clergymen would have aroused unwelcome suspicion."

"Aye, that's possible. But it doesna' signify! Truth is no more than what people *want* to believe."

Rutledge answered, "Or what they fear."

"And ye're as gullible as any man. You canna' face the question about yon Englishwoman's guilt!"

"I haven't forgotten May Trent. But if she killed Father James, there won't be another victim. If it was one of the Sedgwicks, what's to stop the murderer from biding his time until it's safe to kill again? He may already be suspicious of Sims—Holston—or even Miss Trent. Where is my duty toward them?"

"Aye, duty, that's all verra' fine. Ye did your duty in France, too. And I'm dead for it!"

CHAPTER TWENTY-SIX

FINISHING HIS MEAL AS QUICKLY AS he could, Rutledge paid his bill and then walked toward the hotel.

His fatigue had passed the need for sleep. As he had so many times at the Front, he'd ignored it and pushed his body and his mind to their limits—and then pushed both beyond that.

Retrieving his motorcar, he drove to the police station. There, he asked the sleepy constable on duty how to find two people, and left word for Blevins requesting that someone be sent around to speak to the old farmer in the morning.

The constable grimaced. "A year or two back, a lorry hit one of his piglets, out on the road. Odd place for a piglet to be wandering, you'd think, and the Inspector was of the opinion the sow had rolled over on it. But Randal swore it was a lorry. It was three months before we could satisfy him!"

"He has a better claim this time," Rutledge warned, and left.

Dr. Stephenson lived on the main road, toward Hunstanton, in a well-kept three-story house that backed up to the marshes. Rutledge turned into the yard, where a gate led into the flint-walled garden with its flagstone walk up to the door. A black spaniel, waiting on the step to be let in again, greeted him effusively, trying to lick his hand. When the housekeeper answered the knocker's dull *thunk,* the little dog darted past her crisp skirts and disappeared into the hall beyond.

The middle-aged woman, regarding Rutledge with unconcealed interest, as if his reputation had preceded him, warned him that he had interrupted the doctor at his dinner. Stephenson himself, coming out to speak to Rutledge, told him to make his call brief.

"It's brief enough. Tom Randal was bruised in a fall from his horse. It might be best to find out if he's more seriously hurt. I shouldn't be surprised if he'll be more grateful than he'll care to admit. By tomorrow morning, he'll be stiff as a board."

"I've been trying to persuade him to hire a couple to cook for him and help with the farm. He may listen now, but he's as independent and stubborn as they come." Stephenson, his serviette in his hand, sighed. "All right, yes, as soon as I've finished my dinner. And I'll take someone along who can stay the night and see that he has a decent breakfast in the morning. Was it Randal that Priscilla Connaught thought she'd killed?"

"I have every reason to believe it is. Tom Randal is damned lucky to be alive. She was in no state to think clearly about what she was trying to do."

"And whose fault is that?" Hamish asked in condemnation.

Rutledge ignored his voice. "How is she?"

"I've kept her sedated. Mrs. Nutley is staying the night with her."

"I'll look in there on my way."

"Do you have any idea how tired you are? You're slurring your words, man, you ought to be in your bed. Or I'll have a new patient on my hands!"

"Good advice. I'll take it shortly."

Rutledge said good night and strode down the dark path to the road. As he cranked the engine, his chest protested in fiery wires spreading deep.

Ignoring that, too, Rutledge drove next to Priscilla Connaught's house. He was surprised to find that she was awake, drinking a mutton broth that Mrs. Nutley had made.

The nurse had explained to Rutledge on their way up the stairs,

"An empty stomach sees nothing good. I always feed my patients before the next dose of medicines."

Priscilla, wearing a very fetching lavender dressing gown, smiled at him as he walked through the door, but obediently drank most of the broth before saying, "You're here to arrest me." Her voice was matter-of-fact, but her expression bleak behind the smile. "I'd warned Mrs. Nutley the police would come for me soon."

"No." He pulled a chair to the bed and sat down, wondering if he'd be able to get out of it again. "The man you thought you killed is alive, though bruised and bloody. And furious. He must have gone through a hedge headfirst. Still, I'd accept that as very good news if I were you. Nor was it Walsh. Again, good news from your perspective."

"Dear God!" She set the bowl on her tray and stared at him. "Oh, gentle *God*!"

"There's nothing you can do about Mr. Randal tonight. Except to sleep and regain your good sense."

She said faintly, "You look like a dead man yourself."

"Yes, I rather feel like one." He smiled. "Don't you think it's time you told me what lay between you and Father James?"

Biting her lip, she turned away. "I told you once before. It doesn't have anything to do with his death. Only with mine."

"What did he ask you to do? What ruined your life?" he pressed her.

It was unfair to force her in her present state—as Hamish was pointing out—but he was afraid that when she regained her strength, she would be more than a match for the police.

She glanced at Mrs. Nutley. "I'm half drunk with whatever it is she's made me swallow. I can't keep my mind clear!"

He could see it in the pupils of her eyes. Mrs. Nutley, her hands folded in her apron, was unruffled. "It's only what the doctor instructed me to give her."

"I understand." To the patient he added, "Would you like Mrs. Nutley to leave the room? I'm sure she'll be glad to give us a moment."

"Yes. No." Priscilla Connaught fell silent, closing her eyes against his inspection. And then unexpectedly she opened them and said in a despairing voice, "It was so long ago. Nobody cares, nobody remembers. Not anymore. But that doesn't make the *hurt* go away!"

He could see the pain in her face, stripping away what was left of her youth, and turning her almost as he watched into a very different woman. "Do you know what loneliness is, Inspector?"

He answered quietly, "I'm afraid I do. It's how I live."

She embraced herself with her arms, drawing them across her chest as if they offered a measure of comfort, leaning into them as if desperate for human warmth. "I loved a very fine man. We were to be married. I was over the moon with joy."

He knew what she meant. He'd watched the same joy wash over Jean when he'd asked her to marry him. On Saturday next she'd be married to someone else. He didn't want to be in London then—

Priscilla Connaught's voice startled him, stronger now and thick with grief. "And then one day Gerald came to me to say that he had had an—epiphany—of sorts. A revelation. I asked him what it was, and he said he had always been drawn to the Church, and now he knew that that was where he ought to be. It was what God wanted him to do. I told him if this was what *he* wanted, of course he should follow his vision. We could marry when he finished his studies. But he explained that he wanted to become a *Catholic* priest. There couldn't be any marriage, now or later. He broke off our engagement."

"And you blamed Father James for persuading him?"

She squeezed her eyes tightly to hold back the tears, as if on the back of the lids, the past was still vivid and clear. "He wasn't a priest then. He was only John James. But he was Gerald's best friend. I went to him and asked him to persuade Gerald not to do this. He told me the best thing I could do for Gerald if I loved him was to let him go. Let him enter the priesthood."

The tears began to fall, but her eyes were shut still, closing Rutledge out. "So I let him go. I—I truly believed that once he had his way, once he'd embarked on his studies, he'd quickly discover that it wasn't what he wanted after all. I was convinced that he loved me too much for this—this *fancy*—to last. I gave him my blessing *and let him go!*"

Rutledge waited in the bitter silence that followed, uncertain whether or not she had finished. He could imagine how she must have felt, abandoned for what—to a woman—seemed an inexplicable rejection of her and her love.

Finally she opened her eyes and looked across at him.

Her voice was shaking so much he wasn't sure he heard her clearly. "In his last year before being ordained, Gerald killed himself. And neither God nor I had him, in the end. I couldn't torment God. I tormented Father James instead. Gerald's death lay at his door, and every time he looked at my face in his congregation, he was unable to forget how wrong he'd been, how he'd failed Gerald, and me—what, in his sanctimonious *faith* in his own judgment, he'd done to us. Just as I could never forget Gerald. . . ."

Rutledge waited by the bedside until the sedative Mrs. Nutley had given her sent Priscilla Connaught into the comforting oblivion of sleep.

"Keep an eye on her, will you?" he asked as they left the room.

"You can depend on me, Inspector."

As he walked on down the stairs to the door, the older woman, following, said quietly, "In my experience, it helps sometimes to unburden the heart."

But he wasn't convinced that confession would do much for the sleeping figure he'd left in the darkened bedroom.

The only certainty was that Priscilla Connaught's secret had had nothing to do with the priest's death.

Frederick Gifford's house was set well back from the road, just past the school. It stood in a small park of old trees that reminded Rutledge of the vicarage at Holy Trinity. Driving through the gates and up to the door, he could see that the house was gabled and probably very old.

The maid who admitted Rutledge left him in the parlor. From another part of the house he could hear people talking, as if Gifford had guests.

Gifford came in with apologies. "A week ago, I'd invited friends to dine with me. We decided not to let the upheavals of last night affect our plans. Though to tell you the truth, no one is in a festive mood! What brings you here at this hour of the night? Shouldn't you be in your bed? You look like death walking, man!"

Rutledge laughed. "I've heard that enough to believe it. I won't keep you long. I need to learn who arranged for Mrs. Baker—Herbert Baker's ill wife—to have the treatment she required for her consumption. It's rather important."

Surprised by the request, Gifford smoothed the line of his beard with the back of his fingers. "I don't know. That is, I never knew. Nor did Dr. Stephenson. A bank in Norwich sent me a letter instructing me that an anonymous benefactor had requested a sum of money be set aside for the care of one Margaret Baker, wife of Herbert, of this town. I was to use it to pay any medical bills, as required by her doctors, associated with her illness."

"Mrs. Baker wasn't particularly well-known. Her illness wasn't uncommon. Why should she be singled out by a Norwich bank for such a generous gesture?"

Gifford frowned. "I have no idea. I didn't ask. I saw no reason to. The papers were in order—and Mrs. Baker *was* seriously ill. Stephenson told me later that better care extended her life by several years."

"But surely you must have guessed who was behind this generosity. Baker's employer, for one."

"The thought crossed my mind. But I didn't pursue it. Stephenson does what he can on his own, and there are other people in Norfolk who support a variety of charitable activities. The King has been known to act anonymously. And he knew the Sedgwick family."

"I can't imagine how the King discovered that an obscure coachman's wife, living quietly in Osterley, was in need."

"No, no, the King doesn't handle such matters himself; you misunderstand," Gifford answered. "But he has deep roots in Norfolk and apparently feels strongly about them. The staff at Sandringham raised a troop of their own, during the War. He and the Queen took a keen interest in the men. It's not impossible that someone in the Household brought the Bakers to the attention of the staff."

"Yes, I understand. But in my view, they'd be far more likely to have a word with Lord Sedgwick rather than go to the trouble of making arrangements with a bank in Norwich. Is there any way that this—kindness—could be traced through the paperwork?"

"I doubt it. Bankers are worse than stones when it comes to divulging information. Immovable."

Rutledge thanked him and left. Stones could be moved. If Scotland Yard wanted the information badly enough . . .

Hamish said, "Even if his lairdship paid for the sanitarium, it willna' prove much."

"It proves that a debt existed between Herbert Baker and the Sedgwick family. The sort of debt that Baker would have gone to great lengths to repay. As he lay dying, he told the Vicar that he feared he'd loved his wife too much. He could easily have confessed to Father James how he'd demonstrated that love."

"Aye. But yon Trent woman—she has depths you canna' plumb. I wouldna' count her out of the running. You canna' know for certain if she abandoned an elderly woman when the ship was sinking, to save hersel'. She'd ha' killed Father James if he came too close to *her* secret."

Only a few days ago, when Rutledge had seen the connection between Father James and the Watchers of Time, Observers of Deeds, he had remarked that there were no bodies and therefore no murders that the priest could have uncovered.

Now there were two. The woman whom May Trent had accompanied as a companion. And Virginia Sedgwick, who was—possibly—also lost in the sea.

"Or," Hamish interjected into Rutledge's thoughts, "buried here in these marshes. I havena' seen more likely ground for disposing of a corpse!"

On the way back to the hotel, Rutledge spotted a solitary figure walking among the trees just back from the road. As the headlamps of his motorcar flashed across the pale, expressionless face, he recognized Peter Henderson.

He was about to stop and offer the man a lift, and then Mrs. Barnett's words made him drive on. *"I leave him alone now."* Peter Henderson still had his pride.

Rutledge was so tired his eyes were playing tricks on him as the motorcar's headlamps picked out the turning for Water Street, and he came close to swerving into the wall of a house.

He had done all he could this night, and he wanted his bed.

But as he neared the hotel, another thought struck him: May Trent and Monsignor Holston were staying there, too, and if they were waiting for him in the lounge, it would be at least another hour—or more— before he could walk away from them.

He passed the hotel, drove along the quay, and turned toward the main road, considering even a pew in the church as a better alternative. There was something that May Trent had said about a blanket kept there for Peter Henderson. It would do. Soldiers were used to sleeping rough.

But as he went up Trinity Lane, Hamish pointed out another choice, one where his presence might be gratefully accepted. Gratefully enough that no questions would be asked.

The vicarage.

Rutledge had to fight the wheel to turn in through the vicarage gates, like a drunk whose reflexes were starting to fail. He drew up in front of the house, his hands shaking as he switched off the motor.

It was a minute or two before he could make it to the front door and lift the knocker.

After a long wait, the window above his head opened. The Vicar said, "Who is it?" in a flat voice.

"Rutledge. I don't want to go back to the hotel. But I need to sleep. If I keep you company tonight, will you trade me a bed and no conversation?"

There was laughter from over his head. Bitter and without humor.

"I haven't slept myself. All right, I'll let you in. Wait there."

Sims was still fully clothed when he unlocked the door and opened it to Rutledge. He smelled of whiskey. "I'm beginning to think about posting a sign: Rooms For Let," he said. "You look like hell."

Rutledge took a deep breath, unsteady on his feet. "As do you."

"Have you been drinking?" Sims asked suspiciously.

"No. I'm cold sober. Just—nearly at the end of my tether."

Five minutes later Rutledge was deeply asleep in the bedroom that May Trent had occupied only twenty-four hours before.

Her scent still lingered in the room.

Rutledge awoke in the dark, startled by a figure walking close by the bed.

"Who is it?" he managed to ask coherently, after clearing his throat.

"Sims. It's after nine. I brought hot water for shaving, a razor, and a clean shirt. Breakfast will be ready in fifteen minutes, if you're hungry."

"Thanks." Rutledge lay there, an arm flung across his eyes, stunned by exhaustion, his mind working slowly. After several minutes he forced himself out of the bed and across the room to draw open the draperies.

It was pouring rain out of heavy black clouds, a sky that seemed to absorb all light. No wonder he'd thought it was still the middle of the night.

Hamish scolded, "There's no' any need for haste, if you're no' clear-headed."

Rutledge went to the washstand and looked at his face in the mirror, shadowed by beard and the dreary light coming in the windows behind him. It was not a face he was particularly fond of. Lighting the lamp, he set about shaving and dressing.

A quarter of an hour later, he walked into the kitchen.

Sims said, "If anyone came to the door and looked at the two of us, they would be ready to believe we'd had an all-night carousal. My head feels like it." In the lamplight he was haggard, lines bracketing his mouth and heavy circles under his eyes. He had found yesterday unbearably difficult.

"I sympathize." Rutledge reached for the pot of tea, ready to pour the steaming liquid into his cup, and somewhere in the tangle of memories from the day before, one stood out clearly.

There had been *three* cups on the table yesterday morning—

He looked across at Sims, who was putting a rasher of bacon on a plate, while the toast browned.

"Who keeps this house for you?"

"I have a woman who comes in three times a week. Why?"

"She wasn't here yesterday."

"No. She's coming around ten today. That's why I woke you."

"Then who was here—besides yourself and Miss Trent?"

The Vicar became very still. "You were here." But his eyes swept down to the teacups and back to Rutledge. He didn't lie well, as Hamish was busy noting.

Rutledge hazarded a guess. "It was Peter Henderson, wasn't it?"

Sims said carefully, "Peter comes sometimes, yes. When he's hungry. He often sleeps in the church if the weather's foul. I don't know where he sleeps the rest of the time, poor devil."

"A cold roof over his head, the church. With stone walls and stone flooring, he'd not be very warm."

"There's a chest under the tower. I keep clean blankets there. He knows where to find them." He paused. "The church has had a long history of offering sanctuary. I can do no less."

"Miss Trent and Mrs. Barnett tell me that he roams the night more often than not. I've seen him a number of times myself."

"Yes. I expect he does. Perhaps it's easier for him, living in the dark. Fewer people to stare at him."

"What did he see, the night that Walsh escaped?" Rutledge insisted.

Sims put down the plate and retrieved the burning toast from the stove.

"You must ask him."

"I'm asking you."

Sims sat down, reached for the pot, and poured tea for himself. "Look. The man's little more than a vagrant now. Living hand to mouth. Most of the townspeople have no use for him; they think he's beyond the pale. His own father disowned him. I do what I can, and so did Father James. But changing attitudes is much harder than preaching profound sermons on a Sunday."

A silence followed; it was Sims who reluctantly broke it.

"Peter was in the church that night. He wasn't feeling well, and crept in to sleep for awhile. He was still in the church when Walsh came in to hammer off his chains. Henderson heard him dragging them; he didn't know who or what was there. His tally of kills from the War, for all I know. It must have been rather appalling. He slipped into the choir— it's quite dark in there, and no one was likely to find him crouched among the misericords. And he moves like a wraith when he wants to."

"Yes. That's his training."

"When Walsh left, he was on foot. Henderson—who isn't a fool, by any means—had worked out who was in the church and what it must have meant. He followed, and kept an eye on him from a distance. They walked through the woods and past the barn where Trinity Lane ends. Henderson stayed with him for nearly five miles."

"To Tom Randal's farm."

"Walsh didn't go anywhere near the Randal farm. Not according to Henderson. He was moving as swiftly and quietly as he could. Walsh, I mean. Covering the ground faster than most. Peter kept up with him until he was well beyond Osterley. Then he turned back, not wanting to be spotted."

Rutledge shook his head. "That can't be true. The mare at the farm went missing in probably that same time frame. And it was her shoe that killed Walsh."

Sims said, "That's why we didn't tell you, May Trent and I. I've never known Peter to lie to me, but he was very cold and hungry, walking that far, and he might have made up a story in exchange for his breakfast. It seemed—a little less like begging, I suppose."

Rutledge got up and helped himself to the bacon and a slice of burned toast. Sims said, "There are boiled eggs in that covered dish."

Rutledge lifted the lid and set an egg on his plate, cracking it and spooning out the yolk. He said, "What else has Henderson seen, wandering around in the dark?"

Sims buttered his own slice, frowning at the burnt taste. "He seldom talks about his life—or what he's witnessed. I think the only reason he told me about his encounter with Walsh was his need for food and a little warmth."

"Yes, it may be true." Rutledge added pensively, "I should have expected that between you, you and Father James could have found work for Henderson—doing the heavier labor for old Tom Randal, for instance. And Mrs. Barnett must need someone to help with upkeep at the hotel. It's a barn of a place for a woman on her own."

"She doesn't have the custom to hire anyone else, even for a pittance with room and board. Tom Randal refuses to consider help on the farm. No one else in Osterley needs Henderson. Too many people are out of work, that's the trouble—the shopkeepers and farms can find help two a penny without turning to a man with Peter's history. Lord Sedgwick hired him until Dick, Herbert Baker's younger son, was fit again for light duties. The house in Yorkshire is closed while Arthur Sedgwick recovers from his own injuries—if he's not in hospital, he's here in Norfolk or in London. Edwin lives in London most of the year. I've been corresponding with a woman in Hunstanton who may take Henderson on. She and her husband own a small pub, and need an extra man. But he's not local, you see—and she's wary of that." Sims said tentatively, "What are you going to do about Virginia Sedgwick? I don't quite see Inspector Blevins rushing to find out the truth, most particularly if it involves the Sedgwick family. He won't like that!"

"He's already seen to it that most of Osterley believes that Walsh has paid for what he did—that justice has been served. And he has to live here. I can't fault him for trying to put as good a face on the situation as he can." Rutledge grimaced. "The most direct course of action would be going to Lord Sedgwick himself."

"Good God, man, you can't be serious?" Sims's face was the picture of dismay. "I agreed—we *all* agreed—that it was worthwhile speaking to Blevins. Do you realize how powerful Sedgwick is? You'll sink your own career, and possibly mine as well!"

Rutledge considered him. "You still don't wish to know what's become of Virginia Sedgwick, do you? But Sedgwick's son may well have committed murder, and I think it's important to give him an opportunity to refute such a charge. He'll be a worse enemy if half the town hears before he does." He smiled. "Thank you for breakfast—and a night's sleep. I needed both rather badly."

As he went to find his coat, Sims followed him to the hall. "I'm grateful for what you're trying to do. It's just—I'm not sure that I want to stop thinking about her being alive. I—it's given me a kind of hope. . . ." He shrugged, as if embarrassed by the admission. "It's hard to explain."

But Rutledge understood what he was trying to say. He himself had never looked over his own shoulder to find out once and for all if Hamish was there. He didn't want to know—he didn't want to see what was there. And as long as he didn't, he was safe.

As he buttoned his coat against the rain, he said, "What if, against all expectations, we should find that Virginia Sedgwick left her husband of her own accord and is happily settled in a cottage in Ireland, living a life she much prefers to her role as Arthur's wife. Would he welcome her back, do you think?"

"I—don't know. It would depend on the scandal, to a large extent." Sims looked out at the rain and the wet trees overhanging the drive. "The Sedgwicks came from trade—they aren't able to weather the scandals that established families can. They've climbed the social ladder as high as possible in three generations. But they aren't at the top. They've given money generously where it would do the most good. Full acceptance, marrying into the best families, eludes them. Arthur might have, if he hadn't foolishly fallen in love with a cousin. He might still, as a widower. I'm not sure he wouldn't prefer to learn that she's dead."

"Father James pursued her disappearance with unexpected fervor."

"No, not if you'd known him. He had a great capacity for caring. He told me once that every time he looked out at his congregation, he knew that he was not the man they believed him to be. It drove him to strive for a level of service that few of us can ever hope to emulate."

As Rutledge thanked Sims again and walked out into the rain, Hamish said, "Aye, Priscilla Connaught's shadow fell across the priest's pulpit every time he stepped into it."

"A pity he never told her," Rutledge answered silently.

CHAPTER TWENTY-SEVEN

HAMISH SAID, AS RUTLEDGE CLIMBED BEHIND the wheel, "If it wasna' Walsh who killed the priest, you're up against a canny murderer. He kens how to cover his tracks."

"No loose ends to stumble over," Rutledge agreed. "When Blevins allowed himself to be blinded by anger, he tied his own hands. He went looking for a monster." Rutledge turned out of the vicarage gates. "And he found himself one."

Hamish answered, "It willna' be to your credit if you fail."

"I won't fail," Rutledge answered grimly. "Sedgwick should have destroyed that Egyptian bas-relief instead of moving it out to the gardens. It gave me the key to Father James's actions—a Watcher. After that, it was only a matter of time before the rest made sense."

A milk wagon lumbered by on the main road. In the rain the backs of the horses were burnished copper.

Rutledge braked. "In this weather—"

He reversed the motorcar, backing as far as the gate to Holy Trinity. The grass under his feet as he crossed the churchyard to the north porch door was heavy with rain, and his shoulders were soaked by the time he reached the shelter of the church door. Opening it, he brushed the water from his face before he stepped inside.

"Henderson? Inspector Rutledge. I'd like to speak with you, if you're here."

His voice echoed in the silence, almost an obscenity in the peace of the nave and the soft patter of rain against the stained glass. This morning, dark as it was, the colors were deeper and richer, but without life.

Rutledge waited.

Then he heard someone near the choir. "I'm here. Give me a minute."

Peter Henderson, rising from a pew, tried to straighten his coat and brushed a hand over his hair before walking toward Rutledge. "What do you want?"

"Verification. That's all. The Vicar tells me that you saw Walsh the night he came in here to hammer off his chains."

"Yes."

"Was he alone?"

"Yes."

"Why did you follow him, when he left?"

"I knew who he was. I'd seen him at the fair at St. Anne's. I thought it best."

"Where did he go?"

"Up the lane, into that copse of trees. Past the houses. He was bearing west, and south. It's the direction I'd have taken, in his shoes. It's mostly pasturage, beyond the houses, and easy walking."

"He never turned east, while you were following him?"

"No. Why should he? It would be going into a box."

Rutledge nodded. He looked down at Peter Henderson's shoes. They were old. Worn . . .

He said, "Walsh stole a mare from a farmer just east of Osterley. Why would he turn back on himself to do that?"

Henderson shrugged. "I've told you what I saw. I can't tell you what he did after I broke off and walked back to Osterley." He had an odd dignity, standing there in his creased and worn clothes. A man shunned by others because he happened to be very good at killing from ambush. It wasn't deserved, the judgment local people had inflicted upon him. And yet this was his home, and villagers were often tied, emotionally if not financially, to their roots. The money in the tin box at the rectory would have been a treasure trove to him. He could have gone anywhere with ten or fifteen pounds in his pocket. Had it been tempting?

Hamish said, "I canna' believe it. Nor do you. It was a rifle he used in the War. Distant killing, that."

"Fair enough, then. Henderson—" Rutledge paused. "Were you at the rectory, the day Father James was killed? Waiting to see him?"

"Yes."

"Why?"

"I'd heard of work in Wells. I wanted to ask him to write a letter for me."

"Had he written letters before?"

"Once. The Vicar has written them, too."

"Where did you wait?"

"Mrs. Wainer was just leaving. It was growing dark by then. I stood by those overgrown bushes, so as not to frighten her. Someone else came looking for Father James. I left then, not wanting to push myself forward."

He'd stood in the lilacs—"those overgrown bushes." It wasn't one of Walsh's cronies acting as lookout, after all; it was a man wanting help to find a job. Rutledge said, "Who came?"

"Mrs. Barnett, from the hotel, but she only tapped at the door. When Mrs. Wainer didn't answer, she stepped into the kitchen and called, then closed the door and left."

"Mrs. Barnett never went beyond the kitchen?"

"Not as far as I could tell. She wasn't there much above a minute."

"Was there anyone else?"

Henderson said reluctantly, "Yes. Lord Sedgwick came to the front door and knocked."

"You saw his car?"

"No, I never did." His voice was level, a soldier reporting to his commanding officer. "But I saw him walk up the drive. Then he came round to the back. Along the far side of the house, not close to where I was standing. He was looking up at the windows of the conservatory next door. They were dark. Then he went in through the kitchen, calling to Father James. He must have gone on to the parlor, to wait. Or leave a note. That's when I left."

"And you never saw Father James that night?"

"Well, yes, I did. He was on his bicycle, riding back to the rectory. He waved, and I walked on."

"You didn't tell him he had a visitor?"

"It wasn't my place."

Hamish said, "Blevins wouldna' believe it was a local man there in the shrubs. He wished it to be Bolton, the scissor sharpener. Or Iris Kenneth."

Rutledge said, "I'm driving to The Pelican. Would you like a lift?"

Henderson's face brightened. "Give me five minutes. To clear up."

"I'll wait in the car."

Rutledge turned and walked back to the motorcar, hardly noticing the rain.

Once he'd dropped off Henderson, Rutledge drove back to the hotel, retrieved his umbrella from his room, and walking briskly, went directly to the police station.

He found that he was not the only visitor.

A youngish woman in a black coat over a green traveling dress was sitting in front of the Sergeant's desk, her face buried in an overlarge handkerchief, supplied by a red-faced Blevins across the desk from her.

The Inspector looked up as Rutledge came through the door. "Whatever it is, it can wait." He gestured toward his visitor. "This is Iris Kenneth. She traveled up from London to—er—see Walsh. I've just given her the news."

Iris Kenneth raised her face from the handkerchief, her eyes watery and red-rimmed, turning to stare at the newcomer.

Blevins said, "This is Inspector Rutledge, from Scotland Yard."

She nodded a faint acknowledgment and said to Blevins, as if she had been interrupted in the middle of her grief, "I was so *angry* with him! Matthew. For sacking me. But I decided that if I stood by him now, he might take me on again, after. He wasn't a bad man to work for. He enjoyed posing in his costume and being admired. I was jealous."

"He wasn't likely to be taking on a helper ever again," Blevins said. He cast a wary glance at Rutledge. "He was more likely to find himself waiting for the hangman."

Fierce in Walsh's defense, Iris Kenneth cried, "But I told you, Matthew wasn't a *murderer*! He wasn't a bully, he didn't have a temper!"

"Yes, I know, Miss Kenneth. Several times."

She began to cry again. Rutledge, standing by the door, could read the embarrassment in Blevins's face. Over the woman's head, the Inspector shot him a pleading glance for help. "I don't know what you want me to do, Miss Kenneth," he said plaintively. "I can't tell you what the arrangements are for a funeral. Not just at the moment. But if you'd like to take a room—"

She glared at him through her tears. "I don't have the money to stay—or to bury Matthew. I spent nearly every penny coming here— I've barely enough to see me back to London!"

Hamish said, "He's no' a man for the ladies. He doesna' ken that it's no' so much Walsh's dying as it is the disappointment of her expectations. She canna' face what to do now."

Rutledge stepped toward her chair. "Miss Kenneth, it's been a very difficult morning for you. A cup of tea and an hour's rest at the hotel will help. I'm sure Inspector Blevins will meet with you in the afternoon."

Blevins glowered at him, and she caught it.

Iris Kenneth's shoulders slumped. "I could use a cup of tea," she said. "This has been a terrible shock—!"

"I'm sure it has. Mrs. Barnett, at the hotel, is very kind. She'll see that you're taken care of."

She looked more closely at the tall man by the door. He could read her eyes as they swept over his face and across his shoulders, and back again.

With the resourcefulness of her class, she recognized that she would make no headway with the stolid man behind the desk. And she was desperate, willing to try any port in the unsettled climate of her life just now. She got to her feet with some grace and said, "You're very kind. If the Inspector here—" She groped for a name.

"Blevins," he said, relief already spreading across his features. "Inspector Rutledge is right, Miss Kenneth. Take your time and you'll soon see your way clear again." The false heartiness in his voice was almost insulting.

"—Blevins," she acknowledged, "will give me a little more of his time later?"

"Oh, yes, to be sure," he said hurriedly, rising from his chair to escort her to the door.

Rutledge glanced at Iris Kenneth and then said cryptically to Blevins, "I'd come to ask. The doctor was satisfied that it was the mare's shoe that was the cause of death?"

"Oh, yes. There's no doubt. I'm completely satisfied."

Rutledge nodded.

Holding the umbrella over his companion's hat, Rutledge took her arm to guide her toward the hotel. "I'm sorry that you've come so far," he told her, "to hear such tragic news."

"He wouldn't have killed anyone. Much less this priest! Matthew was always on his best behavior at church bazaars, superstitious, if you like. And he never cared for being penned up—I'm not surprised he escaped! A big man like him? In such a small space? It would have been torture!"

Rutledge thought, *God! I'd have tried to escape, too. Shut in away from the air and the light—smothered by the walls—*

Hamish said, "Ye ken, murderers are always locked away. If they're half mad, like you, it's the cell, it's no' the rope."

Iris Kenneth kept up her earnest defense of Matthew Walsh all the way to the hotel, one hand holding her skirts out of the rainwater washing down the street toward the quay. When they reached the door, she looked out at the marshes, and Rutledge could feel her shudder through the arm inside his. "What a dreary place," she remarked. "Enough to turn anybody into a murderer, living here long enough!"

Mrs. Barnett stepped out of her tiny office and said, "Good morning, Inspector, you're about early on such a nasty day. I believe Miss Trent and Monsignor Holston have been waiting for you in the lounge. Shall I bring tea to warm you up?"

"Meanwhile, I've brought you another guest—"

She reluctantly took charge of Miss Kenneth, eyeing her with some dismay. In the calm, gracious lobby of the hotel, Iris Kenneth's style was decidedly out of place, garish, her voice a little loud, her clothes a little shabby, her face rather too heavily made up for a country town. Her rouge and the line of kohl beneath her eyes had run from her tears, giving her a clownish expression of surprise.

Iris Kenneth seemed equally reluctant to give up Rutledge's company. She said, "You *will* take me back to see Inspector Blevins later?"

"Yes. And see you safely on your way back to London," he promised, undone by the fear in her eyes. It was real, not feigned.

This woman had lived a life with little security, on the edge of poverty as often as not, and never climbing to the dizzying heights of the great names of the legitimate stage. It had already taken its toll in her skin and in the hard lines around her mouth. He remembered all too well the woman dragged from the Thames. Had she chosen the water rather than falling into prostitution? If Iris was despairing enough of her future prospects to swallow her pride and anger, and come to offer Matthew Walsh her support, she was desperate indeed.

Hamish said, clicking his puritanical tongue, "You're a fool, and will be taken for one!"

"Hardly," Rutledge answered curtly.

He left Miss Kenneth in Mrs. Barnett's care and walked into the lounge, where May Trent was writing a letter at the small white desk and Monsignor Holston was reading a book. They looked up, their faces mirroring an expression of impatience.

"Where have you been?" Miss Trent asked. "We expected to see you at dinner last night or breakfast this morning!" There was neither censure or anger in her voice, but he detected an undercurrent of strain.

"I've been busy, I'm afraid," Rutledge replied. "I've spoken with the Vicar, for one, and Peter Henderson after that. Peter tells me that Walsh walked away from Holy Trinity through the trees just south of the vicarage, and past the houses there, taking a southwesterly course, where he could make good time in the pastures beyond."

May Trent said, "But you said Walsh hadn't done any such thing! You said he'd taken that poor farmer's horse! That's why we said nothing—"

Monsignor Holston interjected, "If Walsh had come across a search party, he might have doubled back, found himself some faster means of getting out."

"In his shoes, doubling back could mean certain capture. There were farms ahead—"

Mrs. Barnett came in with tea. "I've settled Miss Kenneth for now," she said. "I wouldn't be surprised if she sleeps for an hour or so. She tells me she came all the way from London. It must have been a very difficult journey for her!"

Rutledge said, "Thank you. Er—I understand you went to see Father James, the same day that he died."

"No, that's not true—" She paused. "Oh. You mean to the *rectory*! I stopped to ask Ruth Wainer if I might borrow a roasting pan for the weekend, when there would be a christening party here. I didn't expect to find Father James in—at that hour, he's usually in the church."

"Did you go to the kitchen door? Or to the front of the rectory?"

"To the kitchen door, of course. I was hoping Ruth hadn't left."

"Did you see anyone near the house when you went there?"

She smoothed the collar of her gray dress. "I don't recall seeing anyone else. Should I have?"

"Peter Henderson was there, near the lilacs, waiting to speak to Father James."

"No. But of course I wasn't looking for him, was I? Why didn't he speak?"

"Did you meet a member of Lord Sedgwick's family, by any chance?"

She considered the question. "Not Lord Sedgwick, no. I did pass his motorcar near Gull Street. I didn't see who was in it, the lamps were right in my face, and it was traveling fast. It went on toward Wells, as far as I could tell. Occasionally that chauffeur of his takes it to The Pelican, if Lord Sedgwick is out of town. It could have been Edwin. He's a fast driver, like his brother."

"Do you know the Randal farm?"

"Oh, yes. Everyone does. I used to buy cut flowers from his wife, for the dining-room tables. She was a wonderful gardener."

"Whose property is adjacent to Randal's, to the south?"

"My guess is it belongs to the Sedgwick family. Lord Sedgwick has made a practice of buying up acreage when he can. I shouldn't be surprised to hear he's bought the Randal property, when Tom's too old to run it himself. There's no close family, you see."

What she'd told him agreed with the map he'd seen in Blevins's office. "Thank you, Mrs. Barnett. You've been very helpful!"

"Will you be staying in for lunch?" Her glance ran around the room.

"Yes, if that's convenient," Rutledge answered for them.

"You know something we don't," Holston said, as the door closed behind Mrs. Barnett.

"Little things. Henderson saw Lord Sedgwick arrive at the rectory just after Mrs. Barnett left. When there was no answer to his knock, Sedgwick went inside. Furthermore, if Sedgwick's property adjoins the Randal farm, it's very likely he'd also know about the horses—and that the old man is hard of hearing."

Monsignor Holston said, "I don't follow you—are you telling me that *Sedgwick* arranged for a horse to be available to Matthew Walsh, once he escaped?"

"No," May Trent said slowly, watching Rutledge's face. "No. He thinks someone else rode that mare."

She was quick. . . .

"It's possible," Rutledge agreed. He saw again the hammer wound on the dead wife's temple. All those years ago— Reaching into his experience and deeper into his intuition, he said, "When Matthew Walsh escaped from his cell, it was seen as an admission of guilt. If he was killed before he could be recaptured and tried, all the better. With his death, the investigation would be closed. As it has been! If he'd been retaken and sent to Norwich for trial, anything could have gone wrong."

"Insufficient evidence to convict him?" she asked, intrigued. "Then you're saying that someone went after Walsh, and caught up with him not long after the mare cast her shoe—" Her face changed. "But, look here, if Walsh wasn't riding it, he wouldn't have been the one the mare kicked!"

"Interesting, isn't it?" Rutledge smiled. "After luncheon, I intend to pay a call on Lord Sedgwick."

Monsignor Holston said, "Good God, are you telling me that his son *Arthur* is behind all this killing? I've met the man—you'll never sell him to a jury as a cold-blooded murderer! Charming and very well liked."

"We were all searching for Walsh. And by sheer luck someone caught up with him. In my opinion that's what happened. There's a torn patch of grass, just a few feet from where the body lay. Some sort of struggle went on there. But no one's going to tackle a man Walsh's size, it would be suicide. Unless Walsh was on foot, and his *killer* was on the mare."

"Which brings us back to Lord Sedgwick. If he was at the rectory when Father James was killed," May Trent said, "then he'd want Walsh dead."

Monsignor Holston said, "No. What I think Rutledge is saying is that just as Peter Henderson was a witness, so was Sedgwick. Without necessarily knowing the importance of what he saw."

May Trent's eyes, on Rutledge and speculative, were skeptical.

Rutledge looked at his watch. "We have five minutes before the dining room opens. I should go upstairs and change out of these wet clothes."

As he closed the lounge door behind him, he overheard Monsignor

Holston commenting to May Trent, "When I asked my Bishop to send for the Yard, I thought I was doing something good. *What have I unleashed?*"

Luncheon passed in relative silence, each member of the small party lost in his or her own thoughts.

Over the main course May Trent said suddenly, "I'm going with you. When you call on Lord Sedgwick."

"It's not a very good idea," Rutledge answered.

"It probably isn't," she agreed. "All the same, I'm going."

But they were held up. A fire in one of the houses west of Water Street jammed the road with firefighters and a tangle of buckets, people, and frightened horses. The pouring rain, dropping out of a gray and light-absorbing sky, soon accomplished what the firefighters couldn't, and the smoking, blackened rafters filled the air with the reek of burned wood as they loomed starkly against the clouds. But much of the house survived, and a great many of its contents had been saved.

One of the men fighting the blaze was Edwin Sedgwick, sleeves rolled high, face smeared with sweat and soot. As Rutledge joined the line, passing buckets from the well, Edwin shouted orders and encouragement, taking charge as if by right, and showing unusual skill at coordinating the mob of people.

Observing when he could, Rutledge saw that Edwin's skill lay not so much in cajolery or good-humored bandinage but in the role of the local squire, the natural leader everyone turned to in time of trouble or danger. It was a role Edwin's father played to the hilt, and the son had learned well. He took full advantage of it now.

Hamish said, "He's no' sae overbearing as his father."

As Rutledge spelled an older man needing a breather, he agreed with Hamish. Command came more naturally to Edwin, as if by this generation it was bred in the bone, not learned.

Edwin was everywhere at once, taking as many risks as the next man and not complaining about lending his weight where it was needed. A hand on a tired shoulder, a word of support, swift advice, a cry of warning.

Hamish, whose independent Scottish spirit seldom allowed him to bow his neck to any man, commented, "He's no' the elder brother. He willna' be the laird in his turn."

Rutledge cast a glance around, to find May Trent not in the motor-car watching from a safe distance but busy comforting the distraught woman lamenting the overturned lamp that had started the fire.

Picking up the thread of Hamish's remark again, he found it interesting. While Arthur had been buried in Yorkshire's dales with his young wife or racing across France, Edwin's had been the face that Osterley had seen most frequently.

This presented a different aspect of the man Rutledge had encountered returning from boating in the marshes with his dog and drinking alone in the lounge bar of a tiny hotel outside Norwich. What had taken Edwin there?

Hamish answered, "Mischief." And perhaps there had been a woman with him that night.

Their work done, the firefighters began the onerous task of cleaning up the muddy yard and trying to get the salvaged belongings under cover.

Edwin Sedgwick accepted the gratitude of the householder as if it were his due, *noblesse oblige,* and to satisfy the general euphoria, he shook hands with all comers. When he reached Rutledge, he smiled and added, "Thanks for your help. We needed every man." Treating him casually, as an outsider.

Nothing in his demeanor indicated that he was aware of Rutledge's close observation, but Rutledge had the feeling that Edwin Sedgwick, like his father, was a man used to battling the world and winning. He would be mindful of the smallest detail.

As Rutledge turned to collect May Trent, Sedgwick retrieved a motorcycle from the side of a tree, and roared away toward East Sherham. In the distance, caught by the echoes of the rolling land, the sound dulled from thunder to a quiet chuckle.

It was Hamish who called his attention to that.

Rutledge spent what was left of the afternoon asleep in the chair in his bedchamber. He was awakened by Mrs. Barnett in time to arrange for Iris Kenneth to speak to Blevins again, and it was close to six when he saw her off to King's Lynn in a lorry that had brought boxes of hams to the butcher in Osterley and as far east as Cley. He also made certain that she had money enough to make the journey in reasonable comfort, and she thanked him profusely.

"Matthew wouldn't have hurt anyone," she said earnestly. "That Inspector Blevins won't believe me, but I hope you will. I can't say any fairer than that!"

He helped her into the lorry. "I'll keep that in mind. Thank you, Miss Kenneth."

At the last moment she leaned down, speaking for his ears alone. "I owe you. And I pay my debts. A friend of mine did a bit of work once for a man in Norfolk. I never knew what village, but he was rich, and he paid her well to impersonate a lady. But she never did live to enjoy the money. I always thought he'd killed her. Two months later, they found her in the river, like that poor girl you thought was me. Naked as the day she was born, and drowned."

"When was this?" he asked, his curiosity aroused.

"It was before the War. About two years before the War. I'd like to see you find the bastard yourself, and put that sanctimonious police-man's nose out of joint. Serve him right to be made to look a fool! And a bit of his own back for Matthew."

And she was gone, the empty lorry lumbering down the road in the rain like a drunken walrus. May Trent, who had stepped out in the shel-ter of the hotel doorway, said, "She'll manage, you know. Her kind al-ways does. Somehow."

"We more frequently find them floating in the Thames. I hope to God she's not taken out of the water one day soon."

Rutledge opened the umbrella and held it over her head as they walked to the yard, where the motorcar stood waiting. He was hearing Monsignor Holston's admonition, offered quietly in the lobby of the hotel.

"Don't start something you can't finish," he said. "That's what Father James did."

Hamish had silently answered in Rutledge's mind. "Aye. It's worth heeding."

CHAPTER TWENTY-EIGHT

As he was about to crank the motor, Rutledge said to May Trent, "I've just thought of something. I'll be back shortly."

He turned and walked with long strides to The Pelican.

Ten minutes later, he was back with Peter Henderson, who nodded at May Trent and climbed into the rear seat of the car without a word.

Hamish was a hum of wordless admonition in Rutledge's mind, reminding him that this night's work could become a debacle.

Dusk was falling quickly, the rain shifting for part of the way to a drizzle that seemed to coat the motorcar and its passengers in tiny drops of moisture. As they passed down the avenue of trees in East Sherham that led to the gates of the Sedgwick estate, Rutledge slowed to a walking pace. And Peter Henderson, like a wraith, was out of the car and gone in the mist before May Trent had even turned to see what was happening.

The gatekeeper, reluctant to come out in the rain, called from his doorway, "Who's there?"

"Inspector Rutledge. Lord Sedgwick is expecting me."

The man, a hood over his head, hurried to open the gate and let them through. Rutledge drove on. Halfway down the looping drive to the house, he said to his passenger, "If you've changed your mind, you can stay in the car. I don't expect this to take very long."

"No. I have a stake in this. In a way."

"As you wish." But he was not pleased with her answer.

The house was in darkness, save for lights on the first floor and in the hall. He lifted the knocker on the door and let it fall. The two of them huddled under the umbrella as they waited. Hamish was a constant barrage now in the back of Rutledge's mind, like very distant thunder, warning him to walk carefully.

May Trent said, "I think it's turning colder." As if to prove her words, her breath came out in a small white puff. She shivered.

The door opened, the housekeeper holding the lamp high to see their faces in the shadow of the umbrella.

"Inspector Rutledge and Miss Trent. To see Lord Sedgwick," he said briskly.

She said, "It's such a nasty night, isn't it! Do come in. I'll let His Lordship know you're here."

They stepped into the hall, the umbrella dribbling a tiny stream of water across the floor as Rutledge furled it and left it outside. The housekeeper was gone only a few minutes. She led them to the salon, with its broad windows and the dark, wet sweep of the lawns beyond.

Lord Sedgwick was sitting there, a glass of whiskey in his hand. He rose and greeted his guests with warmth.

"Do sit down! You've come about the reward, have you? Has Blevins made up his mind who should have it?"

"I rather think he's leaving the decision to you. But I haven't come about Walsh. I'm here about your late coachman, Herbert Baker."

Surprised, Sedgwick said, "Baker? What does he have to do with Walsh?"

"Can you tell me who in your family made it possible for his wife to have the medical attention she required?" His expression gave away nothing but polite interest. "It must have cost more than Baker could afford in a lifetime."

"Baker's wife? Ah. I have a feeling that must have been Virginia. My daughter-in-law. She no doubt arranged for money to be sent anonymously. Very much the sort of thing she would do." There was a blandness in his voice that Rutledge found irritating.

Even if she'd had no idea what she was signing, Virginia's name would surely be there, in the bank's file of correspondence. Because that's when the planning must have begun.

Rutledge's glance crossed May Trent's. She smiled pleasantly, as if they were discussing a mutual acquaintance. But her gloved hands gripped each other.

"That brings me to the next question. In regard to your daughter-in-law—"

This time Sedgwick's eyebrows rose. "Virginia? You seem to have a great deal on your mind this evening! Baker and now Arthur's late wife. I don't see how you could have known either one of them."

"As a tangent to Inspector Blevins's efforts to investigate Walsh's role in Father James's death, I've been looking into the priest's background and interests. He did know Virginia Sedgwick, I'm told."

"Can I offer you something to drink? Tea? A little sherry for you, Miss Trent?"

They politely declined.

"Virginia was sweet-natured, and she had half of Norfolk at her feet. Father James was no exception, as I remember." Sedgwick smiled indulgently. "She seemed to feel comfortable with older men. Baker. Myself."

"The priest was quite anxious about her when she disappeared."

Sedgwick crossed his legs and flicked a small bit of mud off his shoe. "Yes, his support meant more than we can say. A great kindness, that was! As soon as we'd learned what happened to her, I sent him word."

"As I understand it, she sailed on *Titanic*," Rutledge said.

"It was some time before we realized that she was among the victims. It came as quite a shock." His voice was heavy. "She'd had a quarrel with Arthur, you know—one of those things that happen in any marriage. Apparently she took it to heart. When she told him she wanted to go home, he told her not to be ridiculous, expecting it to blow over. Tragically, she left anyway."

"Her body was never recovered?"

"Sadly, she wasn't identified when the bodies were brought in. We didn't know, you see, that she'd even sailed. Not until after the fact.

Arthur was the one I worried about—he was frantic. When the police failed to find any trace, we worked through private sources. And in the end, Arthur went straight to Ireland. I'd have accompanied him if I'd realized he was going to be subjected to those pathetic photographs of the dead—imagine, if you will, trying to see a resemblance to someone you loved! But money has its uses. In the end, she came home to us. So many of the dead *couldn't* be identified. It was—rather horrible to think about them." He set down his drink, unfinished. "For a time, I was afraid I'd lose my son as well. I've tried for five years now to persuade him to put her death behind him and marry again. He won't hear of it."

"There's another school of thought," Rutledge said quietly. "That she never sailed at all. That somewhere between her home in Yorkshire and King's Lynn, where she intended to plan a party, she was murdered."

Sedgwick sat forward, his face a picture of dismay. "Good God, man, where did you hear that wild tale! She was *recognized* in King's Lynn!"

"No, she was *seen*. A woman in a veiled hat? It could have been anyone." Remembering Iris Kenneth's parting words, Rutledge improvised. "It could even have been a hired impostor. A shopkeeper might be pleased to say your family patronized his business, whether you did or not. But no one who knew her well ever came forward."

Sedgwick looked over Rutledge's head. He said quietly, "You'd better fetch your brother, Edwin."

Rutledge turned to find Edwin Sedgwick just walking out of the room behind him. Hamish asked, "How much did he hear?"

"Enough," Rutledge answered. "I expected one of them to be listening."

In a moment or two, Edwin returned with his elder brother, the family resemblance between them strong, although Arthur was still quite thin and walked with a distinctly stiff back, as if he wore a brace tonight. He came in and sat down gingerly, as Sedgwick made the introductions.

"You ought to hear this, Arthur," he concluded.

Rutledge said, "This isn't my fancy, Lord Sedgwick." And then to Arthur, he began mildly, "Someone in this family paid for the care of Herbert Baker's ill wife, and he was deeply indebted to you. I can prove that. And you used him in return. After a fashion, I can prove that as well. In the early spring of 1912 you sent him to Yorkshire to fetch Mrs. Sedgwick for a journey to East Sherham. She enjoyed being driven by Baker, I think, with his old-fashioned manners. He didn't know that he was going to be a witness to a staged event: her disappearance. Whatever it was that happened, he was led to believe it was what *she* wanted, and so he agreed. But he was rather a simple man, and it went against his conscience to wreck a marriage. He got drunk when he was supposed to be waiting for Mrs. Sedgwick to return from her marketing. He knew she wasn't going to be meeting him. We can prove that as well."

Arthur Sedgwick nodded. "You've got your facts straight, actually. It's the interpretation that's wrong. Virginia did want to help Baker's ill wife, and the bank can show you the letter she wrote asking for sums to be made available anonymously. And we've believed from the beginning that she cajoled Baker into turning his back while she made good her escape. We couldn't blame him—he punished himself enough as it was."

Hamish said, "A jury would believe this man. . . ."

It was true. But it wasn't a jury that Rutledge wanted to reach just now.

"The only wrong assumption that Baker made in this affair," Rutledge told Arthur, "was believing that your *wife* was the instigator of these arrangements. You'd been planning her death since the November before, hadn't you? And quite cleverly. When Virginia Sedgwick vanished, Baker was hamstrung. His own wife was still in the sanitarium, and he refused to put her at risk by asking questions. After that one bout of drunkenness, he lived an exemplary life until he died of natural causes."

"Yes, we went to the services," Sedgwick put in. *Noblesse oblige . . .*

"Which brings me to the services for Virginia, Mrs. Sedgwick. I can order the exhumation of her coffin, you see. To discover if there's a corpse inside. But I rather think it's empty. When *Titanic* went down, it provided the most unexpected windfall—a marvelous explanation for the disappearance of your wife. You're right, money has its uses, including bribing London clerks and Irish gravediggers. No one would ask a grief-stricken family for proof! And if a coffin silenced Father James and Herbert Baker, who meant well but were persistent in asking for news, then it must have been worth every penny. The scandal of a possible runaway wife allowed you to use great discretion in suppressing the whole story."

Lord Sedgwick started to speak, but Arthur waved him to silence. He said in a strained voice, "It's bad enough to lose my wife the way I did, Inspector. I don't understand why you're tormenting us!"

Rutledge coldly replied, "My guess is that somewhere on that long drive, Baker simply walked away from the motorcar for half an hour. What did you promise Virginia to entice her to come with you? A surprise? A new pony? A trip on a boat you'd borrowed from your brother? If we search the marshes, will we find her rotted bones?"

Edwin and his father had listened to the account with tight faces expressing anger and disbelief. But they'd support Arthur, whatever he'd done. Guilty or not, he was their flesh and blood. Surprisingly, they didn't defend him—

Hamish said, "If it was a lie, you'd ha' been booted out ten minutes ago. But Arthur canna' afford to have that coffin exhumed!"

A flush had risen in Arthur's face. "Perhaps if Baker had met her at the hotel at the hour he'd promised, she wouldn't have taken it in her head to show she could fend for herself! And as for *Titanic*, you don't know what you're talking about!" He got up from his chair and moved about the room, rigidly at first, and then with more ease as the muscles in his back stretched. He was plausible, his voice and his manner carrying indignation and a sense of injustice nicely blended. But was it real? Rutledge couldn't tell. Just as he refused to submit to the pain in his back, Arthur Sedgwick refused to be intimidated.

Hamish said, "He canna' be shaken."

Arthur walked to the rain-wet window, peering out at the dark gardens, his back to the room. His father and brother waited for him to speak again. And Rutledge remembered something that Sedgwick had told him about his elder son—the Watchers of Time had given the boy nightmares. . . .

When Arthur said nothing else, Sedgwick cleared his throat. "Inspector, I think you ought to leave. Miss Trent, we apologize for this distressful business, you shouldn't have been subjected to it."

Hamish spoke swiftly, and Rutledge shifted in his chair to look at Edwin.

Edwin's eyes were still on his brother. As Rutledge had noted once before on the quay in Osterley, they were as cold as the winter sea.

Edwin was the physically stronger now, and harder. He had made no effort to come to his brother's defense, and it had become a telling silence.

His intuition alive and working, Rutledge suddenly realized why. A
jealousy lay like acid under the skin of the second son. It had nothing to
do with Virginia Sedgwick's death. The title would go to Arthur, not
Edwin.

Rutledge was on the point of continuing when May Trent spoke for
the first time. "But it isn't true," she said with conviction to the room at
large, "that the Inspector doesn't know what he's talking about. And it
isn't true that your wife was on board *Titanic*, Mr. Sedgwick. Because I
was, you see, and I'd have met her. Father James made a study of the
ship. That's how he found *me*."

The logs on the hearth crackled and sent sparks flying, but no one
noticed. A gust of rain rattled against the windows. May Trent waited.

Rutledge forced himself not to look at her. But Lord Sedgwick and
Edwin were staring at her with an almost malevolent expression, as if
she had called them liars. And she had.

"My dear lady," Sedgwick said. "Virginia was a wretched sailor—
it's very doubtful that she ever left her stateroom!"

May Trent answered, "But I'd have known that, too. Women gossip
on shipboard, Lord Sedgwick, just as they do at a garden party. We
knew who was assigned to our table, to our lifeboat stations. Who was
available for bridge, who had been confined to bed. Her name wasn't
there." She looked at Arthur and her face twisted with disgust. *"How
could you callously use that tragedy for your own ends? I find it appalling!"*

Arthur's mouth tensed, but he said nothing. His reflection in the
dark glass of the French doors was a study in control. Yet his hands,
locked behind his back, clenched until the knuckles were white.

Rutledge turned to Lord Sedgwick. "And as Herbert Baker lay dying, he couldn't face the prospect that he was taking with him the one
bit of knowledge that might clear up the mystery of what really happened to your daughter-in-law. Trying to set his soul in order, he sent
for Father James, not because he was a priest, but *because this man
cared as much about Virginia Sedgwick's fate as Baker had*. The one
man in Osterley who could be counted on to use the information
wisely! And that's why Father James had to die—there was no way of
knowing whether what Baker confided to the priest was under the seal

of Confession or had been told man to man, with a simple promise binding the priest."

There was the shock of truth in Lord Sedgwick's face now. Arthur and Edwin swung around to look at their father. And he gave them no sign.

Rutledge frowned at Arthur. "I was convinced you killed Father James. I was coming here to break the news to your father. Until today, when I discovered two witnesses who placed not you but your father at the rectory that night. And I realized then that he'd been the killer." Facing Sedgwick, he said, intent on angering the man, "It was quite clever to empty the tin box, to leave a false trail. Certainly Inspector Blevins was convinced by it. You have a flair for planning murder."

Lord Sedgwick met Rutledge's eyes with arrogance. "It doesn't matter if you have a dozen witnesses. I think it's time you left this house."

There was an uneasy moment in the room. Edwin, leaning over the back of a chair, his hands lightly gripping the wood frame, was watching the fire. Arthur started toward a chair and then changed his mind, toying with the photographs on the table.

Hamish said, "Watch your back!"

Indeed, there was an odd intensity in their postures. These three men had spent a lifetime with no leavening to counteract the ferocious ambition that had driven them since the day they were born. It was what their character was all about: the paramount importance of a goal set in the first generation.

Rutledge rose, as if preparing to leave. He wasn't comfortable sitting any longer. He said to Sedgwick, "When Walsh escaped, you sent your sons to search for him, and then borrowed old Tom Randal's mare, and went after him yourself. You found him because you know the land around here better than anyone else—you'd grown up on it, with an old sheepman training your eye. And you killed Walsh—with a hammer—or the shoe Honey had cast. Using it with a polo swing and the full weight of the galloping horse behind your arm. And the Sedgwick luck held—you caught him just right. The police inquiry into the death of a priest was closed."

"Don't be ridiculous! How could I have got to this Randal's farm, without my motorcar being seen as I drove through Osterley? Besides, Arthur was using it, in the search! And there's my gout—" Sedgwick was on his feet. "If you won't leave of your own accord, I'll have my sons throw you out. I won't stand for this in my own house."

"Yes, you've taken every opportunity to remind me of your gout. Your son Edwin rides Arthur's motorcycle. I wouldn't be surprised if you do as well." He turned to the sons.

"If you try to cover up what your father has done, if you refuse to help me, you'll be tarred by the same brush. It will be the end of your family—"

He read cold calculation in hard eyes, an uncompromising facade of unity. They were ranged between him and the door, a solid phalanx of enmity.

Hamish warned, "It's no' what you think—"

Rutledge felt shock. Like cold water thrown in his face.

How could he have got it so wrong?

He said, "May. Will you wait for me in the car, please? I'll be out in five minutes." His voice was pleasant, but there was command in it.

She started to protest, then stood up. The atmosphere had changed subtly, and his order had frightened her.

"If you don't come, I'll drive back to town, shall I?"

"Yes. By all means."

She nodded and walked into the hall, drawing her coat back around her shoulders. They could hear the outer door open—and then shut behind her.

Rutledge walked to the windows, and stood there with his back to them. He could feel the draft coming through the glass, cold and damp. It felt like hope.

"I was wrong," he said, into the waiting silence. "I realize my mistake now."

Sedgwick said, "You won't be able to pursue this. And your career will be destroyed. I have that power. You know I do. If you leave now, I'll undertake to guarantee that your silence will protect that young woman who just left. You would be wise to heed me."

Rutledge said wearily, "Arthur killed his wife, didn't he? And you, Lord Sedgwick, killed Father James. But it was Edwin who killed Walsh. Arthur's back won't allow him to ride that strenuously. And you were busy ordering your staff to search the house and grounds, the outbuildings and the sheepfolds." He paused. He'd blended conjecture and experience and intuition in a unholy weave of truth. But he

didn't want to hear the answer to his last question. "In God's name—
why!"

"She was a pretty ninny who charmed the men around her," Lord
Sedgwick replied, "but couldn't hold a five-minute conversation with
anyone. Much less conduct a household properly. She had the attention
span of a ten-year-old. She had no idea that she could conceive a child
just as half-witted as she was." He shook his head. "Her mother swore
to Arthur after the wedding that she'd had a fever as a child. I discovered later that there had been a cousin and an aunt who were also mentally deficient. It was a trick from the start—*and Arthur here thought
he'd discovered Guinevere!*" Sedgwick's voice was sour with anger. "Do
you have any idea what it's like, living every day of every year with
someone as stupid as she was? The endless repetitions. The tantrums.
The constant refrain of 'But why can't I?' as if God had given her the
keys to the bloody universe! Edwin or I kept an eye on her when Arthur
was abroad. But even that was getting to be difficult. Arthur drew the
short straw, as it were. He'd married her, after all. We never asked how
or where it happened."

"And," said Edwin for the first time, "Baker didn't know either.
Only that she wouldn't be going all the way. The day we buried that
damned empty coffin, he promised my father he'd never speak of what
happened. We expected him to carry whatever he *thought* he knew to
his grave. Instead he made himself the laughingstock of Osterley when
he died shriven by two clergymen! Too many people began to wonder
why."

Rutledge said, his mind working at speed, "When you were playing
night games outside the vicarage windows, to keep Sims silent, did you
see Walsh dragging his chains to the garden shed?"

"Why should I frighten Sims?" Edwin demanded. "I reserved that
for Holston, who knew Father James too well. It was very likely Peter
Henderson who hung about the vicarage, not me. But yes, I was coming
back from Cley on my motorcycle when I saw Walsh hurrying toward
the church." He glanced at his watch. "Your time is up. It doesn't
matter to us what you do with the knowledge you have. The risk is
yours. Your medical history might be of interest in certain quarters.
And prospects for publication of Miss Trent's manuscript may be unexpectedly limited. What else lurks in your future is, of course, unfore-
seeable."

"I spent four years in the trenches," Rutledge answered contemptu-
ously. "I daresay I shall survive the Sedgwick family. I'd set my house in
order if I were you."

He turned to look one last time through the rain-streaked panes
of the French doors and across the wet lawns of the lovely unseen gardens. Then he walked unmolested between Edwin and Arthur and over
the threshold.

CHAPTER TWENTY-NINE

BUT IT WAS ON THE THRESHOLD that Rutledge stopped, facing the elegant room and its three occupants. "Let me remind you, gentlemen, that there are many ways that a man can be judged. I leave you to the tender mercies of the Watchers out there in the dark. When you begin to feel them—and you will—you'll start to turn on each other. It will happen. It's only a matter of time."

A stolid wall of baneful resistance met him. Sedgwick was flushed now, a look of frustration and malevolence in his face. Arthur was resigned, his eyes on the carpet, but there was no remorse in his stance. Edwin, first looking from his father to his brother, turned on Rutledge a hungry glance. He was already bringing to bear a formidable determination.

For an instant, Rutledge thought Edwin might be the first to break ranks.

But the moment passed.

Rutledge leaned against the closed door, feeling the cool rain, breathing in the damp, heavy air.

It wasn't finished yet.

Concerted murder. It was, as Monsignor Holston had claimed, violent and primeval. This family cared for nothing but their power, their will. It had made them implacable, cold-blooded. Virginia Sedgwick had been doomed from the day her husband discovered he'd been deceived. Her family was to blame, too—for their selfishness in pushing a bewildered child into the ranks of Consuela Vanderbilt and Jennie Randolph: a fortune traded for a title, nevermind happiness.

Hamish said, of the night, "I didna' think they would let you go."

Rutledge answered, "They haven't. They just didn't want to dirty the carpets."

A voice out of the rain called tentatively, "Inspector Rutledge?"

He had forgotten that May Trent was waiting in the motorcar.

He found her shivering in her coat. "I'm so very glad to see you!" she exclaimed. "It's been more than five minutes—I thought you weren't coming at all."

"I was safe enough."

She laughed nervously. "It's been frightful, out here in the dark. I've seen and heard all kinds of things! Mostly my overworked imagination, but that's small comfort."

He turned the crank, and when he took his place beside her, behind the wheel, she said, "Where's Peter? We aren't going to leave him, are we? It's a long, wet walk back to Osterley."

"Actually, he was outside the French windows. Just beyond the terrace. He knows where to meet me."

He waited. The rain dripped from the trees as the wind stirred them. And somewhere, they could hear what sounded like a woman crying. It was a peacock, out on the grounds, but May Trent caught his arm. "I'm frightened. More frightened than I was in there!"

"You shouldn't be. That was a very brave thing to do in there. Facing your demons in front of the Sedgwicks."

"I didn't face any demons. I lied, for Father James's sake," she confessed. "Listening to what was being said, I suddenly realized what it was that he'd actually expected me to remember. I did it for *him*. I think he'd already guessed that she wasn't on board. She couldn't have been, could she, if she was already dead? Father James had talked to

Herbert Baker by that time, and he was nearly sure. But he hoped I could give him *proof*—"

Rutledge took out his watch, but couldn't see the face in the darkness.

"Shouldn't we return to Osterley soon?"

"It's barely been a quarter of an hour. Give it a little longer."

"Give what a little longer?" she said, her gloved hands snuggled into her coat pockets for warmth.

"I'm not sure."

It was nearly forty-five minutes later when Hamish, behind him, heard something. Rutledge stiffened, straining to catch the direction of the footfalls.

Then Peter Henderson walked swiftly around the corner of the house and climbed into the rear seat. "He's coming," Henderson said.

"*Who's* coming?" May Trent asked. "It's Edwin you're waiting for, isn't it?"

Still they waited. And then the door of the house opened on a long rectangle of light that seemed to reach toward them. A man stepped out into the silvery path it made across the wet slate walk.

He seemed relieved to find Rutledge there. He came to stand beside the motorcar, looking in at Rutledge, the rain falling harder now, like tears on his face.

It was Arthur Sedgwick.

He handed Rutledge the umbrella he'd left by the door. "I don't want to hang," he said after a moment. "But I'm the one who'll die next. One way or another. My spine is wrecked; I won't live to old age. I'll never father a child. Edwin won't wait very long for the title. He wants it too badly; he has for as far back as I can remember. And my father grieves for a man who raced like the wind, and never thought twice about danger and dying. That's gone, too."

Rutledge said nothing.

Arthur Sedgwick said, "Can you protect me? If I agree to testify against them?"

"I can try."

"They tried to persuade me for the good of the family to take a pistol to my head. 'Driven by despair over my back.' Hush it up. Inspector Blevins doesn't want Walsh resurrected. He wouldn't dare to point a finger at us. My death would be a nine day wonder and then fade away."

He walked around the front of the motorcar and joined Henderson in the rear seat. Rutledge turned on the headlamps. The occupants of the car were ghostly in the reflected glow, after the pitch-black of the night.

As Rutledge turned the wheel and started down the drive, Arthur said, "I've always hated those damned baboons in the garden. They stare at me as if they can look through the flesh and blood into my very soul. I could see them tonight, watching. I always know they're there. I'd promised myself that when I inherited the title, I'd destroy that damned stone. But my father has always had some sort of superstitious regard for it, like the Chastains did."

They reached the gates and drove through.

May Trent asked Rutledge, as if it had suddenly occurred to her, "But what's going to happen now?"

"You'll see. I wish you'd stayed in Osterley. You wouldn't have been dragged through this."

"It was not your choice," she replied. "It was mine. I'd let Father James down once."

Rutledge pulled off the road in a wide patch of brush, the stiff dry fingers scratching against the paint, a shower of raindrops, dislodged from the branches, sprinkling down on the car. Then he drove deeper into the thickest shadows and switched off his headlamps. "Be very quiet."

In a few minutes a motorcar came flying down the road from the direction of the Sedgwick gates, roaring past them like a thunderbolt. It disappeared into the darkness. From what Rutledge could tell, there were two people in the front.

Arthur Sedgwick said, "They're hunting for me already." There was a mixture of resignation and despair in his voice. "There are weapons in the house. Shotguns—"

Rutledge said, "No, they're hunting me. But your turn will come. Where is your wife buried?"

"In the marshes. I killed her, but I couldn't bear to bury her there. Edwin did it for me. He goes out there in the boat from time to time, to be sure she's still there."

Beside Rutledge, May Trent gasped.

After a moment, Rutledge said, "Sedgwick, we're taking you straight to Norwich. Henderson, as soon as we reach Osterley, I'd like you to find Monsignor Holston at the hotel and tell him to come to Holy Trinity. We'll meet him there by the church. Ask Mrs. Barnett, if you will, to send my luggage on to London, and Miss Trent's as well. Then go to the vicarage and stay there out of sight. Will you do that?"

Henderson agreed.

"And thank you," Rutledge added. "For tonight's help."

There was unexpected pride in Peter Henderson's voice. "My pleasure. And I'll keep my mouth shut, you can be sure." He slipped out to crank the engine.

They waited by the church, its towers high and black against the sky. Arthur Sedgwick was morosely silent, Rutledge tense and watchful.

The bark of a fox was sharp and close. May Trent said quietly, "Are you sure this is the right thing to do?"

"There's no choice. The Yard has to make this arrest. If I leave it to Blevins, he'll lose another prisoner. Arthur Sedgwick will be safest in Norwich."

Rain was falling hard again by the time a very wet and somber Monsignor Holston climbed into the seat Peter Henderson had vacated not ten minutes before.

"You'd better get out of here," the priest warned. "As fast as you can! Edwin is searching the town. Peter told me a little of what has happened. He's already gone to ground. They'll never know he was protecting your back outside their windows tonight. He'll be safe enough."

The motor, rumbling quietly in the darkness, picked up a stronger note, and the motorcar drove down Trinity Lane to the main road and headed east, for the turning to Norwich.

But it was a very long time before Rutledge stopped listening for the echo of another vehicle behind him. . . .

ABOUT THE AUTHOR

CHARLES TODD is the author of *A Test of Wills, Wings of Fire, Search the Dark,* and *Legacy of the Dead.* He lives on the East Coast, where he is at work on the next book in the Ian Rutledge series, *A Fearsome Doubt.*

Todd, Charles.
Watchers of time : an
Inspector Ian Rutledge
mystery